Sarita, the Carlist

Arthur W. Marchmont

Sarita, the Carlist

The present edition is a reproduction of previous publication of this classic work. Minor typographical errors may have been corrected without note; however, for an authentic reading experience the spelling, punctuation, and capitalization have been retained from the original text.

ISBN: 978-1-63637-642-4

CONTENTS

Chapter
I   The Victim of a Woman's Preference   1
II   The Gate of Hazard   8
III   Carlists   14
IV   Sarita Castelar   21
V   The Explanation   30
VI   "Counting All Renegades Lovers of Satan"   38
VII   Sarita, the Carlist   45
VIII   Sebastian Quesada   54
IX   The Quesada Version   60
X   In London   68
XI   "The Ways of the Carlists Will be Hard"   74
XII   Sarita's Welcome   81
XIII   The Fight   89
XIV   A Coward's Story   98
XV   The Abduction 106
XVI   After the Rescue 114
XVII   War to the Knife 121
XVIII   At the Opera House 128
XIX   A Carlist Gathering 135
XX   At the Hotel De l'Opera 142
XXI   Sarita's Flight 150
XXII   An Unexpected Meeting 157
XXIII   News of Sarita 166
XXIV   A Check 173
XXV   At Calvarro's 181
XXVI   The Plea of Love 188
XXVII   Sarita Hears the Truth 195
XXVIII How Luck Can Change 202
XXIX   Quesada Again 210
XXX   Suspense 218
XXXI   At the Palace 225
XXXII   Livenza's Revenge 233
XXXIII The Hut on the Hillside 242
XXXIV   A King's Riddle 252

CHAPTER I

THE VICTIM OF A WOMAN'S PREFERENCE

If A won't marry B, ought C to be exiled?

Stated in that bald fashion the problem looks not unlike an equation that has lost caste and been relegated to a nonsense book, or lower still, to some third-rate conundrum column. And yet it was the real crux of a real situation, and meant everything to me, Ferdinand Carbonnell, the victim of a woman's preference.

It came about in this way. The Glisfoyle peerage, as everyone knows, is only a poor one, and originality not being a strong point with us, Lascelles, my elder and only brother, having taken counsel with my father, fell back upon the somewhat worn device of looking out for a wife with money. He was not very successful in the quest, but at length a desirable quarry was marked down in the person of a Mrs. Abner B. Curwen, the young widow of an American millionaire; and great preparations were made to lure her into the net that was spread in the most open and unabashed manner before her very eyes.

But those eyes—bright, merry, and laughing—had a brain behind them that was practical and penetrating, and she saw the meshes quite plainly. She accepted the hospitality with pleasure, did her best to make a friend of my only sister, Mercy, was properly subdued, if not awed, in the presence of my father, and, in fact, did everything expected of her except the one thing—she would not let Lascelles make love to her, and completely out-manoeuvred him whenever he tried to bring matters to a head.

Moreover, a crisis of another kind was in the brewing. Mrs. Curwen herself was not an American, but a north-country Englishwoman, who had used her pretty looks and sharp wits to captivate the rich American, and she took Mercy into her confidence one day to an extent that had results.

"I am very fond of you, Mercy dear, and would give much to have you as my sister; but your brother, Lascelles, is too formal, too stiff in the backbone, for me. I have made one marriage for a reason that wasn't love: but I married an old man; and when I marry again it won't be for either position or money. I should dearly love to have you for my sister, as I say, but I could not marry your brother Lascelles. Ferdinand is just awfully nice—but I suppose he's a dreadful scapegrace."

1

I think Mercy laughed hugely at this—her merry heart laughs at most things—and certainly, when she told me—as being my best particular chum she was bound to do immediately—we laughed heartily over it together.

"She's a bright, jolly, little soul and beastly rich, but I'm not having any," said I, shaking my head. "I don't want to cut out poor old Cello"—this was an unrighteous nickname of ours for Lascelles, with a covert reference to his deep, solemn, twangy voice. "But you'd better tell the father."

"You might do worse, Nand," declared my sister. "Her wealth would give you just the chance you want; and it would be awfully jolly to have a rich brother, and she's a good sort; and you could settle down and——"

"Don't be a little humbug, Mercy. She's all right, I daresay; but I'm not made that way. If I were going to succeed the father I might think about selling myself for a good round sum; but no, thank you, I'm not in the market. You'd better let Cello and the father know that this little net of theirs has got fouled;" and with that I dismissed the matter, and with no thought of trouble went off on a fortnight's visit to an old Oxford friend.

When I got back to town, however, matters had moved fast, and plans were cut and dried. Lascelles had come to the conclusion that if I were out of the way his suit would prosper, and he had grown to like the little widow as much as a person of his importance could care for anyone who did not wear his clothes. My father and he had, therefore, set to work with a burst of Irish zeal, and had succeeded in getting me made a kind of probationary attaché at the Madrid Embassy; and expected me to be mightily pleased at the result of their innocent efforts on my behalf. My father told me the good news on my arrival, and the next morning there came the official confirmation.

My father was in quite cheerful spirits.

"Your foot is on the ladder, Ferdinand," he said, gleefully. He was very partial to this metaphor. Life to him was a maze of ladders, leading up and down and in all directions, of which, by the way, he had made very indifferent use. "You may climb where you will now, my boy. You've a steady head at times."

"I trust I shall not be dizzied by the giddy height of this position, sir," I answered, not wholly without guile, for I was not enamoured of this prospective expatriation in the cause of fraternity.

"I don't think it's a subject for feeble satire," exclaimed Lascelles, sourly. "You've not made such a brilliant success of things on your own account and during your years of vagrancy. I trust

2

you'll remember who you are now, and endeavour to do the family credit, and seek to climb the ladder which our father rightly says is open to you."

"I hope you won't marry a wretched Spanish woman to carry up with you," said Mercy, a little pungently. She resented my exile more than I did.

"Such a remark is scarcely called for, Mercy," said Lascelles, always glad to pose as the much elder brother, and objecting to any reference to the subject of marriage at such a moment. But Mercy was as resentful as a nettle when handled tactlessly.

"You mean we ought to taboo the subject of marriage just at present. Very well, dear," she said, demurely and humbly. My brother frowned and fidgetted on his chair, while I shut down a smile.

"Madrid has a questionable climate, but I believe it is excellent for young strong men," said my father, obviously glad that he had not to go. "It is fortunate you have such a knowledge of Spanish, Ferdinand. It was that which turned the scale in your favour. Sir John Cullingworth told me so. It's what I've always said; all boys should know a language or two. Always lifts a man a rung or two above the crowd when the moment comes. A most valuable mental equipment."

A perfect knowledge of Spanish, the result of years of my boyhood and youth spent in Spain, was the one ewe lamb of my accomplishments; that, and a bad pass degree at Oxford constituted the "valuable mental equipment" of my father's imagination.

"It has come in handy this time, sir," I assented.

"I hope you use less slang in Spanish than in English," said Lascelles, posing again.

"I'm afraid the prospect of our parting has got on your nerves, Cello."

"I wish you wouldn't be so disgustingly vulgar and personal as to use that ridiculous nickname for me," he retorted, angrily.

"I wish to see you in the study, Ferdinand, in about a quarter of an hour. I have something very important to say to you," interposed my father, rising to leave the room, as he generally did when my brother and I looked like having words.

"Very well, sir. I'll come to you."

"Do you know the news, Nand?" cried Mercy, as soon as the door closed behind him, and the look of her eye was full of mischief.

"No. I've only read a couple of newspapers this morning," I answered, flippantly.

"I don't mean news of the stupid newspaper sort; I mean real, private, important news. This will be in the fashionable gossip next week: but it isn't public yet."

"No—and I'm afraid I'm not very interested in it, either. Next week I shall be in Madrid."

"Ah, but this is about Madrid, too," she cried, looking mysterious.

"What do you mean, Mercy?" asked Lascelles, who was of a very curious turn, and not quick. "What news is it?"

"It's about Mrs. Curwen, Lascelles. She is going to stay in Madrid;" and Mercy pointed the little shaft with a barbed glance that made him colour with vexation.

"Upon my word, Mercy, you ought to know better. You are abominably rude, and your manners are unpardonable," he cried, angrily. "I declare I won't allow it."

"Allow it? Why, she didn't tell me she had to ask your permission. But, of course, I'll tell her she mustn't go," returned Mercy, with such a fine assumption of innocent misunderstanding that I could not restrain my laughter.

"It will be a good thing when you are gone, Ferdinand," he turned on me, wrathfully. "You only encourage Mercy in these acts of rudeness."

"Don't be a prig, Cello," said I, good humouredly. "You are a good chap at bottom, and when you don't stick those airs on."

"I shall not stay here to be insulted," he exclaimed, and he retreated, leaving us in possession of the field.

"That was too bad, Mercy. You hit him below the belt," I said, when he had gone.

"But he's just insufferable in those moods, and he gets worse and worse every week. And it's horrid of him to drive you away like this. Positively horrid."

"It's all right, girlie. I'm not the first man by a good many who has left his country for his family's good, even to climb the diplomatic ladder. And when I've got up a few rungs, as the father calls them, and can afford to have an establishment, you shall come and boss it, and we'll have a high old time."

"Yes, but that's just it, Nand."

"What's just it?"

"Why, of course, you're just the dearest brother in the world and awfully good at Spanish and all that, but I don't believe you'll be a bit of good as a diplomatist; and you'll never get on enough to have any place for me to boss."

"What a flatterer you are! For telling the beastly, barefaced, ugly truth, commend me to sisters," and I laughed. "But I believe

4

you're right; and I shall probably never earn bread and cheese rind as a tactician. But I'll have a good time all the same."

"Oh isn't that like a man! For sheer Christian unselfishness, commend me to—brothers."

"A fair hit, and a bull's-eye, too. But we've always been good chums, you and I, and what's the good of chums if they can't slang each other? That's the test of chumminess, say I. I wish Cello was a bit of a chum for you."

"Poor Cello," and Mercy smiled at the notion. "But I think the whole thing's just horrid," she added; and for all her smiles she was not far off tears. That seems to be the way with girls of her sort; so I made some silly joke and laughed, and then kissed her and went off to the study.

There was never anything jocular about my father; and now I found him preternaturally grave and serious. He thought it necessary to improve the occasion with a very solemn lecture about the start of my career, and gave me heaps of good advice, mentioned the moderate allowance he could make me—small enough for me to remember without any difficulty—and then came to the pith of what was in his thoughts.

"I think it necessary to tell you, now, Ferdinand, a rather painful chapter of our family history. You know most good families have these things; and as it concerns some relatives of ours in Madrid, and as you can act for me out there, it's altogether fortunate you are going."

"Relatives in Madrid, sir!" I exclaimed, in considerable astonishment.

"I said Madrid, Ferdinand; and really you cannot learn too soon that concealment of surprise—and indeed of any kind of feeling—is one of the essentials for diplomatic success." He said this in his most didactic manner, and I assumed a properly stolid expression, resolved to make no further sign of surprise let the story be what it might.

"You needn't look like a block of wood," was his next comment; and I guessed that he was in doubt how to put the matter, and therefore vented the irritation on me. "The fact is," he continued, after a pause, "that you had another uncle beside the late peer; junior to both Charles and myself. He lived a very wild, adventurous life—that's where you get your love of wandering—and he had a very stormy time in Spain. He's been dead many years now, poor fellow, and the circumstances are all strange and, I suppose I must say, romantic." He said this regretfully, as though romance had a taint of vulgarity unworthy of the peerage.

"Yes, sir."

5

"Well, it was the result largely of a most extraordinary marriage he made. He was in Spain under an assumed name—the truth is he had made such a mess of things here that the family disowned him, and having, as you have, a splendid knowledge of Spanish, he took a Spanish name—Ramon Castelar. His own name was Raymond. The girl was of the powerful family of the Quesadas; but knowing him only as an adventurer and being quite ignorant of his high birth, they turned their backs on him and wouldn't hear of a marriage. Raymond was a daredevil in his way, however, and the thing ended in a runaway match. A most unfortunate matter."

My father spoke of it as a quite deplorable thing, but I admired my uncle as about the pluckiest Carbonnell I had yet heard of. We all have our own points of view, however.

"The end was a perfect tragedy, Ferdinand, an awful affair. The Quesadas tried by every means to get your uncle's wife away from him and in the end succeeded. He was in England at the time, and when he got back to Madrid, he found his wife shut up as a lunatic, his two children—a boy, Ramon, and a girl, Sarita, named after her mother—gone and himself proscribed. These big Spanish families have enormous privileges, you know; far greater than we have here. Well, he never saw her again. She died soon after, under most suspicious circumstances, and it seemed to quite break poor Raymond's life. He lived only for revenge, and became a moody, stern, utterly desperate man; but he could not fight against them. He found one chance of partial revenge at the time of a Carlist rising. He got hold of the children in some way; and I'm bound to say, although he was my own brother, it was a most unfortunate thing for them. He died soon afterwards, but not before he had ruined the boy's character. The lad was to have been a priest—the Quesadas were seeing to that—but he broke through all control some years ago, and—well, they tell me there is scarcely a crime forbidden in the Decalogue he hasn't committed. The least of his offences is that he is a Carlist of the Carlists; he has more than once attempted violence against the Quesada family, and—in fact I don't know what he hasn't done. What I do know is that he has involved his sister, Sarita, in some of his confounded Carlist plottings, and it seems to be a desperate entanglement altogether."

"Do the Quesadas know of the relationship, sir?"

"No, no, thank goodness, no. At least I think and hope not. There's only one person in Madrid knows of that; a Madame Chansette. She is a Quesada, it's true; but she married against the family's wish. She married a wealthy Frenchman, but is now a widow, and she went back to Madrid some time ago, really to try and take care of Sarita. The family have behaved abominably, I must say; and from what she tells me there seems to be no doubt that they've appropriated all the children's fortune. Well, Madame Chansette has written several times, and lately has pressed me to go over and consult with her about the children's future. She is afraid there will be some big trouble; and what you've got to do, Ferdinand, is just to take my place in the affair. I can't go, of course; and you've got a head on your shoulders if you like to use it: and you can just take a careful look into things and see what had best be done."

"Then I suppose neither the brother nor sister knows about us?"

"God forbid," cried my father, fervently. "Unless, of course, Madame Chansette has told them. But she's a discreet woman, although she is Spanish; and I don't think she'd be so stupid as to tell them."

"It's a rum kettle of fish," I said, meditatively; and my father winced at the expression.

"What Lascelles said is rather true, you know, Ferdinand. You are very slangy in your conversation. I really think, now that you have to climb the diplomatic ladder, you should try to curb the habit. Elegance of diction stands for so much in diplomacy."

"It is certainly a very involved situation, sir, was what I meant," I answered, gravely.

"That's much better, Ferdinand, and quite as expressive. I wish to feel proud of you, my boy, and hope you will be very successful. I have great trust and faith in you, I have indeed, if you will only try always to do your best."

"I will try to be worthy of the trust, sir," I said, earnestly, for he was more moved than I had ever seen him.

"I am sure you will, Ferdinand, God bless you;" and he gave me his hand. Then I was guilty of an anti-climax.

"I think I should like to say, sir, that I know, of course, the reason why my absence is desirable, and I hope that it will serve its purpose. I am not in the least troubled about going."

"I am glad to hear that, my boy. Of course, Lascelles must make a wealthy marriage if possible. We've all known the—the limitations inevitable where there's a title without adequate resources to maintain one's position. It makes such a difference in the world. And, of course, if the thing goes all right, as I trust it will, and you find Madrid unsupportable, why, you must come back. You know what a pleasure it always is to me to have you at home. But this is—is quite essential."

My father was at that moment called away on some political business and our conference broke up. No opportunity of renewing it came in the next busy days of preparation; and before the week was out I was on my way to Madrid, to the new career which promised no more than the humdrum routine of official work; but which, from the very instant of my arrival was destined to negative so sensationally all my anticipations.

My very entrance upon the scene of Madrid was indeed through a veritable gate of hazard.

CHAPTER II

THE GATE OF HAZARD

What Lascelles had termed my years of vagrancy had had one educational effect—I understood the art of travelling comfortably. I thoroughly enjoyed my trip across France, and as I did not intend to take my profession too seriously, I broke my journey at Paris to renew some old and pleasant associations.

I learnt a piece of news there which gave me much satisfaction. An old 'Varsity friend of mine, Silas Mayhew, the companion of many an unsacred adventure, had been removed from Paris to the Madrid Embassy; and the renewal of our old comradeship was an anticipation of genuine pleasure, for our friendship was thoroughly sound, wind and limb.

One incident prior to my leaving London I ought perhaps to mention—the little comedy of leave-taking with Mrs. Curwen. She and my sister had fixed it up between them, and I learned the shameless manner in which Mercy had been bribed to bring it about.

After my semi-understanding with my father I felt myself in a measure bound not to do anything to interfere with the family scheme, and I told Mercy that I should not even call on Mrs. A.B.C.—our name for the widow. She betrayed me to her friend, however, and when I went into her sitting-room for an agreed cup of tea and a chat on the day before that of my departure, Mrs. Curwen was there chatting unconcernedly with Mercy, whose face was guiltily tell-tale in expression.

"What an unexpected pleasure, Mr. Ferdinand," exclaimed the widow, laughing.

"By whom?" said I, as we shook hands.

"What a thing it is to be a diplomatist, and to be able to say so much in just two words. But I can be frank. I mean unexpected to you, of course. Mercy told me you were actually going away on your wanderings without saying good-bye to me—and I wasn't going to stand that. When some stupid mountain or other wouldn't go to Mahomet, Mahomet went to the mountain—like the very sensible person he was. And it was all the same in the end."

"That 'stupid mountain' had no sister to give it away, Mrs. Curwen."

"Mercy's just the dearest friend I have in the world. And now sit down and don't be disagreeable, and we'll have a jolly cosy little chat together, and you shall hear the news and advise us. What's the good of being an ambassador if you can't advise us?"

"Here's your tea, Nand;" and Mercy handed it me with a glance, asking for forgiveness. I accepted the tea and the situation, as I do most good things in this world, complacently.

"What advice do you want?"

"I want to know whether you think it would be quite a safe thing for Mercy to go to Madrid for a time, say—a month or two hence?"

Mercy looked down at the tea cups and laughed. I appeared to consider.

"Yes," I said, slowly. "Yes; but I am afraid my father is not contemplating a trip of the kind. You see, his health is not of the best, and his engagements—" I was interrupted by a peal of laughter from the widow.

"You are the drollest creature!" she cried. "Who said anything about Lord Glisfoyle?"

"I don't fancy Cello has much notion of going out either—at least, not yet," and I pointed this with a look. "And you see, Mercy could hardly come out to me alone."

"Mercy, I do believe he'll make a diplomatist after all. He talks that nonsense with such a perfectly solemn face," exclaimed Mrs. Curwen. "I suppose, Mr. Ferdinand, you haven't the ghost of an idea what I mean, have you? or what we've been planning."

"How could I? But if you have any idea of Mercy coming out to Madrid with anyone but my father or Cello, I should say at once it would be quite unsafe, and quite impracticable. There are a hundred reasons; but one's enough—the equivocal position of the whole Spanish question, owing to the unsettled relations with America."

"Nand, you're incorrigible," cried Mercy; but Mrs. Curwen laughed and clapped her hands, for both saw the double meaning of my words.

"I think that's most lovely. Let me get that sentence—'the equivocal position of the whole Spanish question, owing to the unsettled relations with America'! And then say he won't make a diplomatist! Well, you must know that Mercy and I have already got our plans fixed up. She's going out with me. I suppose I can do as I like. And if I take a sudden fancy to go to Madrid, I suppose I may go. And if I can't go alone, I suppose I may take Mercy with me. At any rate, that's what I'm going to do. I take Mercy's part in this, and agree that it's horrid you should be packed off out of the country and away from her and all your friends in this way, and that it's only right and proper that you should have your sister out just to show people that you're not an Ishmaelite among your own kith and kin. And as she must have someone to look after her, I'm going too. I can't do less than that for my dearest friend."

"I'm sure Mercy is happy to have such a friend, Mrs. Curwen, but——"

I hesitated, and before I resumed, the door opened and Lascelles came in. This was genuinely unexpected by us all, and apparently none too agreeable to my brother, who stopped with a frown on his long, narrow face. But Mrs. Curwen was equal to the occasion.

"Here is another surprise. Do come in, Mr. Carbonnell, and hear all our plans."

"It's too bad of you, Mercy, to monopolise Mrs. Curwen in this way," said my brother, solemnly, smothering his mortification.

"It's not Mercy who arranged this, I assure you; I did. I'm dreadfully unconventional, and I just wanted to say good-bye to your brother quietly and cheer him up with the news that I mean to take Mercy out to see him in Madrid soon; as soon, say, as he has had time to really miss her and feel lonesome."

"That is news, indeed," said Lascelles, looking mightily uncomfortable at hearing it. "And what does Ferdinand say to that?"

"He's rather absurd over it, I think. He says Madrid isn't a very safe place just now. Let me see what was his reason? Oh, I know— because of 'the equivocal position of the whole Spanish question, owing to the unsettled relations with America,'" and she looked up at him audaciously.

"I think that's a very powerful reason," agreed Lascelles, solemnly; he did not perceive the double application of the phrase. "There can be no doubt that the possible war with the States, and the attitude we have been compelled to adopt, might render the position of both American and English people in Madrid fraught with some danger. I think Ferdinand is quite right." He was so

10

earnest that he was entirely surprised when Mrs. Curwen received his remark with a burst of hearty and very mischievous laughter.

"I must be off," I said then, seeing the prudence of retreat. "I have lots to do. Good-bye, Mrs. Curwen. Take my advice and don't go to Madrid. You're much better off in London."

"Good-bye, Mr. Ferdinand—till we meet in Madrid;" and the expression of her eyes was almost a challenge as we shook hands.

She was a good-enough little soul, and pretty and fascinating, too, in her way; but she did not appeal to me. I was perfectly sincere in my advice to her not to come out to Madrid, and the news of her marriage either with Lascelles or anybody else would not have disturbed me in the least.

On my journey I thought over the incidents with no stronger feeling than that of a kind of neutral amusement; and although I would gladly have stopped in London for awhile and regretted sincerely the separation from Mercy, the moving bustle of the journey, the opening of a fresh page of experiences, the anticipation of seeing my old friend, Mayhew, and the general sense of independence, woke my roving instincts, and I was quite ready to forgive the cheery little widow for having been the innocent cause of my exile, and to wish my brother success in his venture.

It was about ten o'clock at night when I arrived in Madrid, and I was standing by my luggage waiting for the porter of the hotel to which I had telegraphed for a room, and looking about me leisurely according to my wont, when I found myself the object of the close scrutiny of a stranger. He passed me two or three times, each time scanning me and my luggage so intently that I was half inclined to be suspicious of him. He did not look like a detective, however, and was too well dressed for a thief; and he puzzled me. At last, to my surprise, he came up, raised his hat, and addressed me by name in Spanish, with a great show of politeness.

"I am not mistaken. Your name is Carbonnell, Ferdinand Carbonnell?"

"Certainly it is. The name's on my luggage," said I. I was not a diplomatist for nothing. He bowed and smiled and gestured.

"It is also here in my instructions;" and he took from his pocket a sheet of notepaper from which he read in Spanish, "Ferdinand Carbonnell, coming by the mail train arriving ten o'clock." Having read this, he added: "I am to ask you to accompany me to No. 150, Calle de Villanueva. May I ask you to do so?"

I looked at him in profound astonishment, as indeed I well might. Then it dawned on me that Mayhew had somehow heard of my arrival and had sent him.

"Do you come from Mr. Silas Mayhew?"

"No, indeed. I am from Colonel Juan Livenza, at your service, senor." This with more shrugs, bows, and smiles.

"Thank you, but I don't know any Colonel Livenza. I can, however, call on him; shall we say, to-morrow?"

"I was to say that the Senorita Sarita Castelar wishes to see you urgently. My instructions are, however, not to press you to accompany me if you are unwilling; but in that case to beg you to name the hotel to which you go, and where Colonel Livenza himself may have the honour of waiting upon you."

"I still don't understand," I replied. I did not; but the mention of the name of Sarita Castelar made a considerable impression upon me.

"It is my regret I can explain no more. I thought perhaps you would know the urgency of the matter, and that it might be the result of the telegram. But I am only a messenger."

"Telegram?" I cried, catching at the word. Could my father have had important news about the Castelars after I had left and have telegraphed to Madame Chansette to have me met? It was possible, for he knew my route and the time I was to arrive. "What telegram do you mean?" I asked.

"Alas, senor, I know no more than I say. I presume it is the telegram announcing your arrival. But I do not know. If you prefer not to come, it is all one to me. I will say you are going to what hotel? I was told it was very urgent. Pardon me that I have detained you."

"Wait a moment. You say the matter is urgent for to-night?"

"I do not know. I believe it is. I was instructed to tell you so. That is all."

At that moment the hotel porter arrived, hot and flurried and apologetic for being late. An idea occurred to me then.

"Look here," I said to the porter; "take my things to the hotel, and listen a moment. This gentleman has met me unexpectedly with a message from a Col. Livenza to go to No. 150, Calle de Villanueva. I am going there first, and do not expect to be detained long. If I am there more than an hour I shall need some fresh clothes. Come to that address, therefore, at half-past eleven, bring that portmanteau, and ask for me;" and to impress him with the importance of the matter, I gave him a good tip.

"Now, I am at your disposal," I said to the stranger.

"You are suspicious, senor?" he said, as we stepped into a cab.

"Not a bit of it. But I am an Englishman, you know, an old traveller—and when I come off a journey I can't bear to sit for more than an hour without putting on a clean shirt." I spoke drily, and looked hard at him.

12

"You are English?" he said, with a lift of the eyebrows. "Some of the English habits are very singular."

"Yes, indeed; some of us have a perfect passion for clean linen—so much so, in fact, that sometimes we actually wash our dirty linen in public."

Not understanding this, he looked as if he thought I was half a lunatic; but what he thought was nothing to me. If there was any nonsense at the bottom of this business, I had arranged that the hotel people should know of my arrival, and where to look for me; and my companion understood this. In the rumbling, rattling, brute of a cab the clatter was too great for us to speak, and after one or two inefficient shoutings we gave up the attempt, and I sat wondering what in the world the thing could mean.

I was curious, but not in the least suspicious; and when we drew up at an important-looking house, I followed my companion into it readily enough. The hall was square and lofty, but ill-lighted, and the broad stairway, up one flight of which he took me, equally gloomy. He ushered me into a room at the back of the house and left me, saying he would tell the Colonel of my arrival.

The room, like the rest of the house, was dimly lighted, and the furniture heavy and shabby, and abominably gloomy and dirty. I was weary with my journey, and threw myself into a big chair with a yawn and a wish that the business, whatever it might be, would soon be over. No one came for some minutes, and I lighted a cigarette and had smoked it half through, when my impatience at this discourteous treatment got the better of me, and I resolved to go in search of some means of bringing this Col. Livenza to me. Then I made a disconcerting discovery. The door was locked or bolted on the outside. I looked about for a bell, but there was none. There was, however, another door, and that I found unfastened.

I had now had enough of this kind of Spanish hospitality, and was for getting out of the house without any more nonsense. The second door opened into a room which was quite dark; but as soon as my eyes had grown accustomed to the darkness, I made out a thin streak of light at the far end, which told of another door, ajar.

I crossed the room very cautiously and slowly, lest in the darkness I should stumble over any furniture, and was close to the door, when I was brought to a sudden halt by hearing my own name pronounced by a heavy, strident, and obviously angry voice.

"I tell you, gentlemen, this Ferdinand Carbonnell is a traitor and a villain. He is playing a game of devilish duplicity, pretending to help the Carlist cause and intriguing at the same time with the Government. He has come to Madrid now for that purpose. There are the proofs. You have seen them, and can judge whether I have said a word too much in declaring him a dangerous, damnable traitor."

In the start that I gave at hearing this extraordinary speech, my foot struck a small table and overturned it. Some kind of glass or china ornament standing on it fell to the ground, and the crash of the fall was heard by the men in the room, who flung the door wide open and came rushing in to learn the cause.

CHAPTER III

CARLISTS

A man does not knock about the world for nothing, and the one or two ugly corners I had had to turn in my time had taught me the value of thinking quickly and keeping my head in a crisis. I looked from one to the other of the men—there were three of them—and asked in a cool and level tone—

"Is either of you gentlemen Colonel Livenza?"

"I am. Who are you, and what are you doing here?"

"Considering the rather free use you've been making with my name, Ferdinand Carbonnell, and that I was brought here by someone who called himself your messenger—and, if I'm not mistaken, is now standing beside you—and was left in a locked room yonder, that question strikes me as a little superfluous. Anyway, I shall be glad of an explanation," and I pushed on through the door into the lighted room.

The men made way for me, and the moment I had passed shut and locked the door behind me. I affected to take no heed of this act, suggestive though it was, and turned to Colonel Livenza for his explanation.

He was a dark, handsome fellow enough, somewhere about midway in the thirties; a stalwart, upright, military man, with keen dark eyes, and a somewhat fierce expression—a powerful face, indeed, except for a weak, sensual, and rather brutish mouth, but a very awkward antagonist, no doubt, in any kind of scrimmage. One of the others was he who had met me at the station, and the third was of a very different class; and I thought that if his character

14

paired with his looks, I would rather have him in my pay than among my enemies.

"So you are Ferdinand Carbonnell?" cried the Colonel, after staring at me truculently, and with a gaze that seemed to me to be inspired by deep passion. The note in his voice, too, was distinctly contemptuous. What could have moved him to this passion I could not, of course, for the life of me even guess.

"Yes, I am Ferdinand Carbonnell, and shall be glad to understand the reason of this most extraordinary reception, and of the far more extraordinary blunder which must be at the bottom of it."

"You carry things with a high hand—but that won't serve you. We have brought you here to-night—trapped you here if you prefer it—to make you explain, if you can, your treachery to the Carlist cause, and if you cannot explain it, to take the consequences."

The gross absurdity of the whole thing struck me so forcibly at that moment, and his exaggerated and melodramatic rant was so ridiculously out of proportion that I laughed as I answered—

"Really this is farce, not tragedy, senor. I have never seen you before; I know nothing of you or your affairs; I am not a Carlist, and never have been; I am not a Spaniard, but an Englishman; I have just come from London; and I assure you, on my honour as an Englishman, that you are labouring under a complete mistake as to myself. I beg you, therefore, to put an end to a false position, and allow me to leave, before you make any further disclosures which may compromise you and these other gentlemen."

Whether this declaration would have had any pacifying effect upon him had I not prefaced it with my ill-advised laughter I cannot say; but the laugh seemed to goad him into a paroxysm of such uncontrollable rage that he could barely endure to hear me to the end, and when I ended, he cried, in a voice positively thick and choking with fury—

"You are a liar, a smooth-tongued, hypocritical, cowardly liar; and having done your dirty traitor's work, you seek to cheat us by these lies. I know them to be lies."

This was unendurable. However much the person for whom this angry fool mistook me deserved this flood of abuse, it was certain that I didn't, and I wasn't going to put up with it. The quarrel, which belonged obviously to somebody else, was fast being foisted on to me, but no man can stand that sort of talk, and my temper began to heat up quickly. I moved a pace or two nearer, to be within striking distance, and then gave him a chance of retracting.

"I have explained to you that you have made a mistake, and in

15

return you call me a liar. I repeat you are entirely in error, and I call upon you, whoever you are, to withdraw your words unconditionally, make such enquiries as will satisfy you of your blunder, and then apologise to me. Otherwise——"

He listened with a smile on his face, and shrugged his shoulders contemptuously, at my unfinished sentence.

"Well, otherwise? I tell you again you are a liar and a perjured traitor to the cause."

I raised my fist to strike him in the face, when the two others interposed, thrust me back and away from him with considerable violence, and then covered me with their revolvers.

"No, no; none of that," growled one of them, threateningly. "You've done enough harm already. If what we believe is true, you're not fit for that kind of punishment. We'll deal with you, for the cursed pig you are."

I was not such a fool as to argue against two loaded revolvers levelled dead at my head and held within a yard. But it struck me that Colonel Livenza was not altogether satisfied with the interruption, and that he had some kind of personal interest in the affair which was apart from the motives of his companions.

"Do as you will," I said, after a second's thought. "And do it quickly. The people at the hotel to which I was going know where I have come. I told them; and a messenger will be here shortly from there." I intended this to frighten them; and for the moment it did so. But in the end it acted merely as a warning, and gave them time to concoct a lie with which to get rid of the hotel porter when he arrived.

One of them kept me covered with his pistol while the others talked together and referred to some papers which lay on a table. Then the man who had met me at the station, and whom I judged to be in some way the Colonel's inferior, turned to me with the papers in his hand, and began to question me.

"You admit you are Ferdinand Carbonnell?"

"My name is Ferdinand Carbonnell; I am an Englishman, the son of Lord Glisfoyle, an English nobleman, and I have come to Madrid from London to join——"

"Enough; you are Ferdinand Carbonnell. You have just come from Paris, haven't you?"

"I came through Paris, from London." A sneer showed that he regarded this admission as a contradiction of my previous statement. "Paris is on the direct route from London," I added.

"And on the indirect route from a thousand other places," he retorted. "Your only chance is to stick to the truth. You shall have a fair trial, and it will go less hard with you if you speak the truth. I

16

am Felipe Corpola, and this is Pedro Valera—you will know our names well enough."

"On the contrary, I never heard your names until this instant, nor that of Colonel Livenza until it was told me at the station."

"Santa Maria! what a lie!" exclaimed the third man, Valera, in a loud aside; and by this I gathered they were two Carlists prominent enough to be fairly well-known in the ranks of that wide company.

"On the 20th of last month you were at Valladolid, two days later at Burgos, and two days later still at Saragossa, urging that a rising should take place there simultaneously with that planned at Berga two months hence in May."

"I have not been at either of those places for three years past. At the dates you mention I was in London; and I warn you that you are giving me information which may prove very compromising for you and those associated with you. I am no Carlist." My protestation was received with fresh symptoms of utter disbelief.

"You were to go to Paris in connection with the funds needed for the enterprise; the two leaders chosen to go with you to receive the money were Tomaso Garcia and Juan Narvaez; and a list of the names of all the leaders in the matter was given to you."

"This is all an absolute blunder," I cried, indignantly. "I know nothing whatever of a jot or tittle of it."

"I warned you not to lie," cried Corpola, sternly. "This is all proved here in black and white under your own name;" and he flourished before me some documents. "This is the charge against you and explain it if you can. Almost directly afterwards our two comrades, Garcia and Narvaez, disappeared; nearly the whole of the men whose names were on that list given to you were arrested at one swoop by the Government; and a secret information in your handwriting together with the original list of the leaders found their way into the hands of the Government. Explain that act of foul treachery if you can"—and his voice almost broke with passion—"or may the Holy Mother have more mercy on you than we will have."

The intense earnestness and passion of the man were a proof of his sincerity, and also of the danger in which I stood. The whole thing was a mad mistake, of course; but that I could prove it in time to stop them taking the steps which I could see they contemplated was far less clear; and for the moment I was nonplussed. Up to that instant I had been so confident the mistake would be discovered that I had felt no misgivings as to the issue. But the sight of Corpola's burning indignation, his obvious conviction. that I was the man who had been guilty of the act which had so moved him, and my intuitive recognition that his fanaticism made him really dangerous, disturbed me now profoundly.

"Speak, man, speak," he cried, stridently, when I stood thinking in silence.

"I can only say what I have said before, that it is all a horrible mistake. I am not the man you think me."

"You are Ferdinand Carbonnell, you have admitted it."

"I am not the Ferdinand Carbonnell you accuse of treachery."

"What! Would you fool us with a child's tale that there are two Ferdinand Carbonnells? Can your wits, so subtle and quick in treachery spin no cleverer defence than that? By the Virgin, that one so trusted should sink so low! All shame to us who have trusted so poor a thing! Can you produce the list that was given you, or tell us something to let us believe that at the worst it was filched from you when you were drunk and so conveyed to the Government. Anything, my God, anything, but the blunt fact that we have harboured such a treacherous beast as a man who would deliberately sell his comrades." The sight of his passion tore me as a harrow tears and scarifies the ground.

"What I have told you is the truth. I am not the man."

"It is a lie; a damnable lie, and you are the paltry, filthy dog of a coward that you were called and shall have a dog's death. What say you, Valera?"

"He is guilty; serve him as he has served our comrades," growled the brute, with a scowl, taking some of the other's vehement passion into his more dogged, sluggish nature.

"Colonel, you are right. He is the traitor you declared, and I give my voice for his death. Aye, and by the Holy Cross, mine shall be the hand to punish him;" and he raised it on high and clenched it while the fury of his rage flashed from his eyes, flushed his mobile swarthy face, and vibrated in his impetuous, vindictive utterance. I had never seen a man more completely overwhelmed by the flood of passion; and for the moment I half expected him to turn his pistol on me there and then and send a bullet into my brain.

Colonel Livenza appeared also to have some such thought for he put himself between us.

"We must be cautious, Corpola," he said, and drew him aside to confer apparently as to the best means of dealing with me, Valera meanwhile keeping me covered with his revolver.

What to do I could not think. I made no show of resistance; that was clearly not my cue at present; but I had no intention of giving in without a very desperate attempt to escape; and I stood waiting for the moment which would give me the chance I sought, and planning the best means. By hook or crook I must get possession of one of the revolvers, and I watched with the vigilance of a lynx for an opportunity; I was a stronger man than either of the three and my

18

muscles were always in excellent trim, and in a tussle on equal terms I should not have feared the result of a scrimmage with two of them. Unarmed, however, I was completely at their mercy; and hence my anxiety.

The Colonel and Corpola were conferring together, arguing with much energy and gesture when someone knocked. The door was opened cautiously and I heard someone say that the porter from the hotel had brought my bag and had asked for me. There was another whispered conference, and then a message was sent in my name to the effect that I was not going to the hotel that night and probably not on the next day, as I had been called away. I would send for my luggage later. I protested vehemently against this, but my protest was disregarded; and I suffered a keen pang of mortification at seeing my precaution quietly checkmated in this way. It impressed upon me more vividly than anything else could have done the reality of the peril in which I stood.

When the messenger left, the discussion between the Colonel and Corpola was resumed, and I began to eye my guard more closely than ever, for some sign that his vigilance was sufficiently relaxed to enable me to make a spring upon him and seize his weapon.

But just when I was in the very act of making my effort another interruption came from without. There was a second knocking at the door, this time hurried and agitated, and a voice called, urgently and vehemently,

"Colonel Livenza, Colonel Livenza! I must see you at once."

It was a woman's voice, and the three men were obviously disturbed at it.

"Quick, you two. Take him into the next room," said Livenza, in a whisper.

Corpola and Valera seized me, and each menacing me with his revolver and pressing the barrel close against my head, led me into the dark room adjoining, Livenza opening the door and closing it again the instant we had passed.

"A single sound will cost you your life," whispered Corpola, fiercely into my ear, giving an additional pressure of the pistol-barrel by way of emphasis.

But he did not succeed in scaring me to the extent he hoped. The circumstances were now as much in my favour as I could expect to have them. It was not a pleasant experience to stand between two desperate fanatics in a dark room with their pistols pressed close to my head; but it was obvious that I had only to jerk my head out of the touch of the pistols to make it exceedingly difficult for my guards to regain their advantage.

19

Despite my awkward plight I was hopeful now, for both were positively trembling with excitement.

"What is the meaning of all this?" I whispered; designing merely to get them off their guard. "That was a woman's voice."

"Silence!" said Corpola, in a fierce whisper.

"Very well," I answered, with a big shrug of my shoulders.

This action was designedly intended to embarrass the two men, and for half a second the pressure of the pistol-barrels was relaxed; but that half-second was sufficient for me. I slipped my head back from between the pistols, and at the same moment caught the two men from behind and thrust them against each other; then turning on Valera, the weaker of the two, I gripped his revolver in my left hand, caught his throat with the other, and dragged him across the room, scattering chairs and tables and bric-a-brac in my course, and having wrested his weapon from him, flung him away from me into the darkness. Then I fired the revolver and sent up a shout for help that echoed and re-echoed through the room.

A loud cry in a woman's voice followed, then the sound of an excited altercation in high tones, the door of the room I had just left was thrown open and Colonel Livenza and a woman's figure showed in the frame of light.

"Have a care," I called. "I am armed now and desperate." But at that moment there was the flash and report of a pistol fired close to me and Corpola, who had used the moment to approach me stealthily from behind, threw himself on me. I had twice his strength, however, and my blood being up I turned on him savagely, and, untwisting his arms, seized him by the throat, and fearing Livenza might come to his aid, dashed his head against the wall with violence enough to stun him. Then jumping to my feet again and still having my revolver, I rushed to square matters with Livenza himself, who alone stood now between me and freedom.

At that instant the woman spoke.

"You are Ferdinand Carbonnell. Have no fear. You are quite safe now. I came here on your account." The words were good to hear in themselves; but the voice that uttered them was the most liquid, silvery and moving that had ever fallen on my ears; and so full of earnest sincerity and truth that it commanded instant confidence.

As she spoke she stepped back into the room and I saw her features in the light. To my surprise she was no more than a girl; but a girl with a face of surpassing beauty of the ripest southern type, and her eyes, large, luminous, dark brown glorious eyes, rested on my face with a look of intense concern and glowing interest.

"You will not need that weapon, Senor Carbonnell," she said, glancing at the revolver I still held.

"I am convinced of that," I answered, smiling, and tossed it on to the table.

"I thank you. You trust me," she said, with a smile, as she gave me her hand. "I am Sarita Castelar, this is my good aunt, Madame Chansette; Colonel Livenza, here, is now anxious to make amends to you for the extraordinary occurrences of to-night."

He was standing with a very sheepish, hang-dog expression on his face, and when she looked at him, I saw him fight to restrain the deep feelings which seemed to be tearing at his very heart during the few moments he was fighting down his passion. He looked at me with a light of hate in his eyes, crossed to the door, and threw it open.

"If I have made a mistake I regret it," he said, sullenly.

"Senor Carbonnell will give his word of honour, I know, not to speak of anything that has happened here to-night," said the girl.

"Willingly. I pledge my word," I assented, directly.

"Then we will go. Our carriage is waiting; will you let us take you to your hotel?" And without any further words we left the room and the house, Sarita insisting that I should lead Madame Chansette while she followed alone, having refused the Colonel's escort.

CHAPTER IV

SARITA CASTELAR

The rapid kaleidoscopic change in the situation, and the surprising means by which it had all been brought about, were so profoundly astonishing that for a time I was at a loss for words to thank the wonderful girl who had come to my rescue.

The palpitating actuality of imminent danger; the vehemence of Corpola's wild, fanatical passion; the tension as I stood in the dark room waiting for the moment to strike; the exertions of the two desperate struggles which followed, and then the sudden transition to the perfect assurance of safety which followed the intervention of Sarita Castelar, were succeeded by some minutes of reaction. I could not instantly reconcile myself to a return to the atmosphere of every-day commonplace.

The mere utterance of an ordinary formula of thanks seemed so inadequate to the occasion that I sat still and silent as we dashed through the now nearly-deserted streets, thinking over the whole mystery and wondering what could possibly be the clue.

Before I had collected my wits the carriage drew up with a jerk at the hotel.

"I have not thanked you," I said, feebly.

"You can do that another time if you think thanks are necessary. We shall be at home to-morrow afternoon. There is much to explain. Will you come then? 28, in the Plaza del Nuovo. But you know where we live."

"Yes, come, Senor Carbonnell," said Madame Chansette, "I am anxious to speak with you—most anxious."

"My dear aunt is in sore need of diplomatic advice to control her turbulent niece," said Sarita, laughing. "We shall expect you, mind."

"I shall certainly come," I answered, eagerly. "But I want——"

"No, no, not to-night. Everything to-morrow. Good-night;" and she held out her hand and dismissed me.

I stood staring blankly after the carriage, and then walked into the hotel feeling much like a man in a dream, dazzled by the beauty of the girl who had rendered me this inestimable service; and when I reached my room I threw open my window, gazed out over the moon-lit city, and steeped my senses in a maze of bewildering delight as I recalled the witchery of her inspiring voice, the glances of her lustrous, wonderful eyes, and the magnetic charm of her loveliness. At that moment the thoughts dearer to me than all else in the world were that she was so interested in me that she had done all this for my sake, that she was my cousin whose future and fortune her guardian wished me to protect and, above all, that I was to see her again on the morrow, and for many morrows. Madrid had become, instead of a place of exile, a veritable city of Blessed Promise.

How long I gazed out into the moonlight and rhapsodised in this fashion I do not know; but I do know that I had a sufficient interval of lucid commonsense to be conscious that I had fallen hopelessly in love with my cousin at first sight, and it was a source of rarest ecstasy to picture in fancy the great things I would achieve to serve her, and to hope that a chance of doing some of them would come my way. And when I got into bed and fell asleep it was to dream that I was doing them.

I am not exactly a rhapsodist by nature; and the lapse into

wistful dreaminess had all the charm of the unusual for me; but the morning found me in a much more practical frame of mind.

I reviewed coolly the strange events which had heralded my arrival in Madrid, and certain points began to trouble me; that there should be someone of doubtful repute of the same name as my own, and that so glorious a creature as Sarita Castelar should be deeply mixed up with Carlists of such a desperate character as those who had menaced my life.

Those were the matters which needed to be cleared up first, and I would ask her freely about them that afternoon. But in the meantime prudence warned me to hold my tongue about everything.

I went to the Embassy to report myself, and afterwards had lunch and a long chat with my old friend, Mayhew. His knowledge on all matters and persons in Madrid was quite cyclopedic, and he told me a hundred and one things that would be useful for me to know. I need only refer to two subjects. We were speaking of Spanish politics when he mentioned a name that kindled suddenly all my interest.

"The man of the hour here is Sebastian Quesada, the Minister of the Interior," he told me. "He is out-and-away the most powerful member of the Government, and, I believe, a most dangerous man. He plays for nothing but his own hand, and allows nothing to stand in his way. The most ghastly stories are told of him; and I believe most of them are true, while all of them might be. He will court you, fawn on you, threaten you, promote you, anything in the world so long as he can use you, and the instant you are useless to him or stand in his way, he kicks you out of it, ruins you, treads you in the gutter, imprisons you, or, if needs be, gets a convenient bullet planted in your head or a knife in your heart. You smile, but he has done it in more instances than one. He is piling up money fast by the most disreputable and dirtiest methods; and Heaven and himself only know how rich he is, for he is a veritable miser in his avarice and secrecy. But he has what so few in this strange, lackadaisical country possess—indomitable will and tireless energy. If you come his way, Carbonnell, give him as wide a berth as you can; or, look to yourself. And if ever you have to cross swords with him, arrange your affairs, make your will, and prepare for failure before you start on the expedition."

"I have heard of him," I said.

"Europe will hear of him, too, unless some one of his victims gets a chance to assassinate him. If this were a Republic, he would be President, and his policy would be pretty much like that of the Moors—he'd make his position permanent by killing off every possible competitor. And I'm not by any means sure that he won't yet be the first President of a Spanish Republic."

And this was the man who had filched the Castelar's patrimony, and it was to be part of my task to try and force him to disgorge it! A hopeful prospect.

"By the way, do you know a Colonel Livenza?" I asked.

"I know of him—Colonel Juan Livenza, you mean. There's not much to know about him. He's a cavalry officer of good family, held in fairly high esteem, and said to be a man of exemplary life. A royalist of the royalists; a bigot in his loyalty indeed, they say; and like all bigots, narrow-creeded and narrow-minded. A follower of Quesada, and either a believer in him or a tool. Presumably, Quesada hasn't yet had need to use him and get rid of him. But that day will come. Livenza is pretty much of a fanatic in his religion, his politics, and his militarism; and like all fanatics, has to be watched, because one lobe of the brain is always too big for the skull, and may lead him into danger. At present, indeed, it is sometimes whispered that he has a much more dangerous fanaticism than politics or religion—a passion for that turbulent little revolutionary beauty, Sarita Castelar. Now, Carbonnell, if you want a type of perfect Spanish beauty——"

"I know of her," I interposed, having no wish to hear his comments. "Her guardian, Madame Chansette, and my father are old acquaintances."

"Oh, well, keep your coat buttoned up and well padded on the left side with non-conducting substance when you come under the fire of the brightest eyes in Madrid. And keep your own eyes open, too," he said, with a glance and a laugh.

I did not think it necessary to tell him how nearly his words touched me, and I am glad to say my looks kept the secret as closely as my lips. But I thought with a smile of his caution when I started a little later for Madame Chansette's house, and found my heart beating much faster than was at all usual or necessary.

I was conscious of a little disappointment when I found Madame Chansette alone, and even the warmth of her very cordial welcome did not make amends.

"I am so glad you have come to Madrid, Mr. Carbonnell. I am in such need of advice and assistance; and Lord Glisfoyle writes me that you know everything."

"He told me something before I left London, but his chief instructions were that I should endeavour to find out precisely the position of things here, and then report to him, with any suggestions that might occur to us."

24

"We sadly want a man's capable head in our affairs," she said, weakly. "I am really dreadfully afraid at times."

"My strange experience of last night has told me something; would it be well for you, do you think, to say quite freely, what you fear, what troubles you, and what you think should be done?"

"I don't understand that affair last night at all. It distressed and frightened me so; but there are so many things I don't understand. What I wish is for Sarita to go away with me, either to Paris or England. She is getting so involved here. She is a dreadful Carlist, as I suppose you know; and believes she can play a great part in the political affairs of the nation. As if that were possible in a country like Spain. How it will end I am afraid to think. But we shall all be ruined;" and she sighed and tossed up her hands with a gesture of despair.

"But women are not taken very seriously in politics here, are they?" I asked.

"This is not politics, Mr. Carbonnell; it is conspiracy. The child worries her pretty head from morning to night, from one week to another, with all sorts of plots and plannings—I don't know a quarter of them—and Heaven be thanked I don't, or I should be in my grave. And then there's her brother. You know Ramon is really dangerous, and does awful things. I wouldn't have him here—but then, thank Heaven, he daren't show his face in Madrid. As if he, a young fellow, little more than a boy, silly enough to commit himself so deeply with the Carlists that he is actually compelled to keep in hiding, and fly about from place to place, always dodging the police and the soldiers, could hope to fight successfully with a powerful man like my nephew, Sebastian Quesada. I tell them both—at least, I tell Sarita, and I suppose she manages to communicate somehow with Ramon, for really she does some wonderful things—I tell them both they had much better give up all thought of trying to get back their fortune. He'll never give up a peseta. I suppose I know my own brother's child's nature. I'm a Quesada—you know that, I think— and I tell them that they might as soon expect to be King and Queen of Spain as to make Sebastian disgorge what he has once got hold of. Besides, there is no need. I have plenty for them both; and who should have it, if not my dear sister's children? At least, Ramon must really behave better if he wishes to regain my favour."

Madame Chansette was as voluble as she was inconsequential, and it was not until I questioned her closely that I could get any grasp of the case. She talked to me at great length, apparently much relieved to have someone into whose ear she could pour the tale of her troubles, and on whom she thought she could lean for support in them.

25

I could get few definite facts. Madame Chansette told me, as my father had done, that Ramon had been intended by his family for the priesthood, but had broken his vows, and had plunged into a life of dissipation, and had attempted to get a reckoning with Sebastian Quesada and recover his and Sarita's fortune. He was a wild, passionate lad, no match for Quesada in any respect, and had been driven by his passion to make two attempts on his enemy's life. As a result he had been proscribed, and had to live in hiding. He had then become a Carlist of the most violent kind, a veritable firebrand; moving from place to place under assumed names, and stirring up rebellion in all directions. He had also drawn his sister into his schemes, and she had so compromised herself that Madame Chansette had written in the last extremity to my father to beg him to intervene.

"There must be some man's capable head in the matter, or we shall all be ruined," she exclaimed dismally five or six times; although what the "man's capable head" was to do to restrain the very wilful beauty was not clear. Madame Chansette, as it seemed to me, meant that she was tired of the sole responsibility, and wished to share it with someone who could be blamed if matters went wrong.

"The position is a very difficult one," I admitted.

"Of course, I told her you were coming; that Lord Glisfoyle was as much her guardian as anyone, and that, as you were representing him, you would have authority yourself. You do agree with me, don't you, that she ought to give up this—this dangerous mischief, and just try to play a woman's legitimate part and get married? Of course, if you don't think that, your coming will only make matters worse than they were before; but I'm sure you will. You must have seen for yourself in that affair last night, whatever the meaning of it all was, how dangerous this conduct is, and how sure to lead to mischief."

"Have you told Sarita that you yourself would leave Madrid if she did not do as you wish?"

"My dear Mr. Carbonnell, how could I?" cried the dear, weak old lady, apparently aghast at the notion. "How could I possibly leave the sweet child here alone? What would she do without me? Besides, how could I? Why, she rules me just as she rules everyone else who comes in contact with her. She wouldn't let me go;" and she smiled so sweetly and feebly—"and I love her so. No one can help it. It would kill me to leave her."

As this was somewhat difficult of reply, I said nothing; and after a few seconds she glanced at her watch and exclaimed—

"Oh, dear, my time is all but up, and I fear I have got so little way with you." Seeing my perplexed expression, she laughed, and added: "Of course, my seeing you alone first is Sarita's arrangement. She does the drollest things. She declared that she would give me every chance of persuading you to side with me, and that she would not say a word of any kind to you to influence you until you and I had had an hour's private conference. And now, what will you do, Mr. Carbonnell?" and she put her white, thin hand on my arm, and looked quite eagerly into my face.

"I will promise to serve you to my utmost, Madeline Chansette," I said.

"Spoken like an Englishman and a diplomatist," exclaimed the voice that had so thrilled me on the preceding night; and, turning, I saw Sarita had entered the room unperceived. "You would make poor conspirators, you two, for you've been plotting against me with an open door," she added, coming forward.

She looked even more lovely than on the previous night, and she gave me as warm a welcome as had Madame Chansette—put both her hands into mine and held them, without a touch of self-consciousness, as she gazed frankly and searchingly into my eyes. She appeared satisfied with a scrutiny that was rather embarrassing to me, and smiled as she withdrew her hands.

"Yes, I am glad you have come, cousin Ferdinand. I suppose I may call him cousin Ferdinand, aunt Mercedes? I don't know how you do in more formal England, but we Spaniards are quicker in the use of the Christian name," she added to me. "I wanted to look closely at you. It is a new thing for me to have a male relation who may be a friend—or an enemy, such as my dearest aunt here. I have only Ramon, whose friendship is more dangerous at times than another man's enmity would be; and my other cousin, Sebastian Quesada." The tone in which she uttered the name was intensely significant. "Yes, yes, I am satisfied. I am glad you have come. You are true. You trusted me instinctively last night; and I will trust you always. My impressions are never wrong. But you will not find me tractable any the more for that; I mean in my dear, dear, dearest aunt's sense of the word," and she kissed the little old lady once for each of the epithets.

"I will try to deserve your words of welcome, cousin Sarita," I said earnestly, but conscious of a clogging tongue.

"I hope so—for you are one of those men who always succeed when they really try. But you have already promised to serve this dear, dreadful, tyrannous, loving enemy of mine. So take care;" and she laughed softly as she was bending over Madame Chansette and settling her more comfortably in her chair. "You are to show that 'capable man's head' which aunt Mercedes is never tired of

27

declaring is so much needed in our affairs." She sat down close to Madame Chansette and took her hand. "I am a sad rebel, am I not, little tyrant?"

"If I didn't love you so much, I should be a far better guide for you, child," was the simply-spoken reply.

"Aye, with a love as sweet and tolerant and true as a mother's," said Sarita, softly. "So sweet that it makes even rebellion like mine difficult and hard at times. You must know, cousin Ferdinand, that we are a most divided pair. In all but our love—which nothing can ever disturb or threaten—we are like the poles, so far apart are our tastes, our principles, our ways, our aims, our lives, everything. You can think, therefore, how we have discussed you. At first aunt Mercedes said Lord Glisfoyle would come; and then I was not interested. I knew what a man of his years would say to me; and there was nothing before me but flat, dogged rebellion. But when we knew that he was not coming, and you were to come in his place— ah, that was different indeed. I warned my dearest that her last hope was gone; that youth—even diplomatic youth—would side with youth, and that if she looked to you for help in her plans, she would be disappointed. We discussed you, analysed you, weighed you, thought of you, talked of you, and, I think, each resolved to win you. I did;" and she smiled frankly.

"Sarita!" exclaimed Madame Chansette, protestingly. "You must have mercy on Mr. Carbonnell. He does not know you."

"I will have no mercy where he is concerned. You would not have me spare you the truth, or hide how much we were interested in you?" she cried to me. "Why should you not know how much you have been in our thoughts, seeing how much you were to influence our lives? I will deal with you perfectly frankly."

"I may hold you to that pledge," I interposed.

"Oh yes, I will tell you everything, presently. But I was so sure of you that I readily agreed Aunt Mercedes should have the first interview with you to poison your ears and prejudice your judgment against me—if this dearest and best of mothers to me could prejudice anyone against me. And, you see, I was right—she has not succeeded;" and she flashed a glance of challenge at me.

"Have I already shown my thoughts?" I asked.

"How gravely judicial and impartial you would be," she retorted. "But I can go even farther. I can put my good aunt's case with greater force than she would put it, I am sure, and yet be confident. I am a Carlist; I am saturated with a love of liberty; I am in league with many dangerous men; I am fighting against a hopelessly powerful antagonist; I am steering a course that aims at achieving ideal happiness for my country, but much more probably may achieve nothing but utter shipwreck for myself; I have an unruly ambition; I am learning to be a man; to think of, hope for, work for the objects of men; I am daring to lead where I should scarcely venture to follow; I am even mad enough to take ideals to my heart and to strive for them; and this best of women believes that in daring to take a man's part I run a risk of ceasing to be a woman. She would have me lay down the task, break with my ideals, leave my country to those who now misrule it, and fly—to safety. Do you think I should do this? or if I should, that I shall?"

"Before I answer I will hear your own side," I said, quietly.

"Ah, there spoke an Englishman—a man with a microscope, to examine, try, inspect, measure, and compare this with that, and that with this, before you venture an opinion. What a wonderful thing is English discretion. But you shall hear it."

Madame Chansette rose at that, and Sarita rose too, and took her arm tenderly and, as it were, protectingly.

"I will leave you. Sarita will speak freely, Mr. Carbonnell; but remember she is steering for shipwreck—her own words."

They went away together then, and presently Sarita came back alone.

"You will think ours a strange household and a stranger partnership. But for all our conventionality we love each other as if we were mother and daughter; and I know how much I make that dear heart suffer at times." She paused, and then said: "And so you are the real Ferdinand Carbonnell. You were surprised to find your name so well known in Madrid? To me amongst others?"

"Tell me what that means," I said.

"It is your own name used intentionally," was the somewhat startling reply.

"My own name? Used by whom?"

"There is no other Ferdinand Carbonnell in all Spain than yourself. You are, as I say, the real Ferdinand Carbonnell."

She looked at my puzzled face with a half whimsical, half doubting expression, and then burst into one of her sweet, musical, witching laughs. "You shall know everything," she said.

CHAPTER V

THE EXPLANATION

Sarita did not speak for some time but sat with a very thoughtful look on her face which she turned now and again toward me, as though some point in her reverie had been reached which concerned me and made her doubtful.

"Yes, I am sorry, deeply sorry, and would undo it if I could!" she exclaimed at last, giving an impulsive utterance to her thoughts, and then jumping up and pacing the floor.

"Sorry for what?" I asked. "If it concerns me, as it seems to, pray do not trouble. I am not of much account."

"I am sorry that we used your name. Had I known what manner of man you were, nay, could I even have guessed you would ever come to Madrid, I would never have sanctioned it."

"Suppose you tell me what the thing means. I am not very quick, and I confess to being very much puzzled."

"It means that part of what you heard last night is quite true. Ferdinand Carbonnell is a Carlist leader—a secret leader, you understand—but held for one of the most dangerous, desperate, and capable of them all. And yet there is no Ferdinand Carbonnell in all Spain but yourself."

"I don't see that that need distress you or disturb me very seriously, whatever the puzzle may mean. A name is only a name, after all. But what is this puzzle?"

"Now that I see you I know that we have wronged you," she cried, vigorously.

"The weight of even that responsibility need not prevent your speaking plainly. Let me hear about it. It's very likely I shall enjoy it as much as you have, probably, up till now—I am not exactly like other men in all respects. I'm no stickler for conventionalities."

"Ferdinand Carbonnell, the Carlist leader, is really an embodiment of Ramon's and my Carlism. Let me tell you the truth. So long as I have known that your father, Lord Glisfoyle, was my uncle—and Aunt Mercedes told me some two years ago—I have bitterly resented his conduct in ignoring us, leaving us to bear the injustice of these Quesadas, our other relatives, and treating us, his brother's children, as though we were outcasts, pariahs, unworthy of his aristocratic recognition."

"You have wronged my father, cousin. I believe he has always held it his business to know that matters were well with you."

30

"Knowing you now, I can believe that. But I thought that some little trouble on his part, for a boy needs a man's hand, would have made my brother's life a far better one. We Spaniards, too, are quick to anger—and do not always stay to think. I grew to hate the names of Glisfoyle and Carbonnell; and when Ramon's great trouble came, when his wildness drove him to seek Sebastian Quesada's life and he failed, and was proscribed and had to take another name, he and I together chose yours—Ferdinand Carbonnell. It was Spanish enough to pass for the name of a Spaniard; and we took a delight—malicious, wrong-headed, unholy delight if you will—in building up for it a character which would at least shock the prudish sensibilities of a noble English family should they ever hear of it."

"I understand, partly; but still I don't see that it was such a very terrible matter," I added with a smile. "As I say, a name is no more than a name." I was anxious to lessen her very obvious concern; and did not in reality take the thing at all seriously.

"It came within very little of being terrible, last night," she replied.

"I don't know that. I had plenty of fight left in me even at the ugliest moment. And at any rate, the ending more than made amends for the whole suspense." She made a quick gesture of protest. "But what was meant by the suggestion that your Ferdinand Carbonnell had been guilty of treachery?"

"Wait, please. When we created the mythical Ferdinand Carbonnell, it was because there seemed no room for me, a girl, in the great work of Carlism; I therefore introduced a new element into the form of agitation. Instead of all the leaders knowing each other and interchanging views personally and openly, only a few of the leaders of the new movement were to know one another; there was to be as much secrecy as possible and Ferdinand Carbonnell was to be the mythical and yet terribly real centre of all. To establish that was our first stroke. Ramon did it under my guidance; going from place to place, now in one name now in another; but everywhere speaking of, and advocating the new departure, and everywhere preaching up the greatness of the new and secret leader, nameless to many, and to the chosen few known as Ferdinand Carbonnell."

"Very mysterious," said I, not quite seriously, despite her earnestness. "But these men spoke of interviews with people, of delegates to go with me to Paris, of lists of names given to me, and so on. As if Ferdinand Carbonnell were anything but an impersonal myth."

"There is something in that I have not probed; but it was false— a tissue of falsehoods. Why, it would make Ramon and me traitors," she cried in a tone of splendid repudiation. I thought a moment.

31

"But it was this same treachery which set these men first to snare and then threaten me. And I am much mistaken if there was not a personal motive of hate at the back of this Colonel Juan Livenza's conduct. Can your brother have used this name anywhere or at any time, and can he and these men have fallen foul of each other?"

To my surprise the question loosed a full rich flood of crimson colour, and the flush spread up to the brow until the whole face glowed like a brilliant damask rose.

"You will have to know these matters," she said, with a touch of embarrassment. "No, Ramon has used the name once or twice, but never in that way. These two have never met; or he would have known last night, of course, you were not Ramon. No, it is this. Ramon and I meet very seldom—though we love one another dearly—and as I am afraid on his account to let people know that he is my brother, our meetings have to be secret, and—might be mistaken for those of a different character."

"I see."

"I have to-day found out that herein our own house there has been a spy; spies here are as plentiful as fools," she cried, contemptuously. "This was a woman whom I trusted somewhat, and she carried news of my concerns to Juan Livenza. She may have told him of my meetings with Ramon; it is likely, for she did not know Ramon was my brother. She has very possibly jumbled up some connection between him and Ferdinand Carbonnell; for Ramon has written to me often in that name, and I to him, sometimes. Then she probably saw here a reference to your arrival here last night, or she may have heard Aunt Mercedes and myself discussing it; and she has carried the news to her employer. It is easy for men in some moods to see facts in either fears or hopes."

"And his mood was?" At my question and glance her colour began to mount again.

"He loves me." She met my look half-defiantly, her eyes fixed on mine as if daring me to utter a word of protest. But the next instant the light died out, her glance fell to the ground, and she added: "I could win him to the cause in no other way."

I had to put a curb of steel strength on myself to prevent my feelings speaking from my eyes, or in my gestures; and in a tone as cold and formal as I could make it, I replied—

"You are not afraid to use sharp weapons. And yourself? Do you care? I had better know everything."

She raised her head, flashed her eyes upon me, drew herself up, and said with great earnestness—

32

"I have no heart for anything but the cause." A very stalwart champion she looked for any cause, and very lovely.

"I begin already to take your aunt's side in the matter, and to think you will get into too deep waters, cousin Sarita." She laughed, easily.

"The deeper the water the greater the buoyancy for those who know how to swim. I am not yet enough of a man to count dangers in advance."

"It is not difficult to despise dangers one doesn't see or credit."

"Nor to take a map and write 'pitfall,' 'abyss,' 'precipice,' 'dangerous,' in blood colour at every inch of a road you mean to travel. Nor with us Spaniards does that kind of timorous dread pass for high and prudent valour." She uttered the retort quickly, almost angrily.

"I am not a map-maker nor colourer by profession," I answered, slowly, with a smile. "But if I were, I confess I should like to have something more about a particular route than the bald statement that, 'This road leads to—blank' or 'That to blazes.' A knowledge of the country is never amiss, and a tip at the crossroads—and there are plenty of them—can come in mighty handy." I spoke coolly and almost lazily, in deliberate contrast to her fire and vehemence, and when I finished she looked at me as if in surprise.

"And you are the same man as last night?" she cried, wrinkling her forehead.

"Oh, that was different. There are moments when you have a stiff bit of country to negotiate, and you have to jam your hat down over your eyes, shove your heels into your nag's side, and take it as it comes, hot foot and all hazards in, and get there. But the pace that wears for everyday work is the jog trot, with a wary eye even for a rabbit hole or a rolling stone."

"Give me the reckless gallop. I am angry with you when you play at being the man with the microscope. I don't want such a man on my side—cold, phlegmatic, calculating, iceful. I would have a cousin, not a lawyer. I am not a microscopic object, to be analysed, probed, peered at, and stuck on a pin for the curious to wonder at. I am a woman, warm flesh and blood, a thing of life and hopes and aspirations, and I want a friend, a sympathiser, a cousin. But a man with a microscope, ah!" and her eyes were radiant with disdain.

"You think I would not—or could not—serve you?" I think my voice must have said more than my words, for she turned upon me swiftly, her face glowing with a different light and softened with a rarely seductive smile.

"Are you trying to dupe me? To hide your real character? Are

33

you posing as a mere piece of investigating diplomatic machinery? Oh, how I wish you were. Do you know you tempt me sorely to tell you what I meant to keep secret? My eyes are not easily blinded, cousin Ferdinand; have a care," and she shook her finger laughingly at me, and then sat down near me, and in a position which, when I looked at her, caused me to face the full light. Not a little embarrassing, considering all things; but I controlled my features carefully. "Are you really cold and calculating and fireless, with just flashes of energy and light; or is the fire always there, and do you know it and fear its effects, and stamp it down with that resolution that now sits on your brow and sets your face like a steel mask?" and she leaned forward and looked closely at me.

"I am full of desire to help you!" I said, controlling my voice.

"Full of desire to help me," she echoed, setting her head on one side whimsically, and pausing. Then she asked, seriously, "What would you do to help me?"

"Surely that must depend upon the case that calls for my help!"

"What an Englishman you are! If only we Spaniards were like you, what a nation we should be!" This with a flash of enthusiasm that was all sincere. "How long have you known of my existence, cousin?" she cried, harking back to her growing purpose.

"A few days."

"And were you told I was in deep trouble? None of your great, lordly house have yet concerned yourselves with us!"

"A proper rebuke perhaps, if you have been in trouble."

"If? Is it not so?"

"You don't wear the trappings of trouble; this house——"

"How English again!" she burst in. "What sort of a coat does he wear? How does she dress? And when you know that, you judge the character!"

"Not all of us."

"You wish me to think you an exception?"

"At least my sympathies with you should guide me right."

"That is pretty and not unpromising; but what was my trouble as described to you? Did it stir your sympathies?"

"I have not yet a clear knowledge of all your trouble. I wish to know."

"That you may help me?"

"That I may help you, if you will let me."

"I believe you would," she exclaimed. "I almost believe it, that is. Why is it that while we Spaniards hate you English, we can't help believing your word?"

"Hate is a strong word," said I, with a glance.

"It is a strong feeling, cousin."

34

"Fortunately our relation is not international."

She laughed, softly, musically, and ravishingly.

"No, not international in that respect."

"So that we are able to make a treaty of alliance," I said.

"Offensive and defensive?" she cried, quickly, and seemed to wait somewhat anxiously for my answer.

"Defensive certainly," I replied. She gave an impatient shrug of her shoulders and half turned away. "And offensive—with limitations," I added. "There are limitation clauses in every treaty of alliance." She turned to me again, and looked at me long and steadfastly; then sighed and rose.

"I have never been so tempted in my life, cousin Ferdinand. But I will not. No—no;" another deep sigh. "I dare not. But while I am in the mood—for I am a creature of moods and a slave of them—let me tell you what you ought to know. I have lately been desperate, and in my desperation I planned to draw you into the snare. I needed you. I wished to make use of you. No, no, don't smile as if the thing were nothing, or as if you were too strong, too cautious, too level-headed, too English, to be caught even in a Spanish snare. Let me finish. We need someone in the British Embassy here; some friend to our cause, who will help us with information, will form a link between us here and our friends in London; and when I heard you were coming, I intended you to fill that role. It was wicked, horribly wicked, and cowardly, too; but for the cause I would do any crime and call it virtue," she exclaimed vehemently.

"And now that you have seen me, you don't think I'm worth the trouble?" I asked, looking at her.

"I should prize your help more than ever," she cried, with equal vehemence; adding slowly, "but I will not take it."

"You would never have had it in the way you planned, cousin. But for anything short of that it is yours at any moment for the mere asking—aye, without the seeking, if the chance comes. It is, however, Sarita my cousin, not Sarita Castelar the Carlist, that I wish to help."

"Do you think you can draw a distinction? No, no; a thousand noes. You cannot; for I can only strike at Sebastian Quesada through my Carlism. If you knew his power and influence, and my weakness, as a girl, you would know that: one individual, unnoticed girl, one puny leaf of millions rustling on the twig to oppose the tempest strong enough to strip the whole tree. What is my weakness to his power? and yet—I will beat him; face him, drag him down, aye, and triumph, and drag from him that which he holds in his thief's clutches, and execute on him the justice which the law is powerless to effect."

35

"You hate this man deeply?"

"Should a daughter love the man who killed her mother, or a sister him who ruined her brother?"

"You cannot fight against him. It is impossible. This time I am but a few hours in Madrid, but I have already learnt the facts of his immense influence and power."

"I don't ask your help," she said, wilfully.

"That is not generous. What I can do to help I am ready to do. But it is a mad chase." I shook my head, as if discouragingly; but, in fact, the very difficulties of the matter appealed to me and attracted me. I recalled Mayhew's caution against crossing swords with Quesada, and the danger of it was anything but displeasing. I did not speak of this to Sarita, however.

"You will not frighten me from my purpose," she said, with a smile of self-confidence; "and I will tell you what no one else dreams—I am certain to succeed. There will always be one door to success open to me if I have the courage to use it—and it will need courage—the courage of a foiled, desperate woman. When all else has failed, that will succeed."

I looked the question, which she answered in her next words.

"He has a secret which I alone possess. The world is full of his greatness, his influence, his power, his wealth, his judgment, his ambition, his fame, and his magnificent future—but only one soul on this dull earth knows his heart."

"You mean——" I asked, slowly.

"That to-morrow, if I would, I could be his wife. That door of revenge will never shut, for he is that rare thing among us Spaniards, a man of stable purpose. And why should I not?" she cried, with a swift turn, as though I had put her on her defence; and her eyes shone and her cheeks glowed. "Between him and me, as he himself has declared, it is a duel to the death. If I will not be his wife he will crush me: he has said it, and never has he failed to carry out a threat. It is true that I hate him: I feed my rage on the wrongs he has done to us. But what then? If we women may be sold for money, traded to swell the pride of a millionaire's triumph, may we not sell ourselves for a stronger motive? What think you of a marriage of hate? A marriage where the woman, with the cunning we all have, hides under the soft laughter of her voice, the caressing sweetness of her glances, the smooth witchery of her looks and simulated love, the intent to ruin, to drag down the man that has bought her, to sear his mind with the iron of her own callousness, to watch, wait, mask, win, lure, cheat and scheme, until the moment comes when the truth can be told and the hour of her revenge strikes."

"It is a duel in which even then you would be worsted; and if you ask my opinion of the scheme, I think it loathsome." There was no lack of energy in my tone now. I spoke hotly, for the idea of her marriage with Quesada was hateful. She changed in an instant, dropped the curt vehemence of manner and smiled at my quick protest.

"Yet the world would see in it a dramatically apt ending to a serious family feud."

"The world will see right in whatever he chooses to do at present. But while you hold that project in contemplation, I cannot help you," I said, and rose as if to go.

"As you will," she answered coldly, and turned away to look out of the window. For a full minute she remained silent, and then, turning back quickly, keeping my face to the light, she placed her hands upon my shoulders and searched my face with a look that seemed to kindle fire in the very recesses of my soul, as she asked in a tone that thrilled me: "And if to gain your help I abandon it, will you help me?"

"Yes, with every power I possess," I cried earnestly, gazing down into her eyes. "On my honour as an Englishman."

She did not take her hands away, and let her eyes linger on my face till I could feel the colour of delight creeping up to my cheeks, and could scarce hold myself steady under the magnetism of her touch and glance. It was not in human nature to bear unmoved such an ordeal; and I think she divined something of the struggle within me.

"You give me your word of honour voluntarily. I know what that means to an Englishman."

"I give you my word of honour, cousin Sarita," I answered firmly and earnestly, feeling at the moment I could have laid down my life for her. But the next moment with a slight push she seemed as if to thrust me and my offer away from her. She moved back and shook her head.

"No. I will not take your word," she cried. "You would go away and would grow cool and reflect, and say—'I am sorry. I was rash. My English prudence was smothered. I am sorry.' I do not want this. I would have your help—Heaven knows how sadly and how sorely I need help; true, sincere, honest, manly, and unselfish, such as I know yours would be; and how I would cherish it. But no, no, no, a hundred noes. There shall be one man at least able to say—'Sarita has always been candid to me.' If you came to me, I should whelm you surely in the flood of my Carlism; and I should drag you down and ruin you. I meant to do it—I told you so; and to you I will be candid. I needed you, not for yourself—I did not know you then; I had not seen you, and it was for the cause that to me is the breath of life. But I release you. Go now. I have seen you—I know you. You are true—aye, cousin, as true a man, I believe, as a friendless, often desperate woman might long to have for a comrade; but no, no, I cannot, I cannot!" she cried wildly and half incoherently, her arms moving with gestures of uncertainty. She covered her face and as quickly uncovered it and smiled.

"You will think me a strange rhapsodist. But when you offered to help me—ah, you can't think how tempted I was. I have resisted it, however;" and she smiled again and almost instantly sighed deeply. "You have come too soon—or too late."

"Too soon or too late? I would do anything in the world for you, Sarita," I exclaimed, scarcely less deeply moved than she herself.

"You are too soon for me to be callous enough to make use of you; I am not yet desperate enough. And too late to save me from myself. But I shall see you again when the hour of temptation is not so sweetly near;" and with that, showing many signs of feeling, she hurried from the room.

CHAPTER VI

"COUNTING ALL RENEGADES LOVERS OF SATAN"

The interview with Sarita excited me greatly, and I was too much engrossed by the thoughts of it to be able to bear with equanimity a second edition of Madame Chansette; so that when that dear and most amiable of women came to me, I pleaded an engagement and left the house.

As I passed through the hall there was a trifling incident, to which at the moment I paid very little heed. A couple of men were standing in whispered conference by the door and did not notice my approach until the servant made them aware of it. Then they drew aside, one with the deference of a superior servant, the other with a quite different air. He looked at me very keenly and apparently with profound interest, then drew aside with a very elaborate bow and exclaimed:

"Senor, it is an honour."

This drew my attention to him, and I set him down for an

eccentric and gave him a salute as well as a pretty sharp look. He was a long-visaged, sharp-eyed, high-strung individual, moderately well-dressed, the most noticeable feature in my eyes being the exaggerated courtesy, not to say obsequiousness, of his manner toward me. I dismissed the matter with a smile, however, and went back to my thoughts of Sarita and her affairs.

I walked back slowly to my hotel revolving them, and while I was standing in the hall a few moments, was surprised to see the man I had noticed at Madame Chansette's house walk past the hotel on the opposite side of the street. For a moment this annoyed me. It looked uncommonly as if he had followed me, and although I tried to laugh at the incident as a mere absurdity, or coincidence, or at worst a result of the fellow's eccentricity, I was not entirely successful; and now and again during the rest of the day it recurred to me, to start always an unpleasant series of conjectures.

The truth was, Sarita's involvement with these confounded Carlists, the extraordinary connection between her and the man who had prepared that welcome for me to Madrid, and the conviction fast settling down upon me that she was rushing full steam and all sails set on the rocks, had got on my nerves; and I was quite disposed to believe the fellow had followed me intentionally, and that the episode was a part of that spyism she had declared so prevalent.

In the evening Mayhew dined with me, and after dinner I took possession of some rooms he had found for me in the Calle Mayor; and the bustle of getting my things in order and the chatter with him served to relieve the strain of my thoughts. But he was quick enough to see something was amiss with me and would have questioned me had I given him the slightest encouragement.

The next morning brought another disquieting incident. I walked to the Embassy, and Mayhew joined me on the Plaza Mutor and we went on together. As we stood in the doorway the spy—as in my thoughts I had begun to term him—passed the end of the building, paused a moment to look in my direction, and then went on.

"What is it, Carbonnell?" asked Mayhew, seeing me start.

"Nothing, old man; at least nothing yet; if it turns into something, I'll speak to you about it," and not wishing him to have any clue I wheeled about and went in.

Then I found something else to think about. There was a letter from my father with very grave news about his health. After a preamble on general matters, he wrote:—

"And now, my dear son, there is something you must know. I have for some time past had serious apprehensions about my health, and some months ago consulted the great heart specialist, Dr. Calvert, about it. He put me off with vague assurances at the time, saying he must study the case; but I have succeeded to-day in getting him to tell me the truth. As I explained to him, a man in my position is not like ordinary folk; he must know things and be prepared. The great responsibility of a peerage requires that its affairs should not be jeopardised or involved by any surprise such as sudden death; and I should be a coward if I could be so untrue to my order as to leave matters unsettled out of a paltry fear of facing the truth. I hope none of us Carbonnells will ever be such poltroons. The truth is, it seems, that my death may happen at any moment. For myself I hope I should never share so vulgar a sentiment as the fear of death, and I let Dr. Calvert see I was really astonished that he should have thought a man of my order and position would be so untrue to the instincts of his breeding—to say nothing of religion.

"Well, that is the verdict; and now for its effect upon you. I am chiefly concerned for you and Mercy; because Lascelles must have every pound that can be spared to maintain the position which the title imposes. Mercy has from her mother about three hundred pounds a year, and this will maintain her should she be so unfortunate as not to marry. For her I can do no more, and for you can, unfortunately, do nothing. The utmost that I dare leave away from the title is one thousand pounds; and this I have left you in the fresh will I have made to-day. I have no doubt that Lascelles, if he marries well, as I hope he will, will always assist you; but you have now the chance of helping yourself—your foot is upon the ladder— and I am very glad that our recent exertions, though prompted by no thought of what we know now about my health, have resulted in your getting such a start. You have abilities of your own, and I urge you to use them to the best advantage in your present sphere, and I pray God to bless you. While I live of course your present allowance will continue.

"Then, lastly, as to the Castelars. Tell Madame Chansette what I have told you about my health, and say that I can do positively and absolutely nothing for them. But if you yourself can do anything, do it by all means. If you can spare me any particulars, however, do so. I do not shirk my duties as head of my house; I hope I never shall shirk them; but the fewer anxieties I have now the better—so, at least, says Dr. Calvert.

"Ours has been a life of many and long periods of separation, Ferdinand, but you have been a dear son to me, and one of my few sorrows is, that I cannot better provide for you."

The letter moved me considerably. My father and I had never been very closely associated, but there was a genuine affection between us; and the courage with which he faced the inevitable, though so characteristically expressed, appealed to me strongly. I did not resent my virtual disinheritance. The lot of the younger son had never galled me much, and I was enough of a Carbonnell to admit the reasoning and to recognise that such money as there was must go to keep up the peerage. But I did not delude myself with any sparkling visions of what Lascelles would do for me if he married well; and I perceived quite plainly that now, indeed, my future lay in my own hands only, and that it would be only and solely such as I could make it.

In one respect solely did this thought sting me. It was a barrier between Sarita and me. I must marry for money or not at all, for the plain bed rock reason that I had not, and probably never should have, money to support a wife.

More than that, the letter doomed me to a continuance of my present career. I should be dependent upon it always for mere existence money; and this meant that I must make it the serious purpose of life, and not merely a means for extracting as much pleasure as possible out of the place where I might chance to be posted. This made me grave enough for a time, for I knew of a dozen men with more brains than I possessed, as qualified for the work as I was ignorant, and as painstaking as I was the reverse, who had toiled hard and religiously for many years to acquire just enough income to enable them to know how many of the good things of life they had to do without.

But Nature had kindly left out the worry lobe from my brain, and I soon held lightly enough the news as it affected my own pecuniary prospects. I took more interest in my work that day than I should otherwise have taken, I think, and found it very irksome. I wrote to my father, and then went off to my rooms with a complete present irresponsibility and a feeling of thankfulness that I had always been a comparatively poor man, and that I should be a big fool if I were to add the wretchedness of worry to the sufficient burden of comparative poverty.

I was whistling vigorously as I opened my door and stopped, with the handle in my fingers, in sheer surprise, at seeing in possession of my rooms the man whom I believed to be a spy. He was sitting reading as he waited, and on seeing me he rose and made me one of his ceremonious bows.

"Who are you, and what do you want here?" I asked in none too gracious a tone, as I frowned at him.

"Senor Ferdinand Carbonnell—you are Ferdinand Carbonnell?"—he repeated the name with a kind of relish—"I could not resist coming. I could not resist the desire to speak to you, to stand face to face with you, to take your hand. I have done wrong, I know; but I shall throw myself on your mercy. I am leaving again to-night; but I could not go without seeing you."

My former impression of him seemed to be confirmed. The man was a lunatic, or at least an eccentric; and a word or two to humour him would do no harm.

"You have been following me; may I ask why?" I asked, in a less abrupt tone.

"I heard your name mentioned at the house where I saw you yesterday. The friend who mentioned it knew nothing; but I knew; and when I heard you were in the house, Senor, do you think I could leave without a sight of you? Ah, Mother of God!"

I was rolling myself a cigarette with a half smile of amusement at the man's eccentricity when a thought occurred to me. I stopped in the act, and looked at him sharply and questioningly. The thought had changed my point of view suddenly, and instead of amusement my feeling was now one of some uneasiness.

"Just be good enough to tell me exactly what you mean; and be very explicit, if you please," I said.

"I am from Saragossa, Senor Ferdinand Carbonnell, and my name is Vidal de Pelayo," he answered, in a tone and manner of intense significance. There was purpose, meaning, and pregnant earnestness in the answer, but no eccentricity.

"I don't care if you are from Timbuctoo and your name is the Archangel Gabriel. What do you mean?" I cried, testily.

The manner of his answer was a further surprise. He plunged his hand somewhere into the deepest recesses of his clothes and brought out a small, folded paper, from which he took a slip of parchment, and handed it to me without a word.

"Vidal de Pelayo. No. 25. 1st Section. Saragossa.
"Counting all renegades lovers of Satan. By the grace of God.
(Signed) FERDINAND CARBONNELL."

The signature was written in a fine free hand utterly unlike my own, of course; but there it was confronting me, and signed to a couple of lines that read to me like so much gibberish. I turned it over and handed it back with a laugh; and my thoughts went back again to my first opinion of the man.

"Very interesting, no doubt; and very important, probably, but it does not enlighten me."

"You mean you do not wish to know me? As you will. Then I suppose I must not open my lips to you? But I have seen you; and it is a great day for me!"

"You are right; I wish you to say nothing," I replied, assuming a very grave look and speaking very severely. "You have done wrong to come here at all," I added, seeing the effect of my previous words. "You must not come again."

"You will wish to know that all is going well?" he said, in a tone of remonstrance and surprise.

"I have other means of learning everything," I answered, with a suggestion of mystery, and rose as a hint to him to go.

"You are at the British Embassy here. It is wonderful," he cried, lifting his hands as if in profound admiration.

"Where I am and what I do concerns no one," I returned, cryptically. "We all have our work. Return to yours."

"I have seen you. You will give me your hand—the hand that has put such life into the cause. God's blessing on you. 'Counting all renegades lovers of Satan. By the grace of God.'" He uttered the formula with all the air of a devout enthusiast; and I gazed at him, keeping a stern set expression on my face the while, and wondering what on earth he meant by the jargon. "And you are indeed Ferdinand Carbonnell?" he said again, fixing his glowing eyes on me as he held my hand.

"I am Ferdinand Carbonnell," I assented, nodding my head and wishing he would go.

"I have made the arrangements required of me. When the little guest arrives he will be in safe and absolutely secret keeping."

"What little guest?" I asked.

"Yes, indeed, what little guest? For what is he now but a guest and a usurper, like a pilfering cuckoo in the eagle's eyrie? Why has it never been done before? Why left to you to propose? But it will change everything—a magnificent stroke," and his voice trembled with earnestness and, as it struck me now, with deep sincerity.

Was he after all no more than a madman? In a moment I ran rapidly over the facts as I knew them, and a suspicion darted into my mind. I resolved to probe further.

"Sit down again, senor. I have thought of something," I said, and placed wine and tobacco before him. We rolled our cigarettes and lighted them; and all the time I was casting about for the best method of pumping him without betraying myself. "It may, after all, be more convenient for you to tell me how matters stand. What precisely have you done in that matter? Assume that I know nothing," I said, with a wave of the hand.

He was seemingly flattered by the request, and answered readily.

"I have done my utmost to organise my district. Of the lists of names given me there is not one I have not sounded, and about whom I cannot say precisely, 'He is for us,' or, 'He is against us.' I

43

know to a peseta what funds would be forthcoming on demand, and what reserve there would be for emergencies. There is not a rifle, sword, or revolver that is not scheduled and listed carefully."

"Good. These things are in your reports," I said, making a shot.

"So far as desired of me," he answered. "The totals."

"Exactly! Well?"

"When the great coup was devised, I was sounded only as to whether there was in my district a place so safe and secret that a little guest, a boy, could be hidden there indefinitely; and I know of just such a spot in the mountains to the north of Huesca, where a guest, little or big, boy or man, can be hidden in absolute secrecy. And so I reported. I know no more; but I have guessed."

"It is dangerous to guess, Senor Pelayo," I said, with an air of mystery.

"If I am wrong, so much the worse for Spain. But if the guest were indeed the usurper"—and here he paused and searched my face as if for confirmation of his hazard, but he might as well have counted the stones in a wall—"if, I say, then the mountain spot I mean would hold him as fast as his officers would hold us in his strongest prison had they wind of this scheme. Do you wonder that my blood burns with excitement for the day to dawn?"

"You have done your task thoroughly," I said, with the same air of reserve; and his face flushed with pleasure at the praise. Then I added with great sternness, "But now I have a word for you. You have done wrong, very wrong, to breathe a word of this even to me. You have been untrue to your duty. For all you could tell I might be a traitor worming this knowledge out of you for evil purposes. You heard my name by chance, you followed me and found me out, and with scarce a word of question from me you have tumbled pell-mell into my lap secrets that should have been kept with the closeness of the charnel house. Shame upon your gossiping tongue and your falseness to your oath. You would have shown yourself worthier of the trust we place in you had you set me at defiance, and, when I questioned, refused even at the dagger's point to breathe a word of answer. From now I shall watch you. I will give you another chance. Go back to your work, breathe no syllable of what has happened here: that you have even seen or spoken to me: look on the very walls of your house and the very stones of the street as listeners, watchers, spies, ready to catch your words and bring them to me; and if you value your life, pluck out your tongue rather than let it ever again betray you."

I have seldom seen a man more thunderstruck and bewildered. He turned white to the lips and trembled violently, and his hands clasped the arms of his chair for support, while his eyes, terror-wide, appealed to me with the prayer for forgiveness his quivering lips refused to utter.

I feared I had overstrung the bow indeed, and filling a tumbler of wine, I handed it to him and said, relaxing the sternness of my looks:

"Do as I bid you, and I will at no distant date send you a sign that you have regained my confidence;" and with this hope to counterbalance his abject fear, I dismissed him.

Then—shall I confess it?—I did a very boyish thing. Full of a curiosity to know how I had looked when frightening the Carlist so successfully, I postured and mouthed and frowned at and rated myself before a mirror much as I had with Pelayo, and laughed with much satisfaction at what I considered an excellent impersonation.

"By Gad, old chap," I exclaimed, with a nod to myself in the mirror, "if diplomacy fails, you'll do something on the stage, and what's more, I'll be hanged if I didn't feel that I meant it all the while I was giving it him."

And then I became serious again.

CHAPTER VII

SARITA, THE CARLIST

There was indeed plenty of food for serious thought in the interview with Vidal de Pelayo. If the man was really one of the provincial leaders of the Carlists, I had stumbled across the track of an intended attempt to abduct the young King, and such knowledge could scarcely fail to place me in a particularly awkward position in regard to my cousin Sarita.

She would as a matter of course be cognisant of the scheme, while it was more than probable that it had sprung from her own nimble and daring wits. My visitor had described it as the proposal of Ferdinand Carbonnell; Sarita herself had said that Ferdinand Carbonnell was the compound of her brother's and her own Carlism; and there was an imagination, a daring, and a reckless disregard of risks in the scheme which all pointed to Sarita as its originator.

But there was also my position as a member of the British Embassy staff to consider. If the thing were done, even if it were attempted and failed, there would be frantic excitement everywhere; Carlists known and suspected would be flung into prison, and questioned with that suggestive and forceful ingenuity which was generally successful in extracting information from the unfortunate prisoners; the name of Ferdinand Carbonnell was sure to come out; and if this Pelayo himself should chance to be among the questioned—not at all an improbable contingency—he would go a step further than anyone else and point me out to the authorities as the actual head and front of the conspiracy.

That was a very awkward position to face. Apart from the decidedly unpleasant results to myself personally, it was very certain that the consequences to the British interests in Spain at such a moment might be gravely embarrassing. It would be argued with much plausibility that the staff of the Embassy could scarcely have failed to know what was going on; and a charge of connivance in an abduction plot might fire a mine that would blow up Heaven only knew what.

All these things I saw as I smoked a pipe of meditation in my room that night; but I saw also something more. I was a soldier of fortune with my way to make. My father's letter had shown me that too plainly for me to misread. What, then, would be my position if I could use this plot, the knowledge of which had been thrust upon me, to my own advantage, while at the same moment saving Sarita from the results of her own wild scheming?

What would be the standing of the Englishman in Madrid who should cut in at the critical moment when the young King had been carried off, and rescue him and restore him to the Queen-mother at the instant of her agonised bereavement? It was a dizzying thought, and I am free to confess the prospect fascinated me. I sat turning it over and over as I smoked pipe after pipe, and the longer I thought the brighter glowed the one picture—the position of the man who saved King—and the colder grew the other—the duty of informing the Embassy of what I had learned.

When I knocked the ashes out of my last pipe in the hour of dawn—for I sat thinking all through the night—I had made my decision. I would fight for my own hand. So far as Sarita was concerned, I would warn her of what I knew, and that the project must be abandoned from her side. If she persisted, then I would take my own measures to save her.

In pursuance of this, I went to Madame Chansette's on the following afternoon to see Sarita. She was frankly pleased to see me, and after a few minutes gave me herself the opening I wished.

"I have made up my mind in regard to you, Ferdinand." She used my Christian name with the unconstrained freedom of relationship. "I will not have your help. You shall not be involved through me in any of these matters. If you can prevail in your way upon Sebastian Quesada to give up what he has taken from us, do so; but you shall not have him for an enemy on my account."

"That is very nice and commonplace of you, Sarita," said I, with a smile.

"I was not quite myself when you were here yesterday. You surprised me out of myself. I was excited, and talked wildly, and you must forget it all."

"What a very charming day it is. Did you notice how blue the sky was at about ten o'clock?"

"What do you mean?" she cried, looking at me in quick surprise.

"Are you going to the Opera to-morrow? I hear that Vestacchia's ballet is wonderfully good," I continued, in a dull, everyday tone. "By the way, I hear that the young Duke of Sempelona is likely to make a mesalliance."

"What is all this rubbish?"

"I thought we were to be commonplace, that's all. I hear, too——" but she interrupted me now with a burst of laughter.

"Ridiculous!" she cried. "As if you and I need talk of such things. I tell you I will not have your help."

"Very well. I'll pack it up and put it away in my trunks against the day it is needed. That is settled."

"So you can be provoking, can you? I thought you were a serious Englishman, with a good deal of the man in you."

"But you don't want the man; and as I can play many parts, I brought with me the society dude in case he should be handy."

"You are angry because I won't let you interfere with my affairs, eh? So you have your pet little weaknesses, too."

"Why don't you care to speak of fashionable marriages? You mentioned one that was in the making when I was here last."

"You think it a pleasant subject for a jest?" she cried, resentfully.

"Scarcely a fair hit. You have just told me you were not yourself then—and I thought and hoped it had been abandoned, and was to be forgotten like the rest of what you said."

To this she made no immediate reply, but after a pause, asked slowly and earnestly—

"And do you take enough interest in my future to feel serious about such a project?"

"There would not be much of the man in me and far less of the cousin, and none of the friend, if I did not," I returned.

"You have seen me once and known me three days."

"You forget the first time I saw you, Sarita. I do not. I never shall—and never wish to. There are some wounds that are long in the making; others that are made in a flash: and the latter may endure longer than the former." She threw a penetrating glance at me, sighed, and turned away again.

"I wonder if you will ever understand me," she said, half wistfully. "I will not have your help. I have told you."

"It is already packed away—waiting," I returned, lightly. But the light tone jarred, and she tapped her foot and frowned in impatient protest. I smiled. "Why play at this game of pretences?" I asked. "I am going to help you, whether you will or no; and you are going to take my help, whether you will or no. And you are going to give up that—well, the need for us to talk about projected marriages, fashionable or otherwise. You know quite well that I am just as much in earnest as you are; and already you have read me well enough to be perfectly aware that having made that use of my name, you have given me the opportunity to help you which I shall not fail to use. Why then pretend? Let us be frank. I'll set the example. I have come to tell you of something that you must abandon—a plan that originated with you: the part of you, that is, that goes to make up half of the mythical Ferdinand Carbonnell. A plan that the real Ferdinand Carbonnell will not sanction."

"You have come to dictate to me, you say? You to me?" she cried, at first half indignantly, but then laughing. "But what is it?" she asked, with a change to curiosity.

"Tell me first the answer to this puzzle phrase, or charade: 'Counting all renegades lovers of Satan.'" I put the question with a smile, but the sudden, intense dismay on her face startled me.

"Where did you hear that?" she asked. "How could it come to you? You must tell me. I must know."

"Tell me first what it means; that is, if it means anything more than a jingle."

"You don't know?" and her eyes lighted quickly.

"No, I don't know—but I suspect. Tell me, however."

"What do you suspect?"

"To question is scarcely to trust, Sarita. I suspect that it is some secret password among you Carlists."

"But how could it come to your ears?" she cried, anxiously.

"Should not Ferdinand Carbonnell be trusted by his followers?"

"Someone has heard your name, has seen you and has mistaken you—oh, Ferdinand, I might have expected it, but scarcely yet. Wait;

48

yes, I know. It will have been Vidal de Pelayo. He has been here from Saragossa: he may have heard your name—ah, I see it was he. And did he come to you—where? Tell me everything." Her speech was as rapid as her deductions were quick and shrewd.

"Yes, it was Vidal de Pelayo;" and I told her generally what had passed at the interview, keeping back for the moment that part of it which referred to the abduction plot. She listened with rapt attention, viewing it much more seriously than I did; as was not, perhaps, unreasonable. "And now, what does that absurdly-sounding phrase mean?"

"You have only half of it."

"You mean, 'By the grace of God;' but that only makes it all the odder."

"If you take the initials of the first sentence you will see the meaning of the second."

"Of course, Carlos, by the grace of God," I exclaimed.

"It is a phrase that Spain will learn to know one day," she said. "It will be the watchword of the New Liberty," and her face lighted with enthusiasm.

"The 'New Liberty,' Sarita; what do you mean by that?"

"The liberty, the greatness that our rightful King will bring back to us. Where do we stand now, but at the very bottom of the scale of contempt? What is Spain, but the doormat on which every upstart country, even this America, wipes her feet? And what were we once—the leaders of the world; the possessors of half the earth, rulers holding sway on sea as well as land? Are we not the same Spaniards to-day as then? What we did once can we not do again? Aye, and Don Carlos will lift from us the shame of our sloth, put blood and fire once more into the veins of apathy, restore us to our ancient standing, and once again give us the strength to show the face of pride to our enemies. Is not that a day for Spaniards to pray for; and to work, scheme, plot, and toil unceasingly; to shed our blood for, if the need demands it? I will give mine freely and without stint;" and her face glowed like the face of a martyr.

"It is a dream, no more. Look at your countrymen, Sarita, and ask yourself where is to be found the power to work this miracle; where the men, the resources, the brains, the energy, everything that is of the very essence of success?"

"Do you think we do not know that? But it is just all that which Don Carlos will alter? What are we now but a people in whose lives the very salt and marrow are withering? I know it; but I know also what will stop the decay; and Don Carlos will give it us. We must free ourselves from the corroding blight of the misgovernment which those who have usurped the throne have forced on us that

49

they might buttress up their own wrongful claims. While we are weak, divided, torn by dissension and undone by mistrust, they can continue to force on us the oppression which they miscall government. They sap the nation's very life that they may pluck for themselves the ever-dwindling fruits from such branches as have not yet been destroyed. But do we not know the cure? Can you yourself not see it? If the forceful blood of true liberty was once again set flowing in the veins of our nation, the change would soon tell. You know, for you are an Englishman. You have the liberty denied to us, and craved by us. You and these Americans, who would now put this last dire shame upon us. You are increasing, we are dwindling. You enjoy the splendours of the achievements of liberty; we are pining on the undigested meal of past greatness. You are what we were once, the very opposite of what we are now; and what you are, Don Carlos would make us—aye, and by the grace of God, he shall yet do it; and if my little life can help him, I shall not have lived it in vain."

So absorbing, so thrilling was her enthusiasm, that I did not wonder at others yielding to her whirlwind influence. I sought to argue with her, to show her the fallacy of her dreams, to convince her that Don Carlos at best was merely struggling to get back the throne from anything but self-less motives, that the destiny of a nation lay not with the leadership of one man, but in the nature of the people themselves—but argument broke itself in vain against her passion and enthusiasm.

"There is nothing before you but disillusion, Sarita," I said at length; "whether it comes in the form of failure to rouse your countrymen—for men more easily fit themselves with a new skin than with a new nature; or in the more tragic form of passing success in the Carlist movement, to be followed by a knowledge that after all your Don Carlos is no more than a man, and a Spaniard."

"I do not expect you to see things with my eyes," she said; then, after a long pause, "If I dream, well, I dream. But I would rather live a dreamer of dreams, and die in striving to realise them, than live and die a drone among drones. But I have told you I will not have your help."

"And I have shown you that you cannot avoid it. For good or ill, the use of my name before I arrived has made it inevitable. You are doing things in my name, and whether you wish it or not, that fact brings us together in close association. What has happened with Vidal de Pelayo may happen at any moment with another; and how can we escape the consequences? But I must make terms, even with you. For instance, you have in the making a plan to carry off the young King——"

50

"What?" she cried, in a tone of profound astonishment.

"Is it not so?"

"Did Pelayo tell you anything of the kind?"

"Can the followers of Ferdinand Carbonnell have any secrets from him—when they find him in the flesh? He told me no more than he knew—that he was to procure a safe place for a little guest; the rest is surmise; but surmise made easy. And I have come to tell you that the project must be stopped."

"Must?" she cried, angrily.

"Must," I answered, firmly. "Stopped either by you or else go on to be checkmated by me."

"That is a word I have never yet heard from anyone," she exclaimed.

"Then it is quite time somebody used it," said I, as firmly and masterfully as I could make my manner. "I mean it."

"I will not listen to you. I won't bear it," and she got up and stared at me with resentment, surprise and rebellion in every feature of her face.

"I am not going because you are angry, Sarita. I care for you far too much to let a passing mood like that ruffle my purpose. I will not let you commit this crime."

"This is ridiculous—monstrous;" and she tossed her head disdainfully. "You are presuming on what passed when you were here yesterday."

"I am doing nothing of the kind, and only your anger would lead you to make so unjust an accusation. What I am doing is to use some of the privileges which you have given to Ferdinand Carbonnell. I have been within an ace of losing my life through the use of the name; I have been recognised by one of your chief agents as the leader himself—and now I intend to use that leadership to save you from the consequences of your own blindness. A moment's reflection will convince you that I am not speaking at random."

"You would make me your enemy?" she asked.

"It would not be the first time that enmity has followed acts which should have generated sincere friendship. Would the Ferdinand Carbonnell of your making be deterred from doing what he deemed right by such a motive? No; and neither will the real man."

"It is the very key-note of our plans," she cried.

"Then you must arrange a different harmony."

"You shall not interfere with it. You shall not, I say," she exclaimed, tempestuously.

"I am absolutely resolved. You shall either abandon the mad project, or I myself will thwart it."

51

"Would you quarrel with me?"

"If you force a quarrel on me because of it; yes." This reply seemed to amaze her more than anything I had said, and her gaze was full of reproach and consternation.

"And you said just now you cared for me," she said, softly.

"How deeply it may never be in my power to tell you, for all said and done, I am only a poor devil with all his way in the world yet to make. But for this you have made me rich in power, and I will use the power you have given me to the uttermost—to save you."

Then she came and stood close before me and putting her hands on my shoulders, as she had done once before, looked pleadingly into my eyes.

"Will nothing move you, Ferdinand?"

"Nothing," I returned, meeting her eyes firmly.

"Not if I tell you——" she hesitated and bit her lip in disconcerting agitation. My heart gave a wild leap at the thought of how the broken sentence might have been finished. I loved her, Heaven knows how deeply, and for an instant I cheated myself with the wild fancy that a confession of answering love was halting on her trembling lips. "Not if I do what I have never yet done to any man—beg and implore you to leave this thing alone?"

Moved though I was I would not let her see anything of my feeling; I changed no muscle of my face, and met her eyes with the same calm, resolute look as I answered slowly and earnestly—

"Sarita, if such a thing were possible as that you love me and that the words which faltered on your lips just now had been a confession of that love, I should still answer you that nothing would move me from my purpose."

She started violently, listened to me at first with such a look as one might give whose heart has suddenly been bared, and then with an expression of dismay which changed at last to almost passionate reproach her hands slipped from my shoulders and she fell into a chair and covered her face to hide her emotion.

But the weakness passed in an instant and she rose and faced me, once again calm, confident, and self-reliant.

"It shall not be abandoned. You have no right to do this. It shall go on, do what you will. You shall not come between me and my duty; between me and my country. I have urged and entreated you, and you have scorned me. It is not in your power to bend me—cold and hard and strong as you may think yourself. I can be cold and hard and strong, too, as you will find. What if I tell you, as I do, that you shall never set eyes on me again if you do not give way?" and she drew herself to her full height, splendid in her flashing, gleaming anger. But I did not yield a jot from my purpose.

"That must be as you will, Sarita," I said, calmly. "Nothing can change my resolve. Because I will not see or say that all you do is right, you are angry. Well, leave it there. Believe me, I will stop this and save you from yourself."

"I do not want your help; and I will not have it. An enemy of Spain can be no friend of mine," she cried, passionately, and was going from the room with all the signs of her anger and emotion flaming in her face when the door was opened and a servant ushered in Colonel Livenza.

As soon as he saw me, his face lowered ominously and the anger deepened and darkened when he perceived by Sarita's face that our interview had been no mere conventional one.

Sarita was for the moment too agitated to stay and speak with him, and with a hasty word of greeting and excuse she hurried past him and left us alone.

He looked after her in surprise and deep annoyance, and then turned with a scowl to me as if for an explanation; looking on me as an intruder.

"I did not expect to meet you here, senor," he said, angrily; but the scene with Sarita had left me in no pleasant mood, and I was glad enough to have someone on whom to vent the temper which I had been keeping under such restraint.

"I am not aware that I am in any way called upon either to anticipate or consider your expectations," I returned, pretty curtly.

"That's a very strange reply."

"To a very impertinent remark," I retorted. I hated the fellow, and was not in the least concerned to conceal the feeling. In my then mood, guessing the object of his visit, nothing would have given me greater pleasure than to have kicked him downstairs and out of the house. I believe he guessed something of this, for he turned aside, pretended not to hear my answer, and made way for me to pass.

As I reached the door, going very slowly and keeping my eyes upon him in that melodramatic manner into which a bad temper will lead the mildest of us, Sarita came hurrying back, and her glance of alarm at us both showed she feared some sort of a quarrel.

"I will see you again, Sarita," I said, with a warmth in my manner which was intended more to displease Livenza than to please her. But she was still very angry, and drawing back, said—

"After what has passed that will scarcely be necessary or desirable." At which the man smiled and shrugged his shoulders contemptuously and with a suggestion of triumph which galled me. And, smarting under the sense of my defeat, I left the house.

CHAPTER VIII

SEBASTIAN QUESADA

The interview with Sarita both distressed and perplexed me, and my uneasiness was considerably aggravated by the fact that she went away from the city leaving Madame Chansette in ignorance of her movements and in much anxiety.

I could not doubt that in some way this absence was connected with the plot which I had declared my intention to thwart, and Madame Chansette and I had more than one consultation concerning her, in which that good soul's fears were largely shared by me.

I was, moreover, doubtful whether to take any further steps in Sarita's affairs until I had seen her again, and, in particular, whether to approach Sebastian Quesada on the subject of his giving up some of the Castelar property.

"He will not do it, Ferdinand; I am convinced he will never do it," said Madame Chansette; "but I wish you to convince yourself also, and then we can together try to bring Sarita to reason."

I was considering the questionable policy of doing something of the kind when a somewhat odd adventure occurred to change this aspect of affairs, and relieve me from the trouble of coming to any decision on the point.

Madrid was growing very uneasy over the Cuban question, and the populace were getting quite out of hand in the mad demand for war. Quesada was far too clear-headed not to understand the infinite danger to Spain of a war with America. He knew, probably, how hopelessly rotten was the state of the army and navy, and he threw the whole of his powerful influence into the scale against war. But the Madrid people went mad, and several riots occurred in which ugly results were with difficulty avoided; and one of these disturbances, directed against Quesada himself, was destined to have weighty consequences for me.

I was in my rooms one afternoon when I heard the sounds of a disturbance in the street, and, looking out, I saw a big crowd hurrying with shouts, and cries, and gesticulations, and with alternate huzzaing and hooting, in the direction of the Puerta del Sol, where Quesada's office, the Ministry of the Interior, stood. I turned out to see what would happen, and soon I found myself in the midst of a mob bent on making a very rowdy demonstration against Quesada and his counsels of peace and prudence.

I hung on the skirts of the crowd, listening to the fierce groans and hisses of those who had reached the Ministry, and wondering curiously what would be the upshot. Then, just as matters were beginning to get very lively indeed, a carriage with a dashing pair of greys came rattling down the Calle de Arenal, and the coachman, being unable to get through the crowd, was idiot enough to lay his whip on the backs of some of the men who stood thronging the roadway.

This fool's act maddened the mob, and with a roar like beasts some of them swarmed on to the box and dragged him off, while others unharnessed the horses, hauled them from the carriage, and with shouts and oaths turned their heads and sent them galloping back along the road they had come.

Meanwhile I had seen that the only occupant of the carriage was a girl, who was almost fainting with fright. I slipped across the road on the chance of being able to help her, and found some of the crowd quite disposed to punish the young mistress for the act of the coachman. One or two of them were already fumbling at the carriage door, and matters had begun to wear an ugly look. The girl was shrinking back in the farthest corner of the carriage, gazing in terror at the rough brutes, who were yelling and shouting in mob temper, as they clustered round the door; and on seeing me she gave a look which I read as a dumb, piteous appeal for help.

By a fortunate chance the carriage had stopped close to the pathway at a point where the pavement was very narrow, and, the crowd being in the road and only a couple of men on the other side, I slipped round to that side, shouldered the men out of the way, opened the door, and said, in a tone of command—

"Quick, senorita. Trust to me; I will protect you. You cannot stay here." A glance at me seemed to assure her that I meant well and not evil; and just as the clumsy louts succeeded in opening the other door, she got up, put her hand in mine, and jumped from the carriage.

Without a word I put her next the wall, and, getting between her and the balked and angry crowd, I hurried with her as fast as I could to the corner where two or three streets open into the Puerta del Sol, the crowd pressing upon our heels and growing more vehement every minute. Most luckily there was a cab standing at the corner of the Calle de la Montera, and I made straight for this. The driver was away seeing the fun, no doubt, and I shoved and shouldered my way toward it, and laid about me so lustily with my stick, getting a fair share of blows in return, that I won the way through and put the girl inside. As soon as that was done I turned at bay for a minute and let drive with my stick and fist in all directions, clearing a path till I could mount the box, when I lashed the horse into so much of a gallop as its weary, weedy legs were capable of achieving. In this way, hatless, breathless, and with my clothes torn and my muscles aching, I succeeded in getting the girl out of the clutch of the mob, who greeted my departure with yells of disappointment.

When I was well out of all danger of interference and the shouts of the people were no more than a distant hum, I pulled up and went to look after my charge. She was lolling against the cushions of the fly in a half-faint condition, and at first did not understand me when I asked where I should drive her. But at length she told me who she was, and I could understand the reason of the crowd's anger. She was Sebastian Quesada's sister, Dolores Quesada, and asked me to drive her to his house in the Puerta de Alcala.

I must have cut a queer-looking figure, but as there was no one else to act coachman I clambered back on to the box and hustled the aged animal in the shafts into as good a pace as I could, choosing the quietest streets for the route. By the time we reached the house my "fare" was better, but asked me to give her my arm, sent one servant to mind the horse, another in search of a Senora Torella, and insisted upon my entering and helping to give an account of what had occurred.

When the colour began to come back to her face I was rather surprised to find she was a really pretty girl. She was disposed to make much of the incident, and thanked me very graciously, although too profusely.

"Do you know to whom you are beholden, Dolores?" asked the duenna, Senora Torella. "May I ask your name, senor?" And when I told her she said—"It is not for us to thank you. Senor Quesada will do that; but now, can we not help you? You will, of course, allow us to place a carriage at your disposal for your return home, or would you rather that we sent some message to your friends? You have suffered at the hands of the mob."

"If you will send a servant with the fly which I borrowed to the police, with some explanation, it will, perhaps, save trouble; and if you will let someone fetch me another fly I can get home all right. But as for thanks, it is sufficient recompense to have been of some service to the senorita. Stay, there is one other matter—give that coachman of yours a severe reprimand. It was his violence in lashing at the crowd which provoked them and led to all this trouble. You are feeling better now, senorita?"

She had been lying back in a low chair, gazing at me with an open-eyed stare which I found somewhat embarrassing, and she now roused herself, sat up, smiled, and coloured.

"Thanks to you, senor, I am better. But for your help and courage what might not have happened to me? What an escape! And what do I not owe you? I shall never cease to thank the Holy Virgin for having sent you to rescue me." She was clearly an emotional creature, but this kind of exaggerated gratitude was not at all to my liking.

"Pray don't make too much of it. I just happened to be on the spot at the moment, but I did nothing more than anyone else would have done under the same circumstances. Besides, it's pretty certain that the crowd only meant to frighten you, and nothing serious would have happened even had I not been there."

"It is clear that the hand of Heaven guided you," said the duenna, with a solemn earnestness which quite disconcerted me. I did not regard myself as exactly the sort of person Heaven would choose for an instrument; and not caring for the turn of the conversation, I rose to leave. They were loth for me to go, however, and urged me to wait until the brother came home; but I had had enough of it, and went away, not sorry to have succeeded in getting a propitious introduction to Sebastian Quesada.

The next day brought Quesada himself to the Embassy; and I met him with deep and genuine interest, heightened considerably by my knowledge of that little secret which Sarita had told me.

"Senor Carbonnell, you have laid my family under an obligation that will end only with death," he said, with Spanish exaggeration, "and the measure of my gratitude is the limitless measure of my love for my dear sister. You must render me another service by giving me your friendship; and though that will add to my obligation, it may afford me an opportunity of showing you something of my gratitude." And all the time he was saying this with exaggerated gesture and elaboration of courtesy, his piercing dark eyes were fixed on my face, seeking to read me, as it seemed, to judge the manner of man I was, to calculate the kind of reward I should appreciate, to gauge whether I made much or little of the service I had rendered; and, in a word, to drag out my inner man to the light so that he might see it and appraise it shrewdly.

"I trust your sister is well after her alarm—it was an awkward two minutes for her; but, believe me, if she tells you that there was anything heroic about the rescue or any real danger for me, it is only because her frightened eyes could not judge calmly."

"Spoken like an Englishman, Senor Carbonnell; but, pardon me, I know what a Madrid crowd can do in less than two minutes when excited. My fool of a coachman was very nearly mauled to death by the roughs, and lies now with a broken leg, a couple of fractured ribs, and a cracked pate. It serves him right, perhaps; but it shows you—or, at any rate, it shows me—that Dolores' danger was no mere imagination. And now I bring you a request—to dine with us to-morrow—and I have come with it in person lest you should be engaged then, in which case you must choose your own day; for we can take no refusal—unless you can name any other way in which our friendship may begin more auspiciously."

"I shall be very glad," said I, cordially. "Indeed, I have wanted to see you on some private matters." A gleam of lightning questioning flashed from his remarkable eyes, until he threw up the mantling veil of as pleasant a smile as ever brightened a human face.

"That will be charming. Myself, all that I have, or know, will be at your disposal, senor. By the way, do you know your very name has interested me immensely, for reasons you could never guess, but I may some day tell you, to your infinite surprise, I am sure. And there are other reasons, too. Are you not the son of Lord Glisfoyle?"

"Yes, the younger son."

"Then do you know that in a somewhat roundabout way you and I are connections? Dolores and I are fascinated by the thought; and we will discuss all this to-morrow, for I intend ours to be really a little family gathering—just ourselves, Senor Carbonnell. And now, as I am a very busy man, will you pardon me if I run away?"

"No mischief was done by the crowd last night at the Ministry of Interior, I trust?"

He smiled at the sheer impossibility of anyone harming him.

"None whatever. My carriage was a little scratched—the rascals recognised it, of course, for mine; a few straps of the harness were lost, and my silly, hot-headed, faithful fool of a Pedro has been laid by the heels for a while. That is all. Ah, would God, senor, that these wild Madrid mobs could always be as lightly turned from the mad purpose on which they are bent!" And as we shook hands his face was very dark with thought.

I went with him to his carriage, not perhaps quite without a feeling of gratification to be seen on terms of friendship with the most powerful man in Spain; nor could I resist the strangely magnetic influence of his personality. I believed him to be one of the most dangerous and treacherous of men; and yet he had so wrought upon me in the course of a few minutes' conversation, that I could not resist the temptation to believe that, whatever he might be to others, to me at least he was sincere in this desire for my friendship.

Mayhew and I dined together, and, as my adventure was now common property and very generally discussed, our talk fell naturally upon Sebastian Quesada's visit.

"You'll have to be careful you don't get your head turned,

Carbonnell," he said. "You'll remember he's a man who never does anything without a purpose."

"What wise chaps they were of old, to have Death's head always handy," I returned, with a laugh. "You're prettier than a Death's head, however, Silas." He was, in fact, a remarkably good-looking fellow.

"Well, a skull has one point over us, after all—it can't affect to hide its expression with any forced laughs. You can see the worst of it at any moment."

"Which means?"

"That A may not always be right, for instance, when he thinks that whatever B may be with other folk, he's sincere with him."

"You've hit it, by Jove, Silas. That's exactly what I did think."

"My dear fellow, it's exactly what everybody thinks with Quesada. I sometimes think he's a bit of a hypnotist. You know the trick. Old Madame Blavatsky, when she had a good subject in tow, could chuck a bit of cord on the floor and make him believe it was a snake. After all, it's only diplomacy a little developed."

"You think I'm a good subject, as you call it, then?"

"We're all more or less good subjects for Quesada; but I do mean that if you believe in him he'll make you see snakes—aye, and feel the sting of 'em, too."

"But I did get the girl out of a fix. Hang it, he can't have any motive in my case."

Mayhew laughed.

"Hasn't a girl ever given you a thing you didn't want at the moment, and haven't you wrapped it up very carefully and put it away somewhere, appreciating the act, and thinking it would be sure to come in handy some day? That's Quesada's policy; and I can think of plenty of things a devoted young friend on the staff of the Embassy here might be useful for."

It wasn't exactly a pleasant view to take of the incident, but I could not help seeing it might be a very true one.

"What an ass a fellow's self-conceit can make of him, Si," I exclaimed, after a pause. "But I shan't forget what you've said."

"Don't, old fellow. I know the man, and I know he's to be labelled dangerous. I don't believe there's any villainy—aye, any villainy of any kind, that he'd stick at to get his way. And he gets it to a degree that astounds those who don't know him. With all my heart, I warn you," he said, more earnestly than I had ever known him speak.

The warning took effect; it pricked the bubble of my fatuous self-conceit, and was in my thoughts all the next day as I was turning over the problem of broaching Sarita's affairs to Quesada. It must mean crossing swords with him, indeed; and the result of such an encounter must at best be doubtful.

I was fully conscious of this; but at the time I had not a thought or suspicion of the infinite hazard and trouble that lay in wait to overwhelm me, and to which I was advancing with the precocious self-confidence of conceited inexperience.

CHAPTER IX

THE QUESADA VERSION

At the Minister's house the cordiality of my reception by both brother and sister was almost embarrassing in its warmth. The Minister was effusive, elaborate, and demonstrative; the sister gentle, solicitous, and intensely earnest in her gratitude. She pressed my hands, thanked me in simple, sincere phrases, but left her gratitude to be expressed chiefly through her eloquent eyes, which were constantly upon me. She had taken a quite exaggerated view of my act, was bent upon setting me up for a hero, and appeared to be resolved to act up to her ideal view of the case.

The Minister was an excellent talker, and, taking the burden of the conversation upon himself, proved himself a most entertaining companion. The one personal touch during dinner was in regard to his previous hint at our relationship.

"Did you understand that hint I dropped yesterday about there being some connection between our families?" he asked.

"Well, yes and no," I replied. "I have had some kind of hint from my father, but I don't know exactly the details."

"It is in some respects a painful story, and one we rarely, if ever, speak of; indeed, it is known to but very few people. But this is a family conclave, and if we may not open the cupboard of the skeleton—as you English very grimly say—who may? By the way, how excellently you speak Spanish. I should not know you for any but a Spaniard."

"I was many years as a youth in Spain."

"You have a wonderful idiom; eh, Dolores?"

"I thought Senor Carbonnell was a countryman at first," she said, her eyes and face lighting as if that were a rare virtue of mine.

60

"No, Dolores, you were wrong there. What he did for you was English work. Had he been our countryman he would have been talking, gesticulating, and scolding the rabble. But, instead, he acted. There was one thing possible to do, and with British practicality he saw it and did it instantly. No one but an Englishman would have thought of it. A Frenchman would have rushed to the door and defied the crowd; but that wouldn't have saved you. A German might have thought of what Carbonnell did; but he'd have been only half-way round the carriage by the time Carbonnell had the door open and had whisked you out. One of these confounded Americans might have done it—but he'd have tried to dash through the crowd, in at the wrong door and out at the right—too much in a hurry to go round the carriage first. He'd have done it, however. But it was the English character to see just what to do, and how to do it most easily, and then to do it in the same moment."

"You are still resolved to make too much of it," I cried, with a laugh at his comparisons.

"Can we make too much of a cause that brings us a new friend, and, indeed, a new relative of such mettle? What think you, Dolores?"

"I think too much for mere words. Senor Carbonnell will feel, I am afraid, that I am very clumsy with my thanks."

"You were speaking about relationship?" I put in, as a diversion.

"It makes a sorry page in our family history; for in truth we committed a series of blunders. Your grandfather had three sons, Carbonnell; and the youngest of them—I fear something of a scapegrace—settled here in Madrid under the name of Castelar, fell in love with my father's youngest sister, Sarita, and married her against the wishes of all our family. You see we regarded him as an adventurer, knowing nothing of his being an Englishman and the son of an English peer. Besides, there was the religious difficulty, I was a lad at the time, about ten or twelve—it's five-and-twenty years ago now—and remember the thing only vaguely; but I know I was as indignant as the rest of us;" and he laughed, frankly and openly.

"The marriage was a very disastrous one, I have heard," said I.

"Very. Could not have been worse; and we did not learn who your uncle really was until after his wife's death. She died professing herself bitterly sorry for her disobedience to the family wishes, and was reconciled to us; but the children——" and he tossed up a hand as though the trouble were too great for words.

"I have seen Sarita Castelar," I said; and the remark brought one of those lightning gleams from his eyes which I had seen before.

"Have you seen the brother, Ramon?" he asked, changing

instantly to a smile. "He should prove interesting to you, if you knew all. But they both harbour the worst opinion of me; and Ramon's opinions have taken the pointed and substantial shape of a dagger thrust uncomfortably close to my heart, and a bullet that proved him, fortunately for me, a very poor shot. But I could not endure that, and when we catch him he will have his opportunities of pistol practice cut short." He made light of the matter in his speech, but there was that in his looks which told plainly how bitterly and intensely he hated.

"Don't speak of it, Sebastian," cried Dolores, shuddering.

"I'm afraid our relationship is a little indefinite," I said. "My uncle married your aunt, and we are therefore—what?"

"Staunch friends, I hope, Carbonnell; closer friends, I trust, than many relatives are."

"With all my heart I hope that too, senor," declared Dolores, and soon after she and Senora Torella, who had scarcely said a word in Quesada's presence, left us. As soon as we were alone and had lighted our cigars, my host returned to the subject of the Castelars, and his open, unembarrassed manner of dealing with it surprised me.

"You have seen Sarita Castelar, you say, Carbonnell? She is a very beautiful girl, don't you think?" and his keen eyes were watching my face as I answered.

"Unquestionably. One of the most beautiful I have ever seen."

"It is a coincidence, too, is it not?—she is the image of her mother in looks; you are not at all unlike your uncle in looks, and you speak Spanish like a—as well as he did; you are here in Madrid. It would be a strange coincidence if the parallel was to be carried a stage farther."

"And I were to fall in love with her and marry her, you mean?" If he could bluff, so could I; and in neither my laugh nor my face was there a trace of anything but apparent enjoyment of a rich absurdity. But it required no lynx eye to see that he did not enjoy my completion of his suggested parallel. "I'm afraid she'd have a poor sort of future. We younger sons of poor peers are not as a rule millionaires. But she is a very beautiful girl."

"She is a very extraordinary one, and her brother has had far too much influence with her. I fear sometimes——" he left the sentence unfinished, pursed his lips, and shook his head dubiously.

"By the way, she and Madame Chansette—who is, I believe, your late father's sister—are hopeful that the family will restore the property which I understand belongs to Sarita's mother and should have gone to her children."

"Say rather you don't understand, Carbonnell," he cried,

laughing and shaking his head. "The good and amiable Chansette has what you English call a bee in her bonnet on that subject; and unfortunately the two children share the delusion. Why, if there was such property I should surely know of it; do you think I should not positively hail the chance of providing adequately for Sarita? Not for Ramon, perhaps. That I grant you. The young dog deserves the whip and worse. My very life is not safe while he is at liberty. But Sarita— why, I like the child. I call her child, although she is four-and-twenty; but as I am seven-and-thirty, and she has always been a child in my thoughts, she seems so now. Wonderfully pretty, wilful, disobedient, resentful, always irresistibly charming, but still a child. Don't take her seriously, Carbonnell; for she is just the type of woman, when taken seriously, for whom men rush even to the gates of hell."

"Then there is no such property?" I asked, quietly.

"How like the practical, pertinacious, dogged Englishman!" he exclaimed, laughing airily. "No, there is no such property, Carbonnell; and anyone who married Sarita Castelar must be content with her beauty as her sole dower." It was impossible to resist the impression that under the words, lightly spoken and with an easy laugh, there lay a sneer and a caution for me. It was the first note of his voice that had not rung true in my ears.

"I am glad to have had that assurance, Senor Quesada," I answered, gravely. "My father charged me to see into the matter and I will report to him exactly what you say." We spoke no more then on the subject, and soon after we had joined Dolores and her duenna, her brother excused himself on the plea of State papers to read.

After an hour or so of music and chatter, in which Dolores showed herself not only a beautiful singer but a most charming little hostess, the Minister came back to us, and did everything that lay in his power to make me feel that in him I had found a sincere friend. But Mayhew's warning, my previous knowledge of Quesada's acts and character, and more than all the sentence of his which had sounded false in my ears, had completely changed my thoughts toward him, and I caught myself more than once listening for the proofs of his falseness even when he was making his loudest professions of good-will and friendship. And I went home saturated with the belief that he was, as Mayhew had declared, a most dangerous man.

As a consequence, I did not believe a word of his version of the story about the Castelars and their property, but rather that he was concealing the facts for his own purposes; and it gave me more than one twinge of uneasiness during the three or four weeks which followed that, despite my feeling toward him, I should have encouraged his persistently maintained efforts to make friend and even close associate of me.

These efforts were indeed a source of constant surprise to me. I was an obscure nobody in Madrid; and yet his overtures could not have been more cordial and earnest had I been the heir to a dukedom or a throne. He invited me constantly to his house, would send me messages to go riding or driving with him, and indeed overwhelmed me with attentions. In truth it seemed to me he was so overdoing his part, supposing it to be mere playacting, that I was almost persuaded he must have some genuine personal interest in me. Certainly he did his utmost to make the time a pleasant one for me, and if I could only have had better news of Sarita, I could not have failed to enjoy myself.

But all the time I did not once get sight of her. When I called on Madame Chansette, Sarita would never see me. She was away from Madrid often, that good lady told me, and would not even hear my name spoken.

"I thought you would be such friends," she wailed dismally more than once; "but Sarita is so wilful. I suppose you quarrelled; why, I can't imagine. I am sure you like her, and in the first day or two when you came, your praises were never out of her mouth. But I can't understand her."

"Couldn't we arrange somehow for me to meet her?" I suggested, presuming on the old lady's good nature; for my heart had warmed at the unexpected avowal.

"She would never forgive me," was her instant and timid reply.

"She need never know," said I. "I will manage that. Let me know where I am likely to see her, say at eight o'clock this evening, and I'll take the risk of walking straight to her. I will come as if with news for you, and will take my chance."

"Why are you so anxious?" she asked, sharply.

"Because I love her, Madame Chansette, and her safety is more to me than my own life. Now that we know Sebastian Quesada will give up nothing"—I had told her of my talk with him—"it is more than ever necessary for her to leave Madrid and abandon this wild business of intrigue."

"You will never persuade her."

"I can at least try;" and after a very little more persuasion she agreed and we arranged a surprise visit for that evening. I went home with pulses beating high in anticipation, and found news awaiting which would make one part of the plan genuine at least.

I should have news for Madame Chansette, and for Sarita. My

father was dead. He had died suddenly, a telegram from Lascelles told me, and I was summoned home with all speed.

I rushed at once to the Embassy, obtained leave of absence, and made my preparations to leave for London that night; scribbled a note to Quesada putting off an engagement with him for the following day and set off for Madame Chansette's house, with an overwhelming desire to see Sarita before leaving Spain.

The simple device effected its purpose well. The front door was open and with a word to the servant I hurried past to the room where I thought I should find Sarita. I paused just a moment before opening the door, caught my breath hurriedly, and turned the handle and entered.

She was there and alone, reading with her back to the door, and thinking probably that it was Madame Chansette she took no notice of my entrance. Then I perpetrated a very thin trick.

"Ah, dear Madame Chansette, I come with grave news;" I got thus far when Sarita jumped to her feet and faced me with eyes flashing and cheeks a-flush.

"How dare you come here?" she cried; speaking in English to emphasise more distinctly the gulf between us.

"Sarita!" I exclaimed, as though in deep surprise; but I kept by the door intending to prevent her escape; and I feasted my hungry eyes upon her glowing beauty.

"My aunt is not here, sir. You must have seen that for yourself the instant you entered. Why then this absurd pretence?"

"Because I would ten thousand times rather see you than Madame Chansette; because I must see you; because—any reason you like. I am too delighted at having at last caught you to care for reasons. You have been avoiding me for many days. Why?" I replied in Spanish, but she kept to English, which she spoke with great fluency.

"Because I do not wish to see you, Mr. Carbonnell. You will please be good enough now to go away." She spoke in her coldest and loftiest tone. "I desire to be alone."

"No, I shall not go away without an explanation. Why have you avoided me purposely for all this time?"

"I have given you the reason. I have had no wish to see you."

"Thank you for your bluntness; but you must carry it a stage further and tell me why."

"Certainly. Because on a former occasion you rendered your presence objectionable to me," she returned in the same cold, level tone.

"I am going to be very rude and objectionable again, Sarita, and ask you not to tell half a truth and then plume yourself on having said something particularly disagreeable;" and I laughed. "I decline to accept that explanation. The truth is that you have been very angry with me, and I think your anger has lasted long enough—far too long, indeed, for relatives and such friends as you and I must be."

"Insult is scarcely the badge which friendship wears," she exclaimed, changing to Spanish in her impetuosity.

"Good. That's a distinct improvement on your cold assumption of callous indifference. Whatever may be your real feeling for me, at least I am sure it is not indifference."

"No, I have told you; you have made yourself objectionable to me," she flashed with spirit.

"Because I told you I would thwart your wrongful intention in regard to the young King. I am still of the same mind."

"I told you you were no friend of mine from that minute, and should never set eyes on me again," she cried, vehemently.

"And here I am, nevertheless, looking at you with eyes of regret that you have treated me in this way."

"I could not prevent your forcing yourself upon me. I meant never with my consent; and I presumed you would observe the common decencies of conduct sufficiently not to force yourself upon me in this way."

"I am sure you never thought that if the chance came my way of seeing and speaking to you, I should be such a traitor to my own wishes as not to use it. But I am here, and have not come to quarrel. I have come with news that may interest even you—for it is bad news for me, and of much trouble."

She glanced at me, and seemed as if to repudiate the intentional ungenerosity of my words; but said nothing, and, shrugging her shoulders, turned away; and, after a moment's pause, substituted a retort, keeping her face averted.

"Why not carry your news where you will find sympathy?"

"You mean?"

"To my enemies, but your new friends. The Quesadas, brother and sister, will surely bind up your wounds best. What their friends suffer can scarcely concern me." I heard this with a tingling sense of pleasure, for it told me much more than Sarita intended.

"I have been to Sebastian Quesada largely on your business."

"You have at least had ample opportunities, and have made the most of them. I should congratulate you upon your successful knight-errantry, too." She said this with a scornful shrug of the shoulders, and a delightful curl of the lip. Was it really possible she had disliked my visits to the Quesadas because I had helped Dolores out of the crowd that day?

"At any rate, my news will have the result you have wished for, Sarita. My father is dead, and I am leaving Madrid to-night." I watched her closely as I spoke, and saw her start slightly, bite her lip, and draw herself together. It did touch her, it seemed, although she was unwilling to show it. After a moment she turned and said, with an effort to be very formal:

"I am very sorry for your personal sorrow."

"Will you shake hands now, Sarita?" I said, going towards her.

"We are not children," she returned quickly.

"I am going away"—and I held out my hand.

"Good-bye." She put hers into mine, and I captured it and held it firmly.

"I am going away—but I shall come back again." She tried to snatch her hand from mine at this, but I held it, and, looking into her face, said firmly, "I will not part in anything but good-will, Sarita. And when I come back to Madrid it must be to find you still my friend. Don't let any cloud come between us. There is no need. God knows I would rather have your good-will than that of anyone else on earth. Don't you believe this?"

"You had better not come back. It can do no good," she said. "You have taken sides against me; you set yourself to thwart me in my chiefest wishes; your closest friends are my bitterest enemies. You know this. You know the wrongs they have done me and mine, and yet you make them your friends. It is nothing to me, of course, whom you choose for your friends, but—you choose them." She looked up and tried to smile as though I had convicted myself.

"Do you really think these people, brother or sister, are anything to me? That their acquaintance or friendship, or whatever you term it, would weigh a hair's weight with me against your good-will, Sarita?"

"There are very few in Madrid who would think slightingly of the friendship of such a man as Sebastian Quesada."

"There is one man in Madrid who would give it up without a thought to secure the friendship of Sarita Castelar."

"Yes; but you make my friendship impossible; you kill it with your violent hostility to my work."

"I shall be away I don't know how long—a week, two weeks, a month may be—but I'll make a suggestion. Let us both use the time to try and think out a solution of that difficulty—how to be friends even while enemies of that kind. We are not children, as you said just now."

She shook her head, still declaring that it was impossible; but she smiled as she said it, and the hardness and anger were gone from her voice, so that when I pressed the point, as I did with all the earnestness at command, she yielded; and when Madame Chansette came into the room some minutes later, she was as intensely surprised as she was pleased to find us both shaking hands over the bargain.

The thought that a complete reconciliation was in the making sent me off on my journey with a much lighter heart than I should otherwise have carried, and I set myself diligently to work to try and think of some means of saving Sarita in spite of herself.

CHAPTER X

IN LONDON

Matters in London were pretty much of the kind customary when so gloomy an event has called together the members of a family; varied, of course, by touches of individuality.

My dear sister Mercy was quite unstrung by my father's death. She was the only one of us who had not been led to anticipate it, and the suddenness of it had roused that sense of awe which, perhaps, the sudden death of a loved one can alone produce. She was as frightened and nervously apprehensive as if she had known that Death had a second arrow fitted to launch at another of us. My arrival did something to cheer her, and Mrs. Curwen, who was with her constantly at the house, joined with her in declaring that Mercy and I must not be separated again.

It was not the melancholy side of the event which appealed to Lascelles. He was now head of the family, and the importance of that position filled his thoughts to the comparative exclusion of any mere personal grief. A peer of the realm was not as other men. The King was dead, long live the King—and the King in the hour of coming to his own had no time for vulgar indulgence in mere emotion.

Three days after the funeral, he explained his wishes in regard to myself.

"Ferdinand, I wish to go into things with you," he said, with quite gracious condescension, having carried me to the study.

"I am afraid I haven't many things worth going into at all, Lascelles," said I. "The father had prepared me for his will. There is a thousand pounds for me, three hundred a year for Mercy—her own fortune, of course—and the rest for the title. I don't complain in the least, and my worst wish is that you may make that good marriage as soon as decency permits. How go matters with Mrs. Curwen?" But this carrying the war into his own country did not accord at all with his point of view. He wished to dictate to me about my affairs, not to listen to me about his; and after fidgetting uneasily, he replied—

"You go very fast, Ferdinand, and I'm sure that in diplomacy you will not find it advantageous to do that. Things are a great deal changed since you left London."

"Alas, yes. It's a way that death has."

"I hope you don't mean that for flippancy, but it sounds like it."

"My dear Lascelles, a long face, a chronic groan, and the white of one's eyes are not essential to real grief."

"Well, it sounded flippant, and it jarred—jarred very much. I have felt very keenly the father's death, although, of course, the duties of my new position have compelled me to face the world with—with a due rigidity of demeanour."

"What was it you were going to say about change?"

"Well, in point of fact I—er—I was referring to—to a match that concerned you as much as myself. Of course I can't do more for you than—than the will provides, and I am glad you recognise that; but there is one thing I can do—and perhaps I ought to do it now—and it will be of great, indeed of the greatest consequence to you."

It was so unlike him to beat nervously about a subject in this way, that I watched him in speculative surprise.

"I think, you know, that you might—that in point of fact you ought to make a wealthy marriage; and I believe that such a thing is quite open to you." What was he driving at?

"Isn't it a bit early to talk of this?" I suggested.

"Under other circumstances, perhaps, it might be," he said, speaking without hesitation now that he was well under weigh; "but as it must affect your plans and movements a good deal, I have thought it desirable to broach the matter at once. I think you ought not to return to Madrid, but to remain here in London in pursuance of this object."

"And who is the object I am to pursue? What's her name?" I could not resist this little play on his awkward phrase.

"I wish, Ferdinand, you wouldn't catch up my words in that way and distort them. I meant project, of course. As a matter of fact, I am disposed to abandon in your favour the project I once had in regard to—Mrs. Curwen." There was a last hesitation in mentioning the name, and a little flush of colour gave further evidence of his

69

momentary awkwardness; but having got it out, he went on rapidly and talked himself out of his embarrassment, giving me a variety of reasons for his decision, and plenty more for my adopting the suggestion.

"Have you somebody else in your eye, then, Lascelles?" I asked, quietly, when he had exhausted himself.

"I think that's a very coarse remark, Ferdinand—quite vulgar; and I am surprised at it." Perhaps he was right to be shocked, but he reddened so nervously that I could see I had hit the target; and for the life of me I couldn't help smiling.

"I can't say that Madrid has improved you," he cried, angrily, seeing the smile. "I am inspired by no feeling but a sincere desire for the welfare of one of the family; but you must do as you please."

"It's all right, Lascelles, and no doubt you mean well. But I'm not going to marry Mrs. Curwen or any one else for her money; and I am going back to Madrid. Is there anything more?" and I got up to show I had had enough.

"No, there's nothing more, as you put it. But, of course, if you place yourself at once in opposition to my wishes, you can't expect me to——"

"Don't bother to finish the sentence. When I turn beggar I won't hold out my cap to you. Don't let us quarrel. I went to Madrid to please you and help your plans, and I'm going back to please myself. And you'll be interested to know that the most powerful Minister in Spain at this moment wishes to be a close friend of mine, and his house always stands open to me. I mean Sebastian Quesada."

"I'm unfeignedly glad to hear it, Ferdinand," cried my brother, instantly appeased. "And if I can do anything to push your fortunes over there, of course my influence is at your command."

"It's very good of you, and I'm sure of it," said I, laughing in my sleeve at the notion of a man like Quesada being influenced by my fussy, pompous, little brother.

When Mercy heard of my resolve to return to Spain she was loud with her protests; and I found that she knew of Lascelles' abandonment of his matrimonial project—and knew the reason too. He had proposed three times to Mrs. Curwen in the short interval of my absence and had been refused; the last time finally, and with a distinct assurance that nothing would induce Mrs. Curwen to marry him.

When Mrs. Curwen herself heard of my return, she met it very differently.

"I am so glad, Mr. Ferdinand. It would have been so tiresome if you hadn't been returning. I don't believe I could possibly have ventured out there alone, and you can be of such use to me. And, of course, now that poor Lord Glisfoyle is dead, Mercy can go with me."

"You are really going to venture out there?" I asked, not over pleased by the news.

"Venture? Of course I am. I'm going on business, you know. My lawyer has put before me a most tempting speculation—a Spanish silver mine; and I'm going out to look into it myself. A poor lone widow must have something to occupy her, you see. Now, you will be nice, won't you, and give me all the help you can?"

"I really think you'd better not go," said I; and I meant it very heartily.

"You know, that's real sweet of you. It's the first nice thing you've said since you came back. It shows you take sufficient interest in me to wish me to keep out of danger."

"If you persist in going I can help you a good deal, I think," I said, gravely.

"Of course we're going."

"Then I can introduce to you just the best fellow in the world— my old friend, Silas Mayhew, and he'll do everything you want."

"I do think you're horrid, and that's a fact," she cried, turning away with a pout of annoyance. But nothing would stop her going, and such was her resolution that she did not rest content until she had arranged to make the journey with Mercy under my escort.

I fixed a date about a fortnight ahead, as I wished certain business matters arising out of my father's death to be settled before I left; but I had a note from Mayhew a week before then with news which I regarded as very serious; and it caused a change in my plans. After giving me some Embassy gossip, he wrote—

"I am writing this mainly because I think you will care to know that some very disquieting rumours are afloat about Sarita Castelar. The Carlists have been unpleasantly active in certain districts, and I hear the Government—Quesada, that is—is meditating a number of arrests. Amongst those listed for this is, I have every reason to believe, the Senorita Castelar.

"By the way, a letter came for you to the Embassy to-day, and I forward it with one or two more I found waiting at your rooms."

The letter filled me with apprehension on Sarita's account, and fired me with eagerness to be back in Madrid. I sat chewing gloomily the thought of her danger; I knew how urgent it might be if Quesada once decided to strike, and I resolved to return to Madrid at once. Then I glanced hurriedly at the enclosed letters. Two or three were small bills, but one bore the Saragossa post mark, and the writing, a man's hand, was unknown to me. But a glimpse of its contents showed me its importance.

71

It was from Vidal de Pelayo, and spoke of the plot which he himself had mentioned, and showed me that all was now ripe.

"I have obeyed your injunctions to the letter. I have never breathed a word to a soul of what passed when, on the greatest day of my life, I saw and spoke with you and held your hand. I have also done everything since that you have directed, and until this minute all was as I reported. But at the last moment those I trusted have failed me. The little guest must not come this way. Someone has betrayed us. You have never told me how to communicate with you under the altered circumstances; and I take this desperate step of writing to the British Embassy to you. If I am wrong, forgive and punish me; but I know not what to do. Only, if the little guest comes here on the 17th, all will be lost."

I knew only too well much of what it meant, and could easily guess the remainder. The Carlists had been pushing forward their mad scheme of kidnapping the young King, and now everything was in readiness. Sarita's absences from Madrid were explained—she had taken alarm at my declared intention to thwart the scheme, and had herself been hurrying things on in the necessary quarters. It was clear that she or someone had communicated with Vidal de Pelayo, and had given him some fresh instructions in the name of Ferdinand Carbonnell—this was how I read his phrase: "I have done everything since that you have directed," and "You have never told me how to communicate with you under the altered circumstances." He had pushed his preparations to the verge of completion, and then had come some hitch; and being at his wit's end, and not knowing how to communicate with anyone, he had taken the step of writing to the Embassy, feeling sure, no doubt, that the authorities would not tamper with a letter addressed there.

The date named was the 17th—the day on which I had fixed to start with Mrs. Curwen and Mercy. I had, indeed, been living in a fool's paradise, but there was, happily, ample time yet for me to interfere and do something. By starting that night I could be in Madrid by the 14th; and I went at once in search of Mercy to tell her of my change of plan.

Mrs. Curwen was with her, as it chanced, and I told them both I was sorry, but that I was compelled, by news from Madrid, to hurry out at once, and must start that night. The widow was a practical little body, and having satisfied herself by a sharp scrutiny of my face that there really had been news which had upset me, she said—

"I thought you were spoofing, you know, but I can see by your face there is something up. Can't you put it off till to-morrow?"

"No, I cannot waste a minute."

"Waste," she cried, with a shrug. "If this thing's bad enough to shake you out of your manners, it must be bad. But I don't think you need be quite so frank in calling it waste of time to wait for us."

"I beg your pardon; I didn't mean that. I mustn't delay."

"That's better; and we won't delay you. But, say, I'll make a bargain with you. It'll be just an awful rush for me to catch any train to-night, and if you'll give me till to-morrow morning, we'll go by the day boat and travel special right through from Paris to Madrid. When a lone widow woman's going silver mine hunting, I suppose it will run to a special train anyhow. And I just love the fuss it makes."

I demurred on the ground of the expense, the trouble, and the possible difficulties of making the arrangements; but she laughed them airily away.

"My dear Mr. Ferdinand, I can fix it up in an hour. One thing I did learn from poor A.B.C., and that was the power of dollars. You can have anything on a railway if you'll only pay for it; and a member of the Madrid Embassy travelling hot-foot to Madrid with his sister and her friend could have twenty specials in twenty minutes, for a due consideration. It's a bargain then? I must be off, Mercy, dearest. Whoop, but we'll scoop some fun in—I beg your pardon, I forgot. But it'll do you good to get out of this gloomy old house, dear, and there is no sin in a laugh or two. And if we don't enjoy our jaunt, may I never have another. Look here, to-morrow ten o'clock at Charing Cross, special to Dover. Good-bye," and she was gone.

"You'll have to marry her, Nand," said Mercy. "And she really is a dear, honest-hearted thing; as good as she is indefatigable and energetic."

"I can do better than marry her, I can find her a husband who can give her what she wants—some love in return." And I was thinking of Silas Mayhew. But the other matters were clamouring for my thoughts just then. Sarita, and the troubles and dangers she was coiling round herself; the plot against the young King; the part I meant to play in it all; and in the background the grim, stern, menacing face of Sebastian Quesada—the thoughtful face of the master at the chess board, moving each piece with deliberate intent, working steadily with set plan as he lured his opponents forward till the moment came to show his hand and strike.

The idea took such possession of me that in the short hours of tossing slumber that night I dreamed of it; and in the dream came a revelation which clung to me even when I woke—that in some way, at present inscrutable, unguessable, Quesada knew all that these Carlists were planning, that it was a part of some infinitely subtle scheme which had emanated by devious, untraceable, and secret ways from his own wily brain, and was duly calculated for the furtherance of his limitless, daring ambition.

I was full of the thought when we reached the station at the time appointed and found the indefatigable widow before us. She had made all the arrangements, and was lording it over the officials and impressing upon everyone the critical affairs of State business which impelled the important member of the Madrid Embassy to travel in such hot haste to the Spanish capital.

I was a little abashed at my reception by them, and disposed to rebuke her excess of zeal; but she only laughed and said:—

"You ought to thank me for my moderation, indeed, for I was sorely tempted to say you were the Ambassador himself. But we shall get through all right as it is."

CHAPTER XI

"THE WAYS OF THE CARLISTS WILL BE HARD"

There is no necessity to dwell upon the incidents of that memorable journey to Madrid. As Mrs. Curwen had said, "we got through all right." We were, indeed, treated with as much consideration during the whole journey as if we had been personages of the most illustrious distinction, and I found that her agents had contrived in some way to have telegrams despatched to all points, advising the officials everywhere on the route to pay particular heed to our special, and to forward it by all available means.

That we were a very distinguished party no one doubted, and Mercy was so excited by the results at different places and so exhilarated by the change of scene and by her friend's vivacity and high spirits, that the roses began to come back to her pale cheeks, her nerves toughened with every mile, and before we left Paris she was laughing with something of her usual lightheartedness.

During the journey, Mrs. Curwen declared that as she was going out on business and I was going to help her, we had better discuss the matter fully. As I had looked upon the story of the silver mine as an ingenious fable, designed only to be a cover for her visit to Madrid, I was surprised when she put into my hands a quantity of papers having reference to the subject, and begged me to study them.

"Shall we leave them until you think seriously of the thing?" I asked, with a smile, having, in truth, little taste for the business.

"Seriously? Why, I was never more serious in my life. If what I'm told is true, there's a big fortune in it. What do you think I'm going there for?"

"To see Madrid and give Mercy a treat."

Mercy laughed and glanced at her friend, who coloured very slightly.

"Partly that, and partly, too, to be there when there's someone I know there—and that's you. But I am also in earnest about this."

"Then I'll read the papers with pleasure," said I, and without more ado I plunged into them, and almost at the outset made a discovery which caused deep surprise and excited my keenest interest. The land on which the silver mine was said to exist was being offered by Sebastian Quesada, and it formed a part of the property which had belonged to Sarita Quesada—my Sarita's mother. In other words it belonged by right to Sarita and Ramon Castelar, and formed a portion of the estate the very existence of which Quesada had denied to me.

I need not say how earnestly I studied the papers until I had mastered every detail of the case. I was, in fact, so absorbed in the work, and gave so many hours to it, that Mrs. Curwen at length protested her regret at having handed me the documents at all.

I assured her, however, that it was fortunate I had read them as I was able of my own private knowledge to say there was a flaw in the title, but that I might be able to make arrangements when we reached Madrid by which matters could be put right. My idea was that the work of developing the mine might after all be done by means of her money, but that the advantage should be reaped, not by Quesada, but by Sarita and her brother; and I resolved to tackle the Minister as soon as practicable after my arrival in Madrid.

As we drew nearer to our destination, the possible embarrassments of Mrs. Curwen's and Mercy's presence in Madrid began to bulk more largely in my thoughts. The first few days after my return were sure to find me deeply engrossed by the work I had to do, and I did not care to explain this to either of them. As soon as I knew for certain the time of our arrival, therefore, I wired to Mayhew to meet us. I was glad to find him on the platform when our special drew up, and we all went off together to the hotel, where rooms had been reserved by Mrs. Curwen. A few words explained

75

the situation to Mayhew, who was glad enough to take charge of my companions.

"If anyone knows his Madrid, it's Mayhew," said I. "And he's a first-class pilot. My duties to the Embassy will be rather heavy for a few days, so you won't see much of me."

I was glad that Mrs. Curwen was very favourably impressed by my friend, and as he was keen for London news, and she and Mercy were eager for Madrid gossip, the evening passed very brightly.

As Mayhew and I walked to my rooms later, he was rather enthusiastic in the widow's praises.

"She's a good sort, Silas, a real good sort—bright, cheery, and chippy," I said, "But keep off spoons; or, at least, don't show 'em. She's beastly rich, and, like all rich folks, thinks everybody's after the dollars. Treat her like any other unimportant woman, show her a bit of a cold shoulder now and then, contradict her, and make her go your way and not her own, put her in the wrong occasionally and make her feel it, don't keep all the appointments you make, and pay more attention to Mercy sometimes than you do to her—in fact, be natural and don't make yourself cheap, and—well, you'll save me a lot of trouble and be always sure of a welcome from her."

"You seem to know a lot about her," he said, drily.

"She's my sister's chum, Si, and I don't want to be on duty for some days at any rate;" and I plumed myself on having given him some excellent advice and started a pretty little scheme for the mutual advantage of them both.

Then I turned to matters that had much more importance for me, and questioned him as to the rumour he had sent me about Sarita's possible arrest. It was no more than a rumour, and he had had it from a man pretty high up at the Embassy, who in turn had heard it whispered by a member of the Government.

"The most I can make of it, Ferdinand, is that there is some kind of coup projected by the Carlists—I believe they are organising one or two simultaneous risings—and the Government are alarmed and will strike, and strike hard. In fact, at the Embassy we are looking for lively times, and I thought you'd like to know it. By the way, there was a queer-looking provincial came asking for you at the Embassy yesterday, and I found he'd been to your rooms."

"He left no name or word?"

"No name, but said he had written you, and that his business was perfectly private and personal, but important."

I jumped to the conclusion at once that it was Vidal de Pelayo, and that, having had no reply to his letter, he had risked another visit to me; and I had no sooner reached my rooms, late though the hour was, than he arrived. He was looking haggard, weary, and anxious.

"Senor, I have been waiting and watching for you three days here in Madrid. When no reply came to my letter and your further instructions reached me four days ago, I knew something must be wrong, and in my desperation I came here."

"What further instructions do you mean? Give them me."

"Confirming the arrangements, giving me the time for the little guest's arrival at Huesca, and directing me to receive him. What was I to do, Senor? I saw ruin to us all and to everything in this false step; I could communicate with no one—what could I do but come here to you?" He spoke wildly, and with patent signs of distress and agitation.

"I have your letter, and have made the necessary arrangements. The little guest will not go to Huesca. Have no further care. You might have known I should not blunder in this way." I spoke with studied sharpness.

"The blessed Virgin be thanked for this," he cried, fervently. "The fear has weighed on me like a blessed martyr's curse."

"You need fear no more," I said, and was dismissing him when the possibility occurred to me that I might still make some use of him in the last resort. "You will go back to Saragossa, and on the 17th you will proceed to Huesca. I may be there and have need of you. Meanwhile, silence like that of the grave;" and with some more words of earnest caution I sent him away. If the worst came to the worst and the young King was carried to Huesca on the 17th, I could yet use this man to get possession of His majesty.

I had still to learn how the actual abduction was to take place, and I had two days only in which to find this out. It was already the 14th; and cast about in my thoughts as I would, I could see no way of discovering a secret which meant life or death to those who knew it and would be guarded with sacred jealousy and closeness.

To me it seemed that any attempt of the kind must certainly fail. The young King was protected and watched with the utmost vigilance; his movements were not even premeditated and were scarcely ever known long in advance even to those in the immediate circle of the Palace; he was never left alone; and the whole arrangements for his safe keeping might have been framed with an eye to the prevention of just such an attempt as was now planned.

Yet here were these Carlists fixing a day well ahead for the enterprise, making all calculations and arrangements, and taking it for certain that they would have the opportunity which to an onlooker seemed an absolute impossibility. It baffled me completely that night.

In the course of the next morning I sent a note to Sebastian Quesada announcing my return and saying I wished to see him; and a note came back by my messenger asking me to call on him at once at his office.

His greeting could not have been warmer and more cordial had I been his oldest friend returned after a long absence. At the moment of my arrival he was engaged, but by his express orders I was shown instantly to him; he dismissed the officials closeted with him with the remark that even that business must wait upon his welcome of me; and had I not discouraged him I am sure he would have kissed me after the Spanish demonstrative style.

"I have missed you, Ferdinand," he said, using my Christian name for the first time, and speaking with the effusiveness of a girl. "I have missed you more than I could have believed possible. Our little chats, our rides and drives together, have become necessary to me—that is a selfish view to take of a friend, is it not?—but they have been delightful breaks in my too strenuous life. When I got your little note an hour ago I felt almost like a schoolboy whose chief companion has just come back to school. I was grieved to hear of Lord Glisfoyle's death."

We chatted some time and then he surprised me.

"I suppose you know the world's opinion of me, Ferdinand—a hard, scheming, ambitious, grasping, avaricious item of human machinery, all my movements controlled by judgment, and conceived and regulated to advance only along the path of my own self-interest. What a liar the world can be—and I am going to show you this. I have been thinking it out while you have been away. You remember in the first hours of our friendship you spoke of the Castelars and their property, and you seemed surprised at my declaration that they had none. Well, I resolved for the sake of this new thing in my life, our friendship, to have the matter more closely looked into. I have done this, and I find I have been wrong all these years. Certain property that I have looked upon as mine, is theirs, and I am getting ready to make them full restitution. It will mean great riches to them; for amongst it is a district, at present barren and profitless, which I believe has most valuable deposits of silver. I shall restore it to them as soon as the formalities can be concluded; and you, my dear friend, shall, if you desire, be the bearer of the news to them; for it is to you, to our friendship, that in fact they will owe it."

"I am unfeignedly glad to hear this," I exclaimed. I was in truth lost in sheer amazement alike at the intention and at the motive to which he ascribed it. But so deep was my distrust of him that I could not stifle the doubts of his candour, even while he was speaking, and my thoughts went flying hither and thither in search of his real motive. Could he in any way have guessed that the facts were in my possession? Did he know that his agents in London had put the matter to Mrs. Curwen, and that she had travelled with me to Madrid?

"It has been a genuine pleasure to me to think of this little act of justice as the outcome of our friendship, Ferdinand—sincere, genuine pleasure. And now let us speak of another matter. Have you ever heard of your name having been used here in Spain?" The question came with such sharp suddenness that I was unprepared with a fencing reply.

"Yes, I have heard something of it," I answered, meeting the keen glance he bent on me.

"It is a curious business. Don't tell me what you have heard; I should not be surprised if I know it already. But if you have played with this thing at all, I beg you be cautious. If I were to tell you the nature of some of the reports my agents bring me, you would be intensely surprised. Happily our friendship enables me to distinguish accurately between my dear friend Ferdinand Carbonnell, and—the other. All do not hold the key to the mystery, however, and—well, perhaps it is fortunate in many ways that I do possess it. I tell you this now, because, while you have been absent from Madrid, strange things have occurred, and we are in the midst of much danger. Even as I sit here talking to you, it is scarcely an exaggeration to say the very existence of the Government, aye, and of the Monarchy itself may be trembling in the balance."

"You mean this?" I cried.

"My dear Ferdinand, on some things I never make mistakes. You know I have opposed this clamour for war with all my power, putting all I have of value to the hazard in that opposition. I have done that because I see as plainly as if the events had already occurred how hopeless would be a war for Spain. We can scarcely hold Cuba as it is, and Manila is but another name for menace. Can we dream then of winning when all the wealth and power of America is thrown into the scale against us? Alas, my poor, infatuated country!"

He leant back in his chair, lost for a moment in deep meditation.

"They prate to me, these fools, of European intervention and help. Who can intervene? Or if intervening, can do aught but dash themselves fruitlessly against the naval might of your country? If only England would speak the word! Then we might hope indeed; and then in all truth I would cry for war. But as it is, what else do we resemble so much as the swine of the Gadarenes inspired by the devils of our empty pride to rush down the precipice of war to sure and certain ruin? Ah, Ferdinand, my friend, pray to God—or whatever you hold for a God, that it may never be your lot to sit in the high places of your people and watch them rushing to ruin; seeing the ruin clearly and yet powerless to avert it. It is a cursed heritage!" he cried bitterly.

"The war could still be averted," I said.

He smiled and shook his head.

"At what cost? Good God, at what cost? At the cost of a revolution, the overthrow of the monarchy, the outbreak of Civil War! And to do what—to overset one feeble family, and prop up another. Was ever a country cleft by such a sharp and cruel sword?"

That he should have spoken to me in this strain surprised me; for though we had frequently discussed Spanish politics, he had never spoken with such freedom—and he seemed to read the thought in my face.

"You wonder why I speak so frankly. I have reasons. The hour is striking when all men will know the truth as I see it now. Then it is a relief to speak: I believe even the highest mountains and tallest trees grow weary at times of their solitude. And lastly, we are on the eve of stirring events, and I must warn you to be doubly circumspect in regard to this coincidence of your name. In the hour of her agony, Spain may prove as unjust as in the days of the Inquisition. Therefore, be careful. I know you English can keep secrets."

"Will you tell me one thing? Is Sarita Castelar in danger and likely to be arrested?"

"She has been foolish, wild and reckless even in her Carlism. And if the outbreak comes and any rising, the 'ways of the Carlists will be hard.' But of this be sure—she may always reckon now that I will try to save her; although any hour may see my power broken. If war comes, Ferdinand, it will be largely to divert the dangers of Carlism. And then, no man can say what will follow." He spoke with apparently deep earnestness of manner; and as he finished, a clerk came with a paper which caused him to end the interview and send me away, urging me to see him again shortly.

I had scarcely been more impressed by any event in my life than by that interview, and for all he had said in explanation, the reason for his conduct was a mystery; and a mystery which after events were to render infinitely deeper, until the hour when the clue came into my hands. I could not shake off the disturbing thought that throughout all he was misleading me and using me for some presently unfathomable purpose.

But one result was clear—he had given me good news to carry to Sarita; and when the time came for me to go to Madame

Chansette's house, the thought of Sarita's pleasure at my news, and the hope that I might use it to induce her to leave this atmosphere of intrigue and danger, found my heart beating high.

Friendship ripens as fast as fruit in that sunny land; would she be as glad to see me again as I to see her? Had she been counting the minutes to the time of our meeting as eagerly as I? I asked myself the questions as I stood on the doorstep waiting impatiently to be shown to her.

CHAPTER XII

SARITA'S WELCOME

If brightening eyes, rising colour in the cheek, radiant looks, smiling lips and the cordial clasp of outstretched, eager hands spell pleasure, then assuredly was Sarita glad to see me.

"We got your message and I have been so impatient," she said, holding both my hands in hers. "And yet so anxious."

It was good to look on her again; to feel the subtle sweetness of her presence; to listen to her voice; to watch the play of feelings as each left its mark on her expressive features; to touch her hand and have it left all trustfully in mine; to have the sunlight of her smiling eyes warming my heart; to revel in the thousand essences of delight which spread around her. Ah me. Life is good, and youth and beauty are good, also; but love is best of all. And my heart told me as I gazed at her how intensely and deeply I loved her, and what a charm there was in the mere loving. But these thoughts do not help the tongue to frame common-places.

"It is good to be with you again, Sarita;" was all I said for some moments; and we just laughed and made believe that this was as good as the most sparkling and brilliant conversation that ever wisdom conceived and wit clothed in phrase.

And for all our silence I believe we understood one another better than ever before. To me I know that the moments of inarticulate nothingism were more eloquent in meaning than any words; for somehow by that subtle instinct or affinity, that strange other sense that has no physical attribute and is all alert and powerful at times in the best as in the worst of us, I felt I did not love in vain, but that this woman, peerless to me among women, who held my hands and smiled to me with all the witchery of loveliness, was swayed by some of the same weird, delightful, thrilling, tantalising emotions which bewildered me.

What stayed me I know not; but the swift, sudden, rushing temptation seized me to draw her to my heart and whisper some of the love thoughts that were whirling with mad ecstacy in my brain; and when I paused as though greatly daring and yet not daring enough, I think my heart must have spoken straight to hers, for with a vivid blush, she shrank, cried "No, no," tore her hands from mine and, breaking away, ran swiftly to the end of the room, and stood, her flashing pride laid by, palpitating, trembling and glancing at me like a timid child.

A long hush fell upon us, and when it had passed, I had retaken control of my emotions and was myself again. But in that instant I know that our hearts spoke and were laid bare each to the other.

"I bring you some very strange news, Sarita. Perhaps the last you would expect."

"From England?"

"No, it was waiting here in Madrid, though I brought out from London something that might have influenced it."

"That is very clear," she laughed.

"Sebastian Quesada has decided to make restitution of your fortune," I said looking for some sign of surprise. But she gave none, and after reflecting an instant said:

"You have him before coming here?"

"I went to him to try and force the act of restitution on the strength of some news I had learned, and he forestalled me by announcing his intention to make it."

"He is very shrewd; but how did he know that you had this news?"

"That occurred to me; but I don't see how he could have known it."

"You are no match for him, Ferdinand. But there is no merit in his act even if sincere. He did not say the matter was already completed and the papers executed, did he?"

"It will be made as soon as the formalities can be complied with."

She laughed again and shook her head sceptically.

"It is a safe promise—for he knows."

"Knows what?"

"What will happen—before the formalities will be complied with." Her tone was thoughtful, and very serious; and she sighed.

"I think I know what you mean, and I am glad to be in time."

She was leaning her face on her hand, and lifted it to look up in surprise. "I want to warn you, too, Sarita—I know you are in danger—and to urge you to abandon this."

"You think I am in danger? Ah, Ferdinand, you do not know the under-currents. What do you think my real danger is?"

"I know you are in danger of arrest; and I urge you to come to England and be free."

"Would that be serving my country and my cause?"

"It would be serving your family." She laughed, and the music of her laughter was indescribably sweet.

"Family," she repeated, half-mischievously, half-earnestly. "I believe you are very much in earnest, Ferdinand, and I forgive you. I am not quite sure you are not foolish. But if anyone else said that, do you think I could hear another syllable from them? It is a counsel of treachery; and such counsel comes ill from the lips of a friend."

"You allow now that I am a friend then?"

"How solemn you English are, when—when you are solemn!" she cried, smiling again. "Do I think you are a friend? Yes, I do, in all truth. I know it. We shall not quarrel again. I believe you are so much my friend that, if I would let you, you would ruin yourself for me. That is how you would read friendship and how I read you. But I will not let my family do that."

"And how may I read you?" I said, quickly.

"How do you read me?" she retorted, with unwonted eagerness.

"How would you have me read you?"

"How would I have you read me?" She paused, glanced away, and then, looking me straight in the eyes, answered seriously and meaningly. "As what I am, not as what I might have been. You of all the world must not make the mistake of confusing the two."

"I do not mistake. What you might have been is what you shall be, Sarita," I said, earnestly—so earnestly that the expression in her eyes changed slightly, and she turned them away and started, and I thought she trembled. She knew my meaning; and after a moment or two, in which she had forced under the feelings that seemed to have surprised herself, she said calmly and almost formally—

"I will tell you what I think you do not know. I am in no real danger, for I am all but pledged to marry—Sebastian Quesada!" Her firmness scarcely lasted to the end of the sentence, and she uttered the last words as if looking for some expostulation from me; but I made none. Instead, I laughed and shook my head. I would not take it seriously.

"There is much virtue in that 'all but.'" She seemed surprised and in a sense disappointed at my reception of the news.

83

"It is true. I have three days left to give my answer. He gave me a week."

"He might as well have given you an hour—or a year. It's all the same. It will never be more than 'all but.' There are those who will never allow it."

"Allow?" she cried with a start, the glance of surprise ending in a smile.

"For one thing your family would bring pressure upon you," I answered, gravely.

"Family, again," and the smile deepened, and then died away, as she added, "But do you know what the marriage would mean to me?"

"I know what it would mean to Quesada. He would never live to lead you to the altar, Sarita."

"You would not do anything so mad?"

"I am not the only man in Madrid who would stop such a marriage. You have sown passion, the harvest may be death." For a moment she looked troubled, then her face cleared and grew very serious.

"You mean Juan Livenza. Yes, he is dangerous; but he is only a man; and after all Sebastian Quesada's man."

"Is Quesada more than a man, and proof against revenge?"

"I cannot tell you all there is in this; nor all that the marriage would mean to me." This perplexed me. Her face was almost stern as she spoke, and after a moment's pause, she exclaimed with a gesture of impatience and irresolution: "Don't question me. It must be."

"You have seen Quesada while I have been away." It was really a question, but I said it as though stating a fact.

"I told you he had given me a week for my reply."

"And you would marry him—loving another?" The colour that rushed to her cheeks was as much a flush of pain as of surprise. For an instant her burning eyes met mine in indignant protest and repudiation, but they fell before my steady gaze. I think she read the resolve that ruled me now, and feared it.

"You have no right to speak like this to me," she said; but there was neither life nor force in her words, and her voice faltered.

"On the contrary, I have the best of all rights. And you know this." She made an effort to assert herself then. Drawing herself up, she met my gaze steadily, and said in a tone she sought to make indignant:

"What right do you mean?"

For the space of a dozen quickened heart-beats we faced each other thus, and then I said, in a tone that thrilled with the passion in me:

"I love you, and I am the man you love, Sarita, and by the God that made us both, I swear no other man shall call you wife."

The masterfulness of my love conquered her, and with a low cry she broke away, sank into a seat near, and sat trembling, her face hidden in her hands. Love's instinct prompted me then to act, while my passion mastered her. I placed my arms about her, lifted her to her feet, took her hands from her face and kissed her.

"Do you think I will lose you, Sarita, in the very moment our love has spoken." At the touch of my lips she trembled violently, and with a cry of love, she wound her arms round my neck. As her head found love's shelter on my shoulder, my passion burst all control and found expression in a lava of words, hot, burning, incoherent, tumultuous and vehement, poured forth in the delirious madness of the moment of love's triumph.

We were standing there, still passion-locked, when a most unwelcome interruption came. The door was opened, and Colonel Juan Livenza was shown into the room.

He stopped on the threshold, his face livid with the rage that blazed up in his eyes at what he saw, and struggling for an instant to regain sufficient self-control to trust himself to speak, he said in a voice husky and hoarse with rage:

"Your pardon; my arrival is inopportune;" and with a bow and a look of deadly hate and menace at me, he went out and closed the door behind him.

Sarita, who had drawn herself hurriedly from my arms, turned pale and gazed at the shut door, trembling with agitation and distress.

"I have sown passion, and the harvest will be death," she murmured, repeating my words. "Heaven have mercy upon us."

"Or upon him," I answered. "But we need not take it quite so seriously. Come, sweetheart," and I held out my arms to her.

"No, no, no. It can never be, Ferdinand. I was mad," she cried distractedly.

"It was a very sweet madness, and shall last our lifetime," I answered, but she would not let me place my arm round her again. "As you will," I said, gently. "The knowledge of your love is all in all to me. The rest I can trustfully leave to time."

"You must go, Ferdinand. I forgot that he was coming this afternoon. You have made me forget everything. Oh, I am mad. Now, all may be lost." The words jarred.

"Lost," I cried; and then a sudden divination of her meaning and of Livenza's visit flashed into my mind. "He was coming, of

85

course, for this business of the day after to-morrow—but you will abandon that now, Sarita?"

"How did you know? Is it guess or knowledge?" and her startled eyes and parted lips told of her surprise.

"I was with Quesada this morning," I answered, the words coming in obedience to an impulse that I could neither account for nor resist.

"I am afraid of you, Ferdinand. How do you learn these things? How much do you know?"

"My dear one, you are playing with weapons of death, and with men who will but use and then fool you. Your one chance of safety and of happiness lies in trusting me. Leave all this seething maelstrom of intrigue, and come with me away from it all." I pleaded with all the force at command and with all the power of love to back the appeal.

But my note was a wrong one. Sarita, my love, would have yielded, but Sarita, the Carlist, was still the stronger; and my appeal fell on ears deadened by the calls of her patriotism and the cause she loved so fanatically. She grew less and less in sympathy as I pleaded.

"You must not tempt me to treachery, Ferdinand, and I cannot, I dare not, I will not listen. I should despise myself. Remember what I told you when first we met. You came too late."

"I will not hear that. I will not let you be sacrificed. You are mine, Sarita, bound to me by the bonds of our love! and, come what may, I will save you from this, despite yourself."

"Do you think I heed myself in such a cause? Then you little know me. What you ask is impossible—the one thing in all the world you should ever ask of me in vain, Ferdinand. But this I cannot grant."

"I will not take that answer. I know you to be in far deeper peril than you dream. If this scheme for abducting the King were to succeed, how would you profit? Can't you see the master-craft that is directing all: the wires that make you all no more than the puppets of the man who does nothing without a purpose, and everything for the one purpose of his own good. If Spain were kingless to-morrow, who would gain? You Carlists? To the winds with such a dream. When has Quesada lent himself to a cause which was not for his own advantage? Have you asked yourself this? How would he stand to gain by any such change? What were his words to me to-day? By heaven, I begin to see his master-stroke now. You are his dupe, Sarita, nothing but his dupe. You told me once you knew his heart—aye, but you have not yet measured the height of his ambition? To 'overset one feeble family in order to set up another'—

that was his phrase. Where, then, is his profit in this? He lets you think you have won him over through his love for you; that you know his heart; that he will help you for this coup if you in return will be his wife. Sarita, are you blind? What think you is the meaning of the careful network of preparations to strike at all you Carlists? What are those copious lists of names already in the hands of his agents? To help you Carlists, or to crush you? By God," I cried, passionately, as a great light burst in on me—"I see the object. He would have the young King out of his path; and yours are the hands by which it shall be done. And when you have done it, do you dream that he will help to set up another King? What would be his chance? Picture it. Once the young King were away, who would be supreme in this Spain of yours? Who is the most powerful man to-day? To whom would the eyes of the people turn in the hour of kingless crisis? To him or to Don Carlos? No, no, I tell you his power in that moment would be all but supreme, and he would use it to crush relentlessly you very Carlists whom he had used to clear the way for him. Surely, surely, you can see now that you would be the dupe and naught else, and that he aims at securing power that shall be nothing less than supreme."

Sarita listened to my rapid, excited speech with gradually paling cheek, and when I finished, her breath was coming fast and her eyes shining brightly.

"If I thought that, I'd—— But no, Ferdinand, he dare not, he dare not," she exclaimed, in quick, bated tones.

"Dare not—Sebastian Quesada?" I cried, incredulously.

"Dare not. A hundred daggers would flash at his heart."

"Aye, but the hundred hands that could thrust them would be rotting in his prisons."

"It is impossible, impossible, impossible. I won't believe it; but I must have time to think. You madden me. I am fevered and frozen in turns by the thoughts you kindle, I must have time."

"Let me make a last appeal, Sarita. Marry me and come away. Leave all——"

"No, no," she broke in, passionately. "I cannot. I cannot. This is no problem that a coward's flight can solve."

"Well then, postpone this attempt on the young King until you have had time to inquire and search and think."

"I cannot think now. I will see you to-morrow—or better, will think over all and write you."

"No, I will come to-morrow," I said. "Promise you will see me."

"If I am in Madrid, I promise," she said; and with that, seeing how deeply she was agitated, I thought it best to leave.

"One word, not from counsellor this, but from your lover,

Sarita. The knowledge we have gained of each other to-day, is knowledge for all our time. My love can never change; neither will yours, that I know. To-morrow, it will be the lover who will come to you, sweetheart. I shall have all in readiness for our departure. Till to-morrow, good-bye." I took her hand and tried to kiss her, but she would not suffer me, and when I looked in her eyes, I saw, to my consternation, they were full of tears. Knowing how intensely she must be excited and agitated to shed tears, and that it would distress her still more for me to remain and see her weakness, I turned away and went out.

I was scarcely less excited than Sarita, and, driving at once to my rooms, sent a messenger with a note to Silas Mayhew, asking him to come to me without fail in two hours' time, and sat down to try and clear the tangle of my thoughts. I had guessed much of the desperate intrigue that lay behind the abduction plot, and felt that I had guessed rightly the part which Sebastian Quesada was playing. But there was more that I did not know, and I had to learn it if the project was yet to be thwarted and his scheme exposed.

More instantly pressing than all, too, was the grave question of Juan Livenza's intentions. The look he had cast at me had murder in it, and I must find him and let him do what he would at once. It was for this I needed my friend Mayhew's help. I dined in my rooms, and sat pondering the puzzle and piecing together the ends until I began to see the meaning of it all.

While I was thus engaged, a note came from Quesada, couched in the usual informal, friendly terms, and pressing me, in his and his sister's name, to go and see them that evening, and adding that he had something particular to tell me. I scribbled a reply that I had an engagement, and had just despatched it when Mayhew arrived.

He came in, smiling and whistling, with a light question on his lips; but, seeing the look on my face, he stopped abruptly, and his face grew serious as mine.

"What's the matter? What has happened?"

"I can't tell you everything, Silas, but I'm in the thick of a quarrel, I fancy, and may want you to see me through with it. The man is that Colonel Juan Livenza I have spoken to you about, and I want you to come with me this evening when I put myself in his way to see what follows."

"I'll come, of course; but I hope it's not really serious."

"I don't know how serious; but I shall know within an hour or two. He goes a good deal to the Café de l'Europe, and I am going there now in the hope of meeting him."

I was too sensible of the gravity of the matter in hand to have any mind for mere commonplace conversation, and Mayhew, seeing this, fell in with my mood. We walked in silence most of the way to the Café de l'Europe, but when the place came in sight I took my friend's arm, and began to chat much in my usual manner. It occurred to me that Livenza might see us, and I was unwilling to let anything in my conduct display a marked difference from my usual demeanour.

We pushed up the broad steps and into the magnificent room that all Madrid knows and admires, but there was no sign of Livenza; and, having assured ourselves of that, we went on into the smaller saloon used by certain of the constant frequenters of the place. He was there, sitting at a table with a couple of friends, away to the right of the door.

I did not appear to notice him, but led Mayhew to a table at some distance from him, and called a waiter. It was not my cue to force any quarrel. I designed merely to give Livenza an opportunity of doing so if he wished. Acting on a hint from me, Mayhew placed his chair so that he could keep the three at the other table under observation, and, having given an order, we lighted our cigars and began to chat quietly.

"He has seen you," said Mayhew, after a minute or two, "and is speaking of us to the men with him. They are getting up, and, I think, are coming over to us. His face is livid, Ferdinand, and his eyes are burning like those of a man with a fever. What's he going to do? Yes, they are moving this way."

I pulled myself together, continued to smoke calmly, and, leaning forward, went on chatting unconcernedly as I waited for the approach of the man whose heart, I knew, was a very furnace of rage and jealous hate of me. And I will confess it was a tense, exciting moment.

CHAPTER XIII

THE FIGHT

The Red Saloon at the Café de l'Europe, as the room they were in was termed, was a well-frequented resort, and at that hour in the evening was generally full of visitors. But that night there were more empty tables than usual, and at one of these, quite close to us,

Livenza and his two companions stopped and sat down. They were well within earshot, and Mayhew, after a warning glance to me, began to speak on indifferent subjects.

I did not for a moment understand Livenza's intention, but it was soon made unmistakably clear. When the three had ordered some fresh drinks, they began to speak on the topic which was in all Spaniards' thoughts at the moment—the strain with the United States and the probable action of England. The conversation began quietly, and Livenza himself took no part in it for some minutes. The references to England grew gradually more bitter, however, until Mayhew was getting restive.

"There'll be a row if we stop here," he leant forward and whispered. "And you know how urgent the chief is about not getting into a mess."

"Wait," I whispered back. "This is only a blind."

"Well, they're talking at us right enough, and I don't like it."

"I don't want to drag you into it. If there's anyone here you know, go and chat with him for ten minutes; but don't leave the room."

"Hullo, there's Pezzia," he exclaimed aloud a moment later. "I haven't seen him for an age. Excuse me, Carbonnell;" and he got up and went to a table at a distance.

I heard one of the three snigger, and mutter something about discretion and that kind of courage which saves the skin by prudent flight. But fortunately Mayhew heard nothing, and I took no notice. There was a paper lying near, and I picked it up and began to read.

Without any conscious intention, I turned to the paragraph of Court gossip for any news of the young King's movements, and my attention was instantly caught and held by the following:—

"We have reason to state that His Majesty and the Queen Regent have been much touched and gratified by the evidences of devoted and affectionate loyalty displayed by the Madrid populace during the recent unattended drives in the streets and suburbs of the capital. These drives are taken with no more ostentation than those of any private citizen, and their unceremonious character affords eloquent proof of the mutual trust and affection which exist between the Royal Family and the people. They are quite unceremonious. The route is frequently decided only at the last moment, and the statement of a contemporary that, although seemingly no precautions are taken, the whole route is under close police supervision, has no foundation. Yesterday, for instance, the route as first planned was changed almost at the instant of starting, and thus no such precautions could have been taken even had they been necessary. But the Royal Family rely upon the loyalty of their subjects, and, thank God, do not rely in vain. Wherever the young King is seen, the populace hail him with delight, cheer him from the heart, and would protect him with their lives. Every day sees his hold upon the affections of his subjects strengthen, and nothing could more clearly prove this than the spontaneous evidence of Madrid's loyalty which these unceremonious incidents evoke. It is well known, too, that the trust in the people thus displayed had its origin in the suggestion of a powerful minister who, better than any of our countrymen, can gauge the stalwart, gallant loyalty of the Spain of to-day to the Monarchy, even in the midst of a national crisis such as the present."

I was so engrossed by this, and by the thoughts it stirred—for I saw intuitively what it might mean to the scheme for the young King's abduction, and I read between the lines the cunning work of Quesada—that for the moment I lost touch with the proceedings of Livenza and his companions; but a remark from him brought me back in a trice.

"Ugh, they make me sick, these English, with their lying hypocrisy and their insolent cant about God and their everlasting bibles. I can stand an American—he is at least an honest man and an open enemy; but your Englishman is all frothy godliness on the top, and rottenness, lies, and cowardice beneath."

One of his companions laughed, and the other said—

"That's pretty strong, colonel, and sounds almost personal."

"It is personal, too, for there is just such a fellow in Madrid at the present moment. A sneaking, lying, treacherous cur, ready to yap at you from a safe distance, but, when faced, all in a quiver, sticks his tail between his legs and runs yelping behind a woman's skirts, or some such safe shelter. Like the rest of the cowards, he has kept out of my way for fear of getting his ears boxed; but all Madrid shall know of his currishness. His name is——"

I pushed my chair back and stood up, and at the same instant the three men sprang to their feet, while the conversation at the tables near us died away and all faces were turned in our direction.

Livenza was still livid with his passion, save that a hectic spot flushed each cheek, the surrounding pallor throwing up the crimson into strong relief. His eyes burned like coals as he faced me, his nostrils dilated, and the corners of his mouth were drawn down in an ugly sneer. Less than an arm's length separated us.

"Oh, are you there?" he cried, insolently.

"I think you knew that," I answered, coolly. It was generally my good fortune to be able to keep my head in a crisis. My coolness exasperated him.

"You heard what I said, gentlemen," he cried, furiously. "This is

91

the Englishman himself. I will show you how to deal with a cur of an Englishman."

He was beside himself with fury, and he raised his hand to box my ears. But the blow never reached me. As he raised his hand—and the whole room could see his intention—I clenched my fist and struck him in the face. His head was turned slightly on one side, and the blow caught him just under the jaw on the left side, and so hard did I hit him that he was knocked off his feet and fell a-sprawl over the table, scattering the glasses in all directions with a noisy clatter.

In an instant the place was in a buzzing uproar, and men from all parts of the room came crowding round, while Mayhew, white and anxious, rushed to my side.

"It's all right, Silas," I said, still perfectly calm. "The brute insulted me grossly, and was going to strike me when I saved him the trouble. Some of these gentlemen must have heard him."

At that a tall, soldierly-looking man pressed forward, and said—

"I heard it all, senor. It was disgraceful. If my testimony can be of any use to you, here is my name;" and he handed me his card. He was a Captain José Pescada.

"Thank you. I am glad to have your word," I replied.

Meanwhile, Livenza's friends picked him up and gave him some brandy, for the blow had shaken him pretty considerably; and after a hurried whisper together one of them left the room with him and the other turned to me.

"This matter cannot end here, of course," he said. "Who will act for you?"

"You mean you are the bearer of a challenge from Colonel Livenza?" He bowed formally. "If you will come to my rooms in a quarter of an hour—I am going there direct—I will have matters arranged." I gave him the address, and with a bow he left me.

"As you witnessed the insult, Captain Pescada, can you come with me now?" He assented readily, and we three drove to my house, the captain loud and angry in his condemnation of Livenza's conduct.

"There is more in this than lies on the surface, gentlemen," I said, "There is a very bitter quarrel underneath it, and Colonel Livenza has chosen this ground for bringing it to a head. You will understand, therefore, that the fight will be no ordinary one, and no doubt when his seconds come they will bring an intimation that the duel must be à entrance. I am prepared for that, but as I am the challenged party I shall make my own conditions. The fight must take place to-night."

"By the Cross, that's quick work," muttered the captain.

"Do you really mean this, Carbonnell?" asked Mayhew, nervously.

"I never meant anything more seriously in my life. It is a very ugly business, and the sooner it is put through the better. My conditions are equally stringent. I am no great hand with either sword or pistol, and have no intention to be a target for a man whose skill is probably twenty times greater than mine. It is his profession. We will settle this thing by luck. We will face one another across a table; of the two pistols, one only is to be loaded; we toss for choice, and the winner of the toss to fire first; the loser, if he draw the loaded pistol, to fire when and how he pleases."

They both protested vigorously.

"I will fight on those and no other conditions. He has called me a coward, and heaped every foul insult on me he could think of. I believe he did it, relying upon his greater skill. If he is now afraid to face the chance of certain death, let him do it. I am not. I will fight on no other conditions. If he refuses, I will brand him as a coward publicly."

They were still endeavouring to dissuade me when Livenza's two seconds arrived, and I left all four together. For an hour they wrangled, and then the two went away to consult their principal, and another hour passed before they returned and announced that their principal had consented, but under the strongest protest.

Then came the question where the duel should be fought, and, when Mayhew asked me, I said at once that the fittest place would be Colonel Livenza's own house, 150, Calle de Villanueva; and in making this choice I had in my thoughts the incidents which had occurred there on the night of my arrival in Madrid. To this Captain Pescada objected on the ground that it was most irregular for a duel to take place at the house of one of the principals, and that it might be to my disadvantage. But this did not turn me a hair's breadth from my resolve.

"I am glad you put it on that ground, for then my opponent can raise no objection. If I am to fall, I care not a jot where it happens. If my opponent, he can ask no more than to die near his own bed," I answered, grimly. "We are wasting time; let us drive there at once;" and in a few minutes we were in the carriage.

On the way scarce a word was said by anyone. I sat wrapped in my thoughts, brooding over my purpose and nursing with jealous care the plans I had formed. I was semi-conscious of the strange sensation that I was acting in obedience to some subtle outside force which was impelling me to pursue my present line of conduct. I was saturated with the conviction that I should come unharmed through the fight; and that great consequences to me were to follow from that night's proceedings.

The result was an indescribable and indeed half-weird sense of comparative detachment from my surroundings. I was moving forward toward an end of tragic importance; and the scene at the Café de l'Europe, the insult, the blow, the strange preliminaries of the duel, the very fight itself, were but so many necessary steps in the due achievement of the far greater end. Once, something of this found expression. I was conscious that my good friend Mayhew was completely baffled by a mood totally unlike any he had ever seen me in before, and I remember thinking that when the strain was over I would reassure him. I caught him looking wonderingly at me, and at length he asked, solicitously and almost wistfully—

"Have you any private arrangements you wish me to make?"

"There will be none to make, Silas. There will be no need. Nothing will happen to me to make them necessary." He received the answer gravely, with a nod of the head and a whispered, "I thought I'd ask;" and looked at me strangely and compassionately, as a man might look at a friend suddenly bereft of his senses. The look made me conscious for a second that my words of conviction must have sounded oddly; but the next instant the feeling passed and I was again considering how to use the victory which I felt I was going to win.

In my manner I was perfectly cool and self-possessed, and when we reached the house I led the way up the staircase to the rooms I had been in before; and finding the first room I looked in empty, I said I would wait there while the preparations were completed.

The task occupied nearly an hour, I was told afterwards, but to me it passed like half a dozen minutes. I was reviewing all I knew of my opponent's character and temper, searching for the key which at present I could not find, and still animated by the irresistible conviction that I was on the eve of a discovery of vital import. I had not solved the problem when Captain Pescada came to fetch me.

"Everything has been done as you wished, Senor Carbonnell," he said, calmly, yet not without some nervousness; for the unusual and apparently deadly character of the arrangements had affected him. "The room beyond has been selected; two pistols, one loaded with a blank cartridge, lie on the table covered by a cloth. You and Colonel Livenza will take your places at either side of the table, with the pistols between you. A toss will decide the choice and will carry the right to fire first. In the choice, the pistols must not be touched, but indicated merely by a pointed finger."

"Good; I am warmly obliged to you," I said; and without even a conscious tremor or the faintest misgiving, I went with him.

I wish to disclaim entirely any credit for courage on this occasion. For the moment I was a fatalist, nothing more. I went into the room possessed by the irresistible conviction that I should leave it quite safe and unhurt; and had no more concern for the issue than if I had been going to keep a mere social or business engagement. My thoughts were not of my safety, but how I was to achieve that other object, the very nature of which I did not then know. I had no need of courage. I was in no sort of danger; and by some subtle instinct I knew this.

But it was very different with my opponent. A glance at his face told me that he was vastly disturbed. The rage and hate of me still flashed from his eyes and turned his cheeks livid; but there was another emotion besides these; and what it was, and all that it meant to me, I was very soon to see. I was surprised to notice, too, that the sight of him no longer filled me with any anger or bitterness. He had become merely a subject for close and minute observation. I was scarcely conscious of the presence of anyone else in the room.

We took our places at the table opposite one another in silence. The fateful pistols, covered by a thick green cloth, lay between us; and two little bulges in the cloth, one to the right of me and one to the left, denoted where they lay. I saw him look swiftly from one to the other of them, and then catch his breath slightly. That gesture was the first indication.

Then his chief second broke the tense silence.

"We have decided that Senor Mayhew shall spin the coin and Colonel Livenza shall call. It is an old Ferdinand dollar with the King's head; and you will please call "Head" or "Value." If you are correct in your guess, you will point to which pistol you choose, and will then fire. If you select the blank cartridge, Senor Carbonnell will have the other pistol and will exercise the right to fire when he pleases. If you lose the toss, Senor Carbonnell will select the pistol and fire, and you will exercise the right to fire when you please. Are you both agreeable, gentlemen?"

We murmured our assent simultaneously; and I saw Livenza catch his breath again, wince slightly, and clutch his left hand nervously—his second indication.

It was now Mayhew's turn, and my friend was so agitated that his hands trembled and he fumbled clumsily with the coin, and for a moment could not toss it up. But he sent it flying up at the second attempt, and while it was in the air Livenza should have called. But

95

the word stuck in his mouth too long, and the coin fell with a dull thud on the thick cloth without his call.

"Something caught my throat," he said, in a low apologetic tone and a shamefaced manner. "I must trouble you again," he added to Mayhew.

I needed no more. I had the clue I sought, and the little incident quickened my interest.

Mayhew spun it again, this time with no faulty preface.

"Head," called Livenza, while it was still high in air, and when it came down he could not restrain the impulse to stoop forward eagerly to see the coin as it fell. That action brought his face in a different angle of the light, and on his brow I saw some beads of sweat.

"It is head," said Mayhew. "Colonel Livenza fires first."

A gleam of satisfaction lighted my opponent's face, followed instantly, however, by an expression of such fateful, almost agonising indecision as I have never seen on a man's face, and hope never to see again. It was beyond his control to hide it. He glanced from one to the other of the spots where the pistols showed, then closed his eyes; his brow drew into deep furrows, and he bit his lips and clenched his hands as every muscle and nerve in his body seemed to grow suddenly rigid with the strain. Then, drawing a deep breath through his dilated nostrils, he flung out his hand and pointed toward the pistol on my right and his left; while the deep breath he had drawn escaped in a rush through the trembling lips with a sound that could be heard all over the room.

Captain Pescada threw back the covering cloth, handed Livenza the pistol he had chosen, and pushed the other to me. I left it lying on the table, and the next instant was looking into Livenza's eyes along the barrel of his pistol, held none too steadily within a few feet of my head.

I was conscious for a moment of the four white anxious faces of the men who were watching us with staring eyes and bated breath, and was kept at the tension long enough to feel a wish that Livenza would fire, when the report rang out and I felt the hot blast of the powder in my face, and was dazzled by the flash as I realised that I was unhurt. I heard an oath and a groan of despair from my opponent, and the first object I could see clearly was Livenza, now salt-white, trembling like a man with an ague, and swaying as he clung to the table for support.

So strong had been my conviction of safety that I had passed through the trying ordeal without even a change of colour, so Mayhew told me afterwards; and was certainly in complete

96

command of my nerves as I entered upon the second stage of the grim drama.

I saw my way as clearly as though written instructions were actually in my hands. He was a coward. Brave enough for the ordinary routine matters of life and of his profession as a soldier, he yet lacked the courage to face the certain death that was waiting for him in the barrel of the pistol lying to my hand; and throughout the whole scene he had been oppressed and overborne by the fear of what such a minute as this must mean for him. It was through his cowardice, his readiness to sacrifice honour for life, that I was to win my way to the knowledge I needed and achieve my purpose.

I began the task with studied cruelty. I bent on him such a look of stern hate and menace as I could assume, and dallied deliberately with his terror before I even laid finger on the pistol stock. Then I smiled as in grim triumph, and picking up the pistol looked carefully at it, and from it across the space between us to him.

His fight for strength was literally repulsive to witness. Terror possessed him so completely that both nerves and muscles refused to obey the direction of the brain, and the pause I made proved the breaking point in his endurance.

"I can't stand; give me a chair," he gasped, piteously.

"Stand back, gentlemen, if you please," I thundered, when his seconds were going to him; and the sound of my voice increased his already crushing fear, so that he swayed and fell forward on the table, like a man collapsed in drink, his arms extended and his hands clenched in a veritable agony of despair and terror.

I allowed a full thirty seconds to pass in a silence that must have been awesome for him, and then let drop the first hint of hope.

"It is my right to fire when I please. I have not said I shall exercise it to-night."

At that I saw the strength begin to move in him again. His fingers relaxed, he drew his arms back and then gradually his body, and at length raised himself slowly and looked at me—question, doubt, fright, appeal, hope, all struggling for expression—a look that, had I been as full of rage and yearning for revenge as he had been and as he believed me to be, would have sufficed to stay my finger on the trigger or have driven me to fire in the air. I have never seen such haggard misery.

There was another pause, in which I looked at him, my face set apparently upon the execution of an implacable resolve to kill him. When it had had its effect and I saw the grey shades of renewed despair falling upon him, I said—

"Gentlemen, I will ask you to withdraw a while. It may be that a way can be found out of this business which may lead to my waiving or indefinitely postponing my right. If Colonel Livenza is willing, I will speak with him privately."

A hurried whispered conference between him and his seconds followed, and then we two were left alone.

CHAPTER XIV

A COWARD'S STORY

After a very short pause Livenza's very shame at his own panic began to give him a sort of firmness of bravado. The worst about him had been made clear; he had shown that he was afraid and was willing to purchase his life; and it was a matter in which he must make the best terms he could. The pressure of imminent death once removed, he could breathe again. In the future he was to be my creature, and he recognised it. That was how I read the sullen, scowling look he gave me as he drew himself up slowly and crossed his arms.

"You can sit down if you wish," I said, curtly, in the tone of a master, to make him feel my authority and to recall to him his former craven appeal.

"I have no wish: I can stand."

"You know your life is forfeit," and I glanced at the pistol in my hand, "and that I have the right to send the bullet crashing into your brain, if I please?"

He winced, and the light of fear glanced again in his eyes. I couldn't have shot him in cold blood, of course, and the thrust was a cruel one. But I knew that he could have shot me under the circumstances, and that he would read my disposition by his own. He was a brute, and must be treated as a brute.

"If you mean to shoot me, do it," he cried.

"I am willing to let you purchase your life, but the terms will be heavy."

"I am in your power and must pay them," he answered, sullenly, but with unmistakable relief.

"First, then, understand this: What has passed here to-night shall never be breathed by either my friends or myself. So far as we are concerned your reputation outside shall stand just where it did

when you entered the room. On that I give you my word of honour—
if you deal straightly with me. A sign of treachery or a single lie from
you, and the truth shall be told."

"I agree to that, of course."

"Moreover, my right to fire this shot is merely postponed, not
waived. You will put down in writing what will justify me should
your treachery ever make it necessary for me to shoot you."

"I will do that." He was beginning to speak fluently and readily
now.

"You will now answer my questions. Are you in Sebastian
Quesada's pay or in his power?"

"In his power. He concocted a false charge against me some
time ago, confronted me with the proofs, and threatened to have me
prosecuted. I dare not face the charge, and from that moment he
has used me for various tasks."

"Amongst them this business of the young King's abduction?"

He started violently as I made this rather bold shot.

"What do you know?"

"Everything—except the details." The reply was perhaps a little
exaggeration; but I was guessing everything very fast.

"If he knows I have spoken of it to you, he will ruin me. I might
as well be dead."

"He will never know, unless you are fool enough to tell him. He
sent you to Senorita Castelar's house this afternoon?"

"Yes. He said you would be there." He was sufficiently
recovered now for his private feelings to reassert themselves
somewhat, and there was a gleam of the old hate of me in his eyes as
he gave the answer which let in such a flood of additional light upon
my knowledge of Quesada's treachery. I made another long shot.

"He has promised to help your suit with the senorita?"

"You are the devil. You do know everything, indeed," he cried.
"Who are you?"

"You are to answer, not question," I returned, sternly. It was
now as clear as the sun at noonday that Quesada had planned this
quarrel of ours, sending Livenza to catch me with Sarita, with the
certain assurance that his jealousy would lead to a duel in which one
of us would be certain either to fall or to be laid by during the
completion of his plans. He stood to gain almost equally by the
death of either. "You took with you some final instructions about
this plot; what were they?" I asked, after a moment's pause.

For the first time he hesitated, and I saw the beads of sweat
standing thick on his forehead, as he looked at me, trembling like a
blade of grass.

"You are asking me for more than my life," he murmured, his very teeth chattering in his irresolution.

"Answer me, or——" I thundered, lifting the pistol a few inches.

"You will never breathe a word of this?" he implored.

"Answer me," I cried again, with implacable sternness.

"He gave me the privately agreed upon route of His Majesty's drive for to-morrow afternoon." He spoke in a voice low and hoarse, and the sentence was broken by three or four pauses, as if the effort to utter it was almost beyond his strength.

"Give it me," I said, instantly.

"I—I dare not," he answered, his voice no louder than a whisper.

"Give it me," I repeated.

"I—I can tell it you," he said, after a long pause.

"Give it me," I cried, sternly. "I shall not ask again."

He plunged a trembling hand into an inner pocket, and without withdrawing it gave me a glance of piteous entreaty.

"Anything but this!" he pleaded. "God have mercy on me; anything but this, senor, I beg you. I was to have destroyed it."

"As you will. Then our conference fails. I will call in our seconds and——"

But he did not let me finish, for with a groan of despair he brought the paper out and laid it on the table.

I picked it up, and a glance showed me what a prize it was. The writing was Quesada's, and it gave the route of the drive and actually suggested the place where the abduction could be made—a spot on the road to Buenavista, close to where the bridge crossed the Manzanares on the way to Aravaca, and specified the time, five o'clock; adding the significant note—"Only one aide in carriage, no escort; coachman and footman."

When I had read it he held out his hand for it, dreaming apparently that I should return it; and when I put it in my pocket he threw up his hands with a deep sigh of despair.

"Why was to-morrow chosen instead of the following day?"

"I don't know. There have been several changes."

I stopped to think. I had indeed made a splendid haul, and there was little else Livenza was likely to be able to tell me. There was one question I had yet to answer; but it was certain that he would not know any more than I. What was Sebastian's object in all this? I had thought of the probable solution when I was with Sarita—that he was playing for his own hand and meant to get rid of the young King and to crush the Carlists by one and the same stroke; and to pit myself against a man shrewd enough to conceive such a policy and daring enough to put it to the actual test, seemed

100

like madness. But I had made up my mind to attempt it; and the document I now had in my pocket would be a powerful weapon if only I could see the means to use it shrewdly.

As I stood a minute or two revolving these matters, Livenza was staring at me with the fascinated gaze with which a hunted animal will watch the beast of prey that threatens its life, and at length said—

"Is there anything more. I am not well, senor."

"No, you have saved your life; but you will remain close in your rooms until I send you word. To all but Sebastian Quesada you will be ill in bed. Any message he sends you, you will immediately forward to me; and he must not know that you are not acting just as usual. I will find someone who will nurse you day and night and watch you."

"I cannot serve both you and Sebastian Quesada. I cannot do it. I must have either your protection or his," he cried, feebly.

"You will have mine," I answered, in a tone I might have used had I been the master of countless legions. "Serve me in this matter, and you will have your reward. Fail me, and I swear I will take your life."

Without giving him time to answer, I called in the other men, and found that Captain Pescada had gone away, leaving many apologies. I apologised for having kept the others waiting.

"Colonel Livenza is ill, gentlemen," I added. "He has given me proofs of his desire to make ample amends for the insult of this evening, offered under what he declares to have been a complete misunderstanding. While he is arranging matters I have consented to withhold my right under the duel. He will put this in writing with an acknowledgment that I shall be entitled to exercise that right should he fail in what he has undertaken to do, and I wish you to put your names to the document."

He was so broken that he could scarcely keep a steady enough hand to write what was necessary; and while he was so engaged, I drew Mayhew on one side.

"You know many people in Madrid: do you know of any young doctor who would undertake to stay here with Livenza for a couple of days at most, but certainly until after to-morrow night, never losing sight of him and seeing that he does not commit suicide?"

"He won't commit suicide," said Mayhew, contemptuously.

"I know that; but it will make a good excuse for us to give to the doctor who is to watch him," I returned, drily. "It must be a man who won't talk either. And you'll give me your word to say nothing of that distressing scene of his cowardice. There's a good deal in this thing—a good deal. And will you look up Captain Pescada in the morning and get a pledge of secrecy from him?"

"Certainly I will; and I think I know the man you want."

"Can you rouse him up to-night? Of course, I'll see he's well paid. I don't want to be here any longer than necessary; and as soon as this thing's done," nodding to where Livenza was writing, "perhaps you could fetch him."

The arrangements as I planned them were carried out without much further loss of time, and as soon as the paper had been read over and signed, and Livenza's seconds had left, Mayhew started in search of his friend. Livenza went to bed, and when the young doctor came and I had given him my instructions, Mayhew and I left the house together.

"It's all very mysterious, Ferdinand," he said, fishing.

"Very, Silas; but I hope things will come right in the end."

"You're well out of an ugly business."

"Or deeper in—it remains to be seen which," I answered, cryptically, and smiled. "But whichever it is, our friendship will have to stand the strain of silence about it. I'm sorry, for I should much like to have you in it with me. But it can't be—at any rate yet. All the better for you, perhaps."

"That brute meant to kill you," he said, after a pause.

"Not the only good intention that's missed fire to-night, probably."

"I couldn't understand you a bit. You were as cool and certain as if you knew you'd come out on top."

"I think I did know it, too, in a way. Anyhow, I felt dead certain, and that was just as good. But I know a lot more than I did, I'm glad to say."

"What do you mean?" he asked, with quick curiosity.

"I know what it means to stand fire at close range."

"All right; I won't question you. But you're a strange beggar;" and he laughed. I thought I could afford to laugh, too, so I joined him. I might not have many more occasions for much laughter, at any rate for a while; and soon after that we parted at the door of his house.

It was very late, but I sat for an hour smoking, studying the route of the young King's drive for the next day, and making my plans; and when I turned in my nerves were still in good enough trim for me to get to sleep at once. I had had a very full and very exciting day, but unless I was mistaken the morrow would prove much more critical for me, and probably a no less fateful one for Spain.

I sent a letter first thing in the morning to the Embassy,

excusing myself from attendance there on the plea of sudden business; and, hiring a horse, rode out to the spot where the attempt on the young King was to be made that afternoon.

It was cleverly chosen, indeed. A very quiet, lonely place, where the road dipped and then ran in a cutting between high banks up a sharp incline—such a place, indeed, as was exactly suited to the work. Fortunately I knew the district well, and where the various roads about there led; and I could form a pretty good idea of how the thing would be done.

I picked out a good spot where I could keep concealed, watch what transpired, and then follow in pursuit. My plan was a very simple one: To let the affair take place and the abductors get away with the King; then to follow, and just when they were confident all had gone well, strike in and act according to circumstances. My danger lay in the fact that I must be alone; but the personal risks of that were less than any attempt to get others to join me.

Of course, a mere word of warning sent to the palace would be sufficient to cause a change in the route for the King's drive, and so check the plot for that afternoon. But that was by no means my sole object. I was bent on making a bold stroke for my own gain; and for this I was as anxious as any Carlist could be for the momentary success of the scheme. I must not only call check, but checkmate, to the desperate man I was fighting.

The knowledge I had gained from Vidal de Pelayo, that the Carlists would attempt to carry the King to Huesca, gave me a clue as to the line across country they were sure to take, and a gallop of a few miles refreshed my knowledge of it, and also showed me where in my turn I could make my rescue.

I returned to Madrid about noon, confident and in high spirits as the result of my ride, and my next task was to secure the fleetest and strongest horse that could be hired; and I had scarcely reached my rooms after arranging this when a very singular incident occurred.

A letter was brought me from Sebastian Quesada, and my servant told me the messenger was waiting for a reply. I opened and read it with great astonishment.

"Time changed. Six o'clock—not five; return route. Same spot. Communicate instantly."

I had had no message from him, or invitation for a drive or ride that day. The letter was just in the brief style of twenty others he had sent me, and it seemed that some former invitation must have miscarried. I was on the point of penning a line to him to this effect when a light suddenly broke upon me.

The letter was not for me at all. It had been put by mistake in the wrong envelope. I saw the address was in Quesada's own hand, and in his hurry he had apparently committed the blunder of mixing the two notes.

This referred without a doubt to the great event of the day, and my pulses tingled at the thought. I sent for the messenger.

"Did Senor Quesada give you this with his own hand?" I asked the man, whom I knew as a confidential servant of the Minister's.

"Yes, senor. I took it first to the British Embassy, but they told me you had not been there to-day, and as my instructions were to await your answer, I came here."

"Quite right," I answered, casually. "I'm sorry I shall not be able to do what your master wishes. I have hurt my hand and cannot write," and I lifted my right hand, round which I had bound my handkerchief. I could not send a written reply, as I did not know what I had to answer, and could afterwards blame his servant if my verbal message suggested any discrepancy.

As soon as his back was turned I was in a carriage driving fast to Livenza's. I guessed that as this letter was for him, mine might have been enclosed to him, thus forming the counterpart of the mistake.

My guess was right, and I found him puzzling over a letter asking me in most pressing terms to join Quesada that afternoon in a long ride, and to dine with him quietly afterwards. I saw the object—to make it impossible for me to interfere in the business of that day, supposing by any chance I had got wind of it.

That being his purpose, how would he act when he got my reply? The story of the injured hand would seem to him to be the result of the trouble with Livenza; but it was almost certain that he would come himself to see me. If he did so, and found me absent, he might suspect, and perhaps even at the eleventh hour postpone the coup.

A question to Livenza showed me how he would communicate the change of time to those whom it concerned, and the moment I had arranged that I rushed back to my rooms, swathed my hand in bandages, improvised a sling under my coat, and sat down to wait. It was then three o'clock, and I must be away in two hours—by five, that was—if I was not to run a risk of being late, or perhaps of being observed.

My guess was right again, and at a quarter past three Quesada was shown into my room. He found me with his letter lying open on my table, while I was trying with infinite pains to write a reply with my left hand. I received him with a welcoming laugh as I flourished my right arm in its sling, and held out my left.

"My dear Ferdinand, Carlos brought me word that you had

104

injured your hand and could not ride with me this afternoon. I was all anxiety, and have cancelled my arrangements that I may give up the time to cheer you. Tell me, are you much hurt? How did it all happen, in the name of misfortune?"

I cursed his solicitude, and saw his object. He had come to see that I did no mischief. But I replied lightly—

"That is the act of a good, true friend. Sit down, light a cigar, and let us chat. I was at that moment writing to you—have you ever tried to write with the left hand? It is the devil's trouble. See here," and I held out the letter, taking care that he should see his own at the same time, and laughed over the stumbling effort. "I have been trying ever since Carlos went to write and thank you, and say how sorry I am I can't dine with you either, because I am engaged for the afternoon with my sister and her friend Mrs. Curwen. We came from England together, you know. But I am not due until four o'clock, so we can smoke, drink, and chatter till then."

"But you're hurt—what is wrong?"

"My dear Quesada, though you are what we at home call Home Minister, and therefore head of everything that pertains to law and order in the capital, as elsewhere—and a most capable head, too—this Madrid of yours is the devil's own place for a brawl. And I am bound to say that when the Spanish blood's up the knife's out, and I can speak from experience that the man who gets his fingers in the way of a Spanish knife is a good many kinds of a fool for his trouble. But don't ask any questions; I shall be right again in a day or so, and meanwhile I mean to take care of my left hand;" and I flourished it, laughed again, and gave him a look which might have been intended to suggest any kind of intrigue.

He accepted the explanation, I thought, and in a few minutes we were chatting much as usual. As the time passed I grew very anxious for him to go, but he sat on for an hour, showing no indication of leaving, and then I gave him a hint, which he didn't take.

"Now do me a favour," I said then. "Come with me this afternoon—I must go, for I am due now—and allow me to present you to my sister?" I said it as earnestly as though I knew Mercy and Mrs. Curwen were really at the hotel waiting for me, and to my dismay he hesitated.

"You tempt me strongly. Your sister must be Dolores' and my friend."

"Good; then you will come? It is excellent, too, for Mrs. Curwen is the American capitalist who is going to take up that silver mine business on the Castelars' property, that you offered in London, you know, and she will be delighted to see you and ask you all kinds of questions about it. She is the most——"

But his face changed then.

"I do not like Americans just now," he broke in, "and I have remembered something I omitted to do at my office. You must excuse me. But I will drive you to the hotel."

"You are a thoughtful friend always," I replied, knowing he did this because his suspicions of me were not yet allayed. Then came another point. I was dressed for riding—Norfolk jacket and riding gaiters—and could not change them. His quick eyes saw this instantly, and he said with a glance and a laugh—

"Your visit is an informal one, Ferdinand?"

"One's sister learns the art of making excuses, and a man with only one hand can surely plead privilege." And in that dress I started, leaving him only a moment while I secured my revolver and some ammunition.

He drove me right to the hotel, and did not leave me until he had actually heard me ask for Miss Carbonnell's and Mrs. Curwen's rooms, and looked after me as the waiter led me away.

A glance at my watch showed me it was then nearly half-past four, but I felt compelled to carry on the farce so far as to go to Mrs. Curwen's room, perilously short though the time was growing.

CHAPTER XV

THE ABDUCTION

It is an experience which I expect most of us have known, to have to clap on suddenly the mummer's mask at a moment of serious crisis, and to play the fool just when one's whole mind and thoughts are claimed by really tragic issues. That was my case when I went to Mrs. Curwen's on parting from Quesada.

The widow was alone, and was annoyed that I had not been to see her on the previous day, and met me consequently in a mood of satirical banter. Looking at me as though she did not recognise me, she said—

"Carbonnell, Carbonnell, I seem to have heard the name; but

surely it is so long since I saw a man of the name. Are you Mr. Carbonnell?"

"I believe I am," I returned, gravely. "And I was actually going to shake hands with you, I think."

"I don't think you can be; because I am sure the Mr. Carbonnell I knew would never have remained away long enough for me to forget his face."

"Ah, you are thinking of Lascelles Carbonnell. I am Ferdinand, his brother, you know."

"I am very angry with you, and that's the truth," she cried, laughing, and colouring at the little thrust. "Lord Glisfoyle would never have behaved in such a way. If this is how Madrid affects people, I wish I'd never come. But what's the matter with your hand?"

"I have come to have a very difficult surgical operation performed by you or Mercy. Where is she?" She came in as I spoke; and seeing my arm in a sling her face clouded, as she kissed me and asked the reason.

"Are you really hurt?" asked Mrs. Curwen, doubtingly, sympathy struggling with annoyance. "You don't look ill."

"Does a man wear this sort of ornament for fun?" and I drew the bandaged hand from the sling.

"There's no accounting for what a man will do—in Madrid," she retorted, with a sniff of battle and a toss of the head.

"Angela!" cried Mercy. "What is the matter, Nand?"

"He wants us to perform what he calls a 'surgical operation,' Mercy."

"The matter is not very serious, I believe," I answered, in deference to the pain on my sister's face, but seeing now how to punish Mrs. Curwen, I added: "They tell me, indeed, that if the bandages are removed very carefully and a particular kind of massage employed, I shall recover the use of the fingers quickly."

"I have had a lot of nursing experience, I can do it," said the widow; and she began to handle the bandages very gently. "But what kind of massage do you mean?"

"That will depend upon the condition in which we find them. I believe they will have to be rubbed by being passed through cloth." This somewhat recondite description of putting them through my coat sleeve puzzled her completely.

"I never heard of anything like that," she said, wrinkling her forehead in perplexity; now quite serious. "But whoever put these on? I never saw anything so clumsy in my life. I must cut this one," and as she turned away to find scissors, I took occasion to give

107

Mercy a glance, which not only relieved her anxiety, but changed her into an accomplice.

"Poor old Nand," she cried, in quite a tearful voice, but laughing to me with her eyes. "Be careful, Angela. Shall I do it, dear?"

"Do you think I can't take a bandage off?" was the reply, with some sharpness, as she came back with the scissors.

"Ah, oh!" I cried, wincing as if she hurt me at the next touch. "Please be careful. I can't bear pain a bit."

"Men never can," she retorted. "I'm sure I scarcely touched you. But if it's as bad as that, I'll be careful," she added, earnestly; and the little farce proceeded, she unwinding the clumsy bandage I had put on, and I wincing and "ah-ing" and grimacing, until the hand was uncovered, and the fingers—bloodless, of course, from the ligature—were exposed to view.

"What's the matter with them?" she said, examining them closely.

"It came on suddenly." I explained. "And now for the cloth massage. Gently."

"What is cloth massage?"

"Why, massage with cloth, of course. Wait, I have it;" and without more ado about nothing, I thrust my arm through the sleeve of my coat, and held out my hand to shake hers. "The most wonderful cure on record. Thank you so much."

Mercy burst out laughing, but Mrs. Curwen coloured with vexation.

"What does it mean? You've been fooling," she cried. "I call it horrid of you;" and as she turned away I saw tears of vexation start to her eyes. Then I repented.

"Forgive me. Honestly, I am sorry and did not mean to vex you. There is a meaning to all this, and some day I'll tell you both, and the tale will surprise you, probably."

"I'll forgive you if you're going to stay and take us nut, and then come back to dinner. Your friend Mr. Mayhew is coming. We're going to the Opera. The young King is to be there, and the Queen. It's to be a real gala show."

"I should like to see the young King," I replied, truthfully enough, indeed. "But I can't manage to dine with you. Give me the number of your box, and if I can get my work done I'll try and join you there. I must be off now, in fact."

"You seem to be very hard-worked at the Embassy," she replied.

"This is not purely Embassy work; it's rather extra-official than otherwise."

"A.B.C. used to say that when a man had out-of-office work there was generally a woman in the case."

"Ah, he was an American; and American customs are very unpopular in Madrid just now;" and as my time was up, I hurried away. A short drive carried me to the stables where my horse was in waiting ready saddled, and not a vestige of the little farce remained in my thoughts as I mounted and rode slowly off on what might be so momentous an errand for me.

I knew the city well enough to pick my way through by-streets till I reached the outskirts and came out on to the Aravaca road, and then I rattled on for a mile to put my horse's powers to the test. He was a splendid animal, and in the pink of condition, very fast, as sure-footed as a mule, and wonderfully obedient alike to voice, knee, and rein. He would have made a magnificent hunter, and when I put him across a bit of country he took as much pleasure in it as I myself. A jewel of a horse for the task I was upon.

I reached the spot I had chosen for my hiding place well before the time; and, tethering my horse securely, I climbed a tree which was to be my observation post, and commenced my vigil. I had about half an hour to wait, for my ride had taken less time than I had allowed; but there was not much fear of the time dragging.

I had with me a pair of folding field-glasses of great power and range, and with these I swept the country round for indications of the approach of the royal carriage or of any Carlist preparations. For a long time I looked in vain; but presently a carriage, drawn by a pair of stalwart horses, appeared about half a mile away to my left on the road from the city. It was travelling rapidly, and I lost it soon afterwards behind a small olive wood, which stood close to the crest of the hill. As it did not appear again, the deduction was easy that it was the Carlist carriage, and had been drawn up in concealment to wait for the coming of the young King. I would have given a great deal to know the number of those in it—but this was, of course, impossible.

Five minutes later four horsemen straggled up one by one, with considerable intervals between them, and as they did not show on my side of the little wood, I set them down as a further instalment of the performers in the coming drama.

As there must be now at least six or eight men, the number of them gave me a twinge of uneasiness. If anything like that number of men were going with the young King after he had been put in the Carlist vehicle, I had made a very grave miscalculation in my plans, which might have the most serious consequences.

Nor was this all. As the appointed hour approached a single horseman came riding at a sharp trot from the other direction; and he, too, apparently joined the group waiting by the wood. He seemed to have brought news, for soon after his arrival a man came on foot from the coppice to the crest of the hill, stood a moment shading his eyes and staring across the deep dip which the road made at the spot. After staring thus for perhaps two minutes, he made a sign to his companions and retraced his steps.

One thing was at any rate certain from this—the young King was expected; and this meant much.

A pause of some ten minutes followed; during which the scrutiny of the road was renewed twice, and the second time the lookout appeared to see what he sought. I turned my glasses upon the road, and saw a horseman spurring with all possible speed in our direction. He dashed down the one hill at breakneck speed, and spurred and flogged his horse up the next to where the others were awaiting him.

Almost directly afterwards I saw them commence their preparations; and I jumped to the conclusion that his news was that the royal carriage was close at hand.

Six men came out on foot. Four went down the hill, concealed themselves in some bushes that grew by the wayside, and two went farther down, almost to the bottom of the dip, and hid there. Presently two others sauntered slowly a little way down the hill, and directly afterwards the carriage I had formerly seen came out from behind the wood and stood drawn up just far enough from the hill brow to be out of sight of anyone coming up.

Altogether a fairly effective disposition of forces. The royal carriage was to pass the first two at the bottom of the decline and to be stopped by the four posted in the middle. If by a mishap it got past the four, the two at the top would stop it: if it was turned back, the two at the bottom would act; while in any case all of them would be almost instantly available for an attack in force.

As I turned my glasses anxiously along the road to see whether the young King was coming toward the trap so cunningly laid for him, I felt my heart beginning to beat with the strain of the excitement, and involuntarily I caught my breath and started when I saw a slight cloud of dust in the distance which told of the King's approach.

The drama now developed quickly enough to satisfy the most voracious lover of incident. The dust cloud grew larger and larger, till at length I could make out the carriage quite distinctly, and saw that Quesada's information had been absolutely correct. There were no outriders, no escort of any kind, and the only servants on the carriage were a coachman and footman, both on the box. What insanity, I thought, to abandon even ordinary precautions at such a time! And what must not be Quesada's influence even at the palace to get this effected on the flimsy pretence of showing trust in the people!

Meanwhile, the men in waiting made a last preparation. When the royal carriage was about half down the hill on my right, three of the Carlists began to move slowly forward and to descend that on my left at a walking pace. Then the driver drew to the side, as though there were not room for the two carriages to pass, and waited. All was now in readiness.

The thing was done with remarkable neatness, sureness of touch, and precision of movement. The instant the royal carriage had passed the first couple of men at the bottom, the driver having checked the horses to a walk, they both came out and followed. As it came abreast of the four half way up the hill they sprang out, the carriage above drew into the middle of the road, and the remaining couple running down swiftly, the eight swarmed almost simultaneously upon the quarry.

The two servants were dragged from the box in a trice and bound with the reins, and just as the young King thrust his head out of the window to see what was wrong, both doors were flung open, the King was seized by one pair, and the attendant equerry, an old man and incapable of any serious resistance, was collared by the other pair. To borrow an Irish phrase, the thing was over almost before it had begun. The young King proved his pluck and did what he could; but that was, of course, nothing against the strength of the men who seized him and carried him to the carriage up the hill.

Then came a delay which puzzled me. The two men got into the Carlist carriage with the young King, and remained in it some three or four minutes, and what they were doing I could not see; but at the end of the time one got out again, shut the door, threw on a footman's livery coat, mounted the box beside the driver, and the carriage started immediately. Two others had meanwhile gone for their horses, and now came out from behind the wood, and followed the carriage at an interval of about a furlong.

A last look before I slipped from my tree showed me that the others were now making all haste to get the royal carriage away. Then I ran to my horse, mounted, and started in pursuit.

My hopes of accomplishing my object had run down with a rush to zero, and for the time I was full of consternation at the course things had taken. No less than five men were told off to guard the young captive, and I knew they were desperate men, who had imperilled their lives to capture the King, and would risk them freely to keep him. How then could I hope single-handed to effect a rescue? Moreover, it was essential to my plans that I should succeed in my purpose without being recognised by the Carlists; and this seemed to be just a sheer impossibility.

The one step which had baffled me was their precaution in having a couple of mounted men to follow the carriage. But for this my task would have been infinitely easier. It made even the work of pursuit vastly difficult. I could not ride on the open road, as this would have roused suspicion; and I had thus to resort to a hundred shifts; now galloping hard straight across country, now waiting in hiding; sometimes crossing the road for better going or to take a straight line where the road curved; and all the time harassed and worried by the constant effort to remain unseen by these men and yet to prevent them from getting out of sight of me.

Splendidly as I was mounted, the work began to tell on my horse almost as much as upon my temper, and I grew not only anxious but positively desperate. Full of difficulty as this scouting work was, it was leading nowhere. Time slipped on as mile after mile was traversed, but I got no nearer my object. So little did I like the prospect indeed that at length I was forced to contemplate an entire change of plan and the abandonment of the now forlorn hope of accomplishing the rescue single-handed.

It was still open to me to stop the business by dogging the abductors in a more open manner until we came to a place where I could get the carriage stopped by the authorities; and when we were about a couple of miles from the large village of Podrida I resolved most reluctantly to take that course. It involved a bitter disappointment; it would have Heaven alone knew what effect upon my after plans; it might mean indeed the frustration of everything; but I saw no other way, and accordingly I got back on to the road and began to close up the distance between me and the two horsemen as we approached Podrida.

I cursed what I called my ill-luck at the turn things had taken, and was riding in a very sullen mood and ill-temper when a little incident occurred which suddenly changed everything, and once more set my hopes beating high.

We were about a mile from Podrida, and I was some hundred yards behind the two men, when the horse of one of them fell as they were trotting briskly down a hill, and pitched its rider head foremost heavily on to the rough stony road. His companion pulled up and dismounted. The fallen horse scrambled up, and I saw he was dead lame, while the rider was apparently stunned for the moment.

In a trice I resolved to attempt the rescue at once. I clapped my heels into my horse's sides and darted forward at the gallop, and then, luck having changed, Fortune tossed me another favour. The

112

second man had left his animal untethered as he bent over his companion, and, excited apparently at the galloping of my horse, it threw up its head, snorted and neighed as I passed, and came rushing madly after me. Thus in a moment both the guards were out of the fight; and as I had been careful to turn my head in passing, I got by without the risk of recognition.

The carriage was some distance ahead, and I had to think quickly of a spot which would suit my purpose. But even in this Fortune continued kind to me. The men with the carriage, finding the horsemen had dropped too far behind them, and not being willing apparently to enter Podrida without them, had halted to wait in just such a spot as I myself would have chosen.

As a precaution against identification, I had brought with me a small flesh-coloured silk mask, a relic of an old fancy-dress costume, and I now slipped this on, slouched the brim of my hat well over my eyes, and drew my revolver from my pocket. The issues to all concerned were too weighty, and minutes, even seconds might be too precious for me to dally with any sentimental considerations. If blood had to be shed, it must be shed, let come what might; and my resolve was now running so high that I meant to carry the thing through at all hazards.

But even then another splendid stroke of luck came my way. The man with the driver on the box seemed to take alarm on seeing the riderless horse, and, mistaking me for one of his mounted comrades, leapt down from the box and came running toward me. Nothing could have served my purpose better. I rode straight at him, and as I reached him struck him with my heavy hunting-crop, putting all my strength into the blow. He fell like a log, and I rode over him, dashed past the carriage, sent a bullet into the nearest horse's head, turned instantly, and with another shot broke the driver's right arm, and sent him toppling off the box on to the road.

The man in the carriage with the King was now ready for me, however, and, leaning out, fired a revolver at me as I dismounted and rushed to the door. The aim was short enough, but the luck was still mine. He missed me, and had no chance of a second shot, for my hunting-crop came down on his wrist, breaking it, and his pistol dropped harmlessly on to the road.

In half a minute I had him out and lying helpless and half-stunned on the road, and had jumped into the carriage to the King, only to start back in amazement and dismay at the discovery that it was not the King at all, but a girl lying prone, faint, and helpless on an invalid's stretcher, her eyes staring up into my face with the glazed, set stillness of unconsciousness or paralysed fright. What could it mean and what had I done? What astounding blunder had I perpetrated? What miracle had happened? Where was the young King?

CHAPTER XVI

AFTER THE RESCUE

What I endured in those first moments after my shock of surprise I cannot tell. A thousand possible consequences in a mounting scale of danger crowded my mind to the exclusion of all coherent thoughts; and I gazed down in sheer stolidity of bewilderment at the inert form of the girl on the stretcher.

I had risked everything, and lost the whole stake through my blundering, selfish stupidity in trying to carry this thing through single-handed. Indeed, I had lost more than all—for I had laid myself open to a charge of having played the highwayman in this reckless fashion; and while the Carlists were speeding off with the young King, I should be hustled off to a gaol for a common thief.

And this was how I was pitting myself against Sebastian Quesada! At this thought my chagrin, my humiliation, and my self-contempt culminated in an acute agony of mortification and disappointment. I was like a man distracted and broken, when in a flash the light burst in on me.

I stooped over the girl and saw that what in my hasty glance I had mistaken for a piece of displaced frilling was in reality the covering for a cunningly constructed gag. In a moment I had torn it off and was looking on the young King's face.

"Is your Majesty hurt?" I asked, and as I spoke my fingers were busy tearing away the dress with which his captors had covered him, my hands positively trembling in excitement.

"I cannot move. Who are you? I am strapped down everywhere," he said weakly.

"By God's grace, I am come to save your Majesty;" and, without wasting time in words, I searched for the straps that bound him to the stretcher and severed them with my knife. The whole arrangement was cunningly contrived in truth; but a sharp blade cut the bonds quickly enough, and I soon had him out of the carriage.

114

"Have you strength to ride, sire?" I said, finding he was staggering feebly on my arm.

"I don't know," he said; and then, being but a lad, the sudden revulsion of feeling proved too great a strain, and the tears started to his eyes, and he stumbled and leaned helplessly against me.

"Courage, sire; all is well now;" and I gave him a sip of brandy from my small pocket-flask. He rallied with a splendid effort, and pulled himself together. "I can try, senor," he said pluckily, and smiled. It was now more than time for us to be off. A glance back along the road showed me one of the mounted men was running toward us, the fellow I had ridden down was coming back to consciousness, while the others had recovered from their surprise and hurts, and were rallying to stop us.

My horse and the other which had galloped up with us I had fastened to the pole of the carriage, and I decided to take up the boy King on my saddle for a mile or two until he had regained sufficient strength to ride.

I mounted, therefore, helped him up in front of me, and, holding him and leading the second horse, started at the best pace we could make. After we had ridden in this cumbersome style for about a mile, my charge said he felt quite strong enough to ride. We dismounted, and I set him upon the second horse, and we were just setting forward again when he said—

"You are wearing a mask, senor?" A touch of fear was in the tone.

"I had forgotten it, sire. I did not wish to be recognised by the men from whom I took you. They might make powerful and secret enemies!" and I took it off and pocketed it.

"It is they who will fear you, not you fear them. And you did this all by yourself!" The earnest boyish admiration was so frank and free that I smiled. "Where are we going?" he asked next, and leaning across he held out his hand. "I trust you, of course, implicitly."

I grasped it warmly.

"I think we can do no better than make our way back by the Coudova road. I know it well, and we can cover most of the way at the gallop. If anything should have been heard of this, Her Majesty will be almost mad with anxiety."

"Ah, my dear mother! You are as thoughtful as you are brave, senor. What a debt do we and Spain not owe to you!"

"Forward then," I said, and urging my horse to a quick canter we pushed on rapidly.

We scarcely spoke as we rode, except when I had a word to say about the direction. I on my side had no wish for conversation, and the young King needed all his strength and attention for his horse.

Twice, however, we had to draw rein to wind the horses up hills and then he asked me the question which I had been anticipating and which I did not know how to answer.

"You have not told me your name, senor?"

"And with your Majesty's permission I will for the present remain unknown. I am an Englishman, and having been a witness of the attack upon your carriage, followed in the hope of being of service."

"An Englishman!" he exclaimed, in great surprise. Then, after a long pause, "I have always read and heard what a brave nation you English are—now I know it for myself. But you must let us know your name. My mother will insist; and I—well, I should never be happy unless I knew it. I am only a boy, senor; but I shall never forget you, and never rest till I have shown what I think of your courage."

"It is more than probable I may some day ask you for some favour; but for the present permit me to remain unknown."

We galloped forward again then, and as we rode I thought the matter over. If it were known at once in the palace that Ferdinand Carbonnell had effected the rescue, there would be two immediate consequences, both likely to be disastrous to my plans. The Carlists would assuredly hear of it, and my life would be in danger; while Sebastian Quesada would know at once, and my chances of successfully fighting him would be almost hopelessly minimised.

When we drew rein the second time, therefore, at a hill just before we reached the city, I carried the plan further.

"Your Majesty was good enough to say that you trusted me; may I at once request a favour?"

"There is nothing you can ask in my mother's or my power to grant, senor, which you may not now consider granted before it is sought," he answered, enthusiastically.

"It is that you will permit me to leave you as soon as we come in sight of the Palace, sire, and that you will grant me an audience at some future time."

"Ah, you strain my gratitude, senor, with such a request," he cried with a right kingly air. "My mother will never forgive me if I let you leave me until she has thanked you. You cannot know her, if you ask this. As for the second request, where I am you will always be a most welcome guest, and my most esteemed and trusted friend." Then, guiding his horse close to me, he put his hand on my arm, and lapsing again into the boy, he said eagerly and pleadingly: "Do let my mother thank you, senor. You must."

"I have more than private reasons, sire. Permit me to press my

116

request." I spoke firmly, for my mind was made up: and perceiving it, he gave way.

"But how shall I know when some senor incognito asks for an interview that it is my friend?" and he laughed.

"We were close to Podrida when I was fortunately able to rescue you; if I send you word that the Englishman of Podrida desires an audience, you will know."

"The Englishman of Podrida!" he repeated, smiling. "The Englishman of Podrida. Yes. That will do. No. Stay, I have a fancy, and will make a request in my turn. You wore a mask. Give it me as a keepsake, and it shall be the sure password to me. When an Englishman wants to see me concerning a mask, I shall know it is you, my Englishman of Podrida;" and he laughed, almost boisterously, as I handed him the silken mask. "But my mother will be sorely disappointed," he added, his face falling.

"There is only one other point, sire. You will do me a further favour if you will suppress the fact that it is an Englishman who has been so fortunate as to help you, and if in giving any version of the facts you will keep that for your own knowledge and for her Majesty's ears only."

"Surely none but an Englishman would ask that," he answered; but he gave me the promise, and a quarter of an hour later the Palace came in sight, and we halted.

"I shall see you again soon. I shall be all impatience."

"If your Majesty keeps to the arrangements for your attendance at the Opera to-night, a scrutiny of the crowd who will welcome you may discover my face among those present. It would be a wise and reassuring step."

"I shall be there, of course," he said, and gave me his hand.

I watched his boyish figure as he rode sharply forward and entered the Palace gates, the sentries saluting with a start of surprise; and then, turning my horse aside, I made my way back to the stables, and from there drove to my own rooms.

I was naturally elated, and indeed exultant, at the success of my scheme of rescue. Come what might, I had made firm friends at the Palace, a result that might be of incalculable value in the crisis that I knew was at hand. But I had still much to do, and in truth scarcely knew what step to take first.

I held in my possession the proofs, in Quesada's own handwriting, of his complicity in the abduction plot, and had seen for myself the precision of his information and the deadly reality of his plans against the young King; but how could I bring it home to him? He would deny everything, and my word against his would be no more than a puff of air against a cannon ball.

Gradually one group of questions disentangled themselves from the rest as of chief importance. How to secure Sarita's safety? I knew that Quesada had everything in readiness to strike a crushing blow at the Carlists, not only in Madrid, but in other centres of disaffection. I believed that he had laid his plans for this in order to stamp out the whole agitation when once the King was out of the way; but how would he act now that half the scheme had failed? More than that, how would Sarita herself act? There was but one means to find this out—to see them both with the least delay; and in the meantime to warn Livenza to fly.

I changed hurriedly into evening dress and drove to Livenza's house; and there I found strange news awaiting me. The place was in possession of the servants only. My uneasiness may be imagined when I learned that the reason for this was nothing less than a visit from Quesada himself.

"The colonel was ill, and the young doctor was in attendance when I came this afternoon," I said to the servant. "How came he to recover so quickly as to be able to leave the house?"

"I do not know, senor. The Senor Quesada came here about an hour and a half since, and insisted upon seeing my master. The doctor protested, but the senor prevailed; and some ten minutes later the doctor left the house and has not returned. Senor Quesada remained some time with my master—he was here perhaps half an hour in all—and some few minutes after he left my master went out. I know no more."

Remembering the doctor's address, I drove there at once, and what he told me made matters appear not better, but worse.

"You did not tell me there was any political intriguing involved in this work," he said, with some indignation. "A pretty mess for me it may be, with mighty ugly consequences. Had I known, I should have left the fees for someone else to earn."

"There is nothing of the kind," I answered pretty sharply. "You can come to no harm. I will hold you harmless."

"Thank you for nothing. I know Senor Quesada's influence and power to hit hard, and I don't know yours."

"This was a matter between Colonel Livenza and myself. Will you tell me what passed this afternoon?"

"Senor Quesada came there in a devil of a temper, and when I tried to stop him seeing my patient, his reply was the pretty one that if I attempted to resist him a minute longer he'd pack me off to gaol for a Carlist. And by the Lord he meant it too: for he hadn't been closeted with Livenza five minutes before he came out to me and told me I was either a dupe or a conspirator, and that if I wasn't out of the house in a twinkling he'd take the latter view and act on it; and that there was much more in the thing than I seemed to think."

"And you left?"

"I'm not quite such a mule as to prefer a gaol to my present quarters, thank you."

"You have not had your fees," I said, pulling out my purse to pay him.

"And don't want any, if you please."

"You explained, of course, that I had retained you?"

"I told him everything that had passed, and thank my patron saint I got out of the place without a police escort."

I made such apology to him as I could, and left him, quite unappeased and still full of indignation, and drove in all haste to Quesada's house, feeling very anxious. Matters were moving very fast, much faster than I had anticipated, and I saw that I must play my card boldly.

I half expected he would deny himself, but I was shown in without hesitation, and his sister came to me. She was looking very troubled and pale, I thought; but she greeted me with her customary warmth and cordiality.

"You have not been to see us since your return from England, Senor Carbonnell. That is not how we interpret friendship in Spain."

"I have been back only two days, senorita, and they have been very full ones. I pray you to excuse me. And even now I have come to see your brother on business."

"That is engagingly frank, at any rate," and she tossed her head.

"I am very clumsy in my phrase, I fear; but very anxious. Do not think it is not a pleasure to me to see you."

"Do you English generally seek pleasure by avoiding it?"

"Scarcely so; but with us self-denial is sometimes counted a virtue," and I made her an elaborate bow to point the compliment.

"Have you practised the same self-denial with all your Madrid friends?" and a sharp little glance told me her meaning.

"I am unfortunate indeed; for all my Madrid friends are making the same complaint."

"I am surprised. For they have not all the same ground as I have. Do you know how much I wish to be your friend, senor?"

"I know that I could not rank your friendship too high."

"Ah, you fence with me; but it is useless, I know. And the time may come when my friendship may be of more account to you than a mere well-turned phrase."

"It must ever be one of my choicest possessions," I answered, wondering what on earth she meant now.

"Sebastian is not at home just now, but he will be here soon. Do you think you are wise in seeing him?"

"I have come for that purpose, senorita," I said, firmly.

"What have you done to alienate him? Don't you know that although he can be a true friend—and he wishes above all things to be one—he can also be a much more powerful enemy?" There was no mistaking her tone now for any but one of solicitude for me. What had he been telling her?

"I should have made poor use of my intercourse with him if I did not know that," I answered. "But will you tell me exactly what you mean?"

"No—I cannot; except that you have angered him sorely in some way, and if you are not careful will stand in great danger."

"That must be as it will, senorita. But I was wrong to put that question to you. I should rather put it to your brother himself, and I will do so."

"Could you not leave Spain for a while?"

At that moment we heard the sounds of someone in the hall outside the room; and the senorita drew a quick breath, bit her lip, and turned to listen.

"That is Sebastian. Oh, senor, be careful, and do what he may suggest to you; be advised by him. You have rendered us such a service he will not forget it, of course he never can. But do not anger him. I too am your friend; and I can help you. Do, do let us be your friends. I can do much with him, and for my sake he will, I know, do what he can. When I think of your possible danger, it strikes me to the heart; it kills me. Let me beg of you," and her agitation was so great that she was scarcely coherent. "But there is one thing you must not try to thwart him in. Oh, I scarcely know what I am saying," and she wrung her hands in such manifest distress that I was deeply surprised.

"I am in no danger, senorita," I answered calmly, to reassure her. "But if I should be, the knowledge of your warning and of your offer of help will always be a welcome thought." To my yet deeper surprise my words appeared to affect her profoundly, and she seized my hand and pressed her lips upon it, the tears in her eyes.

Scarcely a reassuring preface for my interview with her brother, who entered the room a moment later. He gave me a sharp, penetrating look, glanced, I thought angrily, at his sister, and exclaimed in a tone of surprise, "Dolores!" and then, after a pause, "You had better leave us." He held the door for her to leave, and as he closed it behind her he turned to me and said, with a questioning frown on his forehead—

"Are you here as a friend, or in what capacity?"

"I have much to say to you," I returned calmly. "And we can best ask and answer that question mutually when the interview is over."

I met his look with one as firm as his own, and he sat down at his writing-table and waited for me to open the ball.

CHAPTER XVII

WAR TO THE KNIFE

I did not keep Sebastian Quesada waiting, but plunged at once into my business.

"I do not think our interview need be a very long one, and I will state my object at once. It concerns Sarita Castelar. I know that preparations for decisive action against the Carlists have been made, and that all is in readiness for the signal from you. I have just heard very terrible news in the city to-night, concerning a mad wild act of theirs, and being anxious for a reassurance on the senorita's account, I have come to ask you for it."

"You will do more wisely not to interfere in our political matters," he answered curtly, with a frown at the mention of Sarita.

"I am obliged, of course, by your friendly counsel; but excuse me if I say I have not come for advice, but information."

"I have none to give you;" and his tone was even sharper than before. It was as stern and hard indeed as his look was dour. But in a moment a great change came. His eyes softened and his face brightened, and, using the tone of our former intercourse, he added: "Why can't we remain friends, Carbonnell? Why do you come to me like this? It is but an hour or two since we parted, and nothing can have occurred since that need estrange us; and there was no cloud between us then. Don't you think I wish to be your friend now as I did then?"

I looked at him in considerable surprise. His overtures did not touch me in the least; I was searching for his motive and could not find it.

"Before you and I can speak again of friendship, there are matters which must be explained," I answered, coldly. "Since I saw you this afternoon, you have impliedly accused me of complicity in

121

this Carlist business: I have that from the doctor whom you frightened away from Colonel Livenza's house. You have also intervened in the quarrel between Colonel Livenza and myself—a quarrel which had its origin in an errand on which you sent him."

He listened closely, and was too skilled in masking his looks to give any indication of the effect of my words. But I thought he was surprised when I stopped, having said so little.

"Your quarrel with Livenza was the outcome of the scene at the Café de l'Europe, where the hot-headed fool insulted you."

"No, that was the open cause. The real one was the result of his coming to Senorita Castelar's at the time I was there—a visit timed by you."

"Livenza is in love with the senorita, and hopes to marry her; and you know how some of us Spaniards feel on such matters. But what is this to me?"

"You had given me good news to carry to her, you knew when I was going, and you sent Livenza there. What happened afterwards was the direct consequence."

"It is preposterous!" he cried, with a shrug of the shoulders. "As if I could be responsible for what two angry men do when they quarrel. Really!" and he laughed. Clearly he was relieved that I had nothing worse to say. "I am glad at any rate that you have not hurt each other." This with a scarcely veiled sneer.

"When a man who professes to be my friend deliberately tries to embroil me in an affair which may cost me my life, I do not dismiss it with a shrug of the shoulders and a laugh, as something too trivial to be noticed. But if you will give me the information I came for, I will go."

"I have no information to give you;" and he got up.

"To that I answer I am not going without it, nor without an assurance and a proof of Sarita Castelar's safety—and safety without any entangling complications;" and I looked at him as I said the last sentence with a meaning that did not escape him.

"The only information I can give you is that which to-morrow will be public property; that our police and soldiery are even now engaged in hunting out these reckless traitors and conspirators who have carried their audacity to the point of abducting our beloved young King. All those who have had a hand in this dastardly scheme will suffer, and if the Senorita Castelar has been mad enough to meddle with such treason, no power in the State can save her from the consequences."

But instead of being impressed by his vehemence I smiled.

"And you say all would suffer?"

122

"Every man, woman, and child concerned. I have this moment come from a Council of State."

"And the master mind who planned this coup and by whose help and information it was alone possible?" As I half unsheathed this sword of attack, his own weapon leapt at once from the scabbard, and he answered hotly—

"Is one Ferdinand Carbonnell, senor?" He spoke with grim significance, meeting my look with eyes full of fire and threat, and his misinterpretation of my meaning was wilful. "A name that at a word from me will be full of peril for its owner. We Spaniards love our King with a force which the people of other countries cannot fathom."

There was no mistaking his meaning. He knew of the coincidence which had bound up my name so closely with the Carlist intrigues, and he was threatening to saddle the responsibility upon me. Nor was it by any means an empty threat in the present temper of the loyalists. Once get me packed away into a Spanish gaol on such a charge, and I might whistle either for the chance of a fair trial or an opportunity of even communicating with the outside—to say nothing of approaching the King. The scent of personal danger began to come near; and I recalled how on more than one occasion he had warned me against meddling with Carlist matters.

He watched me closely in the short pause, and then broke it to say in a tone conciliatory and temperate—

"I am still willing to be your friend. Leave Madrid to-night and cross the frontier with all speed, and all may be well. I cannot answer for what my colleagues will do when they know who Ferdinand Carbonnell is, and that he is a member of the British Embassy staff. Be advised and go while there is time."

He had flashed the sword of danger in my face, and now, like a clever tactician, dangled the chance of escape before me.

"Do I understand you to mean that, knowing thoroughly who I am and that I am absolutely untouched by these matters, you yourself would be so mean a liar as to say that I am Ferdinand Carbonnell the Carlist?" I spoke with the galling sting of slow, precise deliberation; and even his practised self-restraint could not repress a start of anger nor prevent his sallow face turning pale at this thrust. But my anger had betrayed me into a bad blunder—I saw it the moment the words were out of my lips; and as he recovered himself he shrugged his shoulders and threw up his hands as he faced me. It was a declaration of war from me, and as such he treated it. His tone was as level as my own—stern, official, and hard.

"I know nothing of yourself or your history except what you have told me. You say you came here a few weeks since, and yet I find your name known everywhere. You rendered my sister a service, and then used it to work your way into my confidence. In that confidence I have said many things to you, which you may have used for these Carlist purposes. I gave you my confidence and my friendship because I believed all you told me. If my faith in you was wrongly placed, you have had opportunities of getting information. Things have, I know, leaked out, but I have never thought of you before in this connection. For aught I know to the contrary—for I know only what you have told me, I repeat—you may be this other Ferdinand Carbonnell."

"By God, but you are a blackguard," I cried, my rage leaping quite beyond control, as I jumped to my feet. "The worst that men say of you is not half so bad as this foul conduct. Do your worst. Tell this lie if you will. Fling me into one of your gaols if you dare—and I will leave it to prove that the man who planned this act against the King, which fills you now with such honest patriotic indignation, was not Ferdinand Carbonnell, but you, Sebastian Quesada, and prove it I can under your own handwriting. Stop," I thundered, as I saw him making his way to the bell to summon assistance. "Try to bring your servants here, and I'll fling myself on you and choke the life out of you before they can come. I have yet a word, and you'd better hear it. You wrote me a note to-day to ask me to ride with you." He started and glanced at me as I made an intentional pause. "At the same time you were writing another note giving the latest news of the young King's movements, so that these Carlists might trap him safely. That note I received and possess; the other went to your jackal Livenza for him to make the necessary arrangements. Those notes are in safe hands, and if you dare to lay a finger on me the whole plan will be revealed—the whole truth told, with all your black treachery uppermost."

His answer was more in character than any he had yet made. He turned to his table and sounded his bell vigorously; and for a few moments of tense silence we waited.

"Send Senor Rubio to me," he said to the servant who came.

I knew the name as that of one of the chief police agents; and knew also that he had determined to have me arrested.

"I am a member of the British Embassy, Senor Quesada. If you molest me, I warn you of the consequences."

"I offered you my friendship and protection, and you declined them and heaped abuse on me. You shall now feel my power."

I made no reply, and then the police official entered—a spare, dark, ferrety-faced man, with quick-twinkling eyes.

124

"Senor Rubio, you have a warrant for the arrest of Senorita Sarita Castelar, which I told you to hold back."

"I have, your Excellency."

"You will execute it at once. This is Senor Ferdinand Carbonnell, of whom you know; hold him in custody; the warrant will be made out."

"I am a British subject, and a member of the British Embassy here in Madrid. I shall resist arrest, and hold you responsible for any consequences."

The official heard this with some dismay, and looked at the Minister for an explanation.

"Do your duty, Senor Rubio. You have my orders."

"You must come with me, please," said the man, turning to me.

"I am armed," was my reply.

"Get the help you need," cried Quesada, sternly. "Do you hear?" he added, angrily, for the man paused; but at this he went to the door and opened it to call assistance. It was clear he had little stomach for the task; and he appeared no less relieved than surprised when, instead of his police assistants, Dolores Quesada entered. She was looking pale and very agitated, but said to her brother quite firmly—

"I heard that Senor Rubio had been sent for; and before anything more is done I have something to say to you. Dismiss him for a moment."

To my surprise, her brother sent him away.

"Have you ordered Senor Carbonnell's arrest?"

"This is no concern of yours, Dolores."

"Why have you two quarrelled?" she cried passionately, and turned to me as if demanding an explanation. But I, of course, could give her none, and said so.

"Sebastian, Senor Carbonnell shall not be arrested. I will not have it."

"Senor Carbonnell will scarcely wish to owe his safety to you," he answered, with an ugly sneer. "Nor is this a matter in which I can allow you to interfere. He has come here purely out of solicitude for the safety of his friend—Sarita Castelar. You owe him thanks for what he did for you, and, remembering that, I have tried to induce him to leave the country. He will not, and as he remains he must take the consequences. This is a State matter, and, I repeat, you must not interfere. It can do you no good."

That there was a meaning under his words which she understood was clear by her change of colour; but when he finished she turned upon him as if to retort angrily. She checked herself, however, and instead asked me, in a voice that only with a great

125

effort she was able to keep firm and cool: "Will you not give your word to leave Spain, Senor Carbonnell?"

"Certainly I cannot and will not, senorita," I replied, marvelling much at the turn things were taking.

"You hear?" exclaimed Quesada, lifting his eyebrows. "You know why he stays?"

This seemed to strike right at her heart. She sank into a chair and bent her head on her hand.

"This step is necessary, Dolores. Be warned; and leave us," he continued, in the same meaning tone.

"I do not care; I do not care. This shall not be. I swear it shall not. I swear by the Holy Virgin it shall not." Her words came with almost hysterical vehemence. "I claim his safety. Come what may, I dare you to harm him, Sebastian. I dare you," and she sprang to her feet again. "Senor, the way is open for you. I open it. No one shall harm you. You are a man of honour, and will at least remember that——"

She stopped.

I felt vastly embarrassed; but, reflecting how much my liberty at that moment might mean to Sarita, I turned towards the door to see if I was really to get away.

"Stay," cried Quesada, hesitating in his fear of what I might do.

"You are free to go, senor," said the sister.

"I shall always remember to whom I owe my liberty; and unless I am driven to act, by steps which your brother has threatened, the recollection will guide my own attitude."

"No, you shall not go," cried Quesada again, this time angrily and decidedly.

"Sebastian, if you dare to thwart me in this, I will go straight to the Palace and say what—you know I can say."

"You are ruining us, Dolores."

Her reply was worthy of her brother for its directness. She went to the door, and called in the police official.

"Senor Rubio, my brother wishes you to understand that he has made a mistake in ordering this gentleman's arrest. He is a member of the British Embassy. Permit me, senor," she said to me, holding the door for me to pass.

"Your Excellency's wishes——?" asked Rubio.

The answer was a wave of the hand, and I was free. A minute later, I was driving to my rooms, with a pretty picture of Dolores Quesada's anxious face in my thoughts.

How long I should remain at liberty was another question, however. Owing to the power she had over him, of a kind I could not guess, Dolores had succeeded in defeating his purpose for the

126

moment; but I knew him too well not to think he would instantly set about repairing that defeat by indirect means unknown to her. I was too dangerous to be left at liberty, and he knew it; and probably his agents were even now starting out in quest of me; for Spanish prisons tell no tales.

But I could at least make good use of my liberty, and my first step must be to rush to my rooms and procure a sufficient supply of money for emergencies. I had quite long enough start of the police for this, as a single minute in the rooms would be enough.

Little did I think, however, of the news I should find awaiting me. A telegram lay on the table, and a glance at its contents filled me with surprise, concern, and pain. It was from the family solicitors in London, and ran as follows:

"Deeply regret to announce Lord Glisfoyle thrown from horse this afternoon and picked up dead. Neck broken. Can you return at once, or wire instructions? Writing you fully by this post."

Poor Lascelles! And as I stood staring absently at the message my thoughts went toppling head over heels down the staircase of the years which he and I had climbed in so different a fashion.

We were scarcely a lucky race, we Carbonnells. My father had had a struggle for many years, and had barely held the title long enough to free himself, by the sweating process of rigid economy, from the smarts and humiliations of the debts piled up in time of poverty. Now Lascelles, in the very course of his humdrum, stay-at-home, commonplace life, had been cut over with a side swing of the remorseless scythe; and here was I, the very antithesis of my brother, flying for my liberty, my life perhaps in danger, and at the very moment of becoming head of the Carbonnells, known and likely to be officially labelled as that much more fateful chief, Ferdinand Carbonnell, head of the most dangerous and violent section of the Carlists. At the thought I started, and seemed to catch a gleam of light. I was no longer mere Ferdinand Carbonnell—I was Lord Glisfoyle. Would Quesada dare to pursue me now?

My answer was prompt. I crammed the telegram into my pocket, and rushed to the drawer where my money was and thrust the whole of it into another pocket, got my revolver and a good supply of cartridges, and hurried out of the house. I might be a peer of Great Britain, but for the moment I was a political fugitive in Madrid, and Sarita had yet to be saved.

127

CHAPTER XVIII

AT THE OPERA HOUSE

Now that I was on foot I saw with much concern what a condition of tumult and confusion prevailed in the capital. The streets were thronged with people talking, gesticulating, shouting; some standing in groups, others loitering casually, and others again rushing hither and thither distractedly. The whole city everywhere appeared to have gone almost wild with excitement. Every street corner had its own clamorous group—men, women, and children mingled together, all manifesting the same symptoms of turbulent unrest.

The police were everywhere. Bodies of troops, mounted and on foot, patrolled the main thoroughfares and by-streets alike; and ever and again I met small parties of police or troops, or both mixed, hurrying along with one or two men or women in their midst. The sight of these seemed to goad the populace almost to frenzy; and they broke into hoots, groans, and indescribable cries, mingled with hisses, oaths, and loud vehement execrations.

I had no need to ask the cause of this, for the key was on everyone's tongue, and the cry was everywhere "Death to the Carlists!" Wherever I turned, the air rang with it: in the quavering tone of old age, in the shrill screech of violent women, in the strident cry of strong, angry men, even in the puny squeal of children held up by their mothers to clench their tiny fists and squeak a curse after the Carlist captives as they were hustled by to gaol.

The tale ran with its usual exaggerations. "The young King had been killed, and the Queen Mother—the Holy Virgin preserve her—lay dying from the wounds received in trying to save her son." "No; the King was not dead, only desperately wounded, lying at death's door, shot from a distance by the cowards who had no stomach for an open attack." "No, no; the King had been stolen and the Queen murdered, and the villains had even dared to enter the Palace itself, and, thanks be to the Holy Saints, had been caught by the guard and clapped into gaol, after having been nearly pulled to pieces by the mob. Blessed be the Virgin, the dear young King was safe." "All wrong, the King was safe, and had been saved by the great Minister himself, Quesada;" and so on, through the whole gamut of conjecturing ignorance.

All this I caught as I hurried at such speed as I could make to

Madame Chansette's house in search of Sarita. It was nothing to me on what lies the people fed themselves or were fed by Quesada's agents. I knew that his object was to raise such a popular clamour against the Carlists as would strengthen his hands in the work of stamping them out, and the Spanish temper was already running so high that more than one ugly rush by the mob had been made at some of the batches of prisoners, as if to tear them to pieces. And I trembled as I thought of Sarita in the hands of these furious violence-mongers.

There was some risk for me, too, in going to Madame Chansette's. I had heard the order given to Rubio to arrest Sarita at once, and if he and his men were before me, I knew I might be arrested. The consideration did not stop my going to the house, but it made me keep a very sharp eye for the police agents.

The house wore its customary appearance, however, and when I knocked I was admitted by the servant, whom I knew by sight. All seemed well so far. I asked for both Madame Chansette and Sarita, and was shown at once to the former. I found her weeping bitterly, prostrated, and really ill with alarm.

"I am so thankful to see you. You have heard this awful news. Oh, what shall we do, what shall we do?"

"Where is Sarita?" I asked in alarm, thinking the police had been before me. "Is she safe? Quick, for God's sake tell me."

"What do you mean?"

"I know that she is in danger of arrest. Where is she? Please tell me everything you can. I am on fire with impatience." But my impetuous excitement so heightened her fear that, to my consternation, she grew suddenly hysterical, and I cursed myself for a blockhead, as I looked round for scent and restoratives and did my best to calm her.

"She must be saved, Ferdinand," she cried, helplessly, after precious minutes had been wasted. "Oh, the rash, headstrong, wilful child!"

"If you will be calm and tell me where she is, I can save her," I said, speaking now with forced deliberation and cool firmness. "But you must be calm, and tell me everything."

"I will tell you. I did not know till to-day that she was actually plotting to get the King stolen away by these fearful Carlists; and now it has been done, and she has gone away somewhere, and I know it is to take some other terrible steps. I can endure no more of it, Ferdinand. I love Sarita; but I will not stay another day in Madrid."

"Do you know where she has gone?"

"No—yes—I don't know. All I know is this: She came to me

about two hours ago, her eyes shining and her face on fire with enthusiasm—you know how she would look at such a time—and told me what she had been planning, and that it had all succeeded, and that she had to go away for an hour or two, but would be back as soon as she had finished the great work there was to do. I was so frightened, I nearly fainted. I begged her not to go—but you know her;" and Madame Chansette waved her hands and shook her head feebly, the tears still running down her cheeks.

"Do you know where she has gone?" I repeated, driven almost to my wit's end by the waste of time caused by her weakness.

"I can only make a guess, and I don't know whether I ought to have done it;" an inconsequential enigma which made me bite my lip with vexation in the effort to restrain my impatience. She glanced up helplessly once or twice while hesitating.

"If you know nothing, I can do nothing," I said, as gently as I could, to spur her.

"I am almost ashamed of it, but I had better say, perhaps; I don't know what you will think. When Sarita came to me she had a letter in her hand, and—and before I quite knew what I was doing, I—I had read it."

"Thank God you did, if it told you what we want to know."

"It was only a short note," she said, relieved by my reception of the confession, but still apologetic. Oh, these good, honest, weak, exasperating people! "It said something about all having gone well, and that she was to go at once to——"

"Where?" I cried, on fire, as she paused again.

"I think it was 47, or 147, or 247—I know 47 was part of it— Calle de Valencia. I am certain about the street, and she may be there. Do you think it was very mean—what's that?" She broke off with a start, and began to tremble violently, as a loud knocking at the house door and a great pealing of the heavy bell came to our ears.

"For God's sake be calm for a minute. It is probably the police agents come to arrest Sarita. Listen, please; listen carefully," I cried, as she again showed signs of hysterics. "I will go at once and warn her and save her. They must not know I have been here, and I can get out through the garden, as I have before. Let them search the house, and keep them here as long as you can, but don't breathe a word that I have been here, or of Sarita. You can hear of me and of Sarita through Mrs. Curwen, at the Hotel de l'Europe. Fasten the window behind me."

While speaking, I had opened the window, and, making a great effort, she came and closed it and drew the curtains. I stood a

130

moment in the darkness, my ear pressed to the pane, and heard someone enter the room and ask for Sarita.

"We are the police," said a strident, high-pitched voice, "and call upon you to help us. She is here, we know, and must come with us. Here is the warrant."

Whoever he was, he did his work in the coarsest and most brutal fashion; and, waiting to hear no more, I slipped away noiselessly into the darkness. My fear now was lest the place should be surrounded and my own escape impeded.

There was a gate at the bottom opening on to a back road, but I knew of a spot at the side where, with the help of a tree, I could easily scale the wall, and deemed it prudent to avoid the gate. I climbed cautiously, and, looking over, saw the way was clear, and jumped down. But a man had been posted to watch close by, and, catching sight of me, he sent up a cry and began to run in my direction. My knowledge of the locality stood me in good stead, however, and, running at top speed, I doubled through one or two back ways and passages, and shook off pursuit sufficiently to be able to walk quietly into one of the crowded main streets, where it would have been hopeless to look for me in the throng.

The excitement in the streets was even greater than before, but now there was a perceptible change of tone. A note of thanksgiving and rejoicing was mingled with the curses and groans and execrations; and I soon gathered that doubts about the young King having been even hurt had begun to spread among the people.

My way took me near the Opera House in the Plaza del Oriente, and then there flashed into my recollection the appointment I had made to see Mercy and Mrs. Curwen in their box. I recalled also the necessity of informing Mercy of the news of poor Lascelles' death. When I should have another chance I could not tell, and thus I resolved to snatch a minute, urgent though my errand was, and go to them in the box.

I pushed my way through the crowd, which was now alternately cheering with deafening enthusiasm, and turning to shout out curses and oaths against the Carlists, and, entering the Opera House, asked for Box 9, the number Mrs. Curwen had given me. They would not let me pass for a moment, however, and I was taking out my card to send to Mrs. Curwen, when the possible danger of having my name known at such a time struck me, and I scribbled, "Lord Glisfoyle," on an envelope which I borrowed at the bureau, and sent an attendant in with that. He returned and asked me to follow him, and I walked through the magnificent corridors, half ashamed of what looked like a grim, unnatural jest at such a moment, and thinking how best to break my bad news to Mercy.

Little did I foresee, indeed, what a friend to me that simple precaution would prove; but, then, how few of us can see even an inch beyond the nose-tip!

I had nearly reached the box when a roar like thunder burst out suddenly in the great building, which seemed almost to stagger with the sudden shock and vibration; and, as the attendant opened the box door, the huge volume came rushing out with a deafening crash. A wild passion of excitement, uproar, and tumult possessed the vast audience, making such a scene as I had never witnessed.

Men and women alike were beside themselves in the rush and delirium of positively frantic enthusiasm: standing on the seats, and even rushing over them, leaning on one another, pushing, straining, climbing one on top of another's shoulders to gain a place from which they could catch a sight of one central spot. Even the stage was filled with a heterogeneous crowd of actors and actresses in costume, men and women in evening dress, and scene shifters and employees of all kinds. And the whole congested mass of people were yelling and shouting and cheering as though they would burst their lungs, as they waved anything they could lay hands on—hats, caps, handkerchiefs, shawls, opera cloaks, and on the stage flags, anything and everything that would help them to vent their overwhelming enthusiasm.

The centre of it all was the slight, slim, graceful, figure of the boy King, standing in front of the Royal box, bowing and smiling his acknowledgments; while just behind him, like the guardian angel of his life, was the beautiful Queen Mother, with a light of love, pride, and pleasure on her strong, clever face, as she gazed through eyes bright and shining with rare tears at this marvellous demonstration of a people's thanksgiving for her and their darling's safety.

Minutes passed, and the tumult gave no sign of abatement. If the great hoarse volume of shouting seemed for a second to be dying down, it was quickly noticed, and huge waves of swelling sound arose again, until it appeared as if the very roof would be rent by the strain. Suddenly a voice started the national air, and in a moment the leader of the orchestra seized the occasion, the band took it up, and the whole audience, led by the singers on the stage, sang it with such a chorus as had never before been heard in Madrid.

Then came an unrehearsed and most dramatic scene. There was a movement on the stage as the singing drew to a close, and the Archbishop of Madrid came to the front and stood with uplifted hand for silence.

An intense hush, seeming almost weird after the raging tumult, fell upon the place, and then his powerful voice was heard in half a dozen impressive sentences of thanksgiving for the King's

132

deliverance; and as he finished amid sounds of sobbing from men and women, for all were now so wrought upon that emotion reigned supreme alike over strong men and weak women, a mighty Amen came from every corner of the house, with another moment of weird silence as the great priest stood with bowed head and hand-covered eyes in prayer.

Before the audience could gather strength for fresh shouting he stepped back, the curtain came down on the stage, the band struck up some of the music of the night's opera, and the great scene—a scene to be remembered to one's dying day—was over; and the panting, exhausted, half-hysterical audience struggled back into some semblance of order.

I had been as much carried away as anyone—the fever of contagion was in truth resistless—and I had forgotten everything in the excitement, even the time I was losing, so vital for the rescue of Sarita; and my companions in the box were equally oblivious. But at the close of it they turned to me.

"Why, they said it was Lascelles," said Mercy, who like Mrs. Curwen was sitting back exhausted with the excitement, for they had been shouting and waving as frantically as the rest.

"I used the name to get in," I replied, feebly: realising how incongruous it would be to attempt to break my news to Mercy in the midst of such a scene. "I didn't expect to get here, but as I chanced to be near the place, I came in to say I hope to be at supper with you at the Hotel de l'Opera."

"You're always coming to say you can't come, but will come some other time," exclaimed Mrs. Curwen.

"I am sorry if I seem neglectful," was my apology,

"You look very serious, at any rate, and as if this mysterious business was a very doleful one."

"When I am able to explain it all to you, you will say I am not serious without cause."

She shrugged her shoulders.

"I have no right to any explanation, but Mercy has," she answered.

"Don't mind me, Nand," said Mercy quickly. "I know it must be serious."

"I have some news for you, Mercy, but I can't tell you now. I must go." I was standing almost in the front of the box, between the two, and Mrs. Curwen said—

"Did you ever see such a scene? What a love that boy King is! I should like to kiss him."

I glanced then across at the Royal box, and to my discomfiture saw that his little Majesty was taking my advice, and, with an opera

133

glass, was earnestly searching the audience. As I looked across, the glass was full upon our box. He started, lowered the glass, and looked eagerly at me. Then he turned to the Queen impetuously, said something to her, and handed her the glass; and she in her turn looked across the house at me.

He had recognised me, and I dare not stay another minute, for fear he should send to enquire for me. I turned to Mayhew, who was sitting by Mrs. Curwen.

"I want to speak to you, Silas. Come with me;" and, murmuring an excuse to the widow, we went out.

"Is anything wrong?" he asked anxiously.

"Yes, there's a devil of a mess, and I'm in it up to the neck, and I want you to help me. I've got a nasty job for you. I've had a telegram from London just now to say that my brother is dead. He was thrown from his horse this afternoon. Here's the wire."

"Then that name you sent in——" he began.

"I didn't use it because of that. But my own name has got mixed up with this infernal Carlist business, and I didn't dare send it in. Ferdinand Carbonnell may be proscribed at any moment, and I've scraped my shoulder already once this evening against a prison door. What I want you to do is to break this news of poor Lascelles' death as best you can to my sister, as soon as you get a chance, and just make them both understand that they're to know nothing of any Ferdinand Carbonnell. If I've been recognised here, as I think I have, and anyone comes questioning, just say I'm Lord Glisfoyle, and if they press for any address give them the Hotel de l'Opera."

"I don't quite understand. Why——"

"That's all right; I can't spare another second," and I hurried off, leaving him staring after me with the telegram in his hand, the very picture of bewilderment.

I walked quickly along the corridor, left the building, and turned at a quick speed in the direction of the Calle de Valencia, in search of Sarita. And when I found how much time I had lost through my visit to the Opera, I was troubled with serious misgivings.

CHAPTER XIX

A CARLIST GATHERING

The Calle de Valencia was a sufficiently important street to be well known, and I had no difficulty in finding it. It had a prosperous look; the houses were for the most part of a good size; and their condition and appearance suggested that the occupants were of the well-to-do class.

Madame Chansette had told me 47 was part of the number of the house I sought, and one of the first I saw being 147, I determined to try that first. It was a doctor's house—Dr. Pascual Vedia, and when I rang the bell a maid-servant opened the door, and showed me into a consulting room.

My nerves had been so wrought upon by the events of the day, the scene at the Opera, my fears for Sarita, and now by the extraordinary nature of my present mission, that this commonplace conventional reception seemed quite a ridiculous anti-climax. Despite all my anxiety I caught myself smiling when I was left alone.

"What an ass I am," I exclaimed; "as if I was to expect the long black conspirators' cloaks, the sharp daggers, slouched hats of picture books! This may very well be the place after all." My meditations were broken by the entrance of the doctor, a man of some forty years of age, with the most approved medical manner. A comfortable-looking person in complete keeping with his conventional surroundings, who smiled encouragingly while he looked me over with a professional eye. If he was a dangerous Carlist, danger and Carlism certainly appeared to agree with him.

"You wish to consult me, senor? My servant did not bring me your name." His manner was easy and insinuating.

"I have not called to consult you, but wish to see the Senorita Castelar, who is, I believe, here. I have grave and urgent news for her."

"I am afraid there is some mistake. My name is Pascual Vedia. I am a physician." It struck me he said this to look at me and gain time to think. There was just a second of hesitation; and then he added: "May I ask your name?"

"My name is of no importance if the senorita is not here. But the news I bring is of the utmost gravity—to her and others," and I emphasised the words with a glance of meaning. This time the pause before he replied was longer; then he answered—

"My wife has a few friends this evening, but the senorita is not here."

"You know her?" I asked quickly.

"Really, as I have not the pleasure of knowing your name——" and he left the sentence unfinished, with an uplifting of the hands. He was fencing with me, that was unmistakable. And, more than that, he was suspicious. When I saw that, the means of at once testing and reassuring him occurred to me. I looked him straight in the eyes, and very deliberately repeated the formula I had learned from Vidal de Pelayo.

"Counting all renegades lovers of Satan, by the grace of God."

"By the grace of God," he repeated instantly with deep earnestness, and gave me his hand. His manner underwent a remarkable change; his easy, matter-of-fact, medical practitioner air dropped like a mask, and his looks, eyes, and voice were charged with enthusiasm.

"I could not know, of course," he said, in explanation. "The senorita is here, but on the point of leaving. Will you come to her with me? Or shall I bring her here? You are from Saragossa—or, better, from Huesca? And all is well, I hope. We have been waiting for this."

His reply showed me there would be no danger of identification if I went with him, since it was clear that none of the men whom I had outwitted that afternoon had yet returned with the news. I was doubtful, moreover, whether Sarita would come to me without hearing my name, while if I sent it to her she might raise delay or difficulty.

I decided to go with him therefore, and he led me to a drawing-room at the back of the house where there were some dozen people. The eyes of all were turned upon us as the door opened, and the doctor, having misinterpreted my silence, exclaimed joyously—

"News at last from Saragossa!"

The words were not off his tongue before Sarita, who was sitting close to the door, jumped to her feet, looked at me in the deepest consternation, and, turning pale to the lips in the greatness of her surprise, faced me with a look of such unmistakable fear and dismay that it brought gathering clouds of suspicion to the faces of many of those present.

"You here!" she said at length, in a tone that was scarcely more than a whisper.

I paused for one supreme moment of doubt, while I glanced at the faces bent anxiously and now sternly upon me, and then answered in a firm voice—

"Where should Ferdinand Carbonnell be at the crisis of peril

136

such as this, if not here?" and I looked at her as though daring her to betray the secret of the double meaning of my words.

The impression created by the announcement of my name was unmistakable. A murmur of astonishment passed from lip to lip, while glances were travelling backwards and forwards from me to Sarita, who stood battling with her agitation.

I could understand her trouble well enough. She had either to denounce me as an impostor and a traitor to the cause, and with probable consequences to me from which would shrink with fear; or she had to cover and confirm the fraud and vouch for my truth to her companions. To distract attention from her while she made her decision, I went on after a short pause, speaking deliberately and incisively, wishing to create the deepest impression possible—

"Only such an emergency as this could have induced me to throw aside my incognito and come to you openly. I bring you the worst possible news. Everything has failed; and the cause never stood in higher peril than at this present moment, when the success we have striven, worked, and fought for seemed actually in our grasp—seemed?—nay, was actually in our grasp. The great event of to-day, so cunningly planned, so patiently waited for, was successful. The young Pretender was captured by our comrades, and was actually in their hands; I myself was present—as I strive to be everywhere in the moment of crisis—and saw it done. They carried him away, and all seemed to have gone gloriously, when just before the village of Podrida was reached, by means which have yet to be discovered, the whole scheme was wrecked; our comrades were struck down, overborne probably, after fighting valiantly, by a vastly superior force." (I reckoned that this was the account of the rescue the men would be likely to bring back.) "The young Pretender was snatched from them and brought back to the capital. I returned when I knew of it, and I come now hot foot from the Opera, where he has just made a public appearance, amid the cheers of those sycophants among the people who persist in upholding his wrongful claim to Our Master's throne."

I did not look once at Sarita while delivering this harangue, and by the time I had reached that point the news I brought had not only convinced everyone of my sincerity, but had set them quaking on the score of their own safety.

"You saw this with your own eyes?" exclaimed the doctor, excitedly. "Holy Mother of God, what will it mean?"

"I saw it, and much more. I was this evening closeted in the house of the master fiend to whose devilment the wrecking of everything may well be due—the Minister, Sebastian Quesada. I heard there the order given for my own arrest. I saw the warrant for

137

the arrest of Senorita Castelar, and heard the order for its instant execution given to his police spy, Rubio, and I know that lists upon lists of our friends' and comrades' names have been handed to the police with orders for their immediate arrest. While you have been sitting here in your snug council of plan-making and scheming"—I threw a good slice of contempt into the reference, for it is rarely ill to be a little contemptuous towards those whom you are seeking to impress and convince—"the streets without are resounding under the tread of armed men, broken by the wailing cries of hundreds of our brave friends, men and women martyrs alike, who are being hustled to gaol amid the curses and howls of the passion-ridden mob. Quesada's avowed policy is now to use this failed attempt of ours to stamp our cause under his feet, and to crush it so utterly that no vestige of strength remains. His plans have been maturing for weeks"—here again I glanced at Sarita—"and he has been deliberately working towards this end. For this he pretended to give us aid—the aid of a traitor—that by it he might find the means to further his own end. And that end was the doubly cunning one, to use us Carlists to overthrow the Monarchy, and then seize on our act as the pretext for crushing us into impotence."

The men present broke into bitter imprecations of Quesada, and for a time much confusion prevailed, as the party discussed the momentous news. I turned then to Sarita, by whose side the doctor was standing.

"What do you advise, senor?" he asked me anxiously.

"There is but one course, so far as we in Madrid are concerned. We cannot hope to resist. The present plans have failed hopelessly, and the one chance is to do what has had to be done before—bow to the tempest, and wait until it has passed. By this time hundreds of Carlists are crowding the gaols to overflowing, and to-morrow every known or suspected Carlist in the capital will be under lock and key, guarded by Quesada's agents. The one hope of safety for those who cannot clear themselves is in flight. Meanwhile every compromising document and paper should be destroyed or burned."

The panic was complete, and already most of those present were preparing to leave.

"Why did you venture here?" asked Sarita, as the doctor was called away. "What right had you to come and act this part and force me to play the traitor by keeping silence?"

"I came to save you; and my coming will have been in vain if you do not instantly leave the house with me. Every word I said of these doings is true, and it is true also that Quesada has denounced me as Ferdinand Carbonnell, the Carlist leader, and ordered my arrest in that character. I think I can save you yet, if you will fly at once."

"I will not go with you. I am not a coward."

"Then we will stay together and wait for the police to come to us."

"You must not stay. You shall not," she cried, quickly.

"I shall not leave you again."

"But you have no right here. You are not of us, and have no right to share our dangers. You shall not stay. I will tell them here that you are not one of us."

"They are too intent on saving themselves to bother about the nice little chain of circumstances which has linked my name to the cause. But as you will. I came to save you, and if I can't do that I don't care what happens. I left Madame Chansette overwhelmed with distress, and I only escaped from the house as the police agents entered it in search of you. I heard Quesada himself give the order for your immediate arrest. You must come. Quesada has only duped you as he has duped hundreds before you. And, mark you, when he gave that order, and when he was busy packing the gaols with Carlists, he believed that the King had actually been abducted. I know that; for I had it from his own lips. Surely you see his double cunning now."

"How do you know all you have told us?"

"I cannot tell you now; but I know it, and more. I believe, too, that I can bring this home to him. Many strange things have happened since I saw you yesterday, and with your help I can drag him down and can expose his treachery to the King as well as to you all. If you will not save yourself because I ask you, will you do it to help in punishing him?"

"I am not a coward to fly," she answered; but I could see that I had touched her. "I will denounce him."

"From where? From the inside of one of his prisons? As what? As a well-known leader of the Carlists? Think, Sarita, and for God's sake think quickly, for every minute may make your peril greater; and not yours only, but mine as well. What heed would be paid to anything a Carlist might say against him at such a moment?"

"I will come," she cried then, impetuously; and in a minute we had explained our intention to those who still remained, and left the house.

"Where are you going?" asked Sarita, when we reached the street.

"For to-night to the Hotel de l'Opera, where my sister is." I explained the position there, and then the change my brother's death had caused, and that I was no longer to be known as

Ferdinand Carbonnell, but as Lord Glisfoyle; that the next day our whole party would leave Madrid, and that she and Madame Chansette would leave with us. "You can stay if you please in Paris, or anywhere out of Spain, and for the purpose of the escape we must decide in what character you will travel. That's as far as I've got with our plans, but no one will look for you in Mrs. Curwen's rooms at the hotel."

"I will not promise to leave Madrid," she said, firmly.

"Just as you please. No doubt Quesada can find a cell for each of us if we remain," I returned, pointedly. "If you stay, I stay, Sarita: on that I take my oath."

Without waiting for a reply, I told her rapidly so much of what had occurred since I had seen her as I deemed necessary: the quarrel with Livenza, the interview with Quesada, my discovery of his connivance in the Carlist plot, and that I had faced him with it, and then the scene at Quesada's house that evening; and I was at great pains to make it as clear as I could that all the Minister's plans were laid well in advance to deal this overwhelming blow at the Carlists, when the King had once been put away.

Told as the story was now, with all the evidence of police activity in full sight, and broken by more than one pause, as we had to stand aside to avoid the rush of the howling mob as some party of prisoners was dragged past us, it carried conviction.

"This is no chance work of an hour, Sarita. The plans have been ready and the preparations made for days past, merely waiting the signal. The very warrants under which these men and women here are being imprisoned have been lying ready signed in the pigeon-holes of Quesada's office, and the lists have been made out with scrupulous deliberation and method. This was the reception he had in readiness for the friends by whose deed he meant to climb. Success or failure was all one to him. If the plot had succeeded, he would have crushed you Carlists, to leave no one in his path; it has failed, and he can still use it to consolidate his power and strengthen his influence as a jealous Minister of the King. His treachery is the only true thing in him."

As we drew nearer the heart of the city, the throng in the streets increased, and the noise and din of the clamour were incessant. Something of the infection of the wonderful enthusiasm I had witnessed in the Opera had spread to the streets. It was known that the young King was unhurt, and had appeared there; and the vast crowds were giving tongue to their feelings in every key of frantic enthusiasm, vented now in roystering, rollicking shouts of loyalty, and again in fierce, wild curses upon the Carlists and all traitors. A scene to try the strongest nerves; and I was not surprised that even

Sarita's courage began to fail, and she clung to my arm in apprehension.

There was cause indeed, for the mob was growing dangerous, and more than one ugly incident occurred close by us. The mere cry of "Carlist!" raised against either man or woman, was enough to bring the mob howling round like wolves scenting prey. And, as in all mobs, there were not wanting those who from motives of robbery or personal spite were ready to raise the cry, and so set light to the dangerous fires of violence.

Thus on one occasion we were standing back from the on-pressing crowd as a couple of prisoners were being taken by, when the cry of "Carlist spies!" was raised against a man and woman. It was started in the shrill tone of an old tatterdemalion hag who had begged an alms and had been refused. In an instant the two found themselves surrounded by a cursing, shouting, shrieking throng, their angry faces thrust forward in fierce denunciation, threateningly close to the pallid, fear-set features of the couple, and a hundred outstretched hands were quivering with the menace of violence. Someone gave the man a push from behind, and in a trice the two were separated, the man pulled, thrust, hustled, and whirled away like a leaf on the tempest of passionate ruthlessness, amid a war of oaths and curses; while by a chance the woman, forgotten in the instant of violence, drifted to us, and we let her creep in behind us and hide till the storm had passed.

A cry of "Carlist!" from below us soon carried the mob in search of the fresh victims, and we stood a minute, Sarita whispering to the woman to gather courage, as the danger was passed. And while we waited, the man who had been with her came back, helped by some friend who had found him battered, bruised, bleeding from a dozen hurts, and with the remnants of his clothing hanging on him in rags.

Sarita would have stayed to help the unfortunate pair, but the danger of the streets was too great, and I led her away.

The scene was repeated more than once, with variations mainly in the degree of violence used by the mob. More than once, too, we only just escaped finding ourselves in the midst of one of the innumerable street fights that occurred, where some man against whom the cry had been raised had friends, and, rallying them, shouted a counter charge against his accusers, and followed it up with an attack, in which knives were drawn freely on both sides and blood spilt.

Never was I more thankful in my life than when at length we reached the doors of the hotel, to which at last I had literally to force and fight my way through the mob still surging in the

141

neighbourhood of the Opera House, and swarming all over the plaza where the hotel stood.

No sooner were we safe, however, and I stood a moment in the spacious hall of the hotel to recover my breath, than a fresh difficulty of a quite different character occurred to me. How should I explain matters in regard to Sarita to Mrs. Curwen and Mercy? I had scarcely mentioned her name to either of them; they knew nothing, of course, of the weird undercurrent of events; and yet here was I turning up with her at eleven o'clock at night, in defiance of all the conventionalities, and as the climax of a series of acts which must have appeared to them as the very type of eccentricity.

Besides, there was Mrs. Curwen's own undercurrent motive for her presence in Madrid.

CHAPTER XX

AT THE HOTEL DE L'OPERA

It is, of course, a very simple thing to laugh at the conventions, and to declare that it would be preposterous to give the least thought to them in the face of the really serious pass to which matters had come. I was trying to do that all the way to Mrs. Curwen's room as we followed the waiter, to whom I had given my name as Lord Glisfoyle.

But, as a matter of fact, I felt more nervous and uncomfortable at having to subject Sarita to the sharp inquisitive fire of the widow's eyes, than if I had been going to face a roomful of armed men. My companion saw my embarrassment.

"You are anxious how your sister will receive me?" she whispered with a quick discernment.

"My sister, Mercy, is one of the best, staunchest little souls in the world."

"Ah, then it is this friend of hers?"

"It will be all right," I answered evasively; and as the waiter threw the door open and announced me at that moment, there was no time to say any more. Our entrance could scarcely have been at a more inopportune moment. My sister had taken the news of Lascelles' death very badly, and was lying on a sofa overcome by grief. Mrs. Curwen was kneeling by her with scent and smelling salts, and Mayhew was standing near in the helpless attitude usual with men under such circumstances.

Mrs. Curwen did not get up or look round for a moment, but an exclamation from Mayhew, who recognised Sarita and bowed to her, and then stared at her with an expression of bewilderment, drew the widow's attention.

"Mercy is,"—she began in a tone of warning but glancing round, then seeing I was not alone, and that my companion was an exceedingly lovely girl, she stopped, jumped up and looked at Sarita with eyes and face that appeared to harden rapidly from surprised confusion to indignant anger. She seemed instinctively to divine enough of the case between Sarita and myself to make her exceedingly uneasy and angry; and she was never in the habit of concealing her feelings.

"I have brought my cousin, Senorita Castelar, who is at this moment in deep trouble, Mrs. Curwen, to ask you and Mercy to help her." I must admit Sarita did not wear the appearance of trouble to bear out my words. She met Mrs. Curwen's most sarcastic look with one of almost queenly hostility, held her head high and had a light in her flashing eyes which augured ill for peace.

"Any friend of yours is welcome, of course,"—oh, the sting of that "of course," and the wicked bow that accompanied it—"but the hour is very late and unfortunately Mercy is prostrated with grief at the terrible news which you left to Mr. Mayhew to tell us. Will you be seated, senorita?" Mayhew glanced across at me, shrugged his shoulders very slightly, and then like, a good fellow plunged in to the rescue.

"Thank God, you are safe, senorita," he said, coming forward. "You must have had an awful experience in the streets to-night. They are almost impassable for the frantic excitement of the mob. You will not have forgotten me, I hope. I have had the pleasure of meeting you more than once; the last time I think was at the French Embassy ball. No? Well, it must have been at some other, for I know that we danced together. My name is Mayhew. I'm at the British Embassy, you know—at least you would know if my good friend Ferd—Lord Glisfoyle, I mean, hadn't got his head too high in the clouds just now to tell you who I am."

His glib chatter was a wonderful relief and broke the exceedingly awkward strain at the moment when everything seemed to spell crisis; and he bustled about and went on chattering in an unconcerned and irrepressible manner, for all the world as though there was no electricity in the air, and the visit at such an hour and under such circumstances was just the most usual thing in the world.

Under cover of this fusillade of small talk I crossed to Mercy's side and bent over and kissed her.

"Mercy, dear, I am in sore trouble and perplexity. If you can make an effort and rally now and help me, you will do me the greatest favour in the world. Both Sarita Castelar—who is your cousin—and I are in imminent danger of being arrested and sent to gaol, and I want your woman's wit, and that of our good friend here—to get us out of it. Mrs. Curwen, you have often declared your friendship for me, will you show it now in this?"

I knew my sister well enough to be sure that such an appeal would be the finest tonic in the world, and that it would stir up every scrap of pluck in her to face the emergency. And I was right. She pulled herself together, and kissing me, sat up.

"This awful news about Lascelles——" she began.

"You must put the thought of it away for the present, Mercy, and face the danger here," I interposed, earnestly. "There is no time for the indulgence of grief."

Mrs. Curwen had stood in silence during the short by-scene with Mercy, and the catchy breathing, slightly paled cheek, firmly pressed lip, and quick glances flashed from me to Sarita, told me she was moved. She bent forward as Mercy sat up in answer to my appeal, laid a hand on my arm and looked into my face with more earnestness and feeling than I had ever known her display, as she asked—

"What is this girl to you, Ferdinand?" and her eyes searched mine keenly for the truth.

"As I live, she is more to me than life itself," I answered in a low whisper that trembled with suppressed passion.

At the reply, she drew her hand hastily from my arm, closed her eyes, bit her lip as she drew one deep breath, and clenched her hands in a moment of intense agitation. But in the moment she had herself in hand again, a smile broke the set pallor of her face, she gave me her hand.

"Then, of course, we'll do all we can. What queer, clumsy creatures you men are sometimes. Why on earth didn't you tell us before?" and like the plucky little soul she was, the smile quickened into a rallying laugh.

I had no words ready for a reply. I was too much moved; and I held out my hand in silence and pressed hers. Mercy had been scarcely less moved by my news, and getting up now, put her arms round her friend's waist and kissed her.

"What a fuss you two make about a trifle," said the widow,

144

shrugging her shoulders. "Come, Mercy, we must do something, instead of chattering here; and let poor Mr. Mayhew off duty. I hope he isn't as awfully uncomfortable as he looks;" and she and Mercy crossed to Sarita.

"Lord Glisfoyle wants you a minute, Mr. Mayhew," she said, and then earnestly to Sarita, "My dear, let me call you that, I want to apologise to you, but I didn't know. Will you forgive me? Lord Glisfoyle is a very dear friend of mine—and you must be too."

"I didn't know that I had a cousin in Madrid," chimed in Mercy, kissing Sarita. "And you in such trouble too." And at that point Mayhew and I went out of the room on his suggestion, that if we left the three together while we smoked a cigarette, we should find them thick friends by the time we returned.

"This is a ticklish touch-and-go thing, Ferdinand," he said, as we lighted our cigarettes in the corridor.

"My dear Silas, it's a devil of a job, and how to get out——"

"I meant Mrs. Curwen," he said, drily. "You didn't tell me she'd ever cared for you; and to bring your cousin,"—with a distinct emphasis—"here was a bit risky, wasn't it? But I must say you have a devil of a way with you. I couldn't have done it."

"My dear fellow, Mrs. Curwen is a shrewd, level-headed, clever commonsense little woman, who is not of the type you seem to think. Her liking for me is much more platonic than romantic, and—well, I'm thundering glad it's all right. But I couldn't have done anything else if I'd wished to, for I had nowhere else to go. And look here, you behaved like a brick and just saved the situation. And now listen while I tell you something of the mess we're in." I told him pretty well everything, except my rescue of the young King, as shortly as I could, and very grave it made him look.

"You're in deep, sure enough," he said when I finished. "But there's a way out, and if I were you I should take it. I suppose that as your brother's dead you won't stay on at the Embassy here; well, I should go to the chief, tell him pretty well the whole show and just stop at the Embassy until you can get safely away. Quesada can't touch you, of course; and even he won't dare to try any games when he learns through official channels, of course, that the chief knows the facts. But you must give up the fight with him. You can't beat him. No one can."

"And Senorita Castelar?"

"I should get that plucky little widow-woman and your sister to smuggle her out of the country. It's no good blinking things, and there's no doubt that the Carlists will have a mighty bad time for a while; while those who took an active part in the abduction business have—well, they've put their heads in a noose, and that's the truth.

145

It's a life and death matter for some of them: and you say she was a sort of leader?"

"Your plan won't do, Silas. We must get something better. I can't make up my mind to separate from her."

"Then you'll double the danger for you both. Quesada will have a double trail to follow, and he's a sleuth-hound at the game."

"I shall not leave her," I said, firmly. "I couldn't. I have still something in reserve for Quesada if need be, and I won't give in. Oh, by the way, did any one come to the box to-night?"

"Yes, of course, they did. I'd forgotten it in this hubbub. It was somebody from the royal box too, for you to go there. What on earth does that mean?"

"I think there was some mistake or other. What message did you send?"

"That you had left the house; and when they asked for your address in Madrid, I gave them this hotel, as you said. Are there any more mysteries about, Ferdinand?"

Mercy came out then in search of us and saved me from replying, and as we were entering the room she kept me back a moment and pressed my arm as she looked up and whispered—

"I like her, Nand, and she is beautiful. And it's all right now, but we had such trouble. She's as proud as Lucifer, and we could do nothing with her until Angela—hasn't she behaved splendidly?—kept declaring that if she didn't do what we wanted she'd bring you into all kinds of trouble. For herself, I believe she'd go to the stake with a smile on her face. But she loves you, Nand, and that settled things. You'll see a change in her."

"You're a true little chum, Mercy," I said, kissing her for her news. She was right; there was a change. Sarita was dressed in sober black, with white cuffs and collar, her glorious hair done with quite severe plainness; a costume that seemed a sort of compromise between that of a companion and superior maid. But no change could hide her looks, and the very plainness of her dress enhanced her beauty, at least in my eyes.

"I am the victim of circumstances, and of these two good souls' solicitude for your safety," she said to me.

"And what does it all mean?" I asked.

"We start for Paris to-morrow," replied Mrs. Curwen; "and while you gentlemen have been smoking and talking, I have been fortunate enough to secure the services of a new companion, whose name to the world is Juanita Sanchez. You will remember that. Mr. Mayhew, who can be trusted to see to any business arrangements, will, I know, kindly arrange for me to-morrow to have a special train through to Paris—I am too frightened by these Madrid mobs to

146

remain longer—and will get passports for Mercy and myself and Juanita; and if Lord Glisfoyle joins us, so much the better. And now as I am desperately hungry let us have supper."

It was a strange feast, and had it not been for Mayhew's ever ready glibness of speech, it would have been an embarrassing business. But he opened a vein of anecdotal chatter, and Mrs. Curwen being very excited, soon began to keep up her end, so that gradually the feeling of strangeness wore away and we came to the discussion of our plans. There is no need to dwell upon them further, for they were all fated to be suddenly checkmated.

We had finished the supper; and in the lull that followed, Mayhew and I, at Mrs. Curwen's request, lighted cigarettes, and Mercy and Sarita having risen from the table, stood talking together at the far end of the room when a waiter came in, and approaching Mrs. Curwen, said in a very apologetic tone—

"I am sorry to disturb you, madam, but someone desires to see you—in point of fact, a police agent." As he spoke, we heard the sound of men moving in the corridor and a whispered word of command; and the next moment the police agent was in the room.

"What is the meaning of this?" asked Mrs. Curwen, indignantly, in English, and the official, not understanding her words but replying to her gestures, bowed and shrugged his shoulders.

"Permit me to interpret," said Mayhew, readily, and he put the question in Spanish; and meanwhile the man's eyes were all over the room, settling finally on me.

"My instructions are to come here—the rooms of Senora Curwen, Hotel de l'Opera—" this he read from his instructions—"in search of the Carlist, Ferdinand Carbonnell."

Mayhew made a show of interpreting this to Mrs. Curwen, and jumbled in a half-coherent caution that he knew the man understood English, so that we must look out.

"Tell him he has made a mistake; and you," she said to the waiter, "go and fetch the manager of the Hotel. I will not stand this kind of treatment."

"In the presence of the police we are powerless, madam," replied the waiter. "The manager is away, I am acting in his place."

Meanwhile Mercy had turned so pale that I was afraid the official would notice it. Then Mayhew answered—

"You are under a grave mistake. This lady is an English visitor to Madrid, has been here only two or three days, knows nothing of any Carlists, and desires you to leave her rooms."

"There is no mistake. That is Ferdinand Carbonnell; or at least he answers to the description well enough for me, and he must accompany me," and he came and stood by my chair.

"I don't know what you're driving at," I said, thinking it time to take a hand on my own account. "If you want me to go anywhere with you, I've no particular objection. But you'll find yourself in a mess if you carry this blunder, or fooling, or whatever it is, any further."

"You speak excellent Spanish, senor. May I ask your name?"

"Is that a crime?" I asked with a sneer, while Mayhew laughed unconstrainedly and most naturally. "If you want to know who I am—I'm an Englishman, Lord Glisfoyle; and if you want anyone to prove it, we'll go and knock up the English Ambassador, and ask him what he thinks of this kind of outrage. I say it's monstrous."

"Lord Glisfoyle," he returned, stumbling over the pronunciation. He was obviously impressed by my coolness and the little touch of indignation. He took out a paper and scanned it closely. "You answer in every particular to Ferdinand Carbonnell's description. These are anxious times, senor, and I have only my duty to do," he added apologetically.

"I can't help that," said I, quietly. "If you want to arrest me because I speak Spanish well and look like somebody else, you must have a queer set of laws here in Madrid. Had we better knock the Ambassador up, for the enlightenment of the gentleman?" I asked Mayhew.

"Nonsense," he said, with another laugh. "The thing's absurd. Here, you probably know me—or some of your men will. My name is Silas Mayhew, of the British Embassy. I tell you, this is Lord Glisfoyle. Don't get yourself into trouble and cause no end of complications by carrying this thing any further."

"May I ask the names of all present?" was the reply, for he was by no means satisfied yet.

"Of course you may. I've told you this is Mrs. Curwen," said Mayhew, coolly. "That is Lord Glisfoyle's sister, and that Mrs. Curwen's companion—maid, Juanita Sanchez." He did it excellently, as though the matter were the merest form. The official was puzzled, and stood pulling his beard in indecision. But he scarcely glanced at the two girls, vastly to my relief. If Sarita was safe, I cared little about myself.

"Excuse me a moment," he said, and going to the door he spoke to one of his men who came back to the room with him.

"You are Ferdinand Carbonnell, we are sure," he said then, and to my consternation he was holding a photograph in his hand. I remembered then that Quesada had obtained one from me.

"There is no room for doubt," and he showed it to Mayhew.

I saw Sarita start at this, while Mercy had to cling hold to her and be helped to a chair.

"I'll go with you, of course," I said. "But I shall hold you responsible for this. My sister is not well, and your clumsy blunder has made her positively ill. It's all right, Mercy," I said, going over to them, and taking occasion to whisper to Sarita, "I shall be perfectly safe if you'll only get away. They can do nothing to me, and by to-morrow they'll have a broadside from the Embassy that'll make them shake in their shoes. But promise to leave Madrid with Mrs. Curwen."

"Should I run away and leave you in danger?" she said.

"I can't stop to argue, but if you care for me and my safety, you'll do what I ask. I'm ready," I said aloud. "Just let me see your documents."

He showed me an order signed by Quesada himself, the alleged offence being high treason; and I read it aloud in order that Sarita should hear it, and I was shaking hands with Mrs. Curwen preparatory to leaving when there came another interruption.

Two officers in very elaborate uniforms were ushered in by a waiter, with every sign of extreme deference. They were complete strangers to me, and my heart leapt into my mouth in fear that it boded mischief to Sarita.

"Pray pardon me, madam," said one of them in English to Mrs. Curwen. "I hope we are not intruding; but we come on a mission of the highest importance. I was told Lord Glisfoyle was your guest, and I see"—this with a most courteous bow to me—"I was not misinformed."

"I am Lord Glisfoyle, but I do not recall the pleasure of having seen you before."

"That is my loss, sir," and he bowed again. "I know you, however, by sight, having seen you to-night in Mrs. Curwen's box at the Opera, and afterwards I learnt from this gentleman, Mr. Mayhew, of your Embassy, that you were staying here. I am Colonel Vasca, this is Colonel Damara," and we all bowed again like willows in a breeze. "We come from the King, and bring His Majesty's earnest request that you will wait upon him at the Palace at eleven o'clock to-morrow, when he desires to present you to Her Majesty the Queen Mother, who adds her request to His Majesty's."

The amazement of everyone in the room was complete, while the police official was lost in bewilderment. I think I rather enjoyed the situation, and answered very gravely—

"Their Majesty's desires would have been commands, but unfortunately I shall be prevented. This person, a police agent, has arrested me, so that instead of being in His Majesty's Palace I shall be in one of His Majesty's prisons, I presume. Perhaps you will be good enough to explain the cause of my absence."

The seriousness of my manner and the incongruity of the reply turned the thing in a moment to broad farce; with results which can be easily understood.

The King's messengers routed the Quesada agent in half a dozen words, and sent him and his men packing about their business. Then they made me a thousand profuse, most elaborate, and somewhat tedious apologies, and took their leave with signs of respect for me that were almost overpowering.

And no sooner were they gone than the other side of the incident was put before me very pungently by Sarita, who asked with a very sharp and searching glance—

"How comes the young King to be so friendly with you, Ferdinand, and apparently under so great an obligation?"

The question showed that even a king's favour may not be without its embarrassments; for in truth I did not know how to answer.

CHAPTER XXI

SARITA'S FLIGHT

Mrs. Curwen, Mercy and Mayhew, were almost as keenly interested as Sarita herself in the question she had asked with such vehemence, and thus my hesitation in answering was the more noticeable. Their motives were, of course, very different from hers, and I could have put them off with some light evasion; but with Sarita that would probably be both useless and dangerous; and her suspicion deepened with every second of my hesitation.

It was all but impossible for me to tell her the truth—that I had thwarted the long cherished plot and saved the young King. I could only tell her that when I was in a position to convince her that Quesada's policy was, as I had described it, to use the Carlist plot and then crush the plotters.

Moreover, the position, so far as I myself was concerned, had been completely changed by the death of my brother. Up till that moment I had been a soldier of fortune with my way to make; and the rescue of the King had offered just the chance of chances which a man with such an aim might most desire. I had meant to make

Spain my home and to build a career on the foundation of my contest with Quesada. There was danger in it, of course; but I was not scared by that; and when I gained my knowledge of his double treachery, the means to success were I felt, practically within my reach.

The fact that Quesada feared me sufficiently to resort to the extreme step of clapping into gaol a member of the Embassy staff on a charge he knew to be false, and one which he could not substantiate, and the extraordinary admission he had made to his sister, that by demanding my release she was ruining them, had given powerful confirmation to my confidence; and this attempted arrest in despite of Dolores' intervention, and probably without her knowledge, was still further corroboration of my view that he feared me.

But the fact that I was now the head of the family had altered everything. From the instant I had known that, my purpose changed, and my object was to save Sarita, and with her get out of Spain at the earliest moment. I had no thought or intention of declaring my identity to the King unless in actual need of His Majesty's protection, and in view of the difficulty of explaining that act of mine to Sarita, I had meant the whole thing to remain a mystery.

And yet here I was faced at the most critical and inopportune moment with the necessity of explaining.

"The question seems strangely difficult to answer," said Sarita, when I did not reply.

"I don't know that I need say that. There seems to be a good deal of misapprehension about me everywhere. Probably I can better answer the question when I have been to the Palace—if I go at all, that is. But I am not particularly anxious for His Majesty's goodwill, and prefer to leave Madrid."

"I shall not leave Madrid now," cried Sarita, instantly. "And I shall go at once to my home." At this Mercy and Mrs. Curwen broke into earnest protests, to which Sarita listened unmoved.

"You are one of us now, Sarita, you must not act in this desperate way, your very life may be in danger," said Mercy, earnestly.

"You do not understand," was the firm, steady reply. "I am in no real danger; and if I were I should care nothing. For what I have done, I am prepared to answer. I have plotted for my rightful King, Don Carlos, and I am not afraid to own it. I had built everything upon this stroke to-day, and it has failed. Why? Your brother knows probably better than any one else; and until that mystery is cleared up, I cannot accept your brother's or your help. I thank you for your offer—from my heart I thank you—but I cannot accept it."

"This is madness, Sarita," I cried warmly, going to her. I spoke in Spanish, and Mrs. Curwen and Mercy left us and with Mayhew went to the other end of the room.

"The name of it does not matter; it is the thing itself I care for. I consented to leave not because of my own risk in remaining. I am not a coward to run away because I have failed. I have always had the possibility, nay, the probability, of failure in my thoughts, and have always been prepared to face the consequences. If I could contemplate the necessity of marrying Sebastian Quesada, do you think I should fear a prison? I consented now, because of the danger to you; but you stand safe under the golden light of His Majesty's favour; how gained you know and I fear; but being gained, my motive for flight is gone. I shall stay in Madrid and shall return to my home."

I knew her too well to entertain much hope that she would change her mind, and what to do I knew not.

"You judge me very quickly," I said.

"Can you explain the King's sudden favour?"

"Is it not clear that this raiding of to-night had nothing to do with the success or failure of the attempt on the King?"

"Can you explain the King's sudden favour?" I paused, and then took the plunge.

"Yes. I took His Majesty this afternoon from the hands of the men who were carrying him off."

"It is enough. I will go, if you please," she said, quietly.

"You will step straight into danger," I cried.

"I would rather be in danger where you are not, than safe where you are, Lord Glisfoyle." The cold, cutting words struck me to the heart.

"That is very hard to hear, Sarita."

"It is harder to say, but it is no less than the truth."

"Yet, I will not believe it. Your heart will not say it. You know how I love you. You know I have not a thought or care but for your good, your safety, your happiness. You have confessed you love me; I know you do. I know that it was your love for me that prompted you just now to think of my danger and consent to leave Madrid. Even now I can read it in your eyes, for all the coldness you would try to force into them. You shall not go like this. I swear to God you shall not. If you speak of truth and mean that we must part, there must be at least some sign from you of that other truth—the heart truth—that you love me, Sarita. I will not let you go else."

She was moved by my passion, although she would not let her

152

own respond to it. But the struggle kept her silent a moment. Then she lifted her head and looked me calmly and still even coldly in the eyes.

"Do you think I would let my love weigh against treachery to the cause of my country that is more to me than life itself? Am I so poor a thing as that? If you wish to give me pain you are causing it. I love you; I know, as you know. I was not ashamed of it; even if I now feel shame that I loved one who could deal Spain this blow. But I shall live it down—I will. But you and I must not meet again." Her firmness began to give out then, and breaking slightly, she said in a quicker tone of agitation, "Let me go now. Nay, I will go."

"You are as hard as steel, Sarita, but before you break both our lives in this wild, impulsive way, you must have time to think. Remember what I have told you, how all that has occurred to-night has long been planned, and that it would have occurred just the same if I had not saved the King. Indeed, it was actually being done while Quesada still believed the attempt on the King had been successful."

"There is no proof of this," she interposed.

"That is the first ray of hope you have given me. If I prove it, will you recall the wild words you have spoken to-night? Give our love at least this one chance, Sarita," I pleaded.

"You cannot prove it," she said wavering.

"When I have proved it, I will put that question again. And now as to to-night. You cannot go out into the streets in the midst of uproar, and no power on God's earth shall make me let you do it. Stay here to-night, promise to see me to-morrow—I will take no refusal; and I have some claim on you, if for nothing else, for the warning I carried to-night to the Calle Valencia. Promise that, and I will see Madame Chansette and relieve her anxiety. She herself is leaving Madrid, broken down by all this trouble, and when we meet to-morrow, you can make your decision. You will do this?" At first she would not promise, but my determination prevailed, and she agreed to stay at the hotel until the morning; but would not promise to see me then.

I accepted the compromise, however, and having hurriedly explained the matter to Mrs. Curwen and Mercy, I left with Mayhew, to go and relieve Madame Chansette's anxiety.

"Did I hear you say you saved the young King?" he asked me as we passed down the stairs.

"Yes, unfortunately."

"Unfortunately! Why, when it's known, you'll be the most popular hero in all Spain."

"And to-night, I am about the most wretched. I could wish His

153

Majesty had gone to the devil before I interfered in the matter;" and feeling half-distracted by my gloomy thoughts, I pushed on through the now clearing streets in the direction of Madame Chansette's house.

We found her waiting up in great distress at Sarita's prolonged absence, and dreading to hear she had been arrested. The news we brought relieved her anxiety, and having stayed with her a short time we left.

"Where are you going now?" asked Mayhew. "Hadn't you better come and turn in with me?"

"No, I think I'll take the risk of going to my own rooms. I don't fancy the police or Quesada will think for a moment that I shall return there. And in fact I don't care if they do."

"Rubbish, man. You come with me. You're hipped now, and want an hour or two's sleep. I'll go to your rooms first thing in the morning;" and not caring, I agreed. I was as tired as a dog after a hard day's hunting, and within a few minutes of reaching Mayhew's rooms I fell into a heavy sleep and did not wake until late in the morning, to find my friend by my bed shaking me vigorously.

I was vastly refreshed, and had my bath and some breakfast while he went over to my rooms.

"Everything seems all right there," he reported. "And I brought over the first things I could find. But I think you may venture there to get something decent to wear for the interview at the Palace."

"My dear fellow, I wouldn't put my head inside my rooms for a pension, till I've been to the hotel."

"But last night you wanted to go and sleep there."

"Last night was last night, Silas, and I felt done; but I'm myself again this morning. Now look here, there are things to do. In the first place, I've written out a wire for the lawyers about matters in London. Poor Lascelles' funeral must wait a day or two if need be. Then you've got to see about the special train for Mrs. Curwen and Mercy to leave, with Sarita, if she'll go. But the others must go, and probably poor old Madame Chansette with them. If Sarita goes, I go; if she stops on, I stop on. I was a fool to leave the hotel at all last night, and my brain must have been addled or in my boots for me to do it."

"Why not go to London and clear the business there out of the way; let things simmer down here, and leave me in charge of them; and then come back and do what has to be done?"

"Have you ever cared for a woman, Silas?"

He smiled, and shrugged his shoulders as he said—

"Too busy and too poor for luxuries of the kind."

"Ah, well, everything comes to those who wait. If you haven't, you don't know how I felt in this; if you ever do, you'll understand me. I'm ready now, and feel fit. I'm off to the hotel."

"You'd better see the chief and tell him. He can do more than you."

"He can't save Sarita from Quesada, and I can, and will. Of course, there's the chance that these agents of his will lay me by the heels, and we must reckon with that. I don't know what's going to happen; but I do know this, that where Sarita goes, I follow; and so long as I'm outside a gaol I'll try and communicate with you twice a day. If a day passes and you don't hear from me, then tell the chief what's wrong; and if he can't get me out of any bother, then let the people at the Palace know. So much for emergencies. As for the rest, I'll cut the knots as I find them."

"You'll come out on top, Ferdinand, I'm sure of that. I wish to Heaven I had your energy."

With that we parted for the time, and a good deal was to happen before we shook hands again.

As I drove to the Hotel de l'Opera I saw the city was as full of soldiery as if it had been under siege; but no one interfered with me, and at the hotel the marks of increased respect with which I was received evidenced the influence of the previous night's message from the King.

Everything else was wrong, however.

Mrs. Curwen and Mercy were waiting for me in a condition of nervous excitement, and Madame Chansette was with them. But as I had more than half dreaded, Sarita was gone. She had slept with Mercy and had got up early, dressed, and written a note for me before Mercy had awoke.

"She was just leaving, and her kiss woke me," said Mercy, who was in sore trouble. "I did my utmost to persuade her to stay, at all events until you came, but I could do nothing against her resolve. I asked her where she was going, but she would not say. 'I am going to my friends, who are in trouble and have need of me. I have work to do, and under no circumstances could I stay with you. Give your brother a note I have written,' was all she would answer. I am so sorry, Ferdinand."

"It is not your fault, Mercy; I more than half feared it, and blame myself for not having stayed here in the hotel. Do you know anything of her movements, Madame Chansette?"

"She did not come home. I sent here the first thing in the morning for news of her, and when word came that she was no longer here, I hurried to the hotel myself. I meant to tell her I will not stay any longer in Madrid. I cannot. I am miserable. It will kill me, this incessant danger," and she wrung her hands.

155

"She will be sure to let you hear from her," I said, quietly, wishing to calm her anxiety.

"How can she if she is in one of those horrible prisons?"

"She is not there, and I shall find her, be assured," I answered, with much more confidence than I felt. "Do you know where Ramon is?"

"I never know where he is," was the helplessly spoken reply. "But I believe some days ago he was somewhere near Saragossa, or Daroca, or some such place. But I don't know. I know nothing."

"Do you know what name he is using?"

"No—yes—I think so. I believe it is Solano."

"Good. I will find him, at any rate. Now I will see what she says to me;" and I opened the letter.

"I have thought over everything, and have decided not to see you again. Do not seek me: it will be useless. To stay here longer would be treachery to those who have been ruined by your act; and for us to meet would cause only pain to both. You cannot prove what you said, for I know the facts. One last request I make you—go to England and forget we ever met. Good-bye. Sarita Castelar."

"Does she tell you anything?" asked Madame Chansette, eagerly, for I had read the letter twice with long pauses of thought.

"Not a word as to where she is going. She tells me only that she does not wish to stay and see me." I spoke calmly, and tried to hide every sign of the feelings of dismay, pain, and anxiety that were gnawing at my heart; and, putting the letter in my pocket, I added: "And now as to your plans. I should like you to return to London, Mercy, with Mrs. Curwen."

"Do you think I am going away under such circumstances?" burst in Mrs. Curwen, in a tone of indignation, "and leave you in this pickle of a mess? If I can't help you find the senorita—and I don't suppose I can do much good in that—I can at least be at hand to help you when you've found her. And here I stop."

"Mr. Mayhew is arranging for a special train," I said.

"Then Mr. Mayhew can travel in it, and take this dear old lady and Mercy. I stop in Madrid, and nothing shall move me—unless you want me to be somewhere else in this detestable country."

"And I can't go without Mrs. Curwen, Nand, can I?" cried Mercy.

"I call it just real mean of her to have gone off in this way; but I will say she is a brick to stick to her friends in a mess. And if ever she wants a friend, I am on call; and that's all about it. Don't you think Madame Chansette had better stay with us until the senorita's found?"

"You are a true friend, and I shall never forget this," I

answered; and, indeed, I was much moved by her spirited declaration, and more by her praise of Sarita. "I will not say another word about it. But I must get to work."

I wrote a letter to the young King, apologising for not being able to go to the Palace, and pleading urgent and most embarrassing business; and, having despatched it, promised Mrs. Curwen and Mercy to let them know how things went, if I could, and said that in any case they would hear of me through Mayhew.

With that I hurried away to commence my search.

CHAPTER XXII

AN UNEXPECTED MEETING

My knowledge of Sarita's real relations with the Carlist leaders was, of course, too slight to enable me to form anything approaching a definite opinion as to where she would go. I could only guess, build up a workable theory, and act upon it until something turned up to guide me.

I had one or two points in my favour, the chief being that her brother was probably to be sought, under the name of Solano, either at Saragossa or Daroca. I regarded it as likely that she would endeavour to join Ramon, if other considerations did not render such a course undesirable.

My plan was quickly formed. I intended to adopt the Carlist character of Ferdinand Carbonnell, and in that name push my inquiries among the Carlists themselves. The name was a sure passport among them, or it would be unless Sarita herself should proclaim me an impostor. That was a contingency which I did not anticipate, but I had no option but to face it.

In this character, there were two men who might be valuable allies—Dr. Vedia, at whose house I had been the previous night, and Vidal de Pelayo, either in Saragossa itself, or at Huesca.

I resolved to go first to the doctor, and hurried to the Calle Valencia. If Sarita had left Madrid, I guessed it would have been by the doctor's help, and I worked on that theory. I found Dr. Vedia in a condition of considerable nervous excitement.

"It is very dangerous to come here, senor," he said, directly.

157

"It is not a time to think of personal considerations, doctor. You have had Senorita Castelar here, and I am anxious to know that she succeeded in getting the disguise she sought to leave the city." I deemed it best to appear to know everything, and I watched him like a lynx for any sign that my guess was right. The start he gave was very slight, but perceptible to eyes looking for it, and without waiting for his answer I made a further shot. "The railway to Saragossa is watched with Argus eyes by Quesada's men—you know that, of course—but I thought she might learn through you if the attempt to get away might be dared."

"She told me you knew nothing of her journey," he said, completely off his guard in surprise.

"That is immaterial," I replied, nodding my head, smiling, and waving the remark aside as a superfluity, seeing that I had already shown my knowledge. "I thought that either a peasant's or a nun's dress would be safest, and knew, of course, that she could get from you one or the other." It was notorious that disguises of the kind were frequently kept in the houses of the Carlist agents. "And she came to you because of all our houses in Madrid, yours will be the least suspected."

"I don't understand you," he said then, cautiously.

"Nor is it necessary," I returned, warmly, with an air of offended authority. "It is your part, senor, to comply with the requests laid upon you, not to question their wisdom or expediency." My sternly-uttered, insolent bluff succeeded where anything else might well have failed.

"I did all that lay in my power," he replied, almost apologetically.

"All I want to know is that she got away. So much depends upon her mission that I came for the news at first hand. Will she get through to Daroca—you know the movement there?"

"I knew nothing of it until I read the news this morning, which the senorita confirmed. I have every hope she will get through. Heaven send she may be in time."

"So we all pray to-day," I answered, mysteriously; for I did not in the least know what news he meant and dared not question him. I had the news I wanted, however, and was turning to leave when he stopped me.

"I ought to tell you, I think, that she warned me particularly against you."

"She was quite right, but she knows no more than you, senor. These are troubled times;" and having given him this conundrum to chew at leisure, I added: "I am glad to tell you the trouble will pass your house untouched," and then left him, congratulating myself

158

that I had completely mystified him and had much impressed him with my importance as a Carlist emissary.

The next problem was how to get out of the city and follow Sarita to Daroca. As I had said to Dr. Vedia, the railways were infested with police, and watched closely. In all probability every applicant for a ticket would be under observation, and would have to give a sufficient reason for his journey as well as a good account of himself; and not only had I no papers of any kind, but I must almost inevitably be the object of embarrassing police solicitude.

As I neared the station, therefore, I entered a restaurant, and calling for some wine, told the waiter to bring me a time-table and a newspaper. A glance at the paper showed me it was full of the Carlist troubles. There was a short official account of the young King's adventure and a dozen unofficial ones, while from all parts of the country were scores of telegrams speaking of Carlist outbreaks, actual and anticipated. Among these was one that arrested my attention instantly.

The Carlist movement was described as being in chief force along the eastern littoral, from Alicante to the north of Barcelona; and spreading over the whole of Catalonia and Aragon; while Huesca, Saragossa and Daroca were referred to as so many central danger spots inland.

The message from Saragossa contained the following:

"Telegrams from Daroca suggest that that secluded place, being so difficult of access, has been used as a kind of headquarters for a strong and active Carlist body; the proximity to the mountains having rendered it especially liked by those bands of wild and lawless mountaineers who are known to be deeply embroiled in the present disturbances. The government agents here (Saragossa) have learnt that a man known as Solano, believed to be one of the most reckless and venturesome of the Carlist propagandists, came here lately from Daroca. He narrowly escaped capture, and in the room he had occupied were found a quantity of compromising documents, such as addresses to the people and stamped brevets of appointments in a Castilian rifle brigade. A quantity of arms and ammunition were also discovered through the papers he left when he fled. The situation here is decidedly serious. A conflict has occurred between here and Huesca, in which blood was shed, and the military beaten by the superior numbers of the Carlists. The authorities have now closed all the known Carlist clubs, have arrested a number of the leaders, and have placed many others under close police and military surveillance. There is every fear of an outbreak."

The news might well make me grave. It was into this hornets' nest I had to follow Sarita, and in following her had to take the double risk of danger from both sides.

If the police agents identified me, I should be clapped into gaol by them as the dangerous revolutionary, Ferdinand Carbonnell; while the Carlists might very probably hold me for a spy and a traitor, the proper mark for either bullet or dagger.

But go to Saragossa and on to Daroca, aye, and on to the end of the world, I would, if necessary, and if I could get there, in search of Sarita; and, putting down the paper, I picked up the railway guide to find the route and the train time.

Then came a very pertinent and unpleasant reminder of the difficulties ahead of me. Chancing to glance into the street, I saw three men in earnest conversation close to the door, and recognised two of them; Senor Rubio, the official who had been at Quesada's house the night before, and the man who had come in search of me to the Hotel de l'Opera. The third was a stranger.

They stood for two or three minutes talking earnestly, and when they parted, the two I knew went together hurriedly toward the railway. I sauntered to the door and watched them enter the station, after exchanging a word with one or two men standing about in front of the building.

How could I hope to get away unrecognised, was my perplexed thought as I returned to my table. These men knew me personally, and had spoken to me; one of them had my photograph, and I did not doubt that it had been reproduced by the hundred and distributed among the police spies. Quesada was not the man to do things by halves, and this Rubio was no doubt both a willing and clever agent.

Still, the attempt must be made, and if they laid hold of me I must rely on the Embassy or the palace to procure my liberty; and I turned up Daroca in the guide. It was a beast of a place to get at and there was no train for some hours.

It was the terminus of a loop-line some forty odd miles south of Saragossa, and could only be reached by going to that place first. It seemed to be a sort of cul-de-sac with the mountains all about it— just the place of all others in the country that would be most difficult to reach, and having been reached, probably a hundred times worse to leave. As I realised the inaccessibility of the spot, and the proportionate increase in my difficulties and risks, my irritation and chagrin found vent in a curse which paradoxically proved most providential.

"Damn the place," I exclaimed aloud, heartily, as I tossed the book on the table.

160

"That's just the sweetest word I've heard to-day, and if it is anything to do with the railway, sir, I'd like to join you in the curse."

The speaker was a florid, flabby-faced, square-shouldered, middle-aged man, who was sitting at the other end of my table, and received my look of surprised and somewhat intolerant protest at his interruption, with a broad, good-natured, knowing smile.

"No offence, I hope," he went on, glibly, "I meant none; but when I heard you swear in dear old English, I couldn't help chipping in. This is an infernal country to do business in at the best of times, but at the worst, and I suppose this is about the worst; it's the most God-forsaken, riotous, bundle-you-about, stick-a-knife-into-you-if-you-say-anything, and run-you-in-if-you-don't cursed hole that ever a man was condemned to travel in. I don't do much in their beastly lingo at any time, and I haven't heard a word of English this day till I heard your 'damn,' and if there's any sympathy in any word of ours, I say it's in a good old hearty damn. And damn the place I say too."

"You put it crudely, my friend, but there's something in the theory, perhaps; though I haven't heard it before," I replied, amused, in spite of myself. "What's your worry? I know what you call the lingo, and if I can help you, well, we're both English, and that's enough."

"My name's Hunter, David Hunter, of the firm of Ross and Catter, the lace people of London, Nottingham, Calais, and everywhere where lace counts. You'll know them if you're on the road, or ever have been;" and he gave me one of his business cards.

"I've been on a good many roads," said I, taking the card; "but never on such a queer one as this."

"May I ask your name, sir?"

"Glisfoyle."

"Glisfoyle, umph, I haven't met it. In any particular line, may I ask?"

"In no particular line at present; travelling for myself, and not exactly on business, commercial business, that is. But all the same, if I can be of any service, I shall be glad."

"I wish you could, but it isn't anything to do with the language, as you suggested. I can patter along in my way, sufficient for what I want. But this isn't the lingo. I wanted to get to Daroca; a big order depends on my getting certain samples there, and now they tell me the place is full of those hot-headed fools of Carlists, and that it's as much as a man's life is worth to poke his head into the hole. I like my firm, and like a good order too, but I like my head a thundering sight better; and so I say, damn the place and the Carlists too—stopping business in this fat-headed way."

161

The mention of Daroca set my ears tingling, as may be imagined. Here might be a chance in a thousand for me to get there, and while he chattered, I thought and planned.

"I am going to Daroca," I said quietly. "If you like we could travel in company, and if one of us chanced to get killed—not, perhaps, a great improbability—the other could deliver your samples. The order might thus reach your firm, and even if you were not fortunate to live and profit by it your widow might be glad of the commission. I know there's danger there, but then a man can only die once, Mr. Hunter, and how better than in the performance of his duty?"

His fat, flabby face paled slightly, and I went on to give a vivid and coloured picture of the risks, until he was obviously very much frightened indeed.

"And you are going to such a place?" he asked, looking at me as though I were a madman.

"Oh yes, why not? It's so difficult to find a little excitement nowadays," I said, in a rather languid, bored tone. "You'll find it pleasant enough after a bit."

"No thank you, sir. David Hunter doesn't travel in bullets and guns and explosives. My skin ain't warranted not to puncture either. It's out of my line altogether. But if you really mean that you are going, that you're really bent on going——" he stopped and looked at me.

"Well?"

"I wouldn't do a blessed thing to persuade any fellow creature to shove his head into such a devil's pit, but if you are going, perhaps you wouldn't mind undertaking a little commission for me."

"Not the least in the world. What is it?"

"It's only to deliver a few samples—they aren't big enough to bother you, and just say they're from me," and he gave me particulars of what he wanted. "It wouldn't take me an hour, and I'd be awfully obliged to you, and so would my firm."

"I don't care a cent for your firm, but I'll do it to oblige you, Mr. Hunter, if you think you can trust me with the samples."

"I hope I know a gentleman when I see one, Mr. Glisfoyle; and you're one of the right sort. Besides, the samples are of no great value;" and this excellent caution made me smile.

"I won't run away with them, anyhow; and if you'll go to the station when the time comes and get me a ticket—get a return if you can, and if any questions are asked just give your own name and the lace business as the reason for the journey, and you may consider the thing settled." I handed him a bank-note.

162

"Oh, you think they mightn't let you go then?" he said, shrewdly.

"They will let a man with definite business to do pass much more readily than one who can plead nothing more than a wish to see the fun."

He gave me a meaning look, a knowing twist of the head, and a wink.

"I twig. I'll soon have a ticket," he said, and went off briskly. He was soon back with the ticket. "It's all right. I gave a card and showed 'em my samples, and that did the trick. And if you don't mind my giving you a wrinkle, you take my case with you and some of my cards. Looks workmanlike;" and seeing the policy of it, I accepted the case.

"We'll go over together when the train's due out," I said; "and as there might still be some questions asked, you'd better appear to be going until the last moment."

In this way we managed. Just before the train was due out we went together and I kept as much out of sight as possible; and taking care to avoid Rubio and the other official who knew me, I succeeded, under the pretence of seeing Mr. Hunter off, in getting away without any difficulty at all. It was so simple a matter indeed that I was disposed to laugh at my careful precautions; but I had ample reason to be glad of them before we had travelled far. Not once only but half a dozen times I had to show my ticket and explain the purpose of my journey, and that I was Mr. David Hunter, representing the great lace firm of Messrs. Ross & Catter.

Nor were those the only exciting incidents of the journey. We made a stoppage of some minutes at a station some thirty miles out from Madrid, Guadalajara, and there I made the unpleasant discovery that the police agent Rubio was travelling by the same train. I caught sight of him as he was walking along the platform scanning the passengers pretty closely. I thrust my head out of the opposite window, therefore, and kept it out until we started again, feeling, I must admit, profoundly uncomfortable.

He did not see me, however, or at any rate recognise me, but I did not breathe freely until we were well clear of the station and again steaming north, when I drew in my head and resumed my seat, with a casual look at the fresh passengers who had entered the carriage at the station. And then I made a discovery, which sent the blood for an instant rushing to my heart and made me catch my breath in sudden dismay.

Right opposite me, their knees almost touching mine and their eyes staring full into my face, were two men, whom I recognised

163

instantly, and who were as unwelcome fellow-passenger's as the keenest scented police spy in Spain could have been.

They were two of the men from whose hands I had snatched the young King on the previous day. One was the man I had ridden down and then knocked unconscious on the road, and the other was he who had come running up at the last moment, whose horse I had borrowed for the young King's use.

If they recognised me, and both were staring at me as though trying to place me in their memory, who could tell what would be the result? We had over 100 miles to travel together, if they were bound for Saragossa; and the thought of it might well set my teeth on edge.

With an effort I pulled myself together, however, and to get my nerves quite steady, I opened Mr. Hunter's despatch case, holding it on my knees with the name turned towards them, and made a pretence of looking through my samples, watching them well the while. I saw them interchange a sneer and a shrug of the shoulders as they rolled fresh cigarettes. I thanked my luck profusely. That little ruse of the small silken mask had kept my secret safe, and they did not know me. Very soon their interest in my features slackened, and they began to talk in low tones.

When I felt safe, my doubts gave place to pleasure; and I set to work to consider whether I could turn the incident to good account and make use of the two men for the purpose I had in view.

What better chance could I ever hope to have of playing my part of Carlist leader? These two were sure to be among the best known of the Carlists; for none but picked men would have been told off for such a task as theirs of the previous day. It was clear they did not know me; and as Ferdinand Carbonnell was to them or to anyone no more than a name, why should I not declare myself to them in that name? That I knew them would be sufficient to impress them greatly; while the interchange of the password would probably convince them of my sincerity.

It was an easy guess that they were on their way either to Saragossa or to Daroca; and they had no doubt come so far on horseback or on foot, deeming it safer to join the train where they had, than to risk going back to do so at Madrid. In all probability their object in going there was the same which had taken Sarita in the same direction. Either it had been pre-arranged that the leaders should gather there in the event of the abduction plot failing, or there had been some summons when the failure was known.

All these thoughts and a hundred other conjectures rushed into my mind as I sat fiddling with the bits of lace and making sham jottings in a pocket-book. And I resolved to take the risk.

Catching one of them looking at a bit of the lace I smiled and, holding it towards him, said casually—

"A pretty bit of work that, senor."

He took hold of it gingerly and nodded with a laugh, as if to humour me.

"Very, senor; but I don't know anything about it; and don't want any."

"I'm not offering to sell it you. But anyone can tell good lace, I should think. That's a bit of a kind—fit for a King's ransom;" and I looked him straight in the eyes. It was a somewhat daring move, but I wanted them both to look well at me with the thought of the King in their minds; and so that I could be quite positive that they did not know me. They both grunted, and one of them swore softly under his breath; but no look of recognition came into his eyes.

"Thank you, I don't want any, senor," was the answer, shortly spoken, as though to close the conversation.

"Ah well, I suppose you've no King to ransom," I returned, and laughed pleasantly; but as the laugh ended, I looked again at him meaningly; and then surprise and question showed on his face.

"Do you travel in this?" he asked, sharply.

"Yes, my name's Hunter, David Hunter, of the great lace firm of Ross and Catter, of London. Here's my card;" and I handed him one; I said this for the benefit of the rest of the people in the carriage who were listening. "If you care about such things, I can find you something of interest."

"I don't, thank you, Senor Hunter. Odd time for such business, I should think," and he returned the card.

"Depends on the business, of course," said I, "and of course on the man. I'm going to Daroca; and expect to do a good stroke there," and while I was speaking, I wrote on the back of the card: "Counting all Renegades lovers of Satan. By the Grace of God;" and covering it with a piece of lace, I handed it to him again. "Now, there's something you might care to see."

The start he gave caused him to let his cigarette fall, and as he stooped down to recover it, he whispered for me to hear—

"By the Grace of God," and when he sat up his face was set like steel in his sudden excitement. He muttered a word to his companion and passed him the card. He in his turn was scarcely less excited.

"It's quite a unique pattern. Very rare;" I said; and when he returned me the lace and card, I scribbled hurriedly my name, "Ferdinand Carbonnell;" and as they read it our eyes met.

"You are right, senor. We have never seen anything like it

165

before, and are more glad than we can tell you to have seen it to-day."

"I thought you would be interested," I replied, lightly; and taking the card I tore it into a hundred pieces, and flung it out of the window; and in silence put the samples away into the case.

All had gone well, so far, very well; for I had turned two of the most dangerous enemies a man could well have, into two staunch allies at the very moment of peril.

CHAPTER XXIII

NEWS OF SARITA

Having made myself known to my two travelling companions, I had next to ascertain their destination and plans. I had not much doubt that they were going to Daroca, and when I had allowed enough time for the impression I had created to have due effect, I began to talk in the casual tone one uses with chance acquaintances, covering the real meaning of my words in the form of business chatter.

"I suppose you gentlemen are in the same line as myself, and going to Daroca by way of Saragossa?"

"We are newspaper correspondents. I represent the 'Puebla,' and my name is Cabrera, senor," replied the elder of the two—this was he whose head I had cracked on the highway. "My friend, Senor Garcia, is of the 'Correo.' We are going up about the Carlist outbreak. We are going to Daroca, of course," and gave me a significant glance, and added in a lower tone, "But we shall ride from Calatayud; much quicker."

"Of course," I assented, trying to rally my scanty geographical knowledge of the place to understand his meaning. I must not show ignorance on such a point, seeing that my character was that of a kind of flying scout who would be presumed to know all such things. "I think, perhaps, I'll join you. They tell me business at Saragossa is seriously interfered with, but that at Daroca something can still be done. I am, therefore, going there."

"Good," said both.

"I suppose there's nothing really serious in this Carlist

business?" I said, in a tone of indifference. "You newspaper gentlemen generally know these things."

"From our point of view you may call it serious, perhaps; seeing that we are ordered to such a place as Daroca. The authorities too are pretty much in earnest."

"Ah, yes, so it appeared at Madrid. By the way, I saw on the station there, the great police agent, Rubio, I think his name is. He is travelling in this very train; I suppose also on Carlist business."

"Rubio in this train, is he?" exclaimed Cabrera. "We must get hold of him, Garcia, and see what he's after. He'll have news;" and both were evidently surprised and somewhat uneasy.

"I suppose you know all these officials by sight?" said I, with a light laugh. "That's the best of newspaper work; at least so it seems to me."

"We have not been long enough in the work to know many people, and we are scarcely known by anyone."

"Then I am more fortunate than you, perhaps, for this Senor Rubio and I have met, and I daresay he would know me again." They were quick enough to read this as a caution that Rubio must not see me; and then I turned the talk to general matters, and one or two other passengers joined in it.

At the next station, the last we were to stop at before we alighted, our fellow passengers got out. Our tickets were examined again; we were once more questioned, and the two Carlists produced credentials from their supposed newspapers, which proved sufficiently satisfactory. But when the matter had just ended and the official was closing the carriage door, an incident occurred that gave me a passing twinge of anxiety. The police agent, Rubio, passed the carriage, and a quick little start as his keen gaze flashed through the carriage showed me that he had recognised me.

"Rubio has seen and recognised me," I whispered hurriedly to my companions, in a sharp authoritative manner. "He may arrest me. In that case do nothing, but go on to Daroca, and make it your chief charge to find and protect, with your lives if need be, the Senorita Sarita Castelar. I can get out of Ruble's clutches again quite safely."

"They shan't take you," said Cabrera, with grim earnestness.

"You will do nothing to prevent it. I can protect myself," and opening my sample case, I began fingering the samples again while I waited during three minutes of as anxious suspense as I have ever endured. Then to my intense relief the train started, and I breathed freely. It was moving along the platform when a young man, protesting excitedly that he must go, opened the door, jumped in and sank breathless in the corner seat, while the porter, swearing generously, ran alongside and fastened the door after him.

"That was a near thing, wasn't it?" he said to me. "Wonder if they got my luggage in;" and putting his head out, shouted vociferously to those on the platform to throw his bags into the luggage break. "Good," he exclaimed, as he sat down again. "They can do things if you only shout at them. They got them in." Then rolling himself a cigarette, he asked me for a light, and began to chat.

"A commercial traveller, I see," he said. He had a pleasant voice, and to keep my character, I went all through the lace business again. In reply he gave a long account of himself, to which I paid little attention, and then he gradually led the conversation to Carlism, and professed a good deal of sympathy with the Carlists who seemed to have fallen on evil times.

"I am an Englishman, senor, and these things can be nothing to me except so far as they are bad for trade," I answered, and commenced to make some entries in a note book as if to close the conversation. He would not be put off, however, and continued to talk, asking a host of questions and trying to draw my companions into the conversation.

To my surprise they would not speak to him, not even replying when he put questions direct to them, and after a while the talk ceased, and we travelled a number of miles in silence. Then he began again, and pestered me with questions as to my journey, where I had come from, where I was going, what business I had done, and soon, and again made strenuous efforts to get my companions to speak.

"We must be within a few miles of Calatayud," he said, at length, and at that Garcia, having exchanged a glance with Cabrera, crossed the carriage, and saying they would have the window closed now, pulled it up and sat down opposite the stranger.

"You have been very anxious to make us talk with you, senor; may I ask why?" he said.

"Merely because I hate travelling in silence."

"You are very interested in the Carlists, too, I notice," and Garcia looking him straight in the face said, "Kindly tell us the nature of that interest?"

"Mere sympathy with them of course. I think they're being very hardly dealt with. That's all."

"Are you one of them?"

"Oh no, certainly not."

"Perhaps you know some of them?"

168

"No, I don't think I do." The answer was lightly spoken, but I noticed that a shadow of anxiety began to show on his face.

"By sight, perhaps?"

"No. No, not even by sight." The tone was growing less firm.

"What did you say you were?"

"Really, I am not here for examination," and I saw his hand go stealing towards his pocket.

"Keep your hand out of your pocket, please. I must know more about you. You are armed, I observe, and I must know why. My friend and I are of the secret police; and our mission is in search of Carlist spies. You are one; and we are going to search you." And almost before I grasped the meaning of the thing, Garcia had whipped out a revolver, and the stranger, now showing unmistakable signs of fear, was looking along the barrel into the strong, threatening face. At that Cabrera crossed the carriage and sat beside him. "The right pocket," said Garcia, coolly; and his companion plunged his hand in and drew out a revolver.

"Put your hands up," cried Garcia, his voice ringing with menace.

"I'm no Carlist spy," cried the fellow, and then appealed to me. "You won't see this done, senor, without trying to help me?"

"It's not my affair. I'm neither police nor Carlist," I answered. And then in my turn I had a most disquieting surprise.

"You evidently know this man," said Garcia, in the same rough, blunt tone, indicating me with a side jerk of the head. "Who is he?" while Cabrera half turned toward me holding his revolver in readiness. "If you won't answer, we'll find the way to make you. I believe you're both Carlist spies." It was so naturally done that for the moment I more than half believed I was really suspected. But I was not long in doubt. While Garcia threatened him with the revolver, Cabrera searched him thoroughly.

"Why, you infernal scoundrel, you are not only a Carlist spy, but you dare to carry papers on you to make you out one of us secret police," cried Cabrera in a voice of thunder.

"I am a police agent," was the reply. "But I don't know you."

"Then who is this man here? You know him. I saw that the instant I clapped eyes on you. You're here to spy on him, if you're one of us. Quick, who is he? You want to keep this capture all to yourself, do you, you selfish dog?"

"He's Ferdinand Carbonnell, and pretends to be an Englishman."

"And who the devil is Ferdinand Carbonnell?"

"Who should he be but one of the Carlist leaders?" was the answer sullenly spoken, the tone showing that the fear for his life was passing and giving place to the minor one of losing an important prisoner and the credit of the capture.

"Good, then we'll see to him. As for you, you're a disgrace to the whole of us, getting in and talking your magpie chatter about sympathies with the Carlists and all the rest of it. Why, if we'd been Carlists ourselves, we should have known you by your lying tongue. You must have a lesson, my friend. If you knew this man, why didn't you arrest him at the last station, or before? Or is the whole thing only a lie to cover some Carlist trick?"

"He was only recognised at the last station, and there wasn't a strong enough body of police there to take him. He may have a lot of friends in the train. These are Senor Rubio's own orders. He is in the train and has wired for help to Calatayud."

"Oh, well, we're going to make the capture now, not you. Now, Cabrera," he said quickly, and they both darted on him, and tied him up hands and feet. "We shall be in Calatayud in a few minutes. Shall we shoot him and pitch him out of the window? Dead men keep silence longest." And Garcia looked so reckless and fierce that I thought he would do it on the spot.

"Is that necessary?" I said, hastily, shrinking from the thought of bloodshed. "Gag him and leave him under the seat. We need no entanglements we can avoid."

For a moment the man's fate hung in the balance, and his bloodless face and staring eyes of terror as he glanced from one to another were sickening to look upon.

"For God's sake, don't kill me," he cried, eagerly. "I won't say a word of what has passed. I swear on my soul I won't."

"He'll know us now by sight," muttered Cabrera, who was clearly of Garcia's mind; and the argument was undoubtedly strong.

But I could not see murder done in cold blood, and in a very firm, authoritative voice and manner I said:

"I will have no blood needlessly shed. Let it be as I say." And somewhat to my surprise, and greatly to my satisfaction, the two yielded to me.

"Mischief may come of a tongue that can wag as his does," growled Cabrera, and his companion gave way with equal reluctance. But I insisted, and the spy's bonds were tightened, he was gagged securely, and laid for the while on the seat, while we held a whispered council.

"There'll be a strong body of men in waiting for us at Calatayud. What are we to do?" asked Garcia; and in all truth it was an awkward puzzle.

It was clear we couldn't hope to make a fight of it. Any attempt of the kind would be the instant signal for us to be surrounded and probably shot. For the moment I was disposed to let my companions escape, and give myself up to Rubio; but against this course were very strong arguments arising out of the scene with the police spy. At the best of it I should have some difficulty in explaining my presence, while the treatment meted out to him constituted in itself an offence of which I could not clear myself. If Rubio arrested me on such a charge and in such an out-of-the-way place, it would be an easy matter for Quesada to instruct him to put me away where the Embassy might not find me, and inquiries even from the palace might prove abortive.

At all hazards I must get away therefore, and the question was—how? I could only think of one means, and I explained it rapidly.

"I think I have it," I said. "Calatayud is an out-of-the-way place with not many police, and probably the men wired for by Rubio will be soldiers—much easier folk to fool. Rubio will reckon that we have no suspicion of his intentions, and will simply have wired to have the men at the station to await his instructions. We'll leave the train as it slows down before entering the station, therefore; and if any attempt is made to interfere with us, we'll play another scene of this farce of yours—that I'm an escaped Carlist and you're the police after me. Then we must hustle things through as chance serves, and get horses as quickly as can be."

"They'll be waiting for us at old Tomaso's," said Cabrera, readily. "Yes, it'll do. Fortunately we're well at the back of the train, and there's a curve through a cutting just before the station that will serve us well; and Tomaso's isn't five hundred yards from the top of it. We can slip out, dash up the side of the cutting, and be half-way there before the train pulls up."

"And give this brute a whack on the head to keep him silent for a while," put in Garcia, who seemed to have a keener appetite for violence than his really sterner comrade.

"It'll serve no purpose, and may only get us charged with attempting to murder him. There must be no violence," I said, and Cabrera agreed, seeing the force of my words.

"We're close there now," he added; and giving a final look at our prisoner to see that he was securely tied and gagged, we thrust him under the seat and made ready to leave the carriage.

The place could not have suited better such a plan as ours. We were in luck, too, for the train slowed down on approaching the curve, so that we were able to leave it quite safely. I jumped out first and sprang rapidly up the high bank, the others following me. I let them catch me up before we reached the top, as I did not, of course, know in which direction to run, and then together we darted off as fast as our legs would carry us.

We had only one incident. Having crossed a field we leapt into the road, and almost jumped on the top of a couple of soldiers who were obviously on patrol duty. Up went their guns as they called us to halt.

"Now we've got you," cried Cabrera, fiercely, clapping his hand on my shoulder. "Tie his hands, Garcia;" and with ready presence of mind he turned to the soldiers and laughed, as he took his hat off and breathed hard.

"They'll want you at the station," he said. "There's half a trainful of these cursed Carlists, and our chief Rubio, from the capital, has only got a handful of men with him, and is at his wit's end for help. But he'll be glad we've netted this bird;" and, turning to me, he shook me, cursing and abusing me with voluble violence.

The soldiers, completely taken in, lowered their weapons, and were obviously interested in the smart capture.

"Who is he?" asked one, with a grin.

"He broke from the train, the brute," answered Cabrera, "and gave us all the trouble. I wish you'd tell the chief we've taken him on, and that he's safe in the lock-up. Come on, Garcia, or the beast may be up to some of his tricks again. Let's get him under lock and key;" and, shoving me forward, they pushed by the soldiers, who drew aside and wished them luck for this good day's work.

"Thank the Virgin, we hadn't to break their heads with their own guns," growled Cabrera; and the moment we were out of sight of the men we set off running again at full speed, and did not stop until we reached the house where we were to find horses. This was an inn, and both my companions were well known to the old man who came out to meet them. A white-haired, exceptionally dark-skinned, and most picturesque-looking old fellow, who greeted the two quietly, but cordially, and looked suspiciously at me.

"Who's this?" he asked.

"The most honoured guest who ever crossed your threshold, Tomaso," answered Cabrera. "Take off your hat to him; and if his name were whispered in your ear, you'd be ready to bow your head to his boots. We must have three horses instantly. The dogs are close on our heels."

The old fellow raised his hat and bowed his head, and the long white locks shone in the mellow light of the now dying sun. To act the part which Cabrera had thus assigned to me, I returned the bow, and in a quick, imperious tone, said:

"The horses, my good Tomaso, the horses, with all the dispatch you can show. Even minutes may spell danger."

"Your lordship can depend upon me," he returned, deferentially, and, turning, gave a sharp order to a groom who stood near. "You will take wine while you wait. It will be but a minute."

We entered the house, and food and wine being laid out in readiness, we ate and drank hastily; and the moment the horses were at the door I paid him liberally, and we mounted.

"Is the road clear, Tomaso?" asked Cabrera.

"Yes, senor, I believe so. Juan and Andreas rode forward with the senorita some four hours ago. I instructed them to ride with their eyes open, and if they saw anything suspicious during the first half-score of miles, one of them is to hide with the senorita and the other return and warn you. After that you will be safe, and among our own people. I wish you all God-speed on the journey, and glorious success at the end of it. If there is any trouble, Andreas or Juan will show you the mountain paths."

"The senorita?" I asked, pricking up my ears at his words.

"Aye, the blessings of the Holy Virgin rest ever on her lovely face—the Senorita Castelar," and he bared his old head again, with a look of deep enthusiasm on his rugged features.

I waited for no more.

"Forward, gentlemen," I cried. "Great work lies ahead of us."

It was full time we started. We had paused but a few minutes at the inn, but already in the distance behind us signs of commotion in the direction of the station were to be discerned.

Only one thought found place in my mind, however. It was not for the danger we had escaped, nor the work that lay ahead, nor the risk inseparable from this close companionship with the two Carlists, of whose desperate character I had had full evidence. Sarita was but four hours ahead of me, and we should meet at latest in Daroca.

CHAPTER XXIV

A CHECK

We were all three well mounted, and we rattled our horses along at a good pace, quickening soon into a smart gallop, until we felt that the risks of pursuit from Rubio's men or the soldiery were over, and then we slackened and took matters more leisurely. We had five and twenty miles to cover, and a good deal of the road was rough and hilly enough to make us desirous to save our horses as much as possible.

But the slower pace gave the greater opportunity for conversation, and in this I knew there must be a certain amount of risk that something might be said which would rouse my companions' doubts of my sincerity. So far they had an absolute conviction that I was heart and soul with them in the cause, that I was a very Carlist of Carlists, and one to whom they owed that kind of rough-and-ready obedience which a recognised leader might rightly demand.

So long as we were engaged together in escaping from the police there was little chance of their making any compromising discoveries about me; but every mile that carried us nearer to Daroca was also bringing me face to face with a very different position, in which a hundred pitfalls would threaten me with discovery in every direction. There were a thousand things I should be expected to know, and any number of people whom I ought to be able to recognise; and failure in any one of them might bring the glaring search-light of suspicion of treachery upon me. A mere hint that I was a spy would expose me instantly to the imminent peril of death.

These considerations made me thoughtful, as well they might, and I rode plunged in deep thought. But I could see no alternative except to leave everything to blind chance and just do what my wits might suggest as each crisis arose. Sarita was ahead, and, as I knew, in danger; and to Sarita I would go, let the peril be what it might, and come from either Government men or Carlists.

"Have you formed any plans, senor?" asked Cabrera, in his strong, deep voice, as we rode side by side. Garcia was riding some hundred yards ahead at my suggestion, to warn us of trouble should any threaten us, and we could only make out his form indistinctly in the evening gloom.

"How can we plan till we know what is happening with our friends? If all is well, we must carry on the fight; if all ill, we can only scatter and hide. A child can plan so far, and the wisest of us no farther. I am very anxious."

"You are right. Things have gone badly. Instead of the simultaneous risings, the Government have got their hands in first, and have dealt us a heavy blow," he answered, rather dismally.

"How came you to let the young Pretender escape? I saw you carry him off, with rare cleverness; and when you drove away with him I believed the day was won for Spain."

174

"In the devil's name I don't know how it was done," he answered, with genuine feeling. "For my part, I am shamed. I know only that once, when the carriage stopped, I saw a horseman and a riderless horse closing in on us, and got down to learn the cause, fearing trouble. It must have been the devil himself, I think, in the flesh, and hell organised a miracle to save the Pretender. The horseman rode me down—me, Juan Cabrera—and stretched me senseless on the road before I had a thought of his intention, and when I came to, the thing had happened. How many men there were with him, I know not—Garcia, who came running up at the close, swears that there was never more than one—but it can't be true. If ever we meet—and I should know him again in twenty thousand men—and there is an ounce of strength left in my arm, I'll use it to plunge a knife into the heart of the man who dealt that blow at me and Spain."

"Good. You were ever a man prompt to action, Cabrera; and you must have been bewitched." This touched his superstition, however.

"The Holy Saints forefend," he said, hurriedly, crossing himself. "But I believe it truth that he was no man, but the devil in the shape of a man. And, mark you, senor," he cried, eagerly, "what else could it be but wizards' work? Didn't Correja's horse fall and stun him at the very moment of all others when this could have happened? Aye, and what but the devil could send Garcia's horse galloping off at the same moment? But I'll never cease to search for him, and if I don't find him on earth I'll wait till I get to purgatory, and bribe the devil with gift of my soul to point him out to me. The curse of all hell upon him!" And then, somewhat incongruously, he crossed himself again, as though to give additional power to his curse.

"Aye, the Fates have been against us," said I: and not caring to push the subject further, and feeling profoundly thankful that his power to recognise me had fallen so far short of his most vindictive desire, I urged my horse to a canter, and we rode on in silence. But his talk made me feel how peril was here always close at my very elbow.

Presently the moon rose, and the brilliant, streaming light flooded the whole landscape until it was as bright as day. The road was fast getting rougher and more hilly; the country wilder and more rugged; and the mountains lay to our left, the peaks towering up to great heights, majestic and grand in the bathing moonlight. The air was solemnly still; only the sounds of our horses' feet, the creaking of the saddle leather, and the musical jingle jangle of the bits breaking the silence.

"We have covered many more than old Tomaso's ten miles, and

should be safe," I said once, as we were walking our horses up one of the steep, short hills which now checked our progress constantly; but the words were scarcely out of my lips when Cabrera laid his hand on my bridle arm and checked his horse.

"Halt, senor. I hear Garcia coming back;" and a moment later his figure and that of another horseman were silhouetted on the top of the hill, and they came down to us at a sharp trot.

"There is danger ahead, senor," cried Garcia, as he rode up. "Andreas has come back to meet and warn us. The soldiers are out in some force between here and Daroca. Young Juan has taken the senorita to a hiding-place until the road is clearer, and Andreas here will guide us by another way."

"Tell me all you know, Andreas," I said to the lad, a sharp, bright-looking fellow of about eighteen or twenty.

"All went well till we were some five miles from Daroca, senor. I was keeping to the main road, not expecting any interruption, when I heard from a friend, who had driven out from the town, that he had passed a number of mounted soldiers, on patrol work, and he believed that all the ways into the town were guarded."

"Did you yourself see any soldiers?"

"Not then, but soon afterwards, senor. I climbed a tree on one of the hillsides, and could make out several parties of them. Perhaps eight or ten soldiers, or a dozen may be, in each."

"Were any riding this way, or were they merely stationary?"

"Riding this way, senor, not fast, just patrol pace; and I saw them stop one or two peasant folk and question them."

"And then?"

"I saw I could not bring the senorita into the town, senor, and thought the best thing to do was to take her to a safe hiding-place and then ride back, as my grandfather told me."

The news set me thinking fast. It was ugly enough from the Carlist point of view, but it promised to prove a perfect Godsend to me. I should catch Sarita before she could get to Daroca and join the rest of her Carlist friends.

"Where is the hiding-place?" I asked next.

"It lies about a league from the main road, senor. The house of the farmer Calvarro; you will know him, senors," he said to my companions, who nodded.

"Very shrewdly chosen," declared Cabrera, readily.

"And very cleverly acted altogether, my lad," I added. "Can you bring us by a safe path to the house, and afterwards guide us into the town?"

"I can bring you to the house, senor; but I doubt getting into Daroca. That depends upon the soldiers' vigilance. I can try."

176

"Forward, then," I cried, eager to get to Sarita.

"It is a very difficult path—a mere mountain track in places—and we must go cautiously and slowly; but it is the only one," said the lad. He trotted back to the foot of the hill, where he put his horse at a low gate, and led us at a smart gallop—he could ride like a centaur, and his horse seemed as fearless as he was—across two or three fields, and away up the hill by the side of some vineyards; behind a wood, where the shadows were as dark as night, and the path absolutely indistinguishable.

"This is ominous news, Cabrera," I said, when the pace slackened.

"About the worst it could be," he answered, gloomily.

"I read it that Rubio has set the telegraph to work, having learnt, or guessed, that we were making for Daroca. And this is the reception prepared for us."

"True; but what are all these soldiers doing round Daroca? It means more than you fear, senor. They are going to strike, and strike hard at our very heart. If the headquarters in Daroca are seized, what hope is there for the cause?"

"We cannot tell yet. It may not be so bad as that. The cause is the cause of righteousness, and must succeed. We must wait."

"Wait, aye, it is always wait, till one's stomach sickens and pines on the diet," he cried, bitterly. "We must get into Daroca before the night's many hours older, let the soldiers swarm where they please."

"My intention is this—to go to this Calvarro's house, join the senorita, and either make a dash for the town with her, or send in on the chance of help getting out to us."

"One plan is as good as another, I fear. The Fates are fighting against us, senor; and when that's so, the best is no better than the worst, and the worst no worse than the best," he replied, growing more and more despondent as matters grew more threatening. That is ever the way with fatalists.

"These Fates have a human shape and a name well known in Spain, Cabrera—the name of Sebastian Quesada. It is his brain, and not fate, that is engineering the destruction of the cause."

"Then why wasn't he dealt with? Are there no arms strong to strike, no blades sharp to pierce, no wit cunning to find the means, no courage ready to give life for life? By the Holy Virgin, are we all cowards? Had I had my way, the young Pretender had never escaped! This comes of woman's work and silly fears and sickly sentiment. What is his life, or Quesada's, or of any one of them, more than that of the meanest of us? My arm, aye, and my life, too, could have been had for the asking. As if you could drive the wild beast of revolution with a silken thread; with your senorita here,

177

and your senorita there! And now, the force we were afraid to use is to be turned to crush us."

"Will railing at what hasn't been done help us to think of what we have to do?" I asked, sternly. "What sort of courage or wit is that which finds its tongue when the hour to act has passed? If those are your thoughts about the senorita, who has risked her liberty and her life to rush now into the thickest of the danger when peril is at its height, go back and save your skin. There is still time to fly; but don't plague us and pollute the air with your doleful cries."

"Good," cried Garcia, who had listened to us in silence. "That crack on your head, Cabrera, has knocked the wit out of you. What is it but the act of a jackass to bray in the face of danger?"

"By the God that made me, I am a fool and have fallen low to be the butt of your clumsy wit, Garcia, and, the Holy Saints help me, to deserve your gibes and have no answer. Senor, I beg your forgiveness; and if I grumble again, put a bullet in my head and I'll say it serves me right. The senorita, the Virgin bless her lovely face, shan't lack help while I can give it. But I'm the better for my growl."

We rode forward again then, the ground offering a little better going; and when we had to walk the horses next, I called the lad Andreas to my side and questioned him more closely as to what he had seen and heard of the doings in Daroca, and about our chance of getting into the town from the farm where he had left Sarita.

"I forgot to tell you, senor, that I hinted to Juan that if the senorita would let him leave her, he should try and make his way into Daroca—no one would suspect him—and find out how things were going there and return to Calvarro's with his report."

"You are a clever, farseeing lad;" and I gave him a liberal reward for his wit. "Now think, is there no way by which we could possibly steal into the town? It is most urgent."

"There is but one possible way, senor, and it is right on the other side of Daroca from Calvarro's. We should have to make a wide circuit over the shoulder of the hills to the north through the thick olive woods there. I know the route, but even on horseback it would take some hours to cover it."

"Still, at the worst it could be done?"

"Yes, at the worst, senor."

"And how long, think you, could anyone lie concealed at Calvarro's?"

"I can scarcely say, senor. It must depend upon how wide the soldiers push out their search parties, and how well those who guide them know the country. But they would have difficulty in finding anyone in Daroca to act as guide; and without a guide the soldiers themselves might pass and repass the place without suspicion."

"Even in daylight?"

"Yes, even in daylight, senor."

"And you think we shall find no soldiers between here and there?"

"I believe there is no chance of it—but Senor Cabrera knows the place and can answer that as well as I."

"Good, push on then with all possible haste," I said, and dropping back to Cabrera I told him that I had made a change in my plan.

"Andreas tells me it is still possible to get into and out of Daroca without being seen, and what I think should be done is this: Send one of the lads by the quickest way into the town to warn our friends and to prepare a party to come to us; and you, or perhaps better, both you and Garcia, go with the other lad to meet them by the longer way, and bring them to us at Calvarro's. We can make the place our headquarters for the time."

"I think you're forgetting one thing, senor," he replied, with a grim smile. "If there's a means of getting into Daroca, the senorita won't stop at Calvarro's, but will insist on going herself. Indeed, I shall be more than a little surprised if we find she hasn't gone before we reach Calvarro's at all."

Knowing Sarita as I did, I felt the truth of this.

"We will see," I said; and as our young guide again hurried us forward then I said no more. The way was more open for a mile or two now, and we rattled forward at a sharp trot in single file. Then came another steep climb up the shoulder of the mountain and down on the other side, both so steep that we had to dismount and lead our horses, and at the bottom I was told we were within a mile of our destination.

Instinctively then we rode in dead silence, keeping to cover for every possible yard of the way, Andreas leading some little distance ahead.

Suddenly we saw him halt, turn in the saddle, hold up a hand to warn us, and then slip from his horse and lead him right under the shadow of some olive trees. We followed his example, and a minute later he came back on foot.

"Soldiers, on the road down there," he whispered, pointing ahead of us. "We have to cross the road and must wait. You may leave your horse, senor, he is trained like the rest, and will stand for hours if need be. We can creep forward and watch them."

He and I went forward then, and he led me to a point from which, ourselves unseen, we could see the road below.

"How came they here?" I whispered, "so close to Calvarro's?"

"I don't understand it; but they are not on the direct road there; merely patrolling, I think, on chance."

"I can see five," I whispered; "how many do you make out?"

"There are seven horses, senor."

"By heaven! you're right. Two must be scouting on foot. And there go two more."

The party had halted, and, as I spoke, two of the men left the rest, and, clambering over a gate on the other side of the road, were soon out of sight among the shadows of a grove of trees. The rest dismounted then, and, holding their horses, lighted cigarettes and stood chatting together.

"Can you hear what they're saying, Andreas?"

"No, senor; but we ought to know where they're going. I can get close down to them, if you wish, and may be able to hear their plans."

"Yes, go, but for God's sake be careful; our lives or theirs may turn on what you do."

Without a word he slipped away from my side, and with the silence and adroitness of a trained Indian scout he vanished, leaving me a prey to deep anxiety.

I watched the soldiers in the road below in a fever of suspense for any sign that they suspected his presence; but they gave none. The voices reached me in an indistinguishable murmur, broken by an occasional laugh and an oath in a louder tone. Now and then the horses moved and the accoutrements rattled and jingled; and once or twice a match was struck as some one or other of the men lighted a fresh cigarette.

This suspense continued for several minutes, and presently two of the soldiers who had been away returned, and were greeted with eager questions by their comrades.

Then a new fear alarmed me: that scouts would be sent up to where we lay concealed; and a confused medley of thoughts of how we should act in such a case and of the possible consequences rushed into my head, increasing my anxiety and alarm a thousandfold.

It was the fear of neither capture nor death that stirred my pulses so keenly. We were strong enough, having the advantage of surprise, to more than cope with so small a party. But if the tussle came and any of the men were killed, as they were sure to be, the consequences to Sarita and myself would be incalculably compromising. If I was to have help from the Palace, I must be able to ask for it with clean hands; and if I were known to have taken part in a fight with the soldiery in which lives were lost, my hope of help would be gone.

Moreover, my own feeling was one of unutterable aversion from shedding blood, or sanctioning it to be shed. Whatever excuse the Carlists might have in their own minds for violence, I had none. I was not one of them, except by the accident of this association for Sarita's sake; and for me to raise my hand to take a man's life in such a case would be murder and nothing short of it.

Many thoughts of this kind beat themselves into my brain in the terrible minutes that followed the return of the two scouts, until I was tempted to go back to my companions and at all hazards order a retreat and find some other plan of getting to Calvarro's farm and to Sarita. Had Andreas been by my side at the moment, I should have done it, but without him we were powerless; and to leave him behind would have been an act of treachery and cowardice as well as folly.

Those minutes of suspense were wellnigh equal in intensity to a death agony.

CHAPTER XXV

AT CALVARRO'S

The tension of suspense was broken at length. I caught sight of the figures of the second couple of scouts on their return as they crossed a patch of moonlight at a little distance, and almost at the same moment a hand was laid on my shoulder, and the lad Andreas stood at my side. He came as silently as a shadow out of the darkness.

"We must fly, senor, there is danger," he whispered. "They will send out other scouts in this direction as soon as the last return. But I can trick them."

We hurried back to our companions, and Andreas, holding his horse's bridle, led the way. I told the other two to follow, and myself brought up the rear, glancing back now and again in great anxiety lest the soldiers should catch sight of us. But the lad knew his business, and a sharp turn up the hillside to the right brought us under the cover of a wood, and gave us an effective hiding-place.

We followed him in silence, and even the horses seemed to share a sense of the danger, so warily did they move. They were indeed, as Andreas had said, perfectly trained animals; and to that training we owed our safety that night.

When we had walked on this way some few hundred yards up the hill, our guide found a track into the wood, and along this we went, the darkness deepening with every step, until it was impenetrable. We were some hundred yards from the entrance, when Andreas stopped so suddenly that we ran one against the other in a confused muddle of men and horses.

"There is a small clearing here on the right," he said in a whisper. "If you leave your horses free they will follow mine." And so it proved; the intelligent beasts knew his voice, and went after him with a sagacity that astonished and delighted me. "You will be safe here, I think, senor; and, with your permission, I will go back and find out the soldiers' movements. There is no risk for me. But please do not touch the horses; they will not be got to move without trouble until I return, and will stand like statues until I tell them; and, remember, voices travel far in such a still air—even whispers."

I told him to go, and then we three stood together and waited.

"What are we to do if they find us, senor?" asked Cabrera.

"Fight," I said, praying fervently there would be no need.

"Good. Knives, Garcia," he returned.

"And till then, silence," I ordered: and not another word was spoken.

The stillness was absolute, and, in the circumstances, awe-inspiring, and there was not a breath of air to stir even a leaf. It was some minutes before our eyes grew sufficiently accustomed to the darkness to discern the moonlight beyond the wood, which gleamed dimly, much like a phosphorescent light, through the thickly-planted trees. Suddenly the stillness was broken by a man's voice laughing and oathing, as he called to a comrade. We all three started and drew together at the sudden sound, so keen was the nerve tension.

"Had enough of this tomfoolery yet, Juan? Seen anything—where there's nothing to see?"

"By the corpse of St. Peter, this is a madman's freak, looking for nothing. I go no further, José," was the reply. "Have you been in the wood?"

"Yes; all the wood I'm going into. We're looking for houses, not men; and shan't find 'em there. Wait while I roll a cigarette, and, when I've smoked it, we'll go back and report," and we heard him strike a match and light it.

"Here, José, here's a path into the cursed darkness," called his comrade, and we heard the twigs snapping underneath his feet as he blundered about in the undergrowth.

"Let it stop," growled the other man. "It might be the pit of hell, without the fire to guide us."

"Holy Saints. I've got an idea. Suppose we set light to the cursed place, and then swear we saw someone in it, and fire our guns and bring up the others. It would be a mighty blaze, and we might get a step for our vigilance," and the scoundrel laughed and swore in unholy glee.

"Hold your tongue, idiot," said his companion, roughly. "If you want to see what's in the wood come with me along the path here;" and to our consternation we heard him coming towards us.

"Knives, Garcia," whispered Cabrera, and I felt them both loosen the knives they carried concealed in their girdles. The faint shadow of one of the men showed between us and the moon gleams, and the sound of crackling twigs came ominously nearer.

"The blight of hell on the place," cried the same voice suddenly, with a sound of heavy plunging among the shrubs, and the thud of a falling body. "What in the devil's name was that?"

His comrade laughed.

"Going to swim through, José? What are you doing on your belly like that?"

"I tripped over some infernal animal, or stump, or something, and struck my head against a tree, you fool."

"Serves you right for not looking where you are going. Put your eyes in your boots, you can't see else. Here, wait while I strike a light, blockhead;" and he lit a match and bent down over his fallen companion.

"Shall we rush on them now?" asked Garcia, trembling with excitement.

"No, no, wait," I said, laying a detaining hand on him.

"Why you're bleeding, José, man. Fine figure you'll cut on parade, with a black eye and a bloody nose. José Balso, promoted sergeant for gallantry in a wood; scouting for nothing and finding it; fought an old olive tree and fell covered with wounds. Here, come out of this, man; I'm going back. I've had enough of this foolery;" and without more ado he went, and we heard his footsteps die away in the distance. His comrade, growling and swearing and abusing him, stumbled to his feet and went after him, staggering about in the darkness as he tried to follow the sound of the other man's calls.

By the lucky chance of his fall we escaped, and I knew peace of mind once more. The men did not stay by the wood, and after a minute or so we heard no more of them; and Andreas came back to tell us they had rejoined the rest of the men, and all had mounted and ridden away on the road back to Daroca.

I told him of the narrow escape we had had from discovery and then he surprised us.

"I did it, senor. I was there when they entered the wood, and I got in his way in the dark and tripped him up when he was getting dangerously close."

"By heavens, but you are as brave as you are sharp, Andreas," I said, enthusiastically, giving him my hand. "And now for Calvarro's."

We continued our journey, riding with the greatest caution, and nothing occurred to interrupt us again. But the unexpected meeting with the soldiers had rendered me profoundly uneasy, and very doubtful of the safety of the place. This evidence that they were patrolling and scouting in the immediate vicinity of Calvarro's farm was very disquieting; and even the indifferent way in which the soldiers were doing the work did not reassure me.

I read in it more than mere chance work; for it looked much more likely that they were acting upon information that some good hiding-places for the Carlists were in the neighbourhood. The remark of one of the pair—"We're looking for houses, not men"— had ominous significance in this respect. They were not merely patrolling the roads in search of me and my two companions in response to messages sent by Rubio from Calatayud, for in that case they would merely have watched the roads and by-paths. They appeared to be one of a thoroughly organised system of search parties sent out to scour the whole country side, to find all the possible hiding-places and farms in the district where any Carlist refugees could possibly be hidden. And if this were so, it seemed to me so improbable as to be virtually impossible for Sarita's hiding-place to remain long undiscovered.

And this brought me once more face to face with a host of disturbing perplexities as to her and my future action. To remain at a place which the soldiers were likely to find was to plunge her into the almost certain danger of arrest; while to leave it in the attempt to steal into Daroca would, if the attempt were successful, bring me into still more imminent peril at the hands of the Carlists who would, unless a miracle chanced, discover my fraud. The dilemma baffled me.

I called Andreas to my side and explained to him fully my doubts in regard to the soldiers' movements, and I found then that to some extent he shared them, as did also Cabrera. But the latter had a plan of his own ready, founded on what I had said previously.

"If we are not to run like rabbits all over the country side and be caught or shot in couples, we must rally and make a stand somewhere, senor. Why not at Calvarro's? The house could be held for a long time, if we can only get a handful of men to it. I own I don't like these soldiers everywhere. It looks to me as if the blow had fallen at Daroca, and we were too late to do anything there. But we are men, I hope, and can fight and die, if need be, like men. For my part I'd rather find a lodging for a bullet in my body than have my whole body lodged in a gaol to rot there until the cursed Government chose to turn merciful and let me out. To hell with their mercy, say I. Give me the word and let me take my chance of getting into Daroca with a message from you to bring help to Calvarro's, and I'll do it and be back before the soldiers can find the place, or finding it, can smoke you out of it."

"Your life would——"

"I'll chance my life," he burst in, impatiently. "I beg your pardon, senor; but there are, or were, plenty in Daroca who are of my mind, and would a thousand times rather fight than go on manifestoeing and scheming and fooling the time and the opportunity away. For the Holy Virgin's sake let some of us do something like men. One good rally, and who knows but the fire will be kindled that will rage all over Spain? It will be the beacon which thousands of eyes are asking to see and thousands of hearts will welcome."

"I'm with Cabrera, senor," said Garcia. "Let us go to the town and bring out our friends. If we fail, well, we fail—but we shall at least have tried, while now——" and he shrugged his shoulders and ended with a sneer: "We might be children or Government men."

Had I been one of them in reality, the plan was just what I would have welcomed; but as it was, I could not counsel it and give my voice for fighting.

"No, not yet. We must wait and hear first, if we can, from Juan how things have gone in Daroca."

"Aye, aye, wait, wait, always wait, till the soldiers have time to get their firing platoons in position, and we can be shot like worn-out mules instead of fighting like men," growled Cabrera, gloomily; and he and Garcia turned to grumble in sympathy, while I rode on.

When we were quite close to Calvarro's—a place that lay indeed most marvellously concealed—and were approaching the farm by a path cunningly masked through a dense olive wood, a lad sprang out of the undergrowth and called to Andreas.

"Juan is here, senor," he said; and the boy, some two years younger than his brother and much resembling him, came to me. "Tell the senor the news in Daroca, Juan."

"It is of the worst, senor. Soon after midday the soldiers began to pour into the town from Saragossa, and special train after special train came loaded with them. They are everywhere; every house in

185

the town has been searched; and they tell me hundreds of prisoners have been hurried away by train to Saragossa. Every road into the town is alive with soldiers, and search parties are spreading out everywhere in all directions. The house of every suspected person is in the hands of the soldiers or the police; and everywhere I heard stories of arms, papers, and property which have been seized."

"We are too late," exclaimed Cabrera. "The only chance will be to rally here, senor. It must be."

"Where is the senorita?" I asked the lad, unable to restrain my anxiety any longer; and I felt that the eagerness in my voice was very patent. When he told me, to my infinite relief, that she was in the house, a fervent "God be thanked for that!" burst from me, and turning I found Cabrera's eyes fixed upon me searchingly.

"So that's it," he growled, half under his breath, and he and Garcia whispered for a moment together. "Your pardon, senor," he said aloud to me, and waved the boys out of hearing. "Stand back a bit, lads. The senorita is much to us all, senor, but the cause is more than any one of us—more than even her safety. Our master first, ourselves after, is the rule; and in this crisis, the cause before all else. We must make the rally here, or all will be lost—so Garcia and I are agreed—and that cannot be."

"Do you think there's a chance of holding a place like this against half-a-dozen regiments? Are you mad? Why the place would be tumbling about our ears in half-an-hour, and every soul inside would be either captured or killed."

"And how could we die better? Your pardon if I speak bluntly and my words offend you, but anyone whose motive is what yours is may be forgiven if his judgment goes astray. A man with his heart in a woman's heart makes an ill counsellor. You are right in your way to think first of the safety of the woman you love; but this is no woman's matter. The thought of the senorita in peril of her life robs you of the power to think freely—we are all like that at such a time; but I for one can't let it influence me now. I'm going to the town, and Garcia with me; and, with the Virgin's help, we'll rally enough to make a stand here. And if you're afraid for her, get her away before we return."

I liked him for his blunt outspokenness, and felt like a traitor as I gripped his hand and wrung it.

"You have heard Juan's news, and you go on a hopeless quest, friend. I cannot leave the senorita."

"Get her away before we're back—if you can, that is; for, like you, I'd sooner she was out of such a scene as, please the Saints, shall make the name of Calvarro's farm ring through Spain; aye, and that before morning breaks, maybe."

"I fear the soldiers will be here before you can return," I said, eager to get them both gone, and yet loth to lose their help in case of need. In fact I was so distracted by my double set of anxieties I scarcely knew what to say or do.

"That must be your risk and hers, senor. Save her if you can; but if you can't, then God's will be done."

"I would rather you stayed in case of need," I said then, weakly.

"So that we three and the senorita be caught like rats in a trap;" and he smiled at my weakness. "No, no, if the soldiers get here before we are strong enough in numbers to hold the place, the fewer they find the better. Good-bye, senor, and the Saints protect you both. Here, Andreas," he called, and gave him his instructions, that one of the lads should lead him and Garcia the nearest and safest way to the town, and the other remain in readiness to give warning on his return if the soldiers came there; and having given me a final pressure of the hand he and Garcia rode off on their desperate business and were soon out of sight.

I gazed after them in a mood of almost desperate indecision; even then half-minded to call them back, risk everything, and bid them wait while I called out Sarita and joined them on the journey to the town. But the mood and the moment passed. I let them go. Their horses' footfalls died away in the distance; and swinging myself from the saddle, I followed Juan to the door of the house, on which he knocked, three times a soft double knock.

An old woman opened it, holding a candle over her head, and peering curiously and cautiously at me.

"Is all well, Juan?" she asked in a deep voice.

"All is well, Mother Calvarro," answered the boy.

"The senor is welcome," and she made way for me to enter.

"Shall I stop outside, senor?" asked the boy.

"And use your eyes like a lynx, my lad, and warn us instantly of anything you notice."

The old crone closed the door carefully after him, and then holding the candle near my face, she said:

"Counting all renegades, senor?"

"Lovers of Satan. By the Grace of God, Mother Calvarro," and I doffed my hat.

"By the Grace of God," she repeated, fervently. "And your name, senor?"

"Is my own, Mother. I would see the senorita at once," I said, putting a note of authority into my voice.

"She is broken by the ill-news that Juan brought. Truly a day of woe. The Holy Virgin save us and protect us all," and she raised her disengaged hand, sighed heavily, turned and shuffled slowly along

187

the narrow bare-walled passage, pausing at a door. "Shall I tell her of your coming?"

"Better not," I replied, and as she opened the door, I entered, my heart beating quickly.

It was a low farmhouse room, very barely furnished; wooden chairs and a bare wooden table on which stood a candle that flickered feebly in the gust of air caused by the opening door.

Near the window and against the wall was a long wooden bench with arms, and on this, her head bowed on her hands which rested on one of the hard wooden arms, was Sarita, crouching in an attitude of deep despondency.

She did not lift her head at my entrance, thinking no doubt it was the woman of the house.

CHAPTER XXVI

THE PLEA OF LOVE

The sight of Sarita crushed down in this way by the load of her hopeless trouble was the most sorrowful my eyes had ever beheld. Knowing as I did her great strength, her buoyant confidence, her intense pride, her indomitable courage, I could gauge the force of the blow that had cast her down, and the depth of the bitterness of this hour of suffering.

For a while I gazed at her, almost ashamed that I had thus broken in upon her. Then a world of intense sympathy welled up from my heart, an infinite remorse even that in a measure I had helped to strike her down by my rescue of the young King, and an overpowering desire to take some of the burden upon myself; and my love for her came to my rescue and prompted me how to act.

I went forward swiftly and knelt down by the settle.

"Sarita, it is I. Let me help you, my dearest;" and I put my arm about her. "I have come to help you, Sarita, with my life if need be."

At the sound of my voice and the touch of my hand she started violently, lifted her face, dry-eyed but all worn and white with pain, gazed at me a second, and then jumped to her feet, and seemed as if about to repudiate my proffered sympathy.

"Ferdinand!" Eyes and voice and face were full of intense

surprise; and as I rose quickly to my feet, she stepped back, and cried, "Why are you here?"

"I love you, my dearest; where else should I be but with you—now?" and I took her hands and held them firmly.

She tried to draw back, and would have struggled against her love, it seemed; but love and the woman in her would not be denied, and in this crisis of her sorrow she yielded to my will, and let me draw her to me.

Her head fell on my shoulder. For the moment at any rate the victory was mine, and I felt with a rare sense of delight that she was glad I had come to her, and that I was giving her strength in her weakness.

I did not attempt to speak. It was enough to have her once more in my arms, to feel that I was a comfort to her, that her love had triumphed overall else in that dread dreary time; and I waited while by slow degrees she battled with her emotion and fought her way back to self-strength.

Once in the long, sweet suspense of that battle she raised her head, looked at me and smiled—a sorrow-laden, anxious, wan smile—as if in deprecation of her own weakness and of her woman's need for aid and sympathy. Then her head sank again on my breast with a sigh of infinite content, such as might have slipped from the lips of a tired and overwrought child.

The sound was music in my ears, for it told me how for the moment at least my coming had eased her misery.

At length she began to stir again in my arms; not away from them, I thanked Heaven, but as though the sense of relieved happiness was passing, and the thoughts of trouble were gathering force again.

"I am shamed, Ferdinand," she murmured.

"I love you, sweetheart," was my whispered reply.

"How did you come here, and alone?" she asked next, after a pause, "You have caught me in my moment of weakness."

"I will tell you all presently," I said. "I have come to help you. Wait."

But her curiosity was rising as her composure returned.

"Tell me now."

"I knew you would be in trouble, dearest, and I followed you."

"But how did you find me?" and then a great and sudden change came over her. "What am I doing? I am mad," she cried in a quick tone of alarm; and drawing swiftly from my arms she stood, my hands still holding hers, and looked at me with fear in her face. "You must not stay here. You are in danger, Ferdinand. There are those coming here, will be here instantly may be, who will know you and—oh God, what shall we do? they will kill you."

The fear was for me, and had quickened her into active thought, as no fear for herself had done. I guessed her meaning instinctively, and allayed the fear.

"No, there is no danger. You mean the two men, Cabrera and Garcia. I came here with them, and Cabrera himself urged me, in his last words, to try and save you."

"But they—I can't understand. How could that be?" she cried, her face a mask of perplexity.

"Simply as I say. I recognised them, but they did not recognise me. I made myself known to them—as Ferdinand Carbonnell—in the train; we escaped from it together at Calatayud, and together we have ridden here. We were going to Daroca, when we heard that you were here, and that the roads were blocked with troops, and we came here."

"You were going to Daroca? Are you mad, too, Ferdinand?"

"Mad, if you will; or very sane, as I prefer. I was going to find you, Sarita. Do you think anything would have stopped me? I went where love called me."

"But nothing could have saved your being discovered—nothing—and your death would have been certain. This was rank madness."

"Had I not heard you were here, I should have been in Daroca at this minute, searching for you, Sarita."

Her hands tightened on mine, and her eyes were full of pain; but their light changed suddenly and grew radiant, and the soft colour streamed over her face.

"And you love me so well as that?" The question, the tone, the love in her eyes, the wondrous magic of her beauty, thrilled my every nerve and set my heart pulsing with passion; and for answer I drew her, now unresisting, to me, and pressed my lips to hers.

"You love me, dear one?" I whispered, passionately, like a child in my longing to hear an avowal from her lips. She seemed to read the thought, and, putting an arm on each shoulder, she looked up and smiled.

"Is this the garb of hate, Ferdinand?" she asked; then sighed and said gently, "If I do not love you, then am I really mad; and yet what is it but madness for us to talk of love? See! I kiss you of my own will—will, do I say?—of my own intense desire;" and reaching up she kissed me tenderly, half coyly; but growing suddenly bolder, closed her arms about my neck and pressed my face to hers, kissing me many times with feverish, passionate, intense fervour. "And if it be madness to love you, then, dearest, there was never so mad a

190

heart and brain as mine. You make me burn out all else in the world when you kindle the flame of this love of mine." She drew back again and looked at me. "And I thought and meant never to see you again. What a creature of feebleness this love makes me!"

"We will never part again, Sarita," I said, fervently.

"Ah, that is different, that is all different;" and she unlocked her arms and fell away a pace, but I caught her hands again and held them.

"We will never part again," I repeated earnestly. "You will let me save you. I can do it. I have come to do it."

"How can you save me? Can you save me from myself? Would you tear me from my duty? Do you know what has happened? Ah, Ferdinand, when you make me think of aught else but our love, you force into my mind the barriers that stand between us."

"There shall be no barriers that can keep me from you? Yes, I know much of what has happened. I know that by Quesada's treachery this whole movement, on which you have built so much and laboured so hard, has collapsed like a house of cards. I know that through some treachery he had learned how matters stood in Daroca, and that his iron hand has closed on the place, and every hope you could have had there is crushed and ruined. And I know, too, that your only hope—as it is the only hope of any one of those whom he has duped—lies in flight. It is not too late for that, Sarita. But it is the only hope."

"It is the hope I can never grasp. Ask me anything but that—anything but the cowardice of flight. If the people who have trusted and followed me are in this plight, can I leave them? Would you wish your secret heart to be ever whispering to you, 'Sarita was true to her love, but false to her courage, a traitor to her honour, a deserter of her friends in trouble'? Is that your ideal of the woman who would be worthy of your love? Would you do it were my case yours, and you had led these people into the slough of ruin? Would your ears be deaf to their cries from behind the prison bars—wives calling for their husbands, husbands for their wives, children for their parents—aye, and widows mourning for their dead?"

"This is not your work, Sarita; it is Quesada's doing."

"And should they say—ah, dearest, how it pains me now to say it!—'Sarita ruined us, and then fled—for what?—to marry the man who ruined all by thwarting the one means that could alone have saved everything; by saving the usurper whose tyrant agents have wrought this havoc'? Can you save me from that!"

"It is not you, but Quesada," I cried again. "I tell you, as I have told you again and again, all this was planned and in readiness. Do you think that this raid on Daroca, with all the special knowledge shown in it of the Carlist plans there, with all the wide and detailed arrangements for police and military movements, with its swift and dramatic action, was the work of a moment? And not in Daroca only, but in every centre where you were strong. In Saragossa, Alicante, right up the seaboard even to Barcelona, and inland to every spot where you were in strength, Sarita, listen to reason. You were but as a child in his strong, ruthless hands. It was his scheme to use you Carlists to get the King removed from his path, and then crush the life out of your whole Carlist movement, even as he is doing at this hour, that there might be none to stand between him and the power at which his ambition aimed. The plans were laid weeks and probably months ahead. His spies and agents have been everywhere, even in your midst, working, prying, scheming, and so getting together the information that has made this day's work possible."

"Then, if I have been the dupe, I must suffer the dupe's fate. I cannot fly. No, no, Ferdinand," she cried with reviving energy. "Let us face the full truth. Our love must be strong enough to bear the strain of truth. Between us there stand two bars: my duty to my friends, and—I must say it, dearest—your act in rescuing the young King. Even if it be true that Quesada has aimed all through at our destruction, how can that make your act less a betrayal of us Carlists? He was in our power, you took him from us; what question of Quesada's treachery can alter that fact, or wipe it away? Nothing. Nothing can alter it. Nothing could make me leave my people to be happy with you, with that fact between us. In truth, I am almost distracted when I think of it."

"Will not your love lead you to pardon me and forget it?"

"The woman in me throbs with desire to do so, but—I am a Carlist, too, dearest; and the Carlist in me can neither pardon nor forget. You break my heart by this pleading. Will you believe I can never alter, and speak no more of it? I do love you; the Holy Virgin knows that in my woman's heart there is no room for thought of another man but you. Dearest, ever to be dearest to me, you believe this?" and she again put her arms about me, and lifted her face to mine.

"I know it, Sarita," I answered, infinitely moved.

"Then you will know something of what I suffer in parting from you. Life would be so welcome, such sunshine, such glorious happiness for me by your side, that the shadows of the thought that it can never be chill and gloom and almost frighten me with their desolateness. But our love can never be more than a memory, my dearest; to be cherished as the one lovely thing of my life, the one consolation in my pain; but no more. You must leave me, and at once. There must be danger for you here, whatever happens. Whether my friends or my enemies come, there must be danger for you. Let me be able to think that at least to you I have not brought ruin. Go back to Madrid; you will be safe there, for you are great enough now, as an English peer, to be free from danger; and even if they try to arrest you, you have the Court to help you; the young King and the Queen. My ambition, my care, my patriotism, have been so fatal to those who have trusted me; let not my love be equally fatal. Leave me that one solace. Go, Ferdinand; go and leave me. I beg of you, I implore you by the love you have for me."

"You must not ask that, Sarita."

"I do ask; nay, I will not have it otherwise. It must not be. You shall not stay here. The thought of what would happen if my friends came back and knew you were not of us, drives me mad. You must go. Ferdinand, dearest, you must."

"I do not fear your friends, Sarita; they will not harm me. I am Ferdinand Carbonnell, and known already to some of them as the Carlist leader; and the Carlist leader I will be to the end. You cannot come with me, you say; you cannot desert your friends. As you will. Then I stay with you, and become one of you. To me the world is nothing without you. You tell me I have lost you because of what I did against you in taking the young King away. So be it. I will win you back again by what I can do for your cause."

"No, no; it is impossible. It is madness. You are not of us, and must not do this."

"I will do no less, Sarita. Cabrera and Garcia have gone to the town in the desperate hope of getting together a sufficient number of comrades to return and make a last stand here for your cause. I urged them against the attempt; but I am glad of it now. It will give me the chance I need; and, my word on it, they shall not find me less staunch than the rest of you. God knows your cause never stood in direr need of recruits than now; and I'll be one."

"You are cruel. You will kill me," she cried; and urged me with entreating and fervent prayers to alter my decision, and make my escape; but I would not yield.

"If you will go with me, I will go; but if you stay, I stay," I said again and again. From that I would not be moved; and she was protesting, urging, and entreating, and I refusing, when someone knocked hurriedly at the door, and the lad Juan rushed in, followed closely by the old woman.

"A party of soldiers have found the house, senor. They are coming to surround it. There is yet a moment to fly, if you will come at once," he cried, excitedly.

"The senor will fly, Juan. You can get him away. You must go instantly," exclaimed Sarita.

"You will come with me. I will go then."

She looked at me earnestly and imploringly.

"For the Holy Mother's sake, save yourself," she cried, in a voice of pain.

"If you will come, yes. If you will not come, no. Where you are, I stay, Sarita."

The old woman and the lad stood staring at us in dismay.

"Come, senor, come," he said.

"We are not going, Juan," I answered, quietly; and Sarita put her hands to her face distractedly, and then she cried again impulsively—

"Oh, you must go. You must go."

"Come, then," and, grasping her hand, I led her toward the door.

"Quick, senor, quick," said the boy again.

"Quick, Sarita," I repeated. "Every moment lost may be fatal."

"I will go. Yes, I will go. Quick, Mother Calvarro, my things;" and, smiling to me with every sign of agitation, she took them from the old woman's hand. "It is for your sake," she whispered, as we hurried out into the passage.

But the chance was lost. We had delayed too long. Outside, the sound of horses' feet, the clang of arms, and the jingle of bits, told us the soldiers were there at the door already, and a strong voice uttered a word of command.

"This way, senor, by the back," cried Juan; and he darted down the passage, and opened the door. But as he did so we heard a man's gruff voice, followed by a heavy step, as a soldier entered. At the same moment a loud knock, as from the butt end of a musket, sounded on the front door, and a stern voice demanded admittance.

"It is too late, Sarita," I said, quietly. "We will wait for them in the room there;" and I led her back.

CHAPTER XXVII

SARITA HEARS THE TRUTH

Sarita went to her old place on the settle, where I had found her so disconsolate on my arrival, and I stood nearer the door, which purposely I left ajar that I might hear what passed. She was pale, but quite calm, and her only sign of agitation was when she whispered to me, with a gesture of regret—

"You should have gone, Ferdinand. I have brought this upon you."

"Nothing has happened yet. They may not know us," I said, in reply; and was in the act of whispering a further word of reassurance, when I stopped and started, held silent by surprise at recognising the voice of the questioning soldier.

"Is this Calvarro's farm?"

Sarita recognised it too, and with a quick catch of alarm she said—

"It is Colonel Livenza, Ferdinand. You are lost. Holy Mother have pity on us! how can he have come here?"

"More treachery probably, somewhere," I replied, with an inward curse at the mischance; but then a thought occurred to me. There was a cupboard close to the door, and whispering hurriedly to Sarita, "Not a word to him of me; I believe I can save us;" I went into it, and closed the door upon myself.

Meanwhile the colloquy at the front door was proceeding.

"Yes, senor, I am the Mother Calvarro. Does your Excellency want provisions for your men, or forage for the horses?"

"No. I want the Carlists you have hidden in the house here."

"Carlists? I don't understand your Excellency. We are no Carlists here, but simple farming folk, and for the King, God bless him," said the old crone.

"Aye, King. I know your jargon. Which King? You're near enough to the grave, I should have thought, to speak the truth," answered the bully, roughly.

"Your Excellency can speak freely. I am an old woman, and have none to protect me here," was the retort, quietly spoken.

"My men will search the house; and look you, it will pay you best to help, not hinder us."

"I am too old either to help or hinder. Do your will."

"Who is in your house? Answer plainly, and with no more sneering," he said, in a truculent voice.

"The house is small to search; and there is none to resist."

"Well, no matter; I'll soon know;" and, giving some order which I could not catch, he came along the passage, and, pushing the door wide open, entered. "Ah, it is true, and you are here, Sarita. I could scarcely believe it true. Who else is in the house?"

"For one there is a swaggering bully of old women, and his name is Colonel Juan Livenza," answered Sarita, scornfully. "Another is the good woman of the house whom you found it so easy and safe to insult."

"Thank you for that," he cried, stung to anger. "And I'll show my gratitude by taking good care of all we find here."

"Like the gallant gentleman and King's officer that you are."

"I won't let your gibes anger me," he said. "It is for you I came; and I must speak with you. I have come in friendship."

"I have no wish to speak with you. I am ready to go at once. I can be your prisoner, but not your friend; the saints forbid that!" she cried, with intense bitterness. And I saw the purpose in a flash. To get him and his men away with her so that I might escape. And I blessed her for the thought, even while I resolved to frustrate it. I had another plan, and all unwittingly Livenza helped me.

"I intend to speak to you and have an understanding, and we can have it here without fear of interruption," he said.

"You were ever a chivalrous gentleman," she retorted, trying hard to goad him to anger.

But he paid no heed to the sneer, and, going to the door, called up one of his men and ordered him to keep the house surrounded, but not to disturb him. Then he closed the door, locked it, and put the key in his pocket, and, feeling secure, said, "Now we can talk, Sarita, without any to overhear us."

"A very prudent precaution, Colonel Livenza, and one for which I am infinitely obliged to you," I said quietly, as I pushed open the door of the cupboard and stepped out, revolver in hand.

The look of exultant triumph changed to one of craven fear, as he gave a violent start and stared at me, his lips livid, and his face white with the whiteness of death. He tried to answer, but for the moment could force no words, and his lips moved in a soundless question inspired by his overpowering dismay at my appearance.

Sarita gave me a look of reproach.

"Why did you do this?"

"That we three may talk without interruption," I answered, not taking my eyes from Livenza's face. "Without interruption," I repeated, meaningly and sternly. "Colonel Livenza knows me, and he knows that as he has the key of the door in his pocket there must be delay, even were he to summon his men; and that the minute of that delay would be his last on earth."

"I shall not call anyone," he said, his voice no longer jaunty and truculent, but hoarse, broken, and abject, the voice of a coward in deadly fear.

"I am glad to hear it. You will therefore show your confidence in me further by laying your weapon on the table."

"There is no need for that. I don't wish——"

"On the table, there," I said sternly, pointing to it.

"I have no objection," he declared, with a start at my stern tone; and with trembling fingers he drew his sword and laid it down, and then put his revolver by the side of it, and sighed.

"Hand the key of the door to Senorita Castelar," I bade him next, and without a murmur he obeyed. "Now we can talk without restraint," I said, and put his sword and revolver on a chair behind him. "Be good enough to answer my questions fully. How comes it you have found your way here to this out-of-the-way place at this precise moment?"

"I heard that this was a house where Carlists were likely——"

"Wait," I broke in, angrily. "Tell the truth, the full truth; no half lies and generalities and equivocations; and don't forget that I also know much—more than enough to test every word you say. If you lie, the interview ends—and the end will not be well for you. Now, answer my question."

"Sebastian Quesada's spies in Daroca found out that Senorita Castelar was here, and I came in search of her."

"That's better. Now, what secret arrangement has there been between you and Quesada affecting your relations with the senorita? Remember, I know it, but wish her to hear it from you." The question set him trembling in dire agitation, and for some moments he stood hesitating and perplexed, trying vainly to speak.

"What do you mean?" he muttered.

"Answer," I said, sternly. "And mind, the truth."

Again he wrestled with his feelings, and then in a low voice: "He knew of my passion for her, and—and thought that if she was to be arrested, I had best do it."

"You are lying, Colonel Livenza," I said.

"I am unarmed," he muttered, shifting his eyes uneasily.

"I, too, was unarmed once before your weapon; and afterwards you swore to tell me the truth. You know why. But if you mean that I am insulting an unarmed man, here, take your revolver;" and I put it on the table and pushed it toward him. "You lied, Colonel Livenza," I repeated.

The sweat broke out on his forehead in the intensity of the

strain. "I don't want it," he said, hoarsely and feebly, pushing it back to me. "I will say it. The senorita is to be my wife."

I put the pistol on the chair again; for the experiment had answered, as I knew it would.

"You mean that your marriage with Senorita Castelar was part of the price with which Quesada bought your help and silence?"

"If you put it so, yes," he murmured.

"This is infamous," cried Sarita.

"But it is not all. Wait, please," I said to her; then again to him—

"In regard to the Carlist plot for abducting the King, what part did he give you to play?"

"I was the intermediary between him and the Carlists. Sarita knows this," and he looked across to her.

"Be good enough to answer me, and not to speak to Senorita Castelar, nor use her name. He promised you that she should be your wife. How was that to be, and what was to happen if the abduction plot had not failed and the Carlist movement had been successful?"

"It was not meant to succeed. His object was to get the young King away, the Monarchy overthrown, and at the same time to crush the Carlist risings as they are now being crushed. He then intended to set up a provisional Government, as a Republic, with himself at the head of it, and his own friends filling all the offices; and then to proclaim war with America, in order to consolidate all classes in favour of the Government."

"And you were to be——? what besides the senorita's husband."

"I was to be Minister of War."

"Spain has lost a brilliant servant, then, and you a portfolio and a wife, by the failure of the plot against the King. Of course, you were not fool enough to go so deep in without something more substantial than Quesada's word. You knew him too well for this. What proofs of his sincerity did he give you?"

He hesitated again, and showed once more the signs of extreme agitation, and at length answered in a tentative, doubtful tone—

"I had only his word; nothing could be written."

"What proofs had you?" I cried again, sternly. "Do you think I don't know what I am saying?"

"We discussed it frequently. I was in his confidence. I had no need of——"

"What proofs had you? I shall not ask you again."

"He gave me the provisional promise in a letter." The words seemed to be wrung from him like drops of blood, and when he had spoken he sighed heavily, and threw up his hands in despair.

"Where is that letter? You have it with you, for you know it would be safe nowhere else. Give it to me," and I held out my hand. I could read him now easily enough, and saw my guess was right.

"It is with my bankers, in my safe, at Madrid," he protested; but I paid no heed, and insisted, disregarding alike his protests, declarations, oaths, and entreaties, and at length made him give it me. He was carrying it sewn up in his clothes, and when I made him part with it, he was so unstrung that he could no longer stand upright, but sank helpless into a chair.

A glance at it showed me the prize I had secured, and the weapon it would be against Quesada, if only I could get it safe to Madrid and lay it before the King's eyes.

"I have nearly done with you," I said then. "And you have my word that I will keep the document safely, so that when the Republic is proclaimed you may claim your seat in the Ministry. But first tell us what arrangements were made, and when, for the suppression of the Carlist risings?"

"All has been in readiness for weeks past. For months, Government agents of all nationalities and classes, men and women alike, have been at work in all directions, and by every possible means worming out secret information. Many of the men who to-day are among the trusted leaders and supporters of Don Carlos are Government agents in Government pay; every movement planned and made, every council and thought almost, every act and speech, have been carried to Quesada, and actor and speaker alike listed, watched, shadowed, tested in a hundred subtle ways, and marked as either suspect or actual revolutionary. Never in the world was such a net devised, and never spread with subtler cunning or more implacable purpose. What chance could you have against such a man?" he cried, turning to Sarita. "Surely never before was such an iron strength, invincible will, fathomless depth, and consummate judgment found in a Spaniard. His spies were everywhere, in your most secret councils; he had your strength to a man; your secrets were his daily knowledge; and you only remained free to plot and plan because he knew that at a signal he could crush your whole revolution as I would pinch a fly between my fingers. A week ago every man was in his place ready to pounce the instant the signal was given; nay, the very prisons and cells were marked out to which the Carlists were to be taken; and in every town where the slightest trouble was anticipated, soldiers outnumbering you five to one were ready at hand. What more proof do you want than what has happened? He built his plans on the success of the abduction plot, and yet when it fails he is found stronger than ever."

"This is mere statement," cried Sarita, stung into the protest by the lingering refusal to believe she had been so duped.

"Proofs? The proofs are written all over Spain at this moment. Am I not here? Is not that a proof? Why was I at Daroca before you thought of coming? Why, except that he allowed you all to fool yourselves with the belief that your stronghold here was not known to the Government, and that you yourself would be sure to fly here when the trouble fell upon your friends at Madrid? But if you want proofs, they exist not by the hundred only, but by the thousand, in the orders given to every regiment of soldiers and every body of police. There is no hope for you, Sarita, but surrender. You cannot fight a man like Sebastian Quesada."

Then I saw the reason of his earnestness, which for the moment had puzzled me. He was bent upon getting her to renounce Carlism and upon filling her with hate of Quesada, that she might the more easily be pardoned and given to him as his wife. He could not have rendered me more effective aid, indeed, had I prompted him in every word he said. And then I went on to play the last card I had in reserve.

"You were in Quesada's confidence, you tell us, and it is plain that you were to some extent, for he was going to help you in winning a wife. Did he ever tell you his own intentions in regard to marriage?"

Sarita started and looked at me hurriedly, but I would not see the glance.

"They were nothing to me."

"You have told us how these Carlists were outmanoeuvred and duped by him; do you think there were no dupes among those nearer to him?" And I spoke with an emphasis that impressed him.

"What do you mean?"

"Do you know that he himself also thought of marrying a Carlist, one high in their councils, and that he made the price of his collusion in this abduction plot a pledge from her to marry him?"

I had not miscalculated the effect of the stroke. Poltroon as the fellow was in the abject regard for his life, he was a true Spaniard in his love and his hate; and the jealousy in his nature was a devil that could be roused easily. It put new strength into him now, and he sprang to his feet again and glared across the table at me with eyes of fire.

"Do you mean I was his dupe in this? By the living Cross if I thought that——"

"Ask the Senorita Castelar the name. She can tell you."

"Is this true, Sarita? Can you tell me?"

There was a pause of tense silence, and then she answered with slow deliberation:

"After what you have told us of his falseness, there is no reason why I should not say. I was to be his wife."

He stood glaring, at her like a man stiffened suddenly in the rigidity of death, save that his eyes glowed like coals; and for a full minute he seemed scarcely to breathe, so unnatural was his stillness. Then with a deep-drawn sigh which shook the whole frame till he trembled, and I thought would fall, he regained self-mastery.

"On your honour, and by the Holy Virgin, you swear that is true?" he said, in a tone ringing with suppressed passion until it sounded utterly unlike his own.

"I do not lie, Colonel Livenza. On my honour and by the Holy Virgin, I swear that that is the truth," replied Sarita, slowly and solemnly.

There was another pause, this time much longer, and then he seemed to force his agitation under control. And in the pause a thought flashed upon me. Sarita's solemn oath had meant Quesada's death-warrant as surely as though the warrant were in fact in existence and bore the sign manual of the King. He was a completely changed man when he next spoke with an altogether unnatural calm.

"Can I go now, Senor Carbonnell? I have work to do."

"And your men?"

"I shall withdraw them; the way is free to you. I would warn you to escape if you wish to go, for the soldiers are everywhere; and above all things avoid every Carlist haunt, for each of them is known. Sarita, we shall not meet again. Will you bid me good-bye?" and he went toward her as if expecting her to give him her hand; but not feeling quite sure of him, I stepped forward. Sarita said, in a cold hard tone:

"No. You are less than nothing to me, Colonel Livenza. I can have no kindly thought of, or for, a traitor like you. I hope we never shall meet again."

Believing what I did of his intention, and that if I was right, he was surely going to his death, I regretted her sternness.

"As you will. Some day, perhaps, you will think less harshly;" and without a word or a glance to me, he picked up his arms, and, while I unlocked the door, he sheathed his sword and thrust the revolver into the case he wore about his waist, and went out.

We heard him call to his men, and give them a sharp short command; the jingle of accoutrements as they mounted was followed by the sound of the horses' hoofs as they wheeled round and trotted away.

"What had we best do now, Ferdinand?" asked Sarita, when the sound had quite died away.

"You are convinced at last?"

"Don't," she cried, wincing in anguish. "I am so humiliated. To be set up for barter by these villains, and cheated and fooled. For the Holy Mother's sake don't let me think of it. Give me something to do. Take me somewhere, anywhere that I may try to forget my shame."

"By God's help that shall be to England, Sarita; and we will know no pause or stop till we are safe. We'll blunt the edge of this business by the excitement of the journey," I cried, little perceiving what the excitement would prove to be; and calling for Juan, I told him we would start at once, and that he must find us a way through the web which the soldiers had spread all round.

One precaution I took, due more to the fortunate accident that we had to wait a few minutes for the horses, than to any foresight of mine. I took the letter which Livenza had given me, and sealing it in an envelope which I obtained from Mother Calvarro, I addressed it to Mayhew at the British Embassy, with instructions to keep it with the papers I had previously entrusted to him.

Before we mounted I drew Juan aside.

"See, my lad, if anything happens to me and I get caught by the soldiers, I shall pass this envelope to you. You must guard it jealously, for it may mean life and liberty for hundreds of us; and take it to Madrid and place it in the hands of him to whom it is addressed, Mr. Mayhew, at the British Embassy. Here is money; and if you have to deliver the letter and do it safely, I will pay you very liberally." He gave me a faithful promise, and then I mounted.

"What were you saying to Juan?" asked Sarita.

"I was giving him some instructions in regard to our safety," I answered; not caring to start the fears of capture which were already present to my mind in disquieting force. With that we started.

CHAPTER XXVIII

HOW LUCK CAN CHANGE

As we left Calvarro's I rode with the utmost caution, for I felt by no means certain that Livenza, even in his changed mood, might not attempt some treachery. But I wronged him in that thought. He had cleared right away and had taken his men with him; and so soon as I was convinced of this, I drew rein and questioned Juan as to the possible roads that were open for us to take.

The position of Daroca made our difficulties vastly greater. The mountains were on three sides of us, and Juan admitted that he knew the passes very indifferently, while it was certain that the chief of them would be blocked with the soldiery. The one bit of open country was that by which I had ridden from Calatayud, and as that was also the country which our young guide knew well, I determined to go there.

From Calatayud I resolved to use the railway, not to Saragossa or Madrid but to work our way north through Old Castile and the Basque Provinces, and across the frontier to Bayonne; and I directed Juan therefore to make for Calatayud by the road I had travelled earlier in the night.

"Do you think you can hold out for a twenty-mile ride, Sarita?" I asked her, as I explained generally my plans.

"I could ride for five hundred if I could only get away from my racking thoughts," was her instant and vehement response; and with that I directed Juan to travel as fast as the ground and the condition of the horses would allow. I knew that a good remedy for her mental distress would be found in physical fatigue, and we rattled along therefore at a strapping pace and for a long time most part in silence. One caution I gave her.

"If you have any papers or anything on you which might cause you to be identified, you had better destroy them in case we are interfered with and you are searched. Until we are out of Spain I shall say you are my sister, and that we are leaving the country because of the troubled state of things."

"I have nothing. I came in this disguise," she answered, referring to the peasant's dress she wore. "Scarcely a convincing dress for Lord Glisfoyle's sister. But it doesn't matter. Nothing matters now," she added, with a sigh.

The truth of this reference to her incongruous dress became more apparent when the dawn broke and lightened. I had not given it a thought while we were at Calvarro's, nor while the darkness made the matter of costume a thing of no importance; but in the daylight it was altogether different. Still, as riding habits didn't grow on Spanish hills, there was nothing to do but to make the best of it, and get a change of dress at the first available opportunity. After all, there was that well-known excuse to fall back upon—the eccentricity of the English traveller.

I left Sarita almost entirely to her own thoughts, and for some hours we scarcely spoke to each other, until, as I had dismounted and was leading my horse up a hill by her side, she looked down and said with a smile:

"You are very good to me, Ferdinand, and very thoughtful for me. I cannot bear to speak much yet."

"That's all right. We shall have many years of chatter to make up for a few hours' silence," I answered, cheeringly. "I can guess pretty well how it is with you. Don't worry. Let's get out of this mess and we'll have all the more to talk about. What a young brick that Juan is. I don't know what we should have done without him. He'll pull us through yet," and it really began to look as though he would, for we were within a mile or two of Calatayud.

"And do I owe nothing to you?"

"We won't shout till we are out of the wood. But here we are at the top of the hill, and forward's the word again;" and soon after that we came in sight of Calatayud nestling down in the valley a good way below us, the smoke from a few early fires curling up lazily in the breezeless air.

"Thank God, there's the railway," I said, pointing to where a sinuous line of white steam marked the course of a train just leaving the station on its way to Madrid. Then I called Juan back. "I am not going to your grandfather's if I can help it, Juan. I have reason to know it will be dangerous. Is there a Royalist house in the place?"

"Yes, senor, there is Angostino's. But if there are any soldiers in the town they are sure to be there."

"All the more reason for them not to think I should go there, too. Now remember, the senorita and I are English people, brother and sister. I am Lord Glisfoyle"—and I made him repeat the name several times, and warned him to tell anyone who might question him that that was my name, and that I was an eccentric English nobleman. "You won't ride with us up to Angostino's, but as soon as we are close enough to the house to find our way, you'll take the horses—they might be recognised—and we shall walk there. And now I'm going to trust you. Take this letter and keep it. If you hear that I have been arrested, go as quickly as you can to Madrid and give it yourself to Mr. Mayhew, and tell him that I am arrested. But if I am not, then I shall want you to be ready to go on a journey with me later in the day or in the evening; I'll find means to let you know the time." He promised me, and when we came near enough to our destination Sarita and I dismounted, and he rode away with the horses.

"Now, Mercy—that's your name now, remember—for a bold face on things and no language but English; no character but that of eccentric English folk; and a prayer from the bottom of our hearts that my friend Rubio is not within a dozen miles of Angostino's. In that case we'll soon be at breakfast, and you'll soon be in bed—and the best place for you."

Scarcely anyone was astir in the narrow street, or in the inn itself, and swaggering in with the assurance of an irresponsible tourist, I asked for breakfast and a couple of rooms for myself and sister. I took care to put a good broad English accent into my Spanish, showed my money with vulgar ostentation, and made the most of my title.

Everything went smoothly. A single gold piece converted a sleepy serving maid from a wondering and contemptuous critic of Sarita's dress into an obsequious servant, who led her away at once.

"Don't be long, Mercy, for I am as hungry as the deuce," I called after her, loudly.

"All right," she cried in reply, in a most winsome accent that no English girl could have copied to save her life.

Then the landlord, having heard that a rich Englishman had arrived, came hurrying out to me with a mouthful of breakfast, a rich smell of garlic, and a whole person eloquent of a desire to do my bidding and earn my money; and a few minutes saw me in the only private sitting-room in the place, a guest of less importance having been promptly dispossessed in my honour. There is nothing like a combination of impudence, money, and a character for English eccentricity if you want your own way on the Continent. And I never wanted mine more badly in my life nor got it more promptly.

"You are a magician, Ferdinand," said Sarita, as we sat at breakfast.

"But you are not Spanish," I whispered, warningly; "and an English brother and sister don't carry their eccentricity so far as to talk in any language but their own, Mercy."

"Then we can talk very little," she replied, in English.

"Which is precisely how English brothers and sisters do behave," said I, with a laugh.

"What about clothes?" she asked in some little dismay.

"I'll see to that. After breakfast you must go to bed. I don't want anyone to see you for one thing and I do want you to get some sleep; and while you sleep, I'll work the oracle."

"You will what?" she asked, wrinkling her brow at my slang.

"I'll get hold of some clothes somehow, if I steal them;" and as soon as breakfast was over, I went out to forage.

Juan was right in one respect. What soldiers were in Calatayud were at the inn, and sticking to my principle of the value of impudence, I went up to the two officers who were in command of the party, bade them good-day, and asked them if they spoke English. One of them replied that he did.

"Good," I said, heartily, and offered him my hand and asked him to give me a cigarette. "I can speak Spanish a bit, but our English tongues don't seem to fit the words somehow. Let me introduce myself, for I want a little advice. I am Lord Glisfoyle, an Englishman, travelling with my sister, and we have just heard of the death of a relative in London, and have to get there quickly. Which is the best way to go? I mean, considering the mess and excitement of all this Carlist business. I was at Daroca, and wanted to get up to Saragossa by rail; but yesterday you gentlemen had taken possession of the line, and I'll be hanged if I could get tickets. So we rode over here and left our baggage there. Here is my card;" and, as if searching for one, I pulled out a roll of English bank notes, which impressed them as much as I desired. "I haven't one, I see; I must have left my card case when I changed, I expect. Anyhow, it doesn't matter."

The officer was as obliging as courtesy demanded he should be to a rich English nobleman in a difficulty, and very soon we three were discussing my route over a bottle of the best wine which Angostino could find in his cellar.

The Madrid route was suggested; but I said I had thought of the other, and then my two companions worked out the train service in that direction. After that was settled we went out together and strolled about the streets chatting and smoking; and in the course of an hour I had acquired a good deal of useful information about the doings and plans of the military; while on my side I took them to the telegraph office and let them see the telegrams I sent off to London and to Mayhew at the British Embassy in the name of Lord Glisfoyle.

That business completed, they went off to their military duties, and I found shops where I could get some clean linen for myself and a costume of a kind for Sarita, to whom, trading on Spanish ignorance of such things, I ordered them to be sent in the name of Lady Mercy Glisfoyle. Then I sauntered in the direction of old Tomaso's house, and finding Juan on the lookout for me, I told him to be at the station that afternoon at four o'clock, to watch me but not to speak to me; and to take a ticket for the station where we had to change into the train for the north.

Having done this good morning's work, I went back to the inn to have a couple of hours' sleep before leaving. I paid liberally and tipped royally, so that everyone about the place was sorry for my going. The two officers insisted upon accompanying us to the station to see me off; an attention which would have been very pleasant, had I not feared that he who spoke English might detect Sarita's accent; but I put a bold face on matters, and explained that my sister, Lady Mercy Glisfoyle, was very much fatigued, and had so bad an attack of neuralgia that she had to bandage her face and could not speak. And such was the confidence in me that even that simple ruse was not detected, and no suspicion was roused.

At the station the officer was good enough to take our tickets for us, and he thus saved me all troublesome questions. In fact every difficulty seemed to vanish as we faced it; and Sarita was actually in the train, and I was standing chatting with my two new friends, when the luck veered, and the crash came all suddenly. Nor was it any the sweeter to me because I had brought it on myself by a single piece of over-acting.

The telegram to Mayhew at the Embassy proved my undoing. It was tampered with or censored or something at Madrid. At any rate it came under the attention of the police there; and the name having been bracketed with that of Carbonnell, when the attempt had been made to arrest me at the Hotel de l'Opera, somebody's suspicions were roused, and instructions were sent to stop me. I was laughing with the officers and just going to bid them good-bye, when someone approached me.

"Lord Glisfoyle, I think."

"Yes, what do you want with me?"

"I am sorry, but there may be a mistake of some kind. I have instructions to ask you not to leave Calatayud for the present."

"From whom are your instructions?" I asked quickly, in very fluent Spanish, forgetting all about my English accent in my chagrin and surprise.

"They come from Madrid; and they speak of a certain Ferdinand Carbonnell in connection with you."

"I am an English nobleman, and at a loss to understand you. Do you mean you intend to stop my going away. You'll do so at your own risk; and unless you use force I shall certainly go."

"I trust you will not compel us to use force. I have no alternative but to obey my instructions."

At that moment I noticed the expression of the two officers and realised my blunder in showing my knowledge of Spanish. I was to pay a heavy price for it, too.

"I repeat I am an English nobleman travelling with my sister, and the English Government will not put up quietly with any interference of this kind. I am called by urgent business of a private character to London, and any delay will be serious. These gentlemen know that I have telegraphed to London announcing my immediate return."

"Your Spanish is far purer than I understood, senor," replied the English-speaking officer, drily. "I think you can explain matters sufficiently to dispense with any reference to me."

"As you please," I answered, loftily; and turning to the official, I said curtly, "I will do as you wish, and will just explain matters to my sister." I could think of no better excuse to get a word with Sarita. Speak to her I must—to urge her to continue the journey, and to give her money as I feared she had none. I turned to the carriage door and said coolly, in English: "I'm stopped, but you can go on; and must take this money. Wire to Mrs. Curwen when you reach Bayonne, and remain there. Please," I urged, backing the appeal with a glance. To my delighted surprise she consented, and with a light nod, I added: "I shall be on by the next train," and turned to the official, "I am at your disposal, senor."

But in the meantime the two officers had communicated their suspicions to the man, and he now said:

"I must ask the senorita, your sister, to alight and remain also. She shall be treated with every consideration."

"This is monstrous," I exclaimed indignantly; but my protests were unavailing, and we had to suffer the infinite chagrin and disappointment of seeing the train steam away without us. I masked my feelings under an assumption of indignation, however, and asked where we were to go.

"You can return to Angostino's, senor," said the official, very politely, "but you must permit that I remain in your company until I have further instructions."

"All places are alike to me after this scandalous outrage," I answered. Then, looking about me, I saw Juan watching us at a safe distance, and as we passed I gave him a meaning glance, and said aloud to Sarita, "We are arrested, you see," and he answered with a look to show that he understood and would do my bidding.

"I wish to telegraph to the British Embassy," I then said to the official.

"I regret, senor, but I can allow nothing to be done until I have further instructions," and there was nothing for me but to comply.

We went back to the inn to wait; but the delay was not long, for in reply to the telegram announcing the arrest there came a message for us both to be taken to Madrid.

"You will give me your word to make no attempt to resist us, senor?"

"Certainly I will not. I won't recognise your action in any way, and you can take the consequences of everything you do," was my hot reply. But it served no other purpose than to cause the man to have two subordinates with him in the carriage, thus preventing all attempt at conversation between Sarita and myself, other than a few words of English.

Sarita played her part well enough, showing a stolid, stoical indifference to everything, and maintaining the pretence of indisposition. But it was all of no avail. I had one consolation. Juan was in the train, and I knew that very soon Mayhew would be acting to effect my release; and I occupied the time and tedium of the journey by thinking out the far more serious problem of Sarita's arrest.

At Madrid the truth came out, of course, as I knew it would. Rubio was on the platform waiting for us when the train drew up. Recognising us both immediately, he rubbed his hands with pleasure over the importance of the arrest. He disregarded my angry protests, and in a few words sent my spirits down to zero.

"You are Ferdinand Carbonnell; I know that, and that would be enough, but there is more. This is Senorita Castelar, a most prominent Carlist, and you were stopped in the act of helping her to escape from the country under the pretence that she was your sister. For that even Lord Glisfoyle would have to answer. You are not in England, senor."

"No; but you'll find the English Government will have a word to say."

"That is for his Excellency the Minister to settle, and for the present you are both prisoners;" and without more ado he put Sarita into one carriage and me into another, with a sufficient guard to ensure our safety. Thus, instead of being well on the road to Bayonne as I had hoped, I found myself locked up in a filthy prison cell in Madrid, with a bitter load of misgivings and fears, and a host of useless lamentations and revilings for the shortsightedness and blunders which I had committed at the moment when Sarita's freedom lay in the hollow of my hand. I could have dashed my head against the wall in the bitterness of my self-reproach and futile regrets.

They would not let me communicate with a soul outside. I asked to send a letter to the British Embassy, and they answered that I was a Spaniard and a Carlist, and would be treated accordingly. I demanded an interview with Quesada, and they replied with the flout that I could see him when he made an appointment. I went so far even as to request that a message be sent to the Palace, and they laughed at me for a madman, and jeered and sneered the louder in proportion as I stormed and fumed and raged. Seeing that, I made up my mind to be sensible, and do the only thing I could do—wait.

Nor did I wait in vain.

The luck which had gone so well with me to a point, only to change at Calatayud with such ruinous consequences, veered round again the moment I reached Madrid, where there had been a witness of my arrest who was soon to bring me help.

I had been about three hours in the cell, and was passing the weary, baffling, irritating time in speculating how long I was to be left like a forgotten dog in the dirty kennel of a cell, and how long it would take Mayhew to get to work to find me and procure my release, when the door of the cell was unlocked and a warder told me to follow him.

"Where to?" I asked.

"There's a visitor for you."

"Bring him here, then," I answered, determined that anyone from the Embassy should see the filthy place in which I had been caged.

"Come with me," he said again.

"I will not," I answered, and curled myself up on the bare bench. At this he growled out an oath, and after a moment banged the door and locked it again. It was probably a novel experience for him to find any prisoner unwilling to get out of such a kennel at the first opportunity, and, in truth, when some minutes elapsed and he did not return, I was disposed to regret my own obstinacy.

But I heard his returning steps later on, the door was once more opened, and the brute said, in a tone of deference:

"The prisoner is here, senorita," and I jumped to my feet in intense surprise to find Dolores Quesada, holding up her skirts, and looking in dismay at the disgusting condition of the cell, and then with distress, sympathy, and concern at me.

CHAPTER XXIX

QUESADA AGAIN

"I must apologise for your brother's taste, senorita, in compelling me to allow you to find me in such a—palace," I said, with a wave of the hand about the filthy cell. "This is the hospitality he considers is my due."

The disgusting stench of the place turned her sick and faint, and anger flashed from her eyes. I was not at all sorry for her to see for herself the hole in which I had been caged.

"You must leave it at once, senor. It is horrible," she cried.

"I am but one of hundreds honoured with the same treatment, and the courtesy of my host is so pressing as to render it difficult for me to leave."

"I have brought the order for your release, senor. It is abominable—abominable! I wish to speak to Senor Carbonnell; take us to some place where we can breathe," she said to the warder.

"I told the prisoner to come before, but he refused, senorita," said the man in a surly tone; and then we followed him along the corridor to a square, bare room near the entrance to the gaol.

"I am ashamed at what you have suffered, Senor Carbonnell. My brother has deceived me, and broken his pledged word."

"I shall ever remember your former efforts for me, senorita, but you will see that the subject of Senor Quesada's conduct is one I can scarcely discuss with his sister," I answered.

"But it is just that which I want to discuss. I have obtained your release——"

"Pardon me," I broke in, "but I cannot accept my release on any conditions whatever. I am profoundly indebted to you for this act of yours, deeply impressed by the motives which underlie it, and can never cease to think kindly of you for it; but, though you found me a prisoner in such vile surroundings, I am not without great influence even here in Madrid—far greater than your brother deems—and my liberation was at most but a matter of hours. I can therefore make no conditions even with one so gracious and so friendly as yourself."

"You have maddened Sebastian against you by threatening him, but you will not think of such things."

"I would do much to please you, I am sure you know that; but you ask me what is impossible," I answered, firmly.

"There is no man in the world for whom I would have done this," she cried, impetuously. "And I had to strain to the utmost my influence with Sebastian to do it. The very fact that he ordered your arrest in defiance of his pledge to me shows how bitterly he feels. I was at the station this evening by the merest chance when you were brought there, and I could scarcely believe my own eyes when I saw you were under arrest. I went at once to Sebastian——"

"Pray forgive me if I interrupt you, but I cannot discuss his conduct with you. If you saw the arrest, however, you will have seen that I was not alone in being arrested; and if you wish to do me a kindness you will use this great influence of yours to secure the liberation of Senorita Castelar."

But at the mention of Sarita she drew herself up, and both anger and surprise, but chiefly anger, were in the look she gave me.

"You ask me that?" she cried, and then as suddenly changed. "You do not think she is in any danger, surely?" she added.

"I know that she was arrested, and you yourself saw the place where I was imprisoned, and can judge of the fitness of such a hole for a girl."

"And you don't know? She has never told you?" she cried, scornfully.

"I am not sure I understand you," I replied.

"She is to be my brother's wife, senor. Do you think he would suffer her to be treated as—as you have been?"

"Senorita, there is a great misunderstanding somewhere; but if anything is certain, it is that she will never be his wife."

"Will you come and see Sebastian?" she asked, suddenly. "I am so anxious to have peace between you."

"It could do no good."

"I ask you to come. If you value what I have done here, you will consent."

"It can do no good; but if you ask it I will go;" and the instant I had consented she led the way to her carriage, which was waiting outside the gate.

"Where is Senorita Castelar?" I asked, as we drove rapidly along.

"I don't know, but she is sure to be well cared for," she answered, as though the subject was no concern of hers; and no more was said until we were close to the house. Then, with some hesitation, she said: "I know nearly everything of my brother's plans, and shall be present at the interview. There must be a full understanding."

I made no reply, for I did not quite know what she meant; but I was certain that if there was to be anything like a full understanding the interview promised to be interesting; and I began to feel glad I had come.

Quesada was at home, and in the room where I had had my last conversation with him and my introduction to Rubio, and I found him looking much more concerned and anxious than I had ever seen him.

"What is the meaning of this visit?" was his blunt greeting.

"I have brought Senor Carbonnell," said Dolores, "that these things may be explained and talked over. I wished it, Sebastian."

"Very well; what does he want to explain?"

"You told me to-night, for the second time, that he could and would ruin you if he was set at liberty. I wish to have peace between

212

you. I told you so, when I insisted on his being liberated; and I have told him so, too. Now that you are face to face, say plainly what this means, and how it is to be avoided."

"When women interfere in matters they don't understand, they always do something foolish. This is mere foolishness. Senor Carbonnell—or, to give him his proper title, Lord Glisfoyle—is bent upon doing his utmost to ruin me, and you have given him the opportunity. Why, then, seek to delay him in his purpose? Let him go and begin his task." He spoke quite firmly, and with great deliberateness.

"This is hopeless, Sebastian," cried his sister, wringing her hands.

"What would you have me do, Dolores? Assume a fear of him which I do not feel? Throw myself at his feet and beg his mercy, when I stand in no need of it? Play at theatricals? You are a woman, we are men; and you don't understand us or our methods. Lord Glisfoyle and I have been engaged in a duel to the death. I had him at my advantage when you interfered—for the second time. You have given him the advantage now, and the cue is with him. He holds, or thinks he holds, weapons which he can use to secure my ruin; and you seem to think you can induce him not to use them by bringing him here to talk over, as you call it, the position. I am sure he did not come willingly, and am surprised he came at all; but here or anywhere else—except, of course, in safe keeping—it is all one to me. We shall continue the duel under the circumstances which you have changed in this way to my disadvantage."

"I was leaving Spain when your men stopped me and brought me to Madrid," I said.

"But not alone," he rapped out, sharply.

"No, with the lady who is to be my wife," I retorted.

For a second his hands clenched involuntarily, and he winced, but instantly recovered himself, and spoke calmly.

"That remains to be seen. But why this interview?"

"I have not sought it," I answered curtly, and got up to leave.

"You must not go," cried Dolores.

"My dear Dolores, do not meddle any more."

"Yes, Sebastian, I will. I must speak. Senor Carbonnell—Lord Glisfoyle, I mean—knows your secret plotting in regard to the King; he holds, as you told me, documents which must compromise you, and may ruin you if he can prove they are genuine. These are what you call his weapons. There must be some inducement that can prevail upon him not to use them. Is that not so, Lord Glisfoyle?" she cried, turning to me in deep distress.

"You are forgetting yourself, Dolores. We are not children or

213

women," said the Minister, sternly. "I will have no more of this child's play. You should not have brought Lord Glisfoyle here. Every word you utter but makes your blunder worse; and God knows you have done enough mischief already to satisfy even a woman."

"I asked you a question, Lord Glisfoyle," said Dolores, paying no regard to his protests.

"A question I find most difficult, I may say impossible, to answer. Your brother knows how he has treated me, and knows also how he would act were our positions reversed. I can say no more."

"But do you mean to use these letters?" she persisted.

"Since obtaining them I have obtained others, and much information. I know the part you have played throughout this business, Senor Quesada,"—I felt it easier to speak to him—"and I shall not rest until I have done my utmost to bring this home to you. In one thing you have wronged your sister. I should not have remained in what you term safe keeping more than a few hours at the utmost; for already there are forces at work for my liberation which even you would find it hopeless to resist. What you term your sister's blunder, therefore—procuring my liberation from the prison—is no more than an anticipation by those few hours of what must have followed."

"That may be. At any rate, you are free, and you owe it to her." This reminder of my obligation to Dolores was the first slight rift in his firmness.

"If it were possible, it would influence my attitude. But nothing can do that—nothing, at least, that you can do."

"I knew there was something. What is it? Tell us that, Lord Glisfoyle. I beg and pray of you, say what it is," cried Dolores, in a tone of fervent entreaty.

"It is useless even to name it. It is nothing less than the undoing of all this wilful and unholy persecution of the Carlists—wilful and unholy because undertaken for the sake of furthering, not the welfare of Spain, but your brother's ambition."

"It is not impossible. I am sure it is not," she exclaimed. "You can do anything, Sebastian; while your influence is what it is, you can do anything. Say that this shall be done, and Lord Glisfoyle will leave Spain—I know he will—and give up these documents you fear so much."

They were the mere wild, idle words of a distracted woman, the cry of a true heart torn asunder by the vehemence of emotion.

To my surprise, her brother did not instantly repudiate them, however, but sat with pent, frowning brows in deep thought for a moment.

214

"Would you go alone?" he asked then, without relaxing the stern, set expression of face.

"Do you mean would anything ever make me consent to see Sarita Castelar your wife?"

"Would you go alone?" he repeated, in the same tone.

"Nothing would make me consent to that," I replied, answering my own question. "And nothing will ever induce me not to hold you responsible for her safety."

He heard me without a sign, and again buried himself in his thoughts. Then he pushed his chair back, rose, and went to the door.

"Leave us a few minutes, Dolores," he said, still in the same set, even tone. "It is possible that we may yet arrive at an understanding."

She looked at him in fear, then at me, doubtingly, and again back at him.

"No, I cannot leave you. I—I dare not."

"Leave us, Dolores. I shall not murder Lord Glisfoyle."

She still hesitated and lingered, but at length yielded, saying as she passed me—

"I shall see you again?"

I bowed, but said nothing; I was too full of surprise at the turn things were taking, and too thoughtful, wondering what was to come next.

Quesada held the door while his sister passed out, and closed and locked it after her, and turned back to his table.

"We are now quite alone, Lord Glisfoyle, and can speak plainly. You love Sarita Castelar, and hope to make her your wife?"

"I decline to discuss her with you, Senor Quesada."

"Well, then, I tell you she is pledged to marry me, and I will suffer no man on earth to take her from me."

"You did not speak so to your tool, Colonel Juan Livenza. I am aware of the infamous bargain you made with him."

"I will not allow anyone to take her from me," he said again, between his teeth, the increased tenseness of the tone being his only notice of my words. "You are an English nobleman, and presumably a man of courage. When you were here last time in my house, you struck me. You are now bent on ruining me, and have set everything on that venture. Owing to my sister's interference, you are free; and because she loves you, she is mad enough to stay my hands in dealing with you, knowing, what you also know, things that must be kept secret. And as a crowning stroke you threaten to rob me of the woman I love. Under those circumstances, what think you is the fitting course for two men—two enemies, if you will—placed as you and I are, to pursue?"

215

"If I understand you, I decline to discuss such a proposal."

"If you are a gentleman and a man of honour, and not a coward, you will find only one answer to my question," he said, his rage deepening in its quiet intensity with every sentence, till each word he uttered was a deliberate insult—an added knot on the lash of his bitter tongue. But I had my temper too well in hand to take fire.

"There are matters you forget. You set your bully, Livenza, upon me first; you used your power as Minister to destroy me; you ordered your police spies to dog me; and you had me gaoled in one of your filthy prisons. In this way you exhausted every means in your power to deal with me officially; and having schemed and tricked and bullied thus in vain, you find yourself at bay, and as a last resource you remember your honour with suspicious tardiness, and think of the means which the gentleman and the man of honour you speak of would have thought of first. I will not fight with you, Senor Quesada."

"You are a coward, then."

"I don't accept your standards in that matter."

"I will make you fight me," he cried; and, his rage breaking beyond all control, he rushed at me, and raised his arm to strike me with the back of the hand across the mouth; but I caught his arm, and thrust him staggering back against his chair, over which he nearly fell. Thinking he might have firearms, and that in his mad fury he would use them, I unlocked the door, and was leaving the room when he called to me; but I paid no heed, and went out.

Dolores was in waiting, and came when she heard me leaving. She was paler even than before, like one distraught with fear and anxiety. I pitied her from the bottom of my heart, and her brother's blunt statement that she loved me, and had been led by that love to insist on my freedom even at the cost of ruin to him, touched me very closely.

"Is there any hope of an arrangement, senor?" she asked, searching my face with haggard eyes.

"None whatever," I replied, shaking my head.

"Can nothing bring you two together again?"

"It is absolutely impossible, senorita."

I spoke as gently as I could, but it was useless to flinch from the truth.

"Can I do nothing to prevail with you? I have tried so hard to serve you," she said, in a tone of despairing wistfulness.

"For you, personally, I would do anything in my power. I am not unmindful of what it must have cost you, and you shall not find me ungrateful."

"I do not ask for thanks; I do not want them. I should have

done the same had the ruin been mine instead of Sebastian's," and she smiled. "I am glad to have done it;" but the smile ended in a sigh at the thought of the price to be paid.

I took her hands and pressed them.

"I am very troubled for you," I murmured.

She returned the pressure, her own hands trembling very much.

"If it had not been for Sarita Castelar, you two would never have quarrelled, and—and all would have been so different." Her lips quivered as she spoke, and her eyes were full of sadness. Her look pained me inexpressibly. I said nothing, and after a pause she added:

"You do not think he will let you take her from him? You know him too well for that; although you do not know him yet. What was it he would not let me hear?"

"I would rather you heard it from him. And I must go." She had roused my fears for Sarita.

"I thought he meditated some act of violence against you, and he is headstrong enough to do anything—even against her."

"You can surely prevent that," I cried, quickly, in alarm. "You were strong to save me."

The look with which she answered me lives in my memory to this hour. Then she drew her hands from mine, and said coldly—

"I can do nothing. You have made him desperate." And with a change of tone, after a slight pause, as though excusing her own hardness of thought and resolve, she added: "Besides, I do not know where she is; so I can do nothing, even if I would."

With that I left her, and hurried from the house a prey to innumerable harassing fears, the stings and darts of which sent me plunging headlong through the streets to go I did not think where, and to do I did not know what.

Sarita was in imminent peril from that reckless, desperate man, and I alone had to save her. More than once I halted undecided whether to return and take up the challenge he had thrown down, and trust to my own strength and skill to render him powerless to harm her. And in this bewildered state of mind I found myself at the door of my old dwelling, half crazed by the thought that hours at least must elapse before I could use hand or tongue for her protection, and that for all those hours she would be absolutely at his mercy.

CHAPTER XXX

SUSPENSE

The moment I entered my rooms I perceived that they had been ransacked. The trail of the police searchers lay over everything. In his eagerness to regain possession of that compromising document which he feared so acutely, Quesada had turned his agents loose in my rooms; and they had done their work so thoroughly that the condition of the place was a silent but most impressive tribute to their skill and his alarm. The rooms had been searched from wall to wall; my trunks had been broken and overhauled; drawers and cupboards had been forced, and the contents diligently scrutinised; not a thing had been left in its proper place; and I smiled with a feeling of grim pleasure that I had had the forethought to put the papers in the safe hands of my friend Mayhew.

For the action of the police I cared nothing, and I stayed in the place only long enough to get such clothes as I might need; and I threw them into a Gladstone bag, and carried them over to Mayhew's rooms.

I had too stern a task before me in procuring Sarita's release to give serious thought to much else. My friend was out, and I guessed I should find him at the Hotel de l'Opera; but, having changed my clothes, I sat down to think over matters before going in search of him.

Affairs were in all truth in an inextricable tangle, and very little reflection convinced me that instead of unravelling them I had made them worse by the course I had adopted with Sebastian Quesada. I had committed the fatal blunder of driving him into a corner, and rendering him desperate enough to resort to any of those violent methods which Dolores had said he would certainly adopt when once his back was to the wall.

It was easy to see now what I ought to have done. Belated wisdom is the curse of a fool, I thought bitterly, as I realised what my clumsy shortsighted tactlessness had achieved. What I ought to have done was to have convinced him of my power to ruin him; have told him even of my influence at the Palace; and have driven in upon him with irresistible force that it was in my power to thwart the ambition and ruin the career that were as the very breath of his nostrils to him. Having done that, I ought to have opened the door of escape by a pledge to do nothing if he would but give up Sarita.

Instead of this I had driven him to desperation. I had left him under the conviction that not only could I ruin him, but that I most assuredly should do so; and had thus given him no alternative but to set his vigorous energies to work to retrieve so much of his position as was possible, and to keep for himself what he prized scarcely less than his position, and what it was already in his power to secure—the woman he loved.

That he could keep Sarita from me, I could not doubt. He needed but to lift a finger to have her conveyed where I might search for her in vain; and a slight knowledge of his resourceful and implacable character was enough to convince anyone that he would act both promptly and resolutely. And I shuddered at the thought of the probable consequences to her.

There was yet another distracting reflection. It was by no means certain that, even if I could wrest her from his grip, I could obtain clemency for Sarita herself. Her actions in this infernal Carlist business had been those of vigorous, bitter, and dangerous intrigue against the King; treason as subtle as it was active. She was an acknowledged leader of the Carlists; and I might be sure that Quesada for his own purposes had accumulated more than sufficient proofs of her intrigues. Great as was the obligation of the King and the Queen Regent to me, I could scarcely dare to hope they would pardon her; and hence, if I succeeded in pulling down the strong pillars at the house of Quesada's reputation, there was too much reason to fear that when the building fell Sarita would be crushed in the ruins.

Moreover, there was the problem of Sarita's own sentiments. In the revulsion of feeling which had followed Livenza's disclosures, she had been willing to leave the country; and while I was with her, and the influence of our mutual love could work upon her, that willingness might have remained. But in the solitude of her imprisonment, wherever the prison might be, she would have long hours of cold thought; and I had seen too much of her infatuated belief that her duty demanded she should stay and share the fate of those who had been misled by her ill-fated plans, not to fear that that infatuation would again assert itself.

Thus, ponder and stew and plan as I would, I could see no clear course. All things contributed to make it a personal struggle between Quesada and myself, in which, while I held the weapons that might ruin him, he had the means of making that ruin fatal to me so far as the only object I cared for, Sarita's safety and well-being, was concerned.

As my head cleared from the whirl of mazing thoughts, the conclusion that I had blundered so badly in my interview with him became plainer and plainer, gradually hardening into the new purpose to return to him in the possible hope of retrieving the mistake. Such a reopening of matters would look like an admission of weakness; and so in truth it was; but I had only one object— Sarita's safety; and that must override all other and lesser considerations.

Going down into the street, I drove back to his house, my distaste for the interview increasing with every yard that brought it nearer, and the difficulties of the task looming ever greater, until I am not sure that I was not rather glad when I was told he had left his house, and that the hour of his return was uncertain. I did not ask for Dolores, but, getting back into the carriage that had brought me, told the man to drive me to the Hotel de l'Opera.

My arrival there was hailed with delight. Madame Chansette and Mayhew were with Mrs. Curwen and Mercy, and, having heard of my arrest, all were deep in anxious discussion of my affairs when I entered.

I gave them a very general and brief account of my doings, and instantly a whole battery of questions was opened upon me.

"You look sadly in need of a good square meal," said Mrs. Curwen, always practical; and she promptly ordered some supper for me. "At the present rate of running, about another week of this will finish you," she added.

"But how did you get away?" asked Mayhew. "You were arrested, and the whole Embassy has been hard at work expostulating, protesting, protocolling, and Heaven knows what. There never was such a pother raised in Madrid before."

"An order came for my release, and I walked out."

"Do you mean you were actually in prison?" asked Mercy.

"And a very filthy prison, too, I assure you. But, so far as I am concerned, that danger is over."

"Well, thank Heaven for that. Another period of suspense of the kind would about kill Mercy, and finish off the family," cried Mrs. Curwen. "I'm off Spanish investments altogether. And what's going to happen next? Of course it'll be something unusual. There's no musty conventionality about your doings just now."

"And where is Sarita?" asked Madame Chansette.

"I wish I knew, my dear madame. She was arrested at the same time as I; and if I knew, I could do something to help her. But that's just the pith and kernel of my trouble. As to what will come next I have not a much clearer idea than you, Mrs. Curwen. But something will probably happen to-morrow."

"We may be sure of that," she returned quickly. "And when can we all go away to some safe un-dynamity country?"

"I think I shall be able to answer that better to-morrow."

220

"It's all to-morrow, it seems to me. And in the meantime don't you think you'd better go to bed somewhere? You're about fagged out."

"I am too anxious to sleep."

"And when was anxiety relieved by sitting up all night and worrying with it? There, I've rung the bell, and you can tell the waiter to have a room got ready instantly for you. We shall all feel easier if we know you're in the place. I'm sure you can't do anything to-night, and by the morning you'll have a clear head, some more plans, and enough energy for another burst of this kind of thing."

When the waiter came I yielded, under protest, and ordered a room.

"I must have a long chat with Mayhew first," I said.

"Not to-night, if Mercy and I have any influence with Mr. Mayhew," she returned, and Mercy agreed. Then, to my surprise, Mayhew, in a half-shamefaced but very serious manner, said: "I think Mrs. Curwen is right, Ferdinand."

"What, you as well, Silas?" and as I looked at him he smiled and shrugged his shoulders.

"No one thinks of questioning Mrs. Curwen's commands," he answered.

"Oh, already? Then I'd better give in, too," and with that I went, feeling indeed the truth of what she said—that I could do nothing that night.

She was right, also, that I was in sore need of rest, and, despite my anxieties and my declaration that sleep would be impossible, my head was no sooner on the pillow than I fell into deep slumber, which lasted until a sluggard's hour on the following morning. It was ten o'clock before I awoke.

I found Mrs. Curwen alone, and my vexation at having been allowed to lie so late must have shown in my face, for she said directly: "There's no one to blame but me, Lord Glisfoyle. I would not allow you to be called. I don't believe in my prescriptions being half taken."

"I have a great deal to do," I answered, somewhat ungraciously.

"That's no reason why you should try to do it with half your energies sapped for want of sleep. Mr. Mayhew has been here for you and tried to get to you; but I wouldn't let him," she said assertively.

"He is learning obedience diligently, it seems," I observed.

"He is a very good fellow, and I strained my influence with him, I can tell you," she retorted, with a smile of some occult meaning.

"He is the prince of good fellows, and the staunchest of friends, and I congratulate you on having such influence to strain."

"Oh, men are not difficult to manage, if properly handled."

"Some of us, that is; but I hope he has been duly attentive in my absence," I said, casually, and with a glance.

"What was the poor man to do? He couldn't very well leave us in the lurch, I suppose? You were away, and we'd positively no one else."

"To say nothing of his own inclinations," I added.

"To say nothing of his own inclinations," she repeated. "Mercy is not exactly the kind of girl to scare a man away from her, I should hope."

"A supposition that might be extended to include——"

"What do you mean?" she asked quickly, as I stopped.

"Whom should I mean but"—looking at her pointedly—"Madame Chansette, shall I say?" She laughed.

"Yes, we'll say Madame Chansette."

"And yet—well, it doesn't much matter whom we say; but at any rate he's a thoroughly genuine fellow, and—you can fill in the rest. But, by the way, where is Mercy?"

"She is having a French or Spanish lesson, I think; I'll tell you all about it when you've finished your breakfast, and not a minute before. But about Mr. Mayhew, tell me, what is he at the Embassy here? He seems to speak as though he was a kind of mill-horse. Are there no prospects for him? Has he no influence to push him on?"

"Yes, he has one, I think I may say two friends now who will see to that. I'm one of the two—and I think I'm speaking to the other," I said, quietly. "And between us we ought to do something. But he's as proud as Lucifer, and a mere hint that we were at the back of anything of the kind would make him kick."

"If poor A.B.C. were alive——"

"Then, my dear Mrs. Curwen, you would never have been in Madrid, and would never have known Mayhew." She shrugged her shapely shoulders, smiled, and then said with unusual earnestness: "And will you really let me help you in trying to get him a step or two up the ladder?"

"I mean to have him in London, and to make the people at home understand that he has a head on his shoulders fit for better things. Why, if Silas only had money to back his brains, there's nothing he might not do or be. But there, I've finished my breakfast!" I exclaimed, getting up from the table, thinking I had said enough. "And now, where is Mercy?"

"Will you shake hands on that bargain, Lord Glisfoyle?" she asked, her eyes bright with the thoughts I knew I had started. We shook hands gravely, as became such a compact, and I looked straight into her eyes, as I said in as earnest a tone as hers: "The woman who marries Silas Mayhew will have a husband in a hundred thousand, true, honest-hearted, straight and good right through. And now, where is Mercy?" She returned my look, coloured slightly, and some reply sprang to her lips, but she checked it, and turning away, said: "Sebastian Quesada's sister came here, and the two girls are closeted together, waiting for you."

"And you have kept me here all this time!" I cried.

"I was bound to see to your health."

"You are as anxious for my health, I believe, as I am for your happiness," and with that I hurried away, leaving her blushing very prettily.

I found Dolores looking very white and worn, and in a mood of deep dejection. She and Mercy had been weeping together in the sympathetic exchange of such confidence and consolation as their ignorance of each other's tongue and mutual indifferent knowledge of the French language would allow.

"She is in terrible trouble, Ferdinand, do try and relieve her. Her heart is almost broken by the fearful strain of her sorrow," said Mercy, getting up to leave as I entered.

"You do not understand things, Mercy, but I will do what I can."

"Your sister is an angel, Lord Glisfoyle," said Dolores, as the door closed behind Mercy. "I am almost ashamed to come to you, but I could not keep away. She has told me what I knew, of course, how good and generous and noble you are. Cannot you do what I asked you yesterday? I heard of your second visit to us last night, and all through the night—such a night of agony for me—I have been feeding my soul with the hope that you came to make some agreement."

"Where is your brother? I am truly pained to see you like this."

"It does not matter about me; nothing of that kind can matter now," she answered in a tone deadened by sorrow. "I should not come to you for such a paltry object as my own troubles. It is for Sebastian I am thinking. But you don't seem to understand how I feel, how this fearful thing has shut upon me like the closing walls of an Inquisition prison cell, until whichever way I stretch out my hands I find ruin crushing in upon me," and she moved her hands like one distraught with terror and trouble.

"What can I do?" I asked, gently.

"Can't you try and see what all this has meant to me?" she asked wildly, ignoring my question. "What I suffered when I knew that Sebastian meant to ruin you, to involve you in this terrible Carlist business, to have you proclaimed as Ferdinand Carbonnell, the desperate Carlist leader, imprisoned and sent Heaven alone knew where, to suffer the fate and the punishment which such a man would rightly suffer? What could I do but step in to save you? You know his reluctance, the struggle we had, the wild words he spoke of your ruining him, and then how he broke his pledged word to me? And yet to save you meant to ruin him! Holy Mother of God, what was I to do?" and she wrung her hands. "I could not see you wronged in this way; and yet as my reward am I to see him dragged down, his reputation destroyed, his position degraded, his very name a foulness in the mouths of the populace? Is this your English sense of honour and recompense? No, no, I don't mean that. I know you are just and honourable. I am crazed with my trouble to speak such words to you."

"Where is your brother?"

"I do not know. You drove him to desperation last night. He left this house almost directly you had gone; and returned late, and was gone again this morning before I could get word with him. He is like a mad-man; and what he will do in his madness, who can tell?" The fears that lay beneath her wild words were the same as had been pressing so keenly on me, yet what to do to avert them was more than I could see.

"If you do not know where he is, what can we do?" I asked.

"Give me those compromising papers, and let me find him and prove that the danger he fears is at an end? He will then do anything you ask. You do not know him. He is stern, hard, implacable when opposed, but he is not dead to feelings of generosity. An act like that would touch him to the core, and he would do anything you asked— nay, let me know what it is you wish, and I would pledge myself that he would do it." She pleaded urgently and almost imploringly, but I could not yield.

"I cannot do that. Only last night he likened this struggle between us to a duel, and you would ask me to disarm myself and throw away the only means by which I can hope to win my way. I am sorry, deeply and sincerely sorry, but this is impossible."

"You would see him dragged into the dirt for the rabble to spit upon!" Her changing mood, as she was swayed first by thoughts for me and then by those for her brother, was painful to witness.

"He did not hesitate to have me treated as a criminal, senorita; he has set me at defiance and refused everything I asked; and I cannot put myself and others at his mercy. But I will do this. Let him set Sarita Castelar free, and stay this Carlist persecution, and I will give up the documents he fears, and say nothing of what I know. More than that I cannot offer you; and even that must depend upon the senorita being free before I am placed in a position which compels me to take action against him."

"What does that mean? How long will you give me? I must have

224

time to find him. I cannot do anything without time. You are iron to me in your madness for this girl."

"Unfortunately I am not free to name any time." I was not. I did not yet know what measures Mayhew had taken, and whether he had communicated with the Palace. My summons to the King might come at any hour, and I was compelled to hold myself free to speak all I knew with regard to Quesada in my interview there. At the same time Dolores' acute distress of mind, and the knowledge of what she had done for me, filled me with a desire to help her; while personally, I was anxious to get Sarita from Quesada's grip at the earliest possible moment, and to leave Spain. Under pressure of these thoughts, I added: "This I can assure you, I would far rather the matter ended as you wish, and will give you every possible moment of time."

"I will go," she answered promptly. "I depend on you. You have given me some hope, if not much. If I fail with Sebastian"—and she closed her eyes and sighed in the agony of the thought—"I will let you know at once."

"And I will do nothing without first sending word to you," I promised in reply.

We parted then, and when she left the room I found Mayhew waiting for me in the corridor.

CHAPTER XXXI

AT THE PALACE

"Your lady visitors call early, Ferdinand," said Mayhew, rather drily.

"Yes, rather embarrassing, isn't it? But what news have you for me? What happened yesterday?"

"More than enough to prove that you are a person of considerable importance, I can tell you. When I got your message by that exceedingly sharp lad, Juan, that you were arrested, I went straight to the chief, and within an hour a protest was in the hands of the Spanish Government, couched in terms calculated to make them sit up, I promise you, and very soon the whole machinery was at work to get you out. They denied all knowledge of you, however;

but I expect a good deal would have happened to-day if you hadn't been set at liberty. I told the chief this morning, however, that you were here, and he wants to see you. And that's about all—unless you want the details."

"Did you send any word to the Palace?"

"No, I kept that in reserve for to-day as a broadside, and, of course, I said nothing to anyone about the papers you left with me."

"Good; just as I should have expected from you. And now, I'm going to tell you the whole mess, and just see what's best to be done;" and I gave him a pretty full account of everything that had happened.

"You're right, it is a devil of a mess," was his comment when I finished. "What do you suppose Quesada's sister can do?"

"I haven't a notion. I'm just at the end of my wits, and can't for the life of me see what's to be done."

"There's one thing you may safely reckon on, and it isn't a pleasant thing anyway—that that beggar is sure to have a trump card up his sleeve that will most likely outplay your best. He's the most cunning beggar in all Spain. He's been in heaps of tight corners before, and wriggled out just when it seemed impossible. And he won't give in now, you bet. I tell you what he's likely to do— he knows just as well as lots of others, that he's the pivot of the whole Government; the one man for instance, who, in the popular view, can wage this threatened war with the States with some chance of success; and I wouldn't be one little bit surprised if he trumps you with a change of front and declares for war. You don't know as much as I do of Spanish politics, and can't, therefore, understand the holy mess that would follow here if the war came. He'd be the only man able to guide things; and in such a case you might hammer at him in vain."

"But these documents, Livenza's statement, my own knowledge, Sarita Castelar's evidence!" I cried, in protest.

"Strong enough in England, perhaps; but he'd deny everything; and do you think anyone's going to care two pence about them if the nation is in danger. He'd say the letters were forgeries; pop Livenza into prison, or bribe or threaten him to change face; the lady is already safe in his charge, and as a Carlist wouldn't be believed even if she were at liberty; and your statement would be listened to politely, and then disregarded as that of an enemy of Spain and a friend of America. I'm sorry to discourage you, but you asked my advice and that is—don't count on your weapons as he called them, and don't believe for a moment that you can really do him any harm. He sits too firm in the saddle."

"But he told his sister that I could ruin him, and he showed the fear by wanting to make me fight him."

"Mere play-acting, Ferdinand, nothing more. He wanted to get the papers back quietly if he could, and the quietest and safest way would have been to have you arrested as Carbonnell, the Carlist, and sent somewhere into the far provinces, and probably knocked on the head by the way or shot in mistake—the kind of mistake that does happen at times. His sister appears to have cut that plan short, and naturally he tells her she must get the papers back, if she could. But if she couldn't, it didn't follow that he wasn't quite prepared to face you. Don't make the mistake of thinking he will give up a jot or tittle of any plan he has, whether public or private; he never has been known to yet, and even you will never make him, strong as your case would be in any other country and against any other man. It's part of his constitution, my dear fellow. He's got all the energy and resource of a present day American with all the confounded pride and stiff-necked doggedness of an Old Castile noble. A rummy combination, but the devil to fight."

"I shan't give in," I said, firmly. "And that I take it your advice is that I should."

Mayhew shrugged his shoulders significantly.

"I'd make it different if I could. I'm very sorry, for I can guess what it means to you; but you've no chance;" and he shook his head, hopelessly. "Shall we go and see the chief?"

"I shan't give in," I said again; but I am free to confess that his counsel of despair had great effect upon me, and I went to the Embassy in a very despondent mood.

I was closeted with the chief a considerable time, while I gave such account of my experiences as I deemed advisable, and was questioned and cross-questioned, and advised and congratulated in the customary official manner, and finally counselled to return to England. A pointed question from me drew the reply that this last advice was the result of a request from the Spanish Government, and I did not fail to see in it the hand of Quesada.

My answer was an evasive one, to the effect that I would go so soon as I had wound up such private affairs as I had to conclude in Madrid.

I rejoined Mayhew, feeling both ill at ease and out of temper. A half-day had passed, and I had done nothing toward effecting Sarita's release; while the hours were flying, and no word came from Dolores. My apparent helplessness in other respects increased my anxiety to hear that she had been successful with her brother; for I was fast coming round to Mayhew's gloomy view of the position.

Then came another complication. When we went to the Hotel

de l'Opera, I found there an urgent summons from the Palace. News of my arrest and liberation had reached the young King, and he desired me to go to the Palace that afternoon. I scribbled a note to Dolores Quesada, telling her I could not wait for news from her after three o'clock—the hour appointed for the interview, and sent Mercy with it, Mayhew accompanying her.

The reply to this put the climax to my anxiety. It ran thus:

"Alas, my friend, I can do nothing. I have just seen Sebastian, who is now in a quite different mood. He laughs at the thought of your doing him any harm. 'Let him do his worst. He can but break himself on the wheel of his own efforts;' were his words. I am distracted with misery."

I showed it to Mayhew, who read it thoughtfully.

"It could not be worse," he said. "He has put the senorita in a safe place, and is going to play the trump card that I was sure he had in reserve somewhere. You should have accepted his challenge and shot him. Only one thing can beat Quesada—and that's death."

"I will do my best all the same," I answered; and in this mood I set out for my interview at the Palace, revolving on the way all the possible expedients that I could adopt to win even part of my purpose against the powerful enemy who held his way with such grim tenacity and inflexible resolve.

My reception at the Palace might have flattered even Royalty itself. When I was ushered into the presence, the young King came running to me, laying aside all attempt at dignity, and smiling with pleasure as he held out his hands liked a pleased child.

"My Englishman of Podrida, at last!" he exclaimed, and he led me to the Queen Mother, who was graciousness itself.

"You have kept the words of gratitude too long prisoners in my heart, my lord. The Queen would chide you, but the mother's heart is too full for anything but welcome for the man who saved her son."

"I trust your Majesties will pardon me. The delay has been due to causes as full of trouble as of urgency."

"My son has told me of your daring rescue, but I wish to hear it again from you. I am so anxious to know all, that I would have the tale even before your own anxieties which, if we can, you must let us help you to dispel."

"I have the mask here, my lord," cried the King, with all a boy's eagerness, bringing it out of a pocket.

"The story is a very simple one, your Majesty," I said, and then in as few words as I could, I told it. She listened with the closest attention, questioning me now and again on such points as interested her most, or where she wished greater detail; and when I described how the King was seized and carried into the carriage,

228

and again how I had found him fastened down and disguised, she clasped the boy to her, and her changing colour and quickened breath gave evidence of her concern and emotion.

"And you were alone through it all?" she exclaimed, when I finished.

"Fortune favoured me or I could not have succeeded, Madame. Had not the two men following the carriage met with an accident, I could have done nothing. As it was, the surprise of my attack did what no strength of arm or skill or wit could have accomplished."

"Do not call it fortune? It was rather the hand of Heaven guarding my dear son's safety, and you were the chosen instrument. And should you know those miscreants again?" Her tone hardened and her eyes flashed, as she put the question; and I thought then I could discern the feeling which had had as much to do with her impatience at my delay in coming to the Palace as her desire to thank me. She was burning with all a Spaniard's hot eagerness for revenge. But it was not my cue to strike at the agents, and my reply was guarded.

"It is possible that if they were face to face with me, I could identify them; but the thing was hurried, the work of no more than a few moments, and my English eyes are not sufficiently accustomed to distinguish between Spanish faces."

"Ah, I am disappointed," cried the Queen, frowning.

"But I can do more than identify the men who actually did the ill-work, Madame; I know by whose hidden hand the wires of the plot were pulled."

"Tell us that, and you will add a thousand times to the obligation that Spain and we owe you, my lord," she exclaimed, strenuously. "Who is the arch-traitor?"

"I shall have need of your Majesty's patient indulgence."

"And you will not ask it in vain, Lord Glisfoyle, if you do not seek it for these villainous Carlists, who would have robbed me of my son and dealt this foul blow at Spain." Then with a quick thought, she asked: "But how comes it that you, an English nobleman, here in Madrid no longer than a few weeks, can have learnt these things?" I believe I could detect a touch of suspicion in her manner; and the King looked up sharply into her face and then across at me.

"By a coincidence in regard to my name, your Majesty. I came to Madrid but a short time ago to join the staff of the British Embassy; I was not then Lord Glisfoyle; and by a chain of coincidences some of the plans of the misguided Carlists became known to me."

"Do you mean you knew of this intended plot against my son?"

"There are always rumours and reports, Madame, and such gossip was, of course, current in your capital—and equally, of course, well known to your Government and officials. But this was different; and the definite tidings came to me at a time and in a form which made it impossible for me to act otherwise than as I did."

"What was your name then, if not Lord Glisfoyle?" she broke in.

"Ferdinand Carbonnell, the younger son of my late father."

"Ferdinand Carbonnell! Ah, then——" the sentence remained unfinished, and I stood in silence watching her and waiting for the conclusion. I could guess her thought.

"Ferdinand Carbonnell is a well-known Carlist leader, Lord Glisfoyle," and she spoke in a tone that augured but ill for my success.

"And for that Carlist leader I was mistaken, your Majesty, and working through that strange mistake, Providence enabled me to rescue your son from a far worse fate than that which any Carlist ever designed. In following this strange double career I carried my life in my hands, risking misunderstanding at the hands of your Majesty's agents, and putting my life to the hazard of any Carlist discovery of my real character."

"You cannot doubt him, mother," cried the King, protestingly.

"You have said too much or too little, my lord. I beg you to speak frankly."

"I would ask your Majesty by whose advice it was that your son came to be in such a case as made this attempt possible?" I said; and the question went home, for she started quickly.

"By the advice of my Ministers, who felt that our confidence in the people should be shown in a way which all could see for themselves. Do you propose to arraign my Government on a charge of treason?"

"I do not arraign your Government as a whole, your Majesty; but what if it were proved to you that one of them, discontented with his present power and influence, great though they be, had aimed to make them greater; had thought that under the Republican form of Government there were wider scope for his ambition; and had planned, therefore, a double stroke of policy— say, for instance, the removal of your son from the Throne, using the Carlists for his purpose, and at the same time preparing to crush their power when he had used them, employing the very pretext of the plot as the cause of his drastic measures of repression? What if there be a man in your confidence who designed to overthrow the Monarchy, and climb on the ruins of the Throne to the place of supreme power in the country as President of a Republic to be

230

proclaimed? What if these plans were all laid and settled in every detail; and yet made with such consummate skill and shrewdness, that even the crumbling of the corner-stone—this attempt on His Majesty—still left him higher, firmer, and stronger in position and influence than ever? What if the subtle organisation by which this Carlist rising has been crushed almost in a day was the outcome, not of a desire to save His Majesty's throne from attack, but of an intention to break down what—should the Monarchy be no longer in existence—would have been the one remaining possible obstacle to this man's success? Would your Majesty say that these Carlists or the arch-plotter were the more to be feared, the more culpable, the more dangerous?"

I spoke with rising vehemence, and my daring words frightened both my hearers. The Queen was almost pale when I ended.

"You cannot make this good, my lord. I cannot believe it."

"Yet every word is true and can be made good. The man I mean is your most powerful Minister—Senor Sebastian Quesada."

"It cannot be. It is impossible," cried the Queen. "You frighten me, my lord. What proofs have you?"

The intense impression created by my charge, emboldened me to go a step farther and place all on the cast. The Queen was so agitated, and the young King so deeply and keenly moved by my words, that I could not fail to see what weight would attach to any request I put while they were in that mood; and taking my fortune boldly in both hands, I resolved to risk everything on the chance of my being able to prove my charge against Quesada. Mayhew's words of despondent caution recurred to me, but my ears were deaf to everything save the one absorbing purpose that swayed me.

"His Majesty was good enough on the day, when under Providence I was able to snatch him from the hands of his enemies, to promise to grant me such request as I might prefer. You, Madame, to-day, with gracious sympathy at the mention of my cares and anxieties, expressed the generous desire to help me. May I entreat you then, remembering what I have done, to grant me a favour should I make good my words, and bring home to the real traitor this treachery against your august family and your throne?"

"You would make conditions, my lord?"

"Your Majesty, I am but a suppliant."

"What is this favour?"

"That your Majesties will be graciously disposed to pardon the unfortunate dupes who have been misled by the man who has used them for his own purpose?"

"It is impossible, Lord Glisfoyle, utterly impossible. You cannot mean this. Stay, I have heard a possible reason for this strange request. I have heard your name coupled with one of the most daring of these Carlists—a Senorita Castelar—by whose influence we are told Ferdinand Carbonnell, the Englishman, took up the role of Ferdinand Carbonnell, the Spanish Carlist. Has this anything to do with this favour you ask?"

"Your Majesty, the dearest wish of my life is to make the Senorita Castelar my wife; as the farthest thought of hers would be to make me a Carlist. I trust that my acts have shown this for me, rendering mere protests needless."

"Mother!" cried the young King, eagerly, like the staunch little champion of my cause that he was.

"These are matters of deep state importance, and we cannot follow only our inclinations," said his mother in rebuke; and the tone was hard and unpromising. "We cannot make any such promise as a condition; but if you prove your charge—and put to the proof it must be—the double claim you will have upon us will make it hard to resist whatever you ask. I can say no more."

"I leave the appeal to your Majesty's heart," I answered, with a deep obeisance. "And I will make good my words now and here." I drew out then the compromising letters in Quesada's handwriting, and placing them in the Queen's hands, I told her at great length and with all possible detail the story of the Minister's treachery.

To this narrative she listened with even more engrossed attention than to my former one of her son's rescue; and as I drove home point after point and saw them tell, I felt that I was winning her to my side all reluctantly and dead against her prejudice in her Minister's favour, until she herself admitted that the route of the young King's drive and the lack of guards on that eventful afternoon had been suggested by Quesada himself.

At the close she was so overcome that, feeling embarrassed, I asked leave to withdraw; but she detained me and gradually put aside her weakness.

"I still cannot believe it, Lord Glisfoyle; but it shall be tested to the uttermost and every means of investigation shall be exhausted. On that you have my word. And now——" she had got as far as that when there came an interruption, and a message was brought that an immediate audience was craved by one of the Secretaries of State on a matter of the deepest urgency.

"You will not leave the Palace, my lord. I wish to see you again," and I withdrew to an ante-room to await her pleasure. I was satisfied with what I had done; and as I sat thinking over the interview, I noticed signs of much excitement and commotion; messengers kept coming and going quickly; high dignitaries and officials were hurrying this way and that, and the number of people

232

in the great chamber increased largely, all talking together in clusters, scared in looks and excited in manner, although subdued in tone.

Presently the infection of the general excitement spread to me, and looking about me I caught sight of one of the two officers who had come to me at the Hotel de l'Opera on the night of the King's rescue, Colonel Vasca, and I went up to him.

"Is there any special news to cause this commotion?" I asked, when we had exchanged greetings.

"Is it possible you have not heard it? The Minister of the Interior, Senor Quesada, has been assassinated within the last hour in his own house."

"Quesada dead!" I exclaimed in profound astonishment. And then by a freak of memory Mayhew's words recurred to me—"Only one thing will ever beat Quesada—and that's death." "How did it happen? Who was the assassin?" I asked.

"Some villain of a Carlist, it is believed, in revenge for the blow which the Government have just struck at them. But they will pay a heavy price for so foul a deed."

My heart sank within me at the news. I realised in an instant what it must mean to my poor Sarita and everyone leagued with her, and I went back to my seat overwrought and half-distracted. She had indeed sown the wind to reap the whirlwind, and I could not hope to save her.

When at length the summons came for me to return to the Queen Regent, I followed the messenger almost like a man in a dream.

CHAPTER XXXII

LIVENZA'S REVENGE

The young King was no longer with the Queen Regent when I entered, and I found two or three of the chief Ministers of State in conference with her.

The news of the assassination had caused profound dismay, intensified in the case of the Queen Regent by the fact that it had followed with such dramatic swiftness upon the heels of my charges against the powerful and favourite Minister.

"You have heard of this fearful deed, Lord Glisfoyle?" was the Queen's question on my entrance.

"I have learnt it within the last few minutes in the ante-chamber, your Majesty."

"I have told my lords here the strange charges you brought against Senor Quesada. Do you still maintain them?"

"In every word and detail, Madame," and, at her request, I repeated to them everything I had said before.

"It is certainly a most extraordinary story," said one of them, the Duke of Novarro, Minister of War, in a tone which suggested unbelief and hostility.

"And the most extraordinary part of it, my lord," I replied, "is the fact that he was enabled to lay all these plans without anyone of his colleagues or associates having a suspicion of the truth. No doubt if the dead man's papers are secured in time, they will yield abundant proof of everything." The hint was acted upon at once, and messengers were despatched to see that this was done.

"Can you throw any light upon the motive for this deed?" asked the Duke.

"I have not heard the actual circumstances, but the Minister was a man who had made many enemies, private as well as public. I should look for the murderer among his private enemies." And even as I spoke, my own words prompted a thought, and the closing scene at Calvarro's farm flashed across my mind.

"Do you mean you would not set this down to Carlist feeling?" he asked next, in the same tone of unbelief.

"It was an act of private revenge, no more and no less," I answered firmly, "and I believe that I can find the means to prove it so." The suggestion was welcome to all present. The murder of a colleague from private motives was obviously a far less disturbing event to Ministers than an assassination designed as a protest against Ministerial policy. But the Duke was none the less hostile to me.

"Her Majesty has informed us that your lordship has gone so far as to request an amnesty for these Carlists as the return for the services you have rendered to the nation and the Throne by the rescue of the King. But you will of course understand that, now at any rate, such a request cannot be conceded."

"His Majesty himself gave me a pledge that such favour as I asked should be granted," I returned.

"His Majesty is too young to understand the needs of policy, my

234

lord; and the pledge was given before this had occurred. Everything is changed by such a deed."

"His Majesty is not too young to keep his word," I retorted, bluntly.

"The pardon of any individual conspirator might still be granted, Lord Glisfoyle," interposed the Queen, pointedly, "provided no complicity in this were found." I understood her meaning, but would not yield my point.

"I have your Majesty's gracious assurance that in the event of my proving the charges I have brought, my claims would be hard to resist whatever the favour I asked."

"You surely cannot think of pressing this, now," was her reply, with a dash of surprise.

"Most respectfully I must press it with all the power and force at my command; and with all submission to your Majesty, I am bound to say, I can prefer no other and no less request. There is no proof that this is a Carlist outrage."

My firmness was altogether unwelcome, and the Queen and her Ministers showed both irritation and impatience at my persistence. But I cared nothing for that. I was fighting for what I believed would be the one certain method of winning Sarita and removing her last objections, and I would not give way.

"Your solicitude for these miscreants is out of place, my lord, and what you ask is a sheer impossibility," said the Duke, haughtily. "Any further insistence must, as you will see, wear a curious look. These wretches are none the less traitors because their first plot failed. This second stroke has not failed."

"Had the man who has met this tragic death succeeded in his project, my lord Duke; if the young King were not only abducted but put to death; if the Monarchy had been overthrown and a Republic proclaimed in its place; if Her Majesty here were an exile from her kingdom, yourselves in danger, and the country in the throes of a bloody revolution, would you have deemed it then too great a price to have paid for the stroke which would have prevented everything? That was what the rescue of the young King meant, nothing less; and it will not be affected by Senor Quesada's death, if I can prove it to have been a private act. But as you will," I said, indignantly, after a moment's pause, "I trusted to the royal pledge, and if you, my lords, advise that the royal word of honour shall be broken, I, of course, can say no more. May I crave your Majesty's permission to withdraw?"

It was a bold stroke, but it did more to help me than hours of argument and wrangling. At the mention of her son's death the

Queen winced and grew suddenly pale, and came over at once to my side.

"What Lord Glisfoyle urges is true, gentlemen," she said, "and he who saved the King, my son, cannot be allowed to find my ears deaf to his plea. What you ask, Lord Glisfoyle, shall be granted, if you can prove this crime to be no Carlist outrage, and if my influence and my son's will stand for aught in the councils of Spain." She spoke proudly and almost sternly, and the others were as much discomfited as I was elated.

"I beg your Majesty to pardon my frankness of speech," I said, with the utmost deference, "and to accept my most earnest and heartfelt gratitude. I believe that already I know where to look for the man who has done this, and with your permission will at once set about the search. May I ask that the powers and services of the police may be placed at my disposal?"

"You shall have anything and every thing you desire, Lord Glisfoyle. If you desire to leave at once the necessary authority shall be sent after you to your hotel."

I bowed myself out then, and drove in hot haste to the Hotel de l'Opera in search of Mayhew. The news of the assassination of Quesada had reached the hotel, and I found them all in a mood of deep concern, and full of anxiety to learn the result of my long interview at the Palace.

"I have not time for a word now, except that I have gained all I wished on one condition—that I trace the man who killed Quesada, and prove it murder and not a Carlist assassination."

"But you cannot," cried Mayhew. "It's all over the city that——"

"I can and will," I broke in. "But listen, my dear fellow. Important documents will come to me from the Palace in a few minutes. I am going now to Quesada's house, and I wish you to bring them to me there the instant they arrive;" and without waiting another moment I was hurrying away, when my sister cried:

"Let me come with you, Ferdinand. That poor girl will be in such sorrow."

"A good thought, Mercy. Quick;" and we drove away together.

But at Quesada's I met with a check. The police were in possession of the house and would not admit me, though I urged and insisted and stormed in turns. Senor Rubio was there in charge, and nothing would move him. There was no option, therefore, except to await the arrival of the necessary authority; and scribbling a hasty note to the Duke of Novarro to tell him the state of matters and to urge despatch, I sent Mercy with it to the Palace in search of him.

Then I tried to curb my impatience while I waited, and to

236

occupy the time I made an examination of the outside of the house in the possible hope of some discovery which might help me.

I was thoroughly convinced that the murder was the act of Juan Livenza, and that I should find he had been at the house and had seen Quesada. I could not get a single question answered, however, and even my scrutiny of the exterior of the house and the grounds brought police interference.

But this was not before I had seen that which set me thinking hard. The window of the library in which I had last seen Quesada, the room he chiefly used, overlooked the garden at the rear, and one of the panes of glass was broken. An examination of the stonework underneath it, and of the ground immediately below, revealed marks which seemed to tell me how such a deed might well have been committed.

One or two branches of a shrub close to the wall were broken and bent, and one of the stones, which projected beyond the rest sufficiently to afford a precarious foothold, was slightly chipped and scraped on the edge. It was just such a mark as might have been caused by a man standing on it to look into the window, and on making the experiment I found that a man of Livenza's height, which was about my own, could easily have grasped the stone sill, looked into the room, and fired a revolver through the broken pane.

Just as I had made this discovery the police ordered me away from the house, and I went back to the front to wait for my tarrying authority. Mercy brought it. The Duke had been at the Palace, and on the receipt of my note had given her a paper which he declared would do all I wished until the more formal authority should be ready.

Armed with this I summoned Rubio, showed it him, and with my sister was admitted to the house. I sent her at once in search of Dolores while I questioned Rubio.

"You see my authority, Senor Rubio; be good enough to tell me all you know of the matter, and as quickly as possible."

"We know very little as yet. His Excellency was alone in the library when I arrived to see him on business. The servant took my name to him, and came running back in alarm, crying that he was lying dead on the floor, having dropped out of his chair where he had been sitting. He was as dead as a coffin, shot through the head, here in the temple," and he put his hand to his own head to indicate the place.

"How do you suppose it happened?"

"No one can tell, senor. He had been dead perhaps half an hour, so the doctors said; no one was with him, and no one was known to have seen him for perhaps an hour before that time. No cry was heard; no sound, indeed; and yet he was dead. The Carlists must have obtained admission to the house secretly, and have escaped as they came."

"Take me to the room," I said, and he led the way in silence. "Show me exactly where he was found." He pointed out the spot. "Now just sit in that chair a moment;" and, much wondering, he took his seat at Quesada's writing table. I stood on the side away from the window, and a glance was enough to show me that his head was in a direct line with the broken pane of glass.

"Was the window fastened?" I asked.

"Yes, I myself examined it."

"That broken pane of glass?"

"It was broken by his Excellency himself to-day, and he had given orders for the repair of it."

The answer surprised me, but a moment's reflection showed me what might have happened.

"How came it broken, and when; do you know?"

"How, I do not know; but it was done when Colonel Livenza was here to-day, closeted with his Excellency. They were, as perhaps you know, senor, closely associated together." There was a furtive, half eager, half alarmed, and wholly cunning look on Rubio's face, which sent the thought flashing upon me that he could say a good deal of Quesada's private matters if he pleased.

"I know much more than you think, Senor Rubio. These two were close friends, you say; did they part to-day on friendly terms?"

"I was not here, senor," was the guarded reply.

But I could read the facts without his help. Livenza had come to demand an explanation, and intended, no doubt, to wreak his revenge on the spot. There had been a quarrel, and probably some kind of tussle, in which this window had been broken. Livenza had for some reason abstained from shooting Quesada there and then; but he had been quick to see that if he left and went round to the back of the house, he could fire at his victim through the broken window, and kill him without anyone suspecting the act. I got some confirmation of this theory by questioning the servant, who had seen his master after Livenza had left the house, and had noticed that he was unusually excited and angry.

There was the fact that no sound of a pistol shot had been heard; but the room had double doors and a heavy portiere curtain, and this might well account for such a thing. I was, at any rate, satisfied with my theory, and while I was with Rubio, Mayhew arrived with the official papers placing the police services at my disposal. I showed them to him, and they increased his apprehension.

"I shall do all I can to help you, senor," he assured me, nervously.

"You will find it safer," said I, significantly. "Have any of Senor Quesada's papers been removed?"

"None," he answered, with a slight start.

"Well, then my friend Mr. Mayhew here, of the British Embassy, will remain and see that everything is sealed. And now tell me, do you suspect anyone of this murder?"

"It is the work of the cursed Carlists, of course. His Excellency's life was more than once attempted by them."

"Put that idea out of your head. This was a private crime, and we have to bring it home to the murderer. Where is Senorita Castelar?" I put the question abruptly, and looked at him fixedly. He started very uneasily.

"She could not do it."

"I am perfectly aware of that, but I must know at once where she is. Understand, your future will depend upon your answering me frankly. You know quite well where she is, for you have been Senor Quesada's instrument in all that business. When you arrested her at the station yesterday, where did you take her, and to what place did you remove her afterwards?"

"She was taken to the prison of San Antonio, and afterwards removed by his Excellency's orders—I don't know where."

"I don't believe you," I said, bluntly. "I know you are lying, indeed, and if you don't tell me the truth on the spot, the first use I'll make of this authority will be to have you clapped into gaol yourself, and the whole of your private papers searched. And you know as well as I what we shall find among them. I'll give you two minutes to choose."

"I don't know, senor, I don't, upon my soul; and, by the Holy Saints, I swear I don't," he cried, eagerly, panic-stricken by the threat.

"One of your minutes is gone. Silas, call up a couple of the gendarmes;" and Mayhew turned to the door.

"Stop, senor, stop for the love of Heaven. I don't know. I wish to help you; I swear I do. But I'm innocent of everything. Give me time to think."

"Your innocence wears a strange dress, Rubio, and I won't give you another second."

"I can tell you what I think, senor," said the bully, trembling like a child. "It is most likely his Excellency would have had the senorita taken to a house at Escorias, which I believe he had prepared for her."

"If your thoughts are wrong you'll find yourself in a hole. Now,

239

a last question. Is it possible that Colonel Livenza can have found this out in any way?"

"Mother of Angels, I believe I see it now," he exclaimed, excitedly, and then was silent.

"You are either hiding some fact or hatching another lie," I said, sternly. "I should have thought you could see the danger of that with me."

"I will tell you, senor, I will, indeed, everything. I came to this house this afternoon in consequence of a message from his Excellency. He had for some time had a suspicion that Colonel Livenza had played him false—there was, I believe, something in which you yourself were concerned with the colonel. A warrant was made out and handed to me, and I was to wait for further instructions before making the arrest. This afternoon his Excellency rang me up on the telephone—his instrument is on the table here, you see—and he was speaking to me when the message broke off suddenly. He had got as far as this—'Go to Escorias and execute the warrant I gave you recently to arrest——' There it stopped, and I remember now there was a sharp noise I could not understand. I thought something was wrong with the wires. I waited for him to speak again, and when nothing came through I spoke to him and rang the bell. But I could get no answer, and in the end thought it best to come to the house for further instructions. I thought he might wish the senorita removed again, and came up to see."

"Then you did know where she was," I said, pointedly. "And I'm glad you see the prudence of treating me frankly. How do we get to Escorias?"

"We can drive in less than two hours, senor." I rang the bell and ordered the fastest pair of horses in Quesada's stable to be put in at once, and while waiting for them, told Mayhew what I wished in regard to the dead man's papers. As soon as the carriage came, I took Rubio and one of his assistants with me, and ordered the coachman to drive at top speed to Escorias.

Everything seemed clear to me now, and this unexpected development filled me with a new fear for Sarita's safety. Livenza, full of his wild passion for revenge, had gone to Quesada, and a fiery interview had taken place between the two, in which the Minister's old ascendancy over the weaker man had so far asserted itself, that the latter had been unable to carry out his purpose in the room. He had either discovered, or Quesada, with the probable object of pacifying him, had told him where Sarita was detained, and had very likely suggested that he should go and take her away at once—calculating with diabolical cunning that the temptation to Livenza to see her again and have her in his power, would prove irresistible. In this way the Minister had saved his life for the moment, and when Livenza had left, Quesada had planned to have him arrested. In the meantime, the murderer had seen his way to achieve both his purposes—to kill his victim secretly, by shooting him from the garden, through the broken window, and then to rush off to Sarita. He had thus probably heard the broken telephone message being spoken, and at the dramatic moment when Quesada's attention would be fixed on the telephone and his ears covered by the receivers, the shot had been fired with instantly fatal results.

So certain was my belief in my theory, and so vivid the impressions I had gathered, that I could picture in my thoughts every step and act in the progress of the tragedy. But there was one question I could not answer: and the thought of it filled me with an acute pang of alarm.

What were Livenza's intentions in regard to Sarita?

In the room at Calvarro's farm, his passion for her had been at first chilled by his fear of me, and then dominated by the even fiercer passion of revenge upon the man who had duped and out-witted him. But this thirst for revenge had now been sated by the death of Quesada, and who could say what wild form the recrudescence of the mad love-passion would assume?

Sarita, as I knew from her own lips, had fooled him. She had allowed him to make love to her; had possibly fed his passion with subtle but dangerous suggestions of a response to his love; and had won him for the Carlists by these desperate means because no others were present to her hand. My own words of warning to her recurred to me; and if he succeeded in forcing his way to her now that his enemy and master was dead, what limit could I believe he would place to his violence?

I had always regarded him as a man liable to be driven by passion across the borderland between sanity and madness; he had passed through more than one crisis of acute mental shock within the last few days; and it was more than probable that the deed of blood he had just committed, itself the act of a madman, would suffice to rob him of the last vestige of sane responsibility.

He would go to Sarita with the blood of their mutual oppressor still hot on his murderous hands, and if we were not in time to save her from him, what hope was there for her? I knew how she would receive him; and the thought maddened me until in my burning impatience I could not sit still, but thrust my head out of the carriage-window to urge the driver constantly to fresh exertions, although we were already travelling at headlong speed.

I was on fire with eagerness, and racked with alarm at the looming possibility of failure, even when all had gone so well.

CHAPTER XXXIII

THE HUT ON THE HILLSIDE

No speed that the driver could get out of the mettlesome horses was swift enough to keep pace with my fears or to ease the pricking of my alarms.

Our route to Escorias lay along the road where I had followed and rescued the young King, and as we flew along, bumping, jolting and swaying, covering the level road at the gallop, dashing down and rattling up the hills, I could measure the distance by the different spots which were fixed in my memory by the incidents of that memorable ride.

"How far is it beyond Podrida?" I asked Rubio, having to shout the question to make myself heard amid the clatter and racket of the jolting carriage.

"At this pace, half an hour," came the reply, in jerks. "If we reach there without a smash." My answer was to lean out once more and shout to the driver to hurry; and then I threw myself back in my seat, folded my arms, and yielded myself up anew to the torture of my distracting thoughts.

I tried to estimate how long a start Livenza would have of us, how far he could be in advance, and what time he would have for the execution of the plan he had formed, whatever that might be. And my lowest calculation alarmed me.

The murder had been committed about two hours and a half before I had got to Quesada's house; I had been there about one hour; and thus Livenza would have three and a half hours' start of us. From this we might deduct the time he would spend in Madrid before setting out for Escorias; but as he would be in fear of discovery, I dared not hope that he would remain a minute longer than would be necessary to procure a horse or some kind of conveyance. His own horses would be at his immediate disposal, of course; and if he had had them at hand, he might have started the instant after he had shot his enemy. This would give him quite three hours' start, even allowing for the quicker pace at which we were following in pursuit. And in three hours what could he not do?

There was, of course, room to hope that he might have had to return to his house to make some preparations for his flight; and I harassed and worried myself with a hundred speculations about this: whether he would not have gone to Quesada's with everything in readiness for flight; or whether he had thought that he would be taken at once, or even killed by Quesada, and had thus set his affairs in order before going. To speculate on his actions in such a case, was, however, of no more value than to count the waves on the seashore; and I got no further than an ever-consuming desire for yet greater speed.

"Close there now, senor," cried Rubio, at last, looking out of the window into the gloom. "A few minutes."

"Thank Heaven for that," I exclaimed, fervently.

"And that we've escaped a smash at that mad pace." We had left the high road, and were going less rapidly along a narrow country lane, and could speak without so much effort. "It's going to be a wild night," he added.

"I wish we were there, or rather that we could have been there two hours ago."

"I think we shall be in time, senor. The place is not easy to find. I think it will be all right there."

When the carriage stopped I sprang out, followed by Rubio, and hurried up to the house, which lay back some distance from the lane, along a rough, ill-kept carriage drive.

"It's evidently all right, senor. If anything had happened we should see some signs of it," said my companion, as he knocked loudly. A man opened the door, and touched his forehead as he recognised Rubio. "Good evening, Carlos. All well here?"

"All well, Senor Rubio;" and at the word I breathed a deep sigh of relief.

"The senorita is well, Carlos?"

"Quite well, Senor Rubio, and in her rooms."

"No visitors, I suppose?" was asked, casually.

"Yes, senor; Colonel Livenza, from his Excellency, has been here."

"Been here?" I cried, in surprise. "Tell us, quickly, what you mean?"

"He came with a letter from his Excellency, to see the senorita. He brought some urgent news, he said, and he was with her about half an hour, and then left."

"How long ago was that?"

"He has been gone maybe an hour, or perhaps less."

"Quick work," muttered Rubio. "Show the senor here to the senorita's rooms," he added, to the man. "Shall I go with you, senor?"

"No, wait, please," I answered, following the man upstairs, my heart beating quickly at the thought of seeing Sarita again. He went up to the floor above, the rooms of which were shut off from the staircase by a door which I saw had been recently placed there. This he unlocked and stood aside for me to pass.

"The first door on the right is the sitting-room, senor," he said, respectfully, and I went to it and knocked. Getting no reply, I knocked again loudly; and again failing to get any response, my fears, that after all something was wrong, began to revive. I knocked a third time, and still getting no answer tried to open the door, and found it locked on the inside. I called Sarita, loudly, by name then, knowing my voice would re-assure her, and when no response came, I tried the other doors and found them locked like the first, on the inside.

I called up Rubio then.

"Does the senorita generally lock her doors?" I asked Carlos.

"I have never known her to do it before, senor."

"Something is wrong; we must break our way in;" and I sent Carlos down at once for tools.

"What can it mean?" he said, in a tone of dismay; and as soon as the tools were brought he set about forcing an entrance.

"Did you see the senorita after Colonel Livenza left?" I asked the man.

"My wife did, senor. She said she was tired, and complained of a headache, and that she would go to bed early, and asked us to keep the house quiet and not disturb her."

"She has gone," I exclaimed, as the meaning of it all rushed upon me. "He brought with him the means for her to escape, and under some pretext induced her to fly, after she had lulled the suspicions of these two with this plea."

And so it proved. The rooms were empty; and an open window, from which hung a knotted rope fastened to a bedstead, told us plainly enough how the escape had been made. For a moment my heart sank with dismay at the sight; but I rallied under pressure of the need for instant action.

"We must follow and find them," I said, promptly. "Which way can they have taken? It is clear that he induced her to escape, and while they were together they were making these preparations. He left about an hour ago, and as the senorita had then to complete her arrangements she cannot have been gone very long. How can we trace them?" A question to Carlos sufficed to show that they must have left by the lane we had come; for it led nowhere but to the house. They had not passed us on the road, and it was clear, therefore, that they must have turned in the opposite direction from the capital.

There were two horses in the stable, and I had these saddled, and rode off with Rubio, ordering the carriage with Rubio's assistant to follow us at such pace as the coachman could get out of the smoking, lathered animals who had brought us so well from Madrid.

At first the trail was broad and easy to follow. We had scarcely turned into the high road when we met some men, who told us enough to show that Livenza and his companion were on horseback, riding at a moderate pace, and were not more than a mile or two distant. We covered four or five miles at the gallop, stopping wherever we met anyone on the road to make inquiries; and it was soon abundantly clear that we were overtaking them fast. They seemed to be keeping to the high road, for what purpose or whither bound it was impossible to guess; nor did it matter much so long as we were rapidly closing up to them.

Then the scent failed suddenly. We had rattled along for a couple of miles or so, and I was expecting to overtake them at any moment, when a carter whom we questioned declared that no one answering to the description had passed him. The news was serious indeed; it was now late, there were few people abroad; the sparsely-scattered houses and cottages were closed, and the inmates abed; we had passed more than one branch road; and thus the chances of our tracking them ran down to zero.

We turned our horses' heads, and at the first of the branch roads drew rein to confer. Rubio had no stomach for the work of further search, and was for doing no more until we could get sufficient help to continue the hunt vigorously the next morning in the daylight. This, no doubt, was a counsel of reason; but I was in anything but a reasonable mood, and would not listen to him—much to his disgust.

"We know just about where they were last seen on the high road," I said. "They can't ride about all night in these by-lanes; if they were making for any definite town they would have had to stick to the main road; and we must take these by-roads in turn, and ride a few miles along each of them. You follow the first, and I'll take the next. We shall find them in that way."

"It is useless, senor. We shall only wear ourselves and our horses out to no purpose," he protested; but I insisted, and sending him down the first lane, I rode on to the next, and dashed along it through the rain that was now falling in gusty, blusterous squalls. But I found nothing to help my search; not a soul did I see, not a cottage or building of any kind; and with something like a groan of disappointment, I pulled up at length, and began to retrace my steps.

Then what might have been expected happened—I lost my way. Puzzled by the darkness I took a wrong turning which, instead of leading me back to the high road, brought me out by a rough zig-zag way on to a wild, bleak hillside, where it ended; and I was stranded, far away from any sign of a habitation, in the pitch darkness, with the wind howling round me and the rain falling in torrents.

For an hour or more I groped about, having at times to dismount and lead my horse, until I realised that I was hopelessly lost, and that I had not only no chance of discovering Sarita that night, but should be lucky if I had not to spend the night in the open.

I was halting for the twentieth time under the shelter of trees to escape some of the pelting rain, when my luck turned, and I caught sight of a glimmer of light faintly quivering through the darkness above me. Where light was, some human being must be also, and if money or force could prevail, that human being should guide me back to the high road and safety; and I led my horse in a bee-line toward the light, stumbling, floundering, and slipping over the sloppy, uneven ground, now blundering into a ditch or sinking ankle deep into a vegetable patch, or almost breaking my shins against stone heaps, until I found that the light came from the window of a cottage.

Then something happened to fill me with the inspiring hope that my good luck was far better than I could have dared to hope. I was close to the cottage when I ran up against a couple of horses tethered to some railings; and on running my hands over them I found both were saddled, and that one carried a side saddle. My excitement at this was intense; for I believed that luck, chance, fate, Providence, call it what you will, had done what no judgment or skill could have had accomplished, and had led me right to Livenza's hiding-place.

In a moment, all my instincts of caution were awake again. I led my horse away from the others, fastened him securely, and crept up to the window where the light glimmered. Although the rain and wind were raging with such violence that no sound I made was at all likely to penetrate within, I picked my way with the utmost care, and stealing up to the window, peered in. I could not see much, as there was a dirty ragged, white curtain, which prevented my getting more than a glimpse at one side; but I saw enough to confirm my belief.

Livenza was there. I could see him plainly, as he stood by the door of the room, leaning against it, his arms folded, his head bent down, and his features moody, frowning, and dogged. As I watched him he looked up toward the corner of the room by the window, and in his blood-shot, haggard eyes was a wild, dangerous light that told all too plainly of the fire of insanity. His lips moved, but I could not hear the words; and at the instant a great gust of wind rushed against the small casement window, and set it clattering and shaking as though to burst it in.

Sarita I could not see, but when he spoke she made a movement forward, which brought her face into the line of light, and her profile was silhouetted for a second on the dirty, wind-rustled curtain.

Turning then, I felt my way to the door of the cottage, only to find it fast bolted, apparently on the inside. I raised my riding whip to knock for admission when a thought stayed me. If I was right, and Livenza's mind had completely given way, what would be the possible effect of any interruption? I scented danger plainly. It might drive him to the instant execution of any plan which might have formed in his mad brain, and the very effort at rescue might be only the signal for him to act. This might mean nothing less than Sarita's death.

I went back to the window, therefore, in deep perplexity, searching my wits for some means of ascertaining how matters stood. He was in the same position as before, and just then another tempestuous gust of wind dashed against the window, the casement of which strained and creaked on its hinges. And this gave me an idea.

Taking off my overcoat I rolled it round my arm and waited for such another gust, when I dashed my arm against the casement, bursting it partially open, and then drew back hastily into the dark.

A cry from Sarita was followed by a shout from Livenza, who came across hurriedly to the window.

"It's only the wind," I heard him say in a strident tone as he tore aside the curtain. "Not the police. You needn't be afraid of interruption." He tried unsuccessfully to shut the small casement, the flimsy fastenings of which I had evidently smashed. He soon abandoned his efforts, with an oath at the storm, and re-crossed the room. But I could now hear what passed, and, as he did not think to rearrange the curtain, I could see everything clearly.

For a time not a word was spoken, and then Livenza broke the silence.

"We may as well end this pretence, Sarita. I have lied to you. Your Englishman is not coming here, he is lying snug, safely caged in a gaol in Madrid, and I have brought you here for my own purposes. To tell you again what you once used to let me tell you freely, and what you know well enough—that I love you; love you, do you hear, as no cold-blooded English dog knows how to love. You are mine now, and shall never belong to another."

I saw Sarita start, and wince at the words. She looked across at him, and appeared to realise in a moment the extremity of the case, her imminent peril, and his wild insanity. She hesitated as if calculating her chance of either outwitting or struggling against him; and I would have given anything to have been able to let her know I was at hand. The dead calmness of her tone, as she replied, told me how clearly she understood her danger.

"I have never let you tell me that, Colonel Livenza," she said, very quietly.

"But you knew it. You could read it in my eyes, in my acts, in how I served you, in my work for the Carlists, in everything," he answered, vehemently. "You are more to me than life—you know that. Life, do I say"—and he laughed—"Why, I have wrecked my very soul for your love, Sarita; and have within the last few hours done murder that you might be free to be mine."

"What do you mean?" she asked, in the same clear, cool, even voice. She was leading him to talk in order to gain time to think and plan.

"What should I mean but that I have killed the only man who stood between us. No, not your Englishman," he cried bitterly, in answer to her changing look. "He never stood between us. A far stronger than he—Quesada. You told me of his treachery. He gave you to me, and all the time was scheming and lying that he might cheat me of you and have you for himself. But he will lie and cheat no more;" and he laughed again, wildly and recklessly. "Unless he does it in hell. He is dead, do you understand, dead, shot through the brain at the very moment when he was setting another cursed trap for me."

I saw Sarita start in fear, then instantly recover herself.

"You did wrong to kill him," she said, quietly.

"Wrong? Is revenge wrong? Is justice wrong? Has he killed no one? Did he not plan my murder? Wouldn't he have ruined you? Were you safe in his greedy clutch? Why chatter of wrong? It was right; a sound, good, true, just act, and had he a hundred lives I would take them all, the hundredth more cheerfully than the first—for your sake, Sarita. God, how I love you!" he cried with mad ecstasy. "When you told me that night at Calvarro's farm how he had cheated me, you signed his death warrant, Sarita. I went away meaning to kill him and then myself, but I saw how to do better. When I taxed him with his treachery he denied everything, and made me more smooth promises. He was afraid to die and told me where you were, that I could go to you and rescue you, and have you for my own, all my own, Sarita. And then I saw what I could do. That I could still kill him, and then escape myself to you and win you; and I went out from his room and crept out to the back of his house and caught him—doing, what think you? In the very act of

248

sending a message to his spies to arrest me at the place to which he was sending me to find you. I knew then he had told me the truth, where you were; and I shot him and saw him fall dead without a word, without a groan even, and I hurried away to you. To you, my love, my last hope in life, my love, my love. God, how I burn for you!" he exclaimed with fresh ecstasy.

Sarita shuddered and drew in her breath, at these evident proofs of his madness.

"You told me Lord Glisfoyle was waiting for me," she said, scarce knowing in her growing alarm what to say.

"Don't speak that name to me," he cried fiercely, his eyes gleaming and his face flushing. "Any name but that. I lied to you, I know it. I am not ashamed. A man must lie when love demands it. I used him to win you away from Escorias; and you came—came, never to leave me again, Sarita. I love you too well. If you will not love me, you shall live to love no other. I swear it. But you don't want to die, and will learn to love me. And if you won't, here is the love draught for us both;" and the brute took his revolver from his pocket, and held it, looking from it to Sarita, with eyes wild with craving, love, madness, and the menace of death.

"You mean you will murder me as you have murdered Sebastian Quesada?" Her voice was perfectly calm as she spoke. No higher proof of her consummate courage could she have shown than this exclusion of fear from her voice. And she smiled and added gently, "I don't think you would do that." But even as she spoke she glanced hurriedly at the broken window in the hope of escape.

I stole away then without waiting for more. I was confident she could hold him in check long enough for me to effect her rescue if only I could get into the house without arousing his suspicions.

I tried the door again, but it was too firmly fastened for me to force it, and feeling my way by the walls I went round to the back, thinking to find there a door or window by which I could enter. But the back door was as firm as that in the front, and I had seen too much not to know that the crash of my entrance, if I burst it in, would be the signal for him to shoot.

There was a small window on the floor level, but this was not made to open, and I was afraid to smash the glass. In the storey above there was also a window, and to my intense satisfaction, I saw the casement was open and creaking in the wind. In a moment I had my plan. I ran to my horse and led him to the back of the house, making a circuit sufficiently wide to prevent his steps being heard, and fastening him under the window I quieted him while I stood up in the saddle. I was still some way below the window, but calculating the distance as best I could in the dark, I sprang up and managed to catch hold of the sill. The rest was easy. I drew myself up, and in a minute was inside the room.

Then I slipped off my boots, and striking a light found my way out of the room and down the narrow rickety stairs, pausing at almost every step, in fear lest the creak of the boards should give notice of my presence. But no one heard me, and as the floor at the bottom was stone paved, I could move with greater freedom. All was still well with Sarita, and when I reached the door of the room where the two were, I heard her voice, still calm and firm with courage, as she reasoned with Livenza.

"Love is sweet and life is sweet," I heard him say in answer to something from her; "but death is sweeter than all if love be denied. If we cannot live and love we can die together, Sarita," he said, in the dreary tone of a crazed dreamer.

I ran my fingers softly and noiselessly round the door in search of the fastening, and when he began to speak again, I lifted the latch noiselessly by imperceptible degrees, and found to my inexpressible relief that it was unlocked. The sands of my patience had now run out, and I drew my revolver and held it in readiness for instant use. The seconds that followed formed a pause of acute suspense. I could hear Livenza brushing against the door on the inside as he moved when speaking, and taking advantage of a moment when he was in the midst of one of his mad rhapsodical harangues, I nerved myself for a tremendous effort, thrust the door open with all my might and main, and dashed into the room.

Thank heaven, the attempt was entirely successful. The door in opening struck Livenza with such sudden violence, that it sent him staggering forward against the table in the centre, overthrowing the candle and extinguishing it. Before he could recover himself, I had found him in the dark, and grappling him dragged him to the floor, where he writhed and strained in a fierce and desperate struggle for the mastery.

Sarita cried out in fear at the darkness and the sudden confusion.

"It is I, Sarita," I called, as I heard her close over us, and feared he would try to escape. "For God's sake, get some kind of light." I could speak no more, having to concentrate every effort to overcome Livenza, who was fighting and wrestling with the wild ferocity of madness. So fiercely did he struggle, and with strength which his madness increased so greatly, that at one time I half feared he would master me; but at length my grip fastened on his throat, and I pressed on it with all the strength at my command, disregarding the blows he rained upon me with frantic violence, and I hung on with a grip which he tried vainly to shake off, writhing, and twisting incessantly. His strength gave out at last; the blows grew fainter and the struggles weaker until he lay passive, choking, and seemingly unconscious in my grasp.

"Can't you get a light, Sarita?" I asked, anxiously, for the whole struggle had taken place in pitchy darkness.

"Are you hurt?" was her reply, her voice trembling.

"Not in the least. Don't be a bit afraid, we'll soon be out of this mess." Finding that Livenza lay still, I plunged my hand into my pocket and found my match-box. "Here are matches;" and when our fingers touched in the dark hers were cold and shaking violently. I pressed them gently and whispered: "It's all right now, sweetheart;" and a moment or two later, the candle was found and re-lighted, revealing by its dim flame a scene of confusion and disorder in the humble little room which bore eloquent testimony to the scene which had just been enacted.

"You must hunt about and find something to tie this mad devil up with; I daren't leave him," I said next; and taking the candle she went out of the room, her face dead white, and her hands shaking so that the candle flickered unsteadily.

Meanwhile Livenza lay so still in the darkness that I began to fear he was dead. I could feel no pulse in his listless wrist, which dropped when I released it like the arm of a corpse. I unfastened his coat and laid my hand on his heart, and then I could just detect a faint fluttering; but it was enough to prove he still lived.

After a few minutes Sarita came back carrying a small length of cord which she had found; and with this I fastened his legs. Taking the candle I looked with a good deal of anxiety into his eyes; and sending Sarita for water I dashed it on his face, and made such crude efforts as I knew of to bring him back to consciousness. For a long time the effort seemed vain, and the apparent difficulty of restoring him, led me to an act of carelessness that came within an ace of proving fatal to everything.

Sarita had been carrying Livenza's revolver which had fallen close to her feet when I had burst in, and now she picked up mine and laid them both on the table; and I, thinking that Livenza would be better if I raised him, dragged him up and set him on a chair close to them. It was the act of a fool. He had evidently been duping me for some time, and now he waited until my hands were off him, when he seized his chance with the cunning of a madman, and snatched up one of the revolvers. A cry from Sarita was my first hint of the peril, and I turned to find the barrel levelled point blank at me.

Her cry came just as he was pulling the trigger and he started and missed me. Quick as thought he turned on her as she moved to

251

the other side of the room; but his hand was too shaky for him to aim correctly, and by the mercy of Providence he missed her. Then before I could interfere to stop him, for the three shots followed in rapid succession, he put the pistol to his own temple and fired. This time the aim was true enough, and with a groan, he fell back off the chair dead.

The revolver dropped close to him, and I kicked it away and bent over him, and laid my hand on his heart.

"He is dead, Sarita," I said, and rose to take her out of the room, but the strain and the shock had been too much for her strength. She had fainted and lay white, wan, and helpless in the chair on which she had crouched when he made his last desperate attempt to shoot her.

CHAPTER XXXIV

A KING'S RIDDLE

The effects of Sebastian Quesada's death were national and dramatic.

For some days the political atmosphere was highly charged with electricity; the utmost confusion appeared to prevail, and in the result the war party emerged triumphant and irresistible. Scarcely a voice was to be heard in favour of peace, even from those who had previously been staunch adherents of the dead Minister.

The reason of this was to some extent a matter of conjecture on my part. How wide-reaching Quesada's conspiracy had been I never learnt precisely; but enough was told to enable me to guess a great deal more. Quite suddenly, and much to my surprise, the policy of a general amnesty for the Carlists embroiled in the recent outbreak found wide and most influential support.

The avowed reason for this was the obvious expediency of uniting all classes in Spain, in order to present a compact front to the common enemy; but I believe the real reason was a very different one. I have grounds for saying that the scrutiny of Quesada's private affairs and papers revealed the fact that so many of the prominent men in the country had been more or less involved in his movement to establish a Republic, that the loyalists were afraid of the results of a strict investigation and rigorous prosecution. The war policy was a good rallying cry, and in view of it the hatchet was to be buried.

This unexpected development was of course all in my favour, although there were some days of acute anxiety and suspense.

So soon as I was in possession of the needed proofs that Quesada's death was due to murder from private motives and was not an assassination in any way concerning the Carlists, I had been confident enough of ultimate success to take Sarita back to Madrid, place her again with Madame Chansette, and then open up communications with the Duke of Novarro.

From my first interview with him I brought away a piece of sorrowful news for Sarita. Her brother was dead. He had been shot at Daroca in the act of escaping from the police who had arrested him. Her grief was very deep, but Ramon's death severed the family tie which bound her to Spain; and when the first pangs of sorrow had passed, it came to be accepted between us that if the amnesty for the Carlists was secured she would go with us to England.

Then, just as matters appeared to be going well, an unexpected thing occurred. I had received a summons to attend at the Palace one day, and went down to tell the others, and as I entered Mrs. Curwen's room I heard her say:

"I'm glad the tornado's over, Mercy. It's a blessing we shall all go back safe and sound to England. Your brother's a regular storm-centre."

"I think the storm-centre is moving at last, and across the Atlantic, as the weather people say, Mrs. Curwen," I said, referring to the war news.

"Ah, did you hear me, Lord Glisfoyle; but you seem to be the storm-centre. Have you brought any more little volcanoes or blizzards with you now? I shall always think of a cyclone when I think of you," she declared, laughing.

"I am summoned to the Palace this afternoon, and hope, with you, to find the tornado is over."

"Have you any news of Sarita's matters then?"

"None, but I expect to hear everything this afternoon. Did you see Dolores Quesada this morning, Mercy?"

"Yes, poor girl; she is awfully broken by her trouble, and holds to her intention to take the veil. She is going to-day to the Convent of the Sacred Heart."

"About the best place for her, poor soul!" exclaimed Mrs. Curwen, "for a time, of course. I'm not surprised there are plenty of convents in this most cut-and-thrust country. I should go into one if I were a Spaniard—which, thank goodness, I am not!"

"I think she would have done better to accept Madame Chansette's offer to go and live with her in Paris," said I. "She's too pretty, too young, and too rich to be shut up for life."

"Madame Chansette was with me this morning, and we both tried to persuade her," replied Mercy, "but she wouldn't listen to us. We hope she will come round. Madame Chansette says she will have at least a year of the novitiate, and a good many things may happen in a year."

"A good many may happen in a week in Madrid," cried Mrs. Curwen. "It must be in the air, I suppose."

"Yes, friendships ripen quickly here, even when people are not Spanish," said I.

"And feelings stronger than friendship, too," retorted the widow, understanding my reference.

"Yes, feelings stronger than friendship," I repeated, with a significant accent and glance at her. At that moment, Mayhew came in and I added, "And here's a friend, I hope."

She smiled, and turned to greet him.

"Well, what news?" she asked, a little eagerly, I thought.

"I've got the leave," he answered.

I looked a question at them both, and Mayhew answered it, with a self-conscious smile of forced indifference. "I'm going for a week or two to London, Ferdinand. I've been a bit overdoing it here."

"Overdoing what, Silas?"

"Work, of course; and as you're all going——"

"It's my doing, Lord Glisfoyle," said Mrs. Curwen. "I hate travelling without someone to look after things; and when we do go I know you will be too much occupied under the circumstances to attend to us, so I told Mr. Mayhew he ought to get leave and come with us."

"I hope with all my heart he'll never come back," I said, very earnestly; and Mercy smiled.

"Not come back? Why?" he asked.

"Because I hope you'll find a sphere in London that will keep you there."

"My dear fellow, a mill-horse like me has no influence."

"What leave will you have?"

"A month."

"Ah, well, one can say of London what Mrs. Curwen said just now of Madrid; a good many things may happen in a month, and many good things too." And in that case the generalism was a prophecy, for Mayhew did not return to Madrid except when he and

254

Mrs. Curwen paid a flying honeymoon visit there some months afterwards.

"Certainly many things have happened here," he replied, drily.

"And the catalogue isn't filled yet; but I'm going to the Palace to-day, and hope to get the remaining items, so far as I'm concerned;" and we were discussing and canvassing my visit to the King, when Madame Chansette arrived, and told us to my infinite consternation that Sarita had been again arrested. I could not at first believe it.

"Arrested? My dear madame, are you sure?" I cried.

"I never feel sure of anything now; but if two officials in uniform arriving with a warrant or a summons or some kind of paper from Government, and the hurrying off of Sarita to some place no one knew where, or at least would tell me where, and taking no denial or excuse and not letting us communicate with anyone, and not even allowing Sarita to make any decent preparations, or even pack a hand-bag with absolute necessaries, not even a brush and comb or a spare handkerchief, and saying no more to me than that they had their orders and must obey them, don't mean arrest, then what can it mean?" She paused for want of breath, and was plunging into another sea of words when I interrupted her.

"Who signed the paper or warrant or whatever it was? What was the charge?"

"My dear Lord Glisfoyle, however can I know when I was not even allowed to look at it, much less take it in my hands; and I was so agitated and frightened, I could not even think coolly. It was in this way——"

"Excuse me, I'll go and see about it," I broke in, and hurried away to the Duke of Novarro in search of some explanation. I had to wait for him, and sat for an hour or more drumming my heels on the floor and controlling my impatience as best I could. It was close to the time of my interview at the Palace when he arrived, full of suave apologies for the delay.

"I learn that Senorita Castelar has been arrested. May I ask the reason for so unexpected a step?" I asked, getting at once to the point.

"I am very glad you have come to me, Lord Glisfoyle, although in this matter I fear I cannot give you much satisfactory information. But I have just completed another affair that you will be interested to learn concerning Senorita Castelar."

"But this arrest, my lord?" I cried, impatiently, irritated rather than appeased by the scrupulous courtesy of his tone.

"Yes, it is undoubtedly singular; but bear with me a moment.

The other matter is also much in point. It concerns the young lady's property, Lord Glisfoyle. An examination of the Quesada papers has convinced us——"

"But the arrest, my lord?" I interposed. "I am burning with impatience."

"This may be in some way connected with it. We are convinced that Quesada was wrongfully withholding from his two relations property which was theirs by right, and it will be restored to Senorita Castelar, of course, if this matter is satisfactorily arranged."

"But the arrest, my lord?" I cried for the third time. "Other matters are nothing compared with this."

"And unfortunately I can tell you nothing about it. I cannot think it is of any serious importance, however."

"But she has been arrested," I urged, insistently. "Such a drastic step must mean something—even in Spain."

"You are severe upon our methods, senor. I wish I could give you a more satisfying answer." And he threw up his hands and smiled.

"To whom can I go for information?" I asked, rising.

"I believe the step has been taken at the instance of the Palace; but it cannot be serious, as I say, for we have definitely settled upon the amnesty for all but a very few of the Carlists—where, for instance, it is clear that robbery rather than politics was the motive."

"This does not satisfy me," I said, ungraciously; for the mention of exceptions made me uneasy.

"I can understand that it should not; but if I may offer a word of advice, I would counsel patience. All will come right, I hope and think. Have you not received a summons to the Palace to-day?"

"Yes. Shall I learn the truth there?" I said bluntly.

"I hope will have no difficulty in learning the truth anywhere in Spain, Lord Glisfoyle," he answered; and the rebuke was none the less telling because of the quiet, courteous tone in which it was administered.

"I beg your pardon, my lord. In my great anxiety I spoke in haste."

"I am sure of that. At the Palace I am convinced you will at least get an explanation;" and he smiled. There was clearly nothing more to be gleaned from him, and in this condition of anxious unrest I went to the Palace.

I was ushered not into any of the public chambers, but into one of the private apartments of the Royal Family, and left there alone, much exercised in mind on account of the strange step which had been taken.

Presently the young King came to me, and I was at once struck by his strange manner and the strange expression on his face. He appeared to be very glad to see me, and yet his manner was unquestionably marked by restraint. At first he came gladly and quickly towards me with outstretched hands, as he had before, but checked himself, gave me his hand to kiss, and then searched my face with precocious shrewdness, mingled, as it seemed, with intentionally suppressed friendliness and a dash of furtive concern. When he spoke it was with a gravity far beyond his years, and without any of his spontaneous boyish frankness.

"I have desired to see you alone, my lord. The Duke of Novarro will have told you of the decision in regard to the amnesty?"

"He has just done so, your Majesty. I went to him to ask the reason of a most unexpected event—the arrest of Senorita Castelar—a matter that has caused me grave uneasiness."

"Did he not tell you that some exceptions had to be made in granting pardons?"

"He did not tell me that Senorita Castelar was to be an exception, and certainly I had never been led to expect it," I answered, rather bluntly. "Nor did I think that such a thing would ever have been done."

He gave me a little eager glance, and was going to reply quickly, when he checked himself, paused, and then in the former tone said—

"We wish to consult your desires so far as possible, my lord; but the senorita took a very active part even in the plot against me."

"I am in your Majesty's hands, of course, but such a step is a strange way of consulting my desires."

"I am not so sure of that," he cried quickly, with a boyish smile. "At least, I mean that you have been such a friend to me that I am convinced you would not wish me to do anything that my advisers consider unwise."

"We did not speak in this strain as we rode back that evening from Podrida. I do not recall any conditions about your Majesty's advisers or even mention of them."

"You are very difficult to deal with, senor, and are making my task very hard," he said, protestingly.

"I have not the honour to know what your Majesty's task is," said I, puzzled by his words.

"It has been found necessary, in the interests which I have at heart, to pass a sentence upon the senorita—in some respects a heavy sentence." He used the same over-serious tone, but as he looked up into my face I saw laughter in his eyes, and when he finished, the smile spread over his face.

"It is your Majesty's prerogative to command," I answered.

"Yes," he cried, eagerly. "Yes, this is my own doing. I have seen Senorita Castelar. I spoke of my advisers just now; but this is not their doing, it is all my work. That may make you agree to it, even if the punishment itself may seem to you severe. And, believe me, I should be very sorry if I thought that—on your account. You will believe that?" and he made a motion to place his hands on mine as if to appeal to me.

"I should be deeply distressed if I thought you of yourself could do anything harsh or unjust. I do not think it possible."

"That is more like my Englishman of Podrida," he cried, gleefully; but, reverting to the grave tone, he added: "The senorita knows her punishment and quite acquiesces in its justice; although it carries with it no less than partial imprisonment for life."

"Your Majesty is not serious?" I exclaimed.

"Do I look otherwise?" he cried; but he could not maintain his gravity any longer, and burst into a merry peal of laughter. "Do you think I would do anything like that? Anything against the man who once wore this for me?" and he pulled out the little mask that he had begged of me that day on the road. "I know more now than I did then of the danger you ran for my sake. Can't you guess my riddle?"

His eyes were dancing with pleasure and mischief, and he put on the mask, and then thrust his hands into mine.

"This is not the only mask I've worn to-day, you see. Can't you guess? Have I really beaten you? That's glorious; and I thought it all out myself," he cried, laughing in high glee.

I began to see daylight then, and laughed with him. "I am not afraid of anything you would think of, sire."

"But you were afraid, you know. I saw it in your face just now, and I could hardly keep it up. I like you too much to wish to hurt you, even in play."

"You said the senorita's punishment carried partial imprisonment for life."

"A golden prison, senor, for this," he cried, laughing again as he held up the fourth finger of the left hand. "Senorita Sarita Castelar is to be exiled from Spain, never to return; never, never, never. But Lord Glisfoyle's wife, Carlist or not Carlist, will always be able to return," he added, slily, "because Lord Glisfoyle, my Englishman, will always be welcome here. Now do you understand it all?"

"And thank your Majesty from the bottom of my heart," I replied, earnestly.

"Have I kept my word?" he added, almost wistfully.

"As a King should, generously," I said.

"And you forgive me my prank—though you could not guess my riddle?"

"It is a riddle, sire, of which the answer could not be better."

"Then I hope Spain and I will always have one firm friend in England," he said, very seriously, as he put his hand again in mine.

"Till the end of my life, your Majesty;" and taking his hand I was pressing my lips upon it when he checked me.

"No," he said, smiling. "I am not the King to you. We are friends, and friends don't kiss hands, they shake them in your England. Good-bye, my friend, my Englishman of Podrida."

"Good-bye," I answered, holding his hand in a firm clasp.

Then he led me, still holding my hand, to the door.

"You are to go there, but—" and his voice shook slightly as he added—"don't forget me, even there; even when you find what you so much desire." He opened the door, and I saw Sarita waiting for me. I went to her with quickly beating heart.

"Good-bye again," came in a whisper, as the boy King closed the door softly behind me, and opened up at the same time all the new smiling love-life that lay ahead for us two.

THE END

www.ingramcontent.com/pod-product-compliance
Lightning Source LLC
Chambersburg PA
CBHW020620260626
47157CB00003B/1093